Akama Vutova

The Goblin Chronicles, Volume 2

S. M. Sutton

Published by S. M. Sutton, 2026.

This is a work of fiction. Similarities to real people, places, or events are entirely coincidental.

AKAMA VUTOVA

First edition. March 13, 2026.

ISBN: 979-8992352948

Written by S. M. Sutton.

Table of Contents

To Val–I am happy to find

After all these years,

That your lifelong friendship

Survived my tears.

I worried about bad decisions,

Rather than counting on

Magical visions.

A SONG OF LEAVING

You left me on the road today,

My fist held to my heart.

I'll count the risings of the sun

As long as we're apart.

If you see a shooting star, know I'm watching from afar.

Every sunset that goes down,

I'll listen for your footsteps

Upon the ground.

If you see a shooting star, know I'm watching from afar.

When I watch the night sky,

A whispered wish I'll send to you.

Come back to me, and we'll build anew.

If you see a shooting star, know I'm watching from afar.

I hope our paths cross again someday.

Perhaps your dreams will turn my way.

I'll be here. Come and stay.

If you see a shooting star, know I'm watching from afar.

If you see a shooting star, know I'm watching from afar.

PROLOGUE: AKAMA VUTOVA

The Rise of the Gugwe

Thana NukPana stood at the edge of a cliff, the drop a thousand feet. A fall off the edge would take long enough for one's life to pass before their eyes; or to count all the regrets of missed opportunities; or to flip through treasured memories of loved ones; or to scream all the way to the bottom, not willing to accept the death rising to meet you.

Thana did not pass up opportunities.

Standing at the edge of this abyss atop the cliff was his favorite view. It was a place to think. To ponder. To find solutions to problems and challenges. It was also the place where he once took advantage of an opportunity when it presented itself.

That opportunity turned out to be the day *he* became the Thana NukPana, Emperor of the Gugwe Tribes.

The Gugwe were creatures of violence. Pugnaciousness is their very nature. But violent streaks could sometimes be born of necessity. Raids by the tribes to steal women or food were something they lived and died by. Villages were spread across the tundra of the far north. Each community had its own KuRuk or chieftain, but all answered to Thana NukPana.

Life for a tribal warrior was short, ever seeking to claim glory. Climbing dead bodies to reach the top, to become the tribe's KuRuk. Most tribal chieftains only held the position for a year, two at most, before they found themselves challenged, a fight to the death. Winner claiming the tribe's KuRuk title.

The process was the same for becoming the Thana NukPana. There was always another who wished to take the mantle as his prize. And it was a prize. The title came with all the Thana's wives, children, slaves, the best meat, the best drink and all the former Thana's possessions. The winner could keep or reject any of the boons.

"Ama, Ama," a young Gugwe cub leaped into his grandmother's lap and looped his arms around her shoulders. "Tell me the story again about our great emperor. Please Ama?" Several other young Gugwe squatted outside the edge of her doorway, content to eavesdrop.

"You must hold your questions until the very end, mind!"

The child nodded in agreement. His grandmother grunted at him, a fierce look on her face. Soon her deep singsong voice was sharing history with her audience.

"Before the current Thana NukPana took the title, he was called Akama of the Vutova Tribe. The Vutova were the fiercest warriors of all the 13 Gugwe tribes. They were survivors of cruel living conditions, a trial all its own. Freezing lands, where little grew that they could eat; hunting a critical skill, death by starvation, the price for failure. The tribes did not look kindly on a mouth to feed if that mouth was unsuccessful in providing some value for the good of all the kin."

"While growing up, Akama Vutova lived and breathed hunting. By the time he became a man under tribal tradition at sixteen, he was the best hunter in his tribe. He had spent his youth tagging along with all the hunt masters. He did not care if he had to haul their water or gather their wood, or carry their dead game back to the village. What he did care about was watching, observing, and learning all their hunting methods. Akama made a study of the hunting theories they applied to various types of prey under differing weather conditions. Witnessing the application of new methods hunters used when a creature's habitat changed, he noted how men used many types of practices. It became his habit to keep track of the kills by each hunter in the village, perceiving which techniques were most fruitful and under what conditions. His study concerned large and small game, and the methods used by old and young hunters."

"Akama asked questions. He found if he was delivering firewood to a huntsman's fire ring or if he offered to sharpen their knives, helped them gut, skin, clean and prepare the meat to cook or to dry, tasks provided an opportunity where the hunt masters were more likely to answer his nagging 'whys'. But patience ran thin with this kind of prodding from a curious boy. When they found his unending questions intolerable, he often received a sharp smack across the back of his head, and he would back away from the hunter's fire, bowing and apologizing for bothering him. But it had never stopped him from returning at a later date to continue gleaning information to enhance his knowledge."

"All his youthful efforts to ferret out each hunter's secrets and their most successful approaches taught him there wasn't only one right way to do something. He found the lesson could apply to many areas of life, coveting the knowledge he gained in his observations. When circumstances, weather, or a prey's patterns changed, he made a note of it. He learned one must detect those changes and quickly adapt to achieve continued success."

"The years rolled by. Eventually, Akama became the Vutova Tribe's Hunt Leader. One day, he had an idea that incentives might increase his clan's health and their survival rate. The tribe had always put all the food hunted and gathered together for community meals. Women assigned the job did the cooking. Those cooks spent their days preparing meals and preserving food for leaner times. It had always been the cook's task to feed all the tribal members in equal shares."

"One evening, putting his idea into play, Akama announced that from now on, the hunter who brought in the most kills each week would receive a reward for doing his job better than all the other hunters to feed the Vutova people. The bonus would be an extra cut of meat for each of the members of the hunter's tent."

"The reaction among Akama's people was mixed. But the tribe's KuRuk didn't interfere with the Hunt Leader's proposed motivation program. The very next day, one hunter came back to the village with three rabbits instead of two, and then produced the same count each day that week. The hunter's success could be attributed to the fact that he had added an hour of hunting in the morning before the others started. He then increased his efforts with another extra hour, when the others were already sitting around their fire rings, the sun going down. As you can imagine, the other hunters were not congratulatory about his enhanced success."

"When the week was over, Akama announced the winning hunter. That night, when the tribal member's bowls were filled with rabbit stew, the victorious hunter, and his family received their equal share from the cook pots. But in addition, the hunter, his wife, and two sons were each given a generous quarter of a roasted rabbit for themselves. Akama himself served the hunter's family the extra share, crediting the hunter for his efforts. After the presentation was done, there wasn't a huntsman seated at his fire ring who didn't make the decision that he, too, wanted to win a reward for his family, doing whatever was necessary to achieve it. The hunting competition became fierce."

The cub's eyes turned a shiny red, and Ama could hear small feet shuffling outside.

"Akama was pleased with the success of this program. So, it wasn't surprising that, not long after, he added the gatherers to the reward system. The one bringing in the most nuts, berries, tubers, etc. would receive an extra cup for each member in their tent at the end of the week. Again, Akama made sure he delivered the bounty personally when the bonuses were distributed."

"Soon, the prizes and the extra boons were connected to Akama, though he always praised the actual hunter or gatherer who had won to each of the lucky recipients who benefitted. Still, it was Akama himself who handed them the life-changing bounty. The community still had enough to eat, actually more, as the number of contributions to the community larder had also increased. The entire tribe benefitted. Not surprisingly, Akama quickly became popular in the Vutova Tribe."

"The Vutova's Hunt Leader was persistent in his studies of all the behaviors among the tribal members. There came a time when Akama found he coveted the Vutova Chieftain's Badge, worn and displayed as the clasp on the KuRuk's leather vest. Soon thereafter, Akama discovered he also coveted the chieftain's fine furs covering the man's tent. Furs that kept out the biting cold that never leaves their land and ever eats at fingertips, toes, and noses. Akama was mindful of his new feelings, acknowledging the fact that he envied all the material things his KuRuk had."

"Chieftains in the Gugwe nation always live with the fear that one day another who thinks they can run the tribe better will challenge them. When the time came, chieftains just took a knife to the gut, or a smash to the skull, or an arrow through the heart. No warning. Death just happened, and the title of Chieftain or KuRuk changed hands."

"Not with Akama. He gave his KuRuk notice of his intentions."

"One night, when all the people had gathered by the fire rings for their nightly community dinner, Akama spoke to the crowd, after he had dispersed the week's rewards, 'Hear me!' he slammed the end of his heavy staff on the ground, commanding the attention of his people. Turning so he could look the KuRuk of the Vutova Tribe directly in the eyes, he announced, 'I challenge you for your Chieftain's Badge, for your title. Fight me now to keep it or die because you don't have the strength to be our KuRuk!' he roared. The crowd roared back as the throng pulled away, forming a circle around the tribal leader and his challenger."

"Hungry for blood, the crush of people growled, howled and chanted, 'KuRuk, KuRuk, KuRuk!' Having come to the evening meal weaponless, surprise lit in the Chieftain's eyes when Akama tossed him a spear, the tip razor sharp obsidian, lashed to a long, smooth stick of Ironwood. Inwardly, the KuRuk laughed at his challenger's stupidity, because he was one of the best spearmen in Vutova. Akama shook his own spear in the air and roared his putrid breath at the KuRuk. They say death danced in his eyes as he lunged."

"As was his way, Akama had also long studied the war moves of this KuRuk. He used every bit of his gained knowledge against his foe. The KuRuk was a huge Gugwe, at least half a foot taller than Akama's thirteen feet. In addition, the Chieftain was five stone heavier because of his habit of taking extra shares of food, a practice warranted by his position. But he was no match for Akama's speed and cunning. Akama used moves he had learned from watching all the skilled warriors in the tribe, having developed a pattern he practiced daily alone in the woods, using all their best techniques. He danced with his spear using both ends, the sharp and the dull, heavy butt. Slicing, then jabbing the KuRuk's chin, shoulders, knees, ribs. Slice, jab, slice, jab."

"The KuRuk swayed, his knees like jelly, his eyes swimming with sweat and blood, trying to keep his sight locked on the devil before him. The KuRuk called out his challenger's name just before Akama leapt, swinging his body in a full arc, the obsidian razor slicing his opponent from ear to ear, blood gushing from his ruined neck, body thudding to the ground."

"A hush fell over the onlookers, and Akama turned in a circle, meeting the eyes of his people, waiting to see if another would challenge him."

"Silence met his stare, and then a female's voice rang out, 'Akama, Akama, Akama!' The tribe took up the chant, changing it to 'KuRuk, KuRuk, KuRuk'. So it was that Akama, who was no longer Akama, bent to his kill, took the dead Chieftain's Badge, hooked it to his vest, raised his spear up in victory, the beast inside him roaring with bloodlust. The weapon came down with a rending crack, breaking apart the lifeless tribesman's sternum. He tore open the dead Gugwe's chest, reaching in with his massive clawed hand, and ripped out his adversary's heart. Blood ran down his arm as he held the heart up for all to see, then he pressed it to his maw and tore a chunk off and chewed. We Gugwe believe that eating the heart of our foe transfers their strength to us."

"The throng surged around their new leader and hoisted him up on their shoulders, chanting his new title 'KuRuk', while he downed the rest of his grizzly prize."

"Vutova began a three-day celebration to honor its new ruler. Again, Akama, now known as KuRuk Vutova, did the unexpected. He ordered the former KuRuk's wives to empty the KuRuk's private larder and shared the spoils among all Vutova's people. When the first night of feasting was done, many drunk on the old KuRuk's fermented liquor, Akama sought his new abode. Opening the flap to enter, he found the fire crackling inside, smoke circling up and out the center vent. He smiled to find each female Gugwe of his new household lying naked, beckoning him to the pile of furs. KuRuk Vutova pointed at his three newly gained wives and ordered them to find shelter elsewhere. He put them aside and had no wish to dine on the former KuRuk's soiled women, sending them from the fur-covered tent, now his."

"The Vutova Tribe continued to thrive under the reward system Akama had created. A year passed, and each day the KuRuk required not just the warriors, but *all* the people to learn his dance of spears, the very best moves he had garnered from other warriors. They practiced these new skills each sunrise, then did their regular tasks to ensure the tribe's survival. When dusk arrived, everyone dropped whatever they were doing and danced the spear patterns again. Strength building, skills sharpening. The KuRuk changed some of his people's tasks, giving both the men and the women opportunities to be reassigned to jobs they desired. Not stuck with whatever they fell into because their parents before them had the same lifelong task. He created a group of women warriors, and when the male Gugwe scoffed at the idea; he assigned them as mentors to each would-be female fighter, offering a boon to those whose skills improved fastest. To determine how those boons were meted out, the KuRuk arranged fights between female opponents; the winner and their tutor rewarded. This practice quickly grew in popularity. Soon, the tribe prepared special food and drink as part of the routine before the weekly matches."

"The community built a fighting pit under the direction of the KuRuk. The sidelines were blocked off with woven rope barriers, where the onlookers could line the pit to watch the bloody action. Inevitably, the tribe began gambling. Bets were placed on the contestants: who would draw first blood, who would maim the other, who would win, and how quickly. Killing was prohibited, but maiming acceptable. Why bother training more warriors just to have them killed off by another member of the tribe in a contest?" Ama laughed.

"KuRuk discovered a young tribesman named Gorloc, with a special talent for making obsidian-tipped spears. He also exhibited the ability to construct good knives, sling-shots and other weapons. So, KuRuk had a special tent set up and materials delivered regularly to speed Gorloc's trade along. The weekly boon paid out to the fight's winner and her trainer was a valuable acquisition, each receiving one of Gorloc's finely made spears. It wasn't long before KuRuk added two additional apprentices to Gorloc's weapon tent."

"The Gugwe tribes across the northern tundra number thirteen. Each tribe with its own KuRuk, all under the rule of the Thana NukPana. Word spread among the tribes of the Vutova's food and weapon rewards, as well as the unusual training of female warriors. These stories made their way to Thana NukPana's throne."

"Curiosity about the Vutova tribe's odd practices took hold of the Thana. He assembled fifty of his fiercest warriors. The chosen group traveled with the Gugwe Emperor, along with a host of slaves he had stolen over time from the Fae, the Goblin, and the Human inhabitants many miles south of the Gugwe territories. The slaves were used to carry the troops' supplies; to cook; to service the Thana's soldiers. A minor offence would find a slave whipped, beaten, raped, and sometimes left for dead during the trip to the northern

Gugwe tribal village, Vutova. Thana NukPana wanted to see for himself what foolishness this KuRuk was fostering."

"The Vutova tribe welcomed the Thana and his troop, but had never seen slaves before. KuRuk quietly arranged for a great deal of secret surveillance of the Thana and his entourage, wanting to understand what role the slaves played in the Thana's life. A feast was prepared. The Thana and his followers had arrived on the same day the weekly pit fight was to take place. Thana NukPana could see for himself that all the members of the Vutovan tribe were muscled and healthy. The tribe's population had nearly doubled to five hundred strong since he had last visited under the former KuRuk. It had been Akama's practice to take in any Gugwe from other tribes who had come to the village to visit and wished to stay, or those who had been banished from their own tribes."

The cub in Ama's arms fidgeted and yawned. She glared at him, and he sat up straight to show she had his full attention, so she continued the story.

"When dusk fell, Thana NukPana's face betrayed his surprise when one of the Vutovas' beat out a drum pattern on a hollowed log. The drummed message caused the Vutova tribal population of men, women, children, old and young alike to drop what they were doing, grab their spears and began their evening ritual of the spear dance practice, a routine complete with guttural growls and a roaring finish."

"Thana NukPana did not hide his disgust at allowing females to take part, even though his eye could see the well-trained fighting skills were honed to deadly moves in the dance. More skill than his own armed men possessed. He held his tongue through the meal, planning to dress down this KuRuk upstart publicly. When the meal was served, KuRuk Vutova informed the Thana he was in luck. His visit coincided with the tribe's weekly games being held in the fighting pit. KuRuk assured the Thana he would see some of their best fighters pitted against one another tonight. Not knowing what this was all about, the Thana was intrigued, deciding his verbal denouncement of the Vutova KuRuk could wait until after these so-called games. He directed his soldiers to intersperse throughout the assembled tribal members in case there was trouble."

"KuRuk placed the Thana on his own carved tree trunk to sit before the pit. The best view and a seat of honor. The gathering filled in all around the pit. Younglings were given a space at the front so they could see. Some sat on the shoulders of a father, or uncle, or brother in the back."

"Using ropes, three men lowered the first two combatants into the fighting arena. Each opponent held a spear in hand as they stepped down onto the sandy floor. A roar went up from the assembly, and the fighters hefted their spears, egged on by the chanting of their names. Thana could see the spectators quickly exchanging stones, a way of making and later collecting on bets."

"The two opponents ran at each other, their powerful bodies slashing and spinning. One drew first blood with a slice across her adversary's shoulder, but took a painful jab to the ribs with the butt-end of her rival's spear shaft. They flew through the pit in a series of movements as if they had been choreographed. It took a keen eye to catch all the bloody damage, while the symmetry ensorcelled the onlookers."

"The end came quickly as the taller of the two thwacked the other on the back of her knees, sending her to the ground and a mouthful of sand. Down, but not defeated, the mob went wild, but her growl echoed out of the pit, she rolled, her hands scrabbling at the ground, her right grabbing her spear once more, as her adversary danced around the pit, drinking in the crowd's approval, shouting her name, not paying attention until the horde went abruptly silent."

"Thana NukPana leaned forward, as excited as everyone surrounding the pit, to see what would happen next."

"The over-confident fighter was taken aback at the sudden hush that fell over the crowd, turned to see her foe up again, running toward her, leaping in an arabesque fashion, spear thrust forward like an extension of her arm, a beautiful movement causing a sharp intake of breath by the watchers, which they held, as the scene played out in front of them. Just when it seemed victory was hers, the other lifted her right arm and threw a handful of sand into her challenger's eyes. The exquisite move ended in an ugly fall, ankle bone shattering as she crashed to the ground, sand blinded. The shorter combatant placed a foot on her competitor's chest, the obsidian point of her spear drawing a small bead of blood at her throat. 'Concede,' she demanded."

"The opponent dropped her spear, and the cluster of spectators thundered their approval. Looking up proudly, the winner nodded first to her mentor, then to KuRuk Vutova, and lastly to Thana NukPana, who frowned back in answer."

"Thana watched incredulously as KuRuk awarded a newly made spear to the winner and one to her mentor."

"The visiting Thana NukPana stood, intending to share his wisdom and denounce their KuRuk's foolishness to the Tribe, but before he could get his first word out, the audience had picked up the mentor and the winner on their shoulders, cheering, whisking them off to the fire rings to celebrate."

"KuRuk Vutova grasped the Thana's shoulder and squeezed, pleased with the performance, and said, 'I hope you enjoyed our competitions, Thana NukPana. Now, there are some serious changes I would like to talk to you about. Come, I know just the place where we can talk uninterrupted; a grand vista of the land I want you to see. There are many ideas I wish to share with you,' he grinned. 'There are many questions in my head that need answers. It is my wish and hope that your great wisdom benefits me.'"

"The Thana's lips curved up with a smile not reflected in his eyes. 'Very well, show me this impressive vista of yours. We can talk on the way.'"

"The two men went west out of the KuRuk's village, and the Vutova leader used the walk to pour out his ideas to the Gugwe Emperor. Expounding on how the hunting and gathering rewards worked, he illuminated how his new weapon's master, now with four apprentices, was making many weapons for the Tribe, rather than each warrior having to make their own. Sharing his success in preparing three units of female soldiers; Akama explained his plans to begin war training at an early age, wherein the younglings would be taken from their mothers when they turned eight. They would live in barracks together. Their training would mold them into a close-knit fighting unit."

"Thana listened attentively as the KuRuk laid out each new idea, his face schooled not to reveal his thoughts."

"A skill you must learn to master, little cub," Ama pinched the boy.

"Anyway, when he finished sharing his notions and plans, Akama pelted the Thana with questions about his slaves. Where did he find them? What was their purpose? How could he get some?"

"At last, they came to the great cliff point, and Thana had to concede the KuRuk had not lied. The vista spread before them just as the moon cast its spotlight, showcasing the valley below, running along the colored rock cliff side, a rushing river crashing through the land and dropping off in a thundering waterfall. The Thana surveyed the panoramic view and was impressed, but his disgust with all he had heard and seen this night bubbled up. He turned his body to face the KuRuk. 'You are not the traditional chieftain,' his words delivered with a menacing growl."

"KuRuk nodded his head, thinking the comment a compliment."

"The Thana crinkled his snout at the fool. He couldn't even tell when he was being insulted! 'You are not fit to rule as the Vutova KuRuk!' his words roared out, spewing his putrid breath with them. 'You've turned your village into a disgrace. Our females are meant for breeding, to give us good, strong sons to train as warriors, not to learn a soldier's ways for themselves. You hand out rewards like sweets instead of claiming the best for yourself to show your strength as a leader. You are foolish and wasteful. I will not permit it!' The ground reverberated with his bellowing, his body trembling on the edge of violence. 'What possessed you to put all these crazy ideas into play?'"

"KuRuk Vutova could hardly believe his ears. 'Did you not see how healthy the tribe was? Are you blind to the power of all the people, their bodies robust with training; their powerful sense of community, but a stronger sense of individualism? I do not limit my people, holding them down under my thumb. Would you take it all from them again? Can't you see how these varied methods could be instilled in the whole of the Gugwe population so we become the strongest, most feared race in the lands?' his own voice reaching an angry boom."

"Thana held up his hand, a gesture striking the KuRuk as child-like, his outline shining in the moonlight, the landscape behind him as he stood in all his perceived glory upon the precipice. 'No,' Thana said in a quiet, firm voice, 'I will not allow you to spread your insanity further. Your foolish ideas will spoil our culture. Kill, eat, breed. Those are the only things we need to survive; you fool.'"

"KuRuk laughed, causing the Thana's eyes to glow red. 'My apologies, Thana. I failed to tell you about my latest discovery, including how such an idea could better life for our people.'"

"Thana's eyebrows raised. The leader of the Vutova continued, 'A strange creature came to our village a few months back. It taught me a new skill before its weak body succumbed to death. You may have noticed, I like to learn new things,' he smiled at the emperor, 'You never know when just the right skill can change your life Thana NukPana, listen...' KuRuk thrust his arms out, fingers pointing at the Emperor of the Gugwe race. A near-invisible thread of power ran from one of the Akama's fingers and attached to the Thana's forehead. 'Your mind is mine,' he declared."

"The Thana's eyes went slack, his rigid muscles relaxed as he stood staring blankly at KuRuk. 'I will demonstrate my new skill to you, Emperor. You see, I have learned to cast a spell of mind-control. Just think what it could mean for our people! Oh, wait, I forgot. You only wish for an endless cycle of kill, eat, breed for the Gugwe nation.' Akama laughed, 'No, Thana. I am afraid I must reject your short-sighted leadership. I do not accept your version of the future for the Gugwe people.' KuRuk sadly shook his head. 'You are a disappointment, Thana NukPana. A fool with a leader's title who does not know how to lead.'"

"KuRuk clucked his tongue three times." Ama demonstrated with her own tongue. "'Turn around, Thana.'"

"The giant beast-man's feet shuffled beneath him, turning his body full circle to face the panoramic view once more. KuRuk tightened his grip on the Thana's mind, ripping, shredding, giving his command in a calm voice, 'Jump, Thana NukPana. Jump. Your life is forfeit.'"

"The emperor of all the 13 Gugwe tribes stepped off the sheer drop. The Vutova KuRuk released his hold, freeing Thana's mind."

"And do you know," Ama poked the cub in her lap in his belly. "Thana NukPana screamed all the way to the bottom."

"'Yes,' Akama said to himself, 'I thought you would be the type to scream all the way down to your death.'"

All the cubs outside Ama's door laughed, thinking Akama clever. Ama pushed the cub off her lap. "There's work to do, but I will tell you the end if you promise to go straight to your chores when the story is done." He nodded. Her eyes looked to the doorway, and the strays put their forefingers and middle fingers together, kissed them and held them to their hearts. Ama nodded her acknowledgement and invited them to slip in to hear the final accounting of the KuRuks' rise to Emperor.

"The new Thana NukPana walked thoughtfully back toward the village, already thinking of another he would appoint as the KuRuk Vutova to take his former place. He smiled pleasantly at the idea of a new tradition. Taking his time, mind occupied with plans for the future, he reviewed all the changes he wished to implement throughout the Gugwe empire. Campaigns to capture many slaves who could do the work of his people, so the Gugwe could thrive and train as an army, able to overcome their enemies. They could get not only what they needed, but anything they wanted. He knew these changes would have to be phased in. There would be much to learn along the way. He was no stranger to trial and error. He would have to study the races he intended to make slaves: the Fae, the Goblins, the Humans, to learn of their strengths, their weaknesses, their ways, and their interactions with one another. It would take a great deal of patience to influence the thinking of the 13 tribes. But he vowed he would see his dreams through to fruition. The Gugwe people would reap the benefits of his ambition." Ama passed each cub a sweet from a wooden bowl and shooed them away from her hearth.

CHAPTER 1: Dream Magic

Kris slept, drifting in a calm, soothing dream. A soft voice captured his attention as he floated in a clear waterhole surrounded by rocky outcroppings. He spotted the small gargoyle sitting above the pool on a flat stone jutting out over the water. It was the same creature he had noticed among the stones in various fireplaces at Robert's hold. His body buoyed, he asked, "What is your name? Why are you here?" Kris sculpted his cupped hands in and out at his sides, maneuvering his long limbs around the water in the circular pool.

"I am known as Dedo. I will help you and your cousins on your quest, young seer."

Kris considered those words, circling the circumference of the water twice. "This is not a vision," he told Dedo.

"No. Not a vision," Dedo agreed. "Originally, when you all set out on a quest, your goal was to find uncles and fathers. Somewhere along the way you got sidetracked, changed your focus to finding your cousin Faith, who before was only ever a whispered rumor to you."

"Yes," Kris acknowledged. "We haven't found the uncles and fathers, but our efforts led us to some clues about the Fae Court. Nor have we been able to find the King or the Queen of the Fae, but I had a true vision about Faith, our Fae Princess. So, we wanted to see where that path would lead us."

"You, your sister and your cousins must find the road again to seek your uncles and their father. Their need for your help is greater than Faith's need." The gargoyle spread his arms, palms up, as if he had decreed the truth of the matter.

"We cannot turn aside, Dedo. Faith is in mortal danger. I have seen it," Kris told him.

"There are many threads within the weave of this cloth. The princess will have the help of others. She has much to learn, but only a select few can teach her the skills she will need to prepare for her future role. Your path points another way. Never fear. You will meet Faith again," the gargoyle spoke with authority.

Kris closed his eyes, letting the truth of Dedo's words fill him. The sun pushed up over the horizon, bathing the small pool in golden sunlight. The young seer told the small creature, "We will go north with the goblin lads."

"Good. You must become the leader of your companions. North is the direction to find your uncles and fathers. This is critical to the weave. Critical for Faith's future. If you need to contact me again, make it private. Here are two agates. Rub them together, speak your message, and I will hear of your need."

Kris's hand closed over the two colorful stones. He felt the mantle of Dedo's command fall across his body like a silk cloak. When he next opened his eyes, the gargoyle was gone. Sleep took him back into her arms and cradled him; his slumber peaceful for another hour.

The sounds of the morning camp woke him. The Goblin lads were stoking last night's fire to life and putting water on to boil. Kris rose and shook out his blanket. Two agates fell to the ground at his feet. Proof of his dream conversation with Dedo. He pocketed the stones. Pouring cold water into the camp's metal washbowl, Kris splashed it on his face to wash the sleep from his eyes. His cousins were in various stages of waking and moving about. Walking to the stump he had stood on the night before, he climbed atop, announcing to one and all, "Change in plan," he stated firmly. "We're going to follow our original quest to find uncles and fathers."

There was a cacophony of questions, demands, and outright declarations against this course from his cousins. The goblin lads looked around at one another, saying nothing. Mariella remained silent.

"Quiet, all of you, and listen," Kristian commanded in a soft voice. For once, they obeyed. "I have it from a reliable source. Faith's safety is in the hands of others. We still must find our fathers and uncles if we are to have any chance of finding the King and...and hopefully Queen of the Fae. We will cross paths with our cousin Faith again in the north." He carefully met gazes with each of his older cousins, then stepped down from the stump.

The collective crowd stood around staring at him. Travis still lay under his blanket, with a dog on both sides. He scrubbed his hand through his hair as he sat up, leaning on his elbows. "Well then, stop wasting time," he said to no one in particular. "Kris has set a fresh course for us. Let's get breakfast going. Best not to travel on an empty stomach, I always say. Master Kristian's compass points north, so north we'll go."

With Travis' approval, action took over the camp. Mariella smiled at her brother, and he granted her one in return. "Why?" she whispered to him.

"I had a visit from the gargoyle we saw at Robert's fortress. Remember him?" he whispered back.

It was all the answer she needed. Mariella nodded at her brother, packed up her things, and helped make breakfast to feed the crew.

ALIAH, GARRETT, CARLISSE, and Delainey had been riding since sunrise; the bright orb overhead now. They stopped by a small stream for a break, watered the horses, letting them drink their fill. Then hobbled the animals in the small field to graze while they prepared a quick meal.

Aliah took advantage of the clear stream. After filling the pot with water to boil, she gathered all their water bladders, found an easy spot to kneel on the bank, filling them. The reflection of the gargoyle appeared in the water without warning; her head jerking up to find his form standing across the small stream, his stance irreverent among the river rocks.

"Well," she said with only minor irritation, "you've certainly taken your time in showing yourself again." She capped the bladder in hand, laid it aside, and grabbed another. "The last time I saw you was the day you warned me to be ready for Val and Faith's secret exit. You said you'd give me more information soon! I haven't had a word from you since. Do you have any idea what we've been through?" she demanded.

Dedo tapped his foot against the stone beneath him. "I do. But I'm here now. I've been busy," he answered curtly. "You, Master Garrett, and your sisters are on your way to rescue your sister Valerie Victoria Pureheart," he raised one eyebrow, and she nodded grudgingly. "It is the path you must continue to follow, though rescue will not be necessary by the time you find her. By then, she will be safe in the company of others willing to help all of you in your next task."

"The next task is to find Faith," Aliah stated. "She's missing too, you know."

"Wrong, Mistress Aliah." They glared at one another. "Faith has others seeing to her rescue. I have a plan for all of you to reunite. In addition, there is a special person who will provide Faith, you and your sisters training in the use of all the magical powers at your disposal, not just those you've stumbled across learning, seer!"

Aliah dragged in a sharp breath, her eyes narrowing at the goyle. He knew she was a seer! How could he possibly have found out? After all her care to keep that information secret, her efforts seemed an obvious waste now.

"Your sister Valerie," he said her name with distaste, "is with several new companions being hosted by the Dream Weaver as we speak. Your entourage will find them." He paused, but when she said nothing, he continued. "You will all take instruction from the Weaver, training until the Weaver deems you ready to leave that special tutelage. This is critical to the weave. Am I clear?" His foot tapped away in irritable annoyance.

Aliah wanted to rage at him, follow her own course, and be rid of the lifelong manipulation she had endured from him. Once, long ago, she was enthralled with Dedo, but in the last year or two he had become a thorn in her side. Deep down, she knew he had always been right about every direction or command, so she nodded her acquiescence, afraid that if she opened her mouth, things would be said that she would later regret.

"Good," he allowed, as if he could hear her churning thoughts, his foot coming to stillness. "You will find the Dream Weaver's house ten miles due west of here. Oh," he turned to address her over his shoulder as he walked away. "Do hurry, or you'll miss afternoon tea. He's expecting you." Dedo had taken three or four steps when Aliah spoke next.

"Wait!" she stammered. "He? He? The Dream Weaver is a woman! I know because I've been to see her before," she bragged.

Once more, those beady black eyes gazed at her from head to toe, making her shiver involuntarily. "Another lesson in proving you don't know everything you think you do, Mistress Aliah. Tuck that nugget away for examination later and learn from it." The haughty gargoyle disappeared right before her eyes.

DEDO RETURNED TO SIR Robert's fortress to the rocks in the fireplace in Faith's room. He found Reatha and the old nurse rocking their chairs in matched time, mending piled in their laps, needles poking in and out of material like they were wielding tiny stabbing weapons.

Lenny and Lester saw him first, turned to one another, hands over their mouths to stifle their laughter, turning back quickly to their staid positions, dripping wax on the mantel.

The old nurse, concentrating on her task, never even raised her head. "Reatha, put aside the shirt you're mending. I believe Dedo has graced us with his presence again."

Reatha's eyes climbed over the rocks above the mantel until she spotted him. "You must be tired."

He nodded, chin resting on his knees.

"Have you completed all your rounds? Come now, tell us what you found?" her request was almost pleading.

"Put your fears aside, mistress. All the threads of the weave are in motion. Our princess is in the hands of Robin Goodfellow. We must trust Queen Aleta's plan. A plan she had taken great care to put into play so many years past will now come to fruition, just as she had foreseen. The spell she cast on Robin Wilum Goodfellow as a child, linking him to Faith through the wake-Robin, the trillium, has been sprung," he announced.

Reatha sighed in relief, though her fears only ebbed a bit. Nursie continued rocking. "At least we don't have to repeat the story, warning her off any longer! I was sick and tired of telling Faith never to pick a spring trillium, drilling the idea into her mind," she stated in fact.

All three of them smiled. Lenny and Lester mimed picking a flower, adding more wax to the mantel in their jest.

"Reatha, you must convince Sir Robert to take the hold's small garrison north to accompany the two of you on a visit to see your sister Mari. The time has come," Dedo told Reatha.

The nurse reached over and patted Reatha's hand. Lenny and Lester mocked an action as if they were riding horses, dripping a fresh coat of wax beneath them.

Dedo pointed at the two small gargoyles. "You two will go with them." They faked biting their nails, then bubbled up in silent laughter. "I have a task that only two fools can accomplish," he told them, shaking his finger in admonishment. They sat stone still.

"I have other things to see to, Evy," Dedo told the old nurse. "But first, I must pay my respects to our queen. Do you have a message for your lady?" he offered.

"Only to send her, my love. She's years beyond needing her old nurse's advice."

Dedo nodded his approval.

"Send her my love as well," Reatha said quietly. "Remember, she still needs us all."

"Make your preparations. I will see you again before you leave for Mari's hold," he told them, disappearing into the stones.

Dedo reappeared in the lowest level of the fortress, touched the stone on the shore of the map shaped like Sapphire Lake, let a wave wash over him among the beach agates, then he touched another and found himself before the shimmering pool at the bottom of the Fae palace in the far north.

He dropped a small pebble into the mirror of water, causing ripples to spread from one edge to the other. When all was smooth again, his Lady Queen's face shone out before him in the pool.

Dedo bowed. She smiled, small lines appearing at the corners of her eyes. Her face looked tired and drawn. "Good to see you, old friend," she told him.

"Are you well, my Queen?" concern laced his words, noting her skin was a pallid gray.

"I am well enough," she assured him. "My jailers' experiment with new tactics. They are always trying to capture the essence of my power, but I am still whole. What news of my daughter?" Her eyes brightened at the asking.

"The Fae Princess has picked a trillium, my lady. Contrary to all our warnings," he let the words wash over her and continued, "It was in the hour of her greatest need, but she sprung the spell you laid so many years before. Robin Wilum Goodfellow answered her call."

Dedo watched as Queen Aleta's relief physically rippled through her, and her skin took on its usual golden pallor.

"A spell cast so many years gone by," she sighed dreamily, "A spell that is still in force today. It would seem my vision was a true one. I always loved the spring trilliums," she admitted. "It's a pity I haven't seen them for so many years."

"Persid is dead," he cut in, as though he were telling her the moon was up.

"Did she..." the Queen started.

"Of course, my lady. The weave was woven, the fortune told. When she realized who the girl was, her long-cultivated hatred of you begged for revenge." Aleta's face rearranged itself in alarm.

Dedo held up his hand, palm out, to stop her fears. "In the end, Persid weighed the value of her children against her desire for revenge. The scale tipped. Unfortunately, the princess had to kill Persid to save herself before all was said and done."

"Persid's children? I promised," she insisted.

"Your daughter has your heart, my queen. She gave the same promise again. Persid's children live."

"What of Persid's twin?" she queried; her face stone hard.

"I used the marker you gave me," he told her.

"So soon, Dedo?"

"It was necessary."

She adjusted her crown; the weight was heavy. "Of course. You must do as you see fit to bring the threads together in the weave."

"Morveena has captured Faith, my queen."

Aleta drew a sharp breath of surprise. "You saved this nugget for last?" she accused.

"Some matters were always unclear in the visions, as you know. You must trust, as we all must. Morveena has hatched a plan to sell our princess to the Gugwe. To Thana NukPana," his voice quivered. He watched the color drain from her face.

"Never!" she whispered. "You must never allow it to happen, Dedo. I beg you, never," her voice trailed off.

"There is no need to make your suffering greater, my queen!" he said with authority. "I have the spider's spinning wheel, and the weaves are in my control. The Gugwe will not have her!" He hadn't realized his voice had risen to a shout. Two spots of color rose to his cheeks, embarrassed by his outburst.

The imprisoned queen calmed him. "Never fear, old friend, if you are pulling the threads in the weave, all will come smooth in the cloth." She wished she could reach out to offer him comfort through touch. "You must go now. I am glad you came and held back no details, however dire. We must trust that the spell given to Robin as a child will do its work as we planned." She turned her head, listening, then looked at Dedo again. "The guards come for me. I must go, and you still have arrangements to make! Take heart and help wherever you can find it. I promise to be strong," she assured him. Her beautiful face fading from the pool, her last question a soft echo in the chamber: "What of my love, Lennox?"

Before Dedo could answer, she was gone, likely to endure tortures he could not fathom at the hands of her captors. His only relief was that there wasn't time to give her the news King Lennox was still missing. Dedo's only hope when they next met was that he could deliver a different response. The clever gargoyle took a moment to be grateful his unspoken answer would keep hope strong in her heart.

AFTER VISITING ANOTHER'S dreams, Ari spun back along the golden thread, reentering his stone house. He stood at the edge of the wide web he had woven throughout his dining room, his prisoners encased, quiet in their cocoons. Exhaling softly, he shifted into spider form. One by one, he touched the foreheads of each of his charges, inserting a slight alteration to their memories using his dream magic. He spent the next several minutes gathering all his webbing from his victims, now his guests, absorbing it back into his sac.

Another shift and he had coalesced back into his man-form. Arnid went about the room, setting the stage just as he wanted it. Satisfied, he took a chair at the table after placing a fresh pitcher of ale and five mugs with varying levels of beer in front of each of his guests. Taking the pitcher in hand, he loudly asked, "Now then, who's ready for a refill?"

The four companions groggily opened their eyes, each holding a mug, looking around the table at one another. There were no webs constricting them now; the evidence was gone. In fact, the four of them didn't remember any imprisonment at all.

Valerie narrowed her eyes, looked suspiciously at the Dream Weaver, then glanced over her shoulder to the shadowed fireplace corner. She turned to Caz. "When did you and Rolland get here? I...I must have dozed off," she said, trying to reconcile her muddled thoughts.

Saffron seemed just as confused as Val. Rolland only acknowledged the relief he felt at finding Saffron safe.

Caz looked from the Weaver to each of his friends. "Wait!" he declared. "I remember you told us we'd found the Dream Weaver. It's you!" he pointed at their host. Ari rewarded him with a smile. "But," Caz scratched his head, "you also told us the girls weren't here, yeah? What's what?"

"You're mistaken, young Touchstone. I merely asked if *you* thought the girls were here." Ari reminded Caz, "If I understand correctly, based on our conversation, seems you all wish to have your fortunes told, hey?"

"Somehow, I missed some parts of the conversation," Val said doubtfully, not trusting Ari's words. There seemed to be a hole in her memory.

"Ah," Ari countered, "no need to feel embarrassed, Mistress Valerie. You and your friend Saffron were nearly exhausted when you arrived. It didn't surprise me when you both fell into a light nap. No harm done. A warm day and a mug or two of good ale can have such an effect. I'm glad I could offer you a respite before your colleagues arrived. These two lads were quite worried about your safety!" he emphasized.

"Asleep? You claim we both fell asleep?" She looked for a second confirmation from him. "But I remember..." her eyes drifted back to the shadowed corner again, but the thought was gone when Ari reached over and patted her hand to comfort her. "Oh, I don't know," she hedged. "I guess it's possible I might have zonked out for a while. But it seems like I would remember something..."

"I know how you feel, Mistress Pureheart, but must be, it was only a dream." Ari offered.

He worked his way around the table, topping off their mugs. "I'll just be in the kitchen getting a meal ready," he told his guests. "Make yourselves at home. Once you're all revived, you can tell me which of you wants your fortune told first, hey?"

CHAPTER 2: Spend Your Own Bacon

Tuck, Zud, and Weasel squatted in a circle with Travis and Shawn. Weasel had an arm around each of the dogs at his sides; stroking their heads as they leaned into him. Travis was using a stick to draw a crude map of Sharas in the dirt. Shawn pointed, stating, "We're right about here. And over here..." he pointed again, "is where our homes are."

Brittany walked up to the small group and kneeled down next to Weasel, offering him a smile, and began petting one dog. "Show us where you lads are heading," she directed to Tuck.

Tuck picked up another stick to use as a pointer. Tapping three places northeast of their current position, he told them, "First off, we know of three gob clans who were there, there and there. At least they were when we last came through this area two years ago. We plan to go to each and see if they're safe, warn them about the Gugwe. Hopefully, they'll send a contingent to a moot to discuss all the problems and help devise solutions."

Zud took the stick from Tuck and drew the shape of Sapphire Lake, then added the outline of the north peninsula. He made ripples like waves in all the vast lakes surrounding the land. Zud waved the stick across the whole peninsula. "Our clans live everywhere up here." He looked up, locked eyes with Travis. "So do the Fae." All the lads nodded their heads in agreement.

Weasel used his finger to point at a spot just between the North and South peninsulas. "This would be a good place to hold the moot."

Brittany took a stick out of one of the dog's mouths and added her own artist touch to the dirt map, creating a vast swath of land above Sapphire Lake. Using her penchant for drama, she looked around the circle at each of them. Taking her time, she drew 13 large Xs across parts of the map. "There, lads," she said to them, "there is the land of the Gugwe nation." Everyone stared at the Xs as though they could come to life and bite them. All the lads and cousins filtered in and out of the group, adding bits and pieces of detail to the map or making comments on what was depicted. The original five were still studying the configuration when Kristian squatted down beside

Travis. Blue eyes moved from side to side, taking in the map the group had created. He had his own pointer, drew arcs across the map connecting different points, and suggested they should travel to the three goblin villages first and then visit their own homes in the mid-lands.

"I say we follow the lads to their clan strongholds, then cut west, stop in at home to let family know we're safe, see if they have any news to share. We can report that we found Faith and bring them up to speed. I like Tuck's plan to hold a formal moot. But I'd like to expand the invitations to include goblins, Fae, really any citizens of Sharas that want to attend. We can check to see if others from home have an interest in joining us for a gathering." Scanning the map again, Kris placed a circle around the area Weasel had shown for the meeting. "Maybe we'll get new information at the moot to direct our next course." Kris looked at Weasel. "Do you think two or three of the lads would want to travel separately? Maybe head to the north peninsula to spread the word up there about the moot to Fae, goblins, and men alike, while we do the same down here?"

Tuck and Zud immediately volunteered, saying they thought Drako would likely go with them. "I can get word to Robert's fortress," Kris told the group. "Robert can spread it south from there. Good work, everyone," Kris told them sincerely. "Let's pack up camp and head out."

Travis smiled at Kristian, surprised to feel a warm glow in his chest, proud his younger cousin had taken on the role of a leader. He was shaking his head in wonder as he grabbed the piece of bacon Shawn was about to put in his mouth, broke it in half and gave a piece to each dog. Shawn punched Travis on the shoulder. "Spend your own bacon to train the dogs," he growled at his brother good-naturedly. "Besides, Britt has already got them trained on her hand."

Travis laughed. "Shawn, dogs always mind the last master who gave the treat."

"We'll see," Shawn countered.

"Hey bro, want to put a wager on it?" Travis urged, a twinkle in his eye.

They all walked away from the dirt map, leaving Weasel and the dogs, their heads in his lap. "Now I know how they do it, eh, fellows?" he asked the dogs as he scratched behind their ears.

It took longer than usual to tear the camp down. They sorted out some supplies — cookware, food, and water bladders — to provide Tuk, Zud, and Drako for their route. Bento advised the three to split the night watch in half every night and rotate, so one of them always got a full night's rest while the other two shared the watch. If they cycled through using his system, it would rest everyone enough to keep alert to dangers. Bento did not want any of them to be taken unaware by a Gugwe again. He shivered at the thought. Brittany gently touched his arm for solace, aware of his fear.

Lehto organized the other groups and was divvying up all the gear equally between them to pack and carry when Brittany marched up to him. "What's going on here, Lehto?"

The goblin cringed, not sure what the tone of her voice meant, wondering if he'd insulted her or broken some Fae rule unknown to gobs. "I'm just dispersing the load evenly between the packs, Mistress, so the weight's fair to carry," he explained and turned back to the task.

"This is definitely not fair," she declared.

"I may be off a few ounces here or there, Mistress." It was clear he'd got his back up a bit from her criticism. "But I've been making up matte'd packs for longer years than you've been born and..." he was sputtering, face turning red.

The argument attracted a small crowd of their companions.

"You're wrong, Lehto. Plain wrong." She poked her finger into his chest to make her point. "How many piles have you got here, Lehto? I count only nine." She tapped his chest with her finger as she counted off from one to nine.

His temper flared again. He took hold of the offending finger poking at him. "Now, see here..." he planned to set her straight.

She shook her head. "Why only nine matte packs, Lehto?"

"As you well know, Mistress, Tuck, Zud, and Drako are splitting off from our group. I already divvied up the loads for those three. You see now?" he demanded, barely containing himself from clenching his fist and shaking it at her.

"What I see, Lehto, is nine packs being matte'd up when there should be fourteen. There are five more of us." She spread her hands out, signifying her brother and cousins. "We don't expect you to carry our load. You're not our slaves, Lehto. We are equal. I'll help you redistribute the loads," she told him, patting his hand and laying out five more canvas squares.

Lehto turned three shades of red, from his cheeks to his knees. He turned to face his embarrassing assumption. Sure that when the alliance formed, the Fae would treat the gobs like their personal servants. It had never entered his mind that the circumstances could be any different. They were equal; she had said. On the same footing. Well, he vowed to reserve judgement, bide his time to see if actions matched words. This could change everything, he mused. But until the full results were in, best not to hope too much, only to have expectations dashed against a stone. In the meantime, he decided he would practice with Brittany–*equality*–and see if this was a concept he could apply to a bigger group than fourteen. It went against everything he'd been taught his whole life about relations between the Fae and the Goblins.

He waved his hand in the air, calling out, "No, no, Mistress Brittany. You can't put those two things together. Here now, let me show you some tricks to making a proper matte," as he hurried over to share the knowledge of his skill. He was delighted to find in her a student willing to listen to his instructions.

Kristian walked along to the far end of their camp and stood by his horse, checking his gear. He pulled two agates from his pocket and gently rubbed them together. Whispering all the plans the companions had made, identifying the place and time the moot was to take place. Trusting Dedo would receive his message.

Vega watched from behind a big white pine, wondering who the young lad was talking to.

CHAPTER 3: Reunion

Aliah followed what she called 'her shimmering thread of love' that only she could see toward their sister Val's location. When they reached the prominent ridges surrounding the stone house Dedo had described to her, Aliah insisted they stay hidden in the trees on the north end. She watched with suspicion as smoke drifted out of the chimney, but could see no movement within the house from her viewpoint. Not that she mistrusted what the bossy gargoyle had told her. But it was the memory of her own vision of Val, trapped in a spider's lair, that was creating her anxiety.

"What is it, Aliah?" Carlisse whispered.

"I'm just being cautious."

Garrett leaned close, causing his horse to side-step, adjusting to his shift in weight. "I'll go down first," he said quietly in Aliah's ear.

"Thank you, Garrett," she said sincerely, "but I think this requires winged reconnaissance. Lainey," she whispered back to her sister, "you're the smallest and our best sneak." Lainey grinned proudly at the compliment. "Spread your wings and fly down there. Have a look at the situation before we all reveal our presence. Be careful! Try not to let anyone see you!"

Without another word, Delainey dismounted, handing the reins of her horse to Carlisse. The slim Fae opened her wings, stretched them, took a running start, and leaped off the edge of the ridge. Her wings, full open, caught the upward draft. Delainey soared in graceful circles round and round the valley on the air currents. Slowly, she made her way to the stone house sitting in the middle of the protected valley. From the ridge above, Lainey looked like a tiny doll as the others watched her land behind the barn. The sun blazed in its afternoon arc, but the forest's shadows allowed her to sneak undetected from tree to tree until she reached the house itself. She pressed her back against the sun-warmed stones, listening, her body tense. She cocked her head to one side, focusing on the sounds from within. Lainey couldn't believe her ears. Did she hear Valerie's laughter? Turning on the ball of her left foot, her hands found holds among the stones that made up the structure's exterior. Pulling herself up so she could peek over the edge of the window sash. Her eyes widened at the scene before her.

The sister they had come to rescue sat around the table with three goblins, two male and a female. There was another muscular man who was placing a platter of cheese and a basket of fresh bread in the middle of the table. The smell of the warm bread made her stomach growl. As Delainey dropped back down from the window, she heard the door open on the other side of the cottage. She silently lowered herself to the ground. Delainey pressed her back against the stones once more, holding her breath, ready to take flight if necessary. Relief flooded her when she saw a black cat round the corner of the house and head toward the barn.

Val's laughter caught Delainey's attention again. She pulled herself up to look once more. The man was no longer in the room. Her sister cut a large wedge of cheese, and one of the male goblins cautioned her, "Remember what Ari said, Val, save some for the other guests he's expecting." Val's face crinkled in mirth as she took a large bite of the cheese and moaned, "Mmmmmm."

Lainey descended, deciding she should go back to Aliah to report their sister didn't appear to be in any danger. Actually, it seemed Val was enjoying herself. Lainey's stomach growled again. She could almost taste the cheese. Suddenly, she startled at the black cat as it rubbed against her legs. She chided herself for her jumpiness, for having let her attention wander and wasn't keeping a good watch on her situation. Reaching down, she absently petted the animal weaving in and out between her ankles. Eventually, the cat walked away. Once again, Delainey registered the sound of the door opening and closing on the opposite side of the house.

Just as she was opening her wings and taking flight, the man she'd seen serving the group inside stuck his head out the window. He called out a cheerful greeting, "Hullo there. High tea is almost over, but you've made it just in time," he told Delainey with a sparkle in his eye. Watching, she saw those same eyes rise to the top of the ridge. "Tell your sisters and Master Garrett to come on down and join us. I've been expecting you for the past hour. There's only one road down. See the tallest white pine up top? Just to the left of where you last saw your travel companions is a steep switchback. Be mindful of taking care with your horses coming down," he warned, then chuckled merrily. "You can stable the horses in my barn. Don't break your necks to hurry!" He cocked his head. "But I worry Mistress Valerie will eat all the cheese before your party arrives!" He noted the surprised look on Delainey's face. "Off you go now," he shooed her away good-naturedly. Lainey found she couldn't form a response, so she said nothing, snapped her wings open and flew straight as an arrow back to Aliah. Her oldest sister grabbed her by both arms when she landed, alarmed by Lainey's straight shot back to them, stealth forgotten. "Is it bad?" Aliah worried, searching Lainey's eyes.

"Bad?" Lainey questioned and laughed. "No. Not if you consider an invitation to tea bad, Aliah." Her older sister gasped, thinking of Dedo's last words, '*Better hurry so you don't miss tea.*'

Lainey took the reins back from Carlisse and led her horse off to the left. "He said the road is a steep switchback to the valley floor, so we'd better walk the horses down." She called back to them over her shoulder, "Val doesn't look like she's in any danger. In fact, just the opposite. Come on! Move along and don't dawdle, because, as usual, Val's eating all the cheese!"

After they unsaddled the horses and put them in stalls, Garrett gave each of their mounts a cup of precious grain and made sure they had a bucket of fresh water. He grabbed Aliah by the arm and turned to hurry from the barn. Garrett was eager to confirm with his own eyes that Val was safe and whole. "Are you sure this isn't some kind of trap?" he asked her in a low voice.

She shook her head, straining against his hold. "One can never be sure of anything, Garrett," he released his grasp, unable to hold her longer. "But I trust Lainey's instincts, if not my own."

Garrett trailed after all three fairies until they came to a stop at the porch door.

Lainey bounced up and down on the balls of her feet as she knocked politely at the door. The man who'd invited her to afternoon tea stepped out from the kitchen door, greeted Lainey's polite curtsy as she gave him a timid, "Hello again."

He swung the door open. "Ah, just in time," he smiled. "I've laid out more refreshments and set a place for each of you. Welcome to the humble home of the Edgewood's Dream Weaver," he waved his hand, inviting them to enter.

Garrett caught the look of suspicion passing between Carlisse and Aliah. He had no way of knowing this was not the house of or the person they knew to be the Dream Weaver. Lainey pushed through, hungry beyond caring about the discrepancy. When she got to the doorway leading into the house, Val spotted her and shrieked her name, running to greet her sister. When Aliah and Carlisse saw their two sisters embracing, they rushed to form a group hug, their voices a joyous cacophony of reunion. Garrett stood back a step as they all danced around in a circle. It surprised him when Val caught his hand and pulled him into their hug. "Garrett Emmon Gladheart," Val crooned, "am I ever glad to see you!" Her eyes searched beyond him, looking for Faith, but Ari was the only one standing there, his arms crossed as he leaned against the dining room wall. "Where is she?" Val asked no one in particular.

Garrett hung his head. "We lost her in the woods getting away from the Gugwe," he confessed, ashamed he hadn't protected their best friend.

"It wasn't Garrett's fault," Aliah said, sticking up for him. "We thought you and Faith escaped together."

Ari clapped his hands, startling the newcomers. "Time for stories to be shared later. Sit now and take refreshments," he encouraged them.

They quickly made introductions while taking seats around the enormous round table. Ari, pitcher in hand, filled all the mugs, topping off the three goblins as well.

The Fae sisters sat staring at the first goblins they had seen since they were children attending the Ostara Festival. The goblins watched in return. Silence ensued. Each taking the other's measure. All were internally reviewing everything they'd been told all their young lives about the hatred between the Fae and the Goblin races.

Val reached for the platter of cheese on the table, but Caz gently grabbed her wrist. "Leave off, Val. You've already had half a wheel of cheese," he teased her.

A wave of laughter rose around the table. It delighted Delainey when Rolland took the cheese platter and passed it to her. Saffron sent the basket of fresh, warm bread along. Caz offered his hand to Garrett. They shook. Rolland proffered his hand, big as a bear's paw, and shook Garrett's hand as well.

Val pointed at Saffron and told the story of how the redhead saved her from the Gugwe. Caz and Rolland relayed their part of the story. Aliah's ears caught the name of Robin Goodfellow and noticed Valerie's face light up at the mention. Then Val took over Caz's story, relaying how Caz and Robin had raced around in circles, binding the Gugwe's legs with rope. Saffron interrupted to add Rolland's heroic attack and how he had actually killed the beast.

Lainey told of her experience, mouth full of cheese. Carlisse plucked another slice of bread from the basket, taking a piece of cheese from Lainey's plate. Then she smoothly took over the telling of how Aliah and Garrett finally found them.

"That was lucky," Val smiled.

"That was love," Aliah corrected. "The same love for you is what led us here."

The Dream Weaver winked at Val, and her cheeks reddened.

Garrett weighed all this information. Sifting through the facts, he asked Caz, "So, you mentioned your friend, Robin Goodfellow, in taking down the Gugwe who attacked us, but I don't see him here."

Val said nothing, as it was Caz's decision to talk about his mate.

Caz's eyes met each person around the table and landed last on the Dream Weaver. He almost sensed Ari knew how they'd lost Robin. Since he planned to have the Weaver give him a fortune anyway, figured he'd have to divulge Robin's curse to get a true weave. So, he told the newcomers about Robin's untimely disappearance. He even disclosed that Faith's name was the last thing Robin had said before he disappeared. The Beaumont shared what little Robin had told him years before of what he referred to as 'the Trillium curse'. That part of the story caused all those who dwelt at Robert's hold to gasp with a sharp intake of breath.

"What is it?" Saffron asked gently. "Caz didn't mean to alarm you."

Val answered for them. "I didn't mention it before when Robin disappeared, but we've all been told time and time again never to pick a wake-robin." She stammered, Ari's eyes bright and piercing, "A Trillium, I mean."

"Our. Whole. Lives," she reiterated.

"We'd been warned that picking the flower would bring the 'evil' Goblin, Robin Goodfellow, down on you."

Caz bolted up, knocking his chair down behind him. "Robin's not evil!" he shouted. "You know that isn't true, Val."

"Calm down, lad," Saffron laid a gentle hand on his arm. Rolland rose and righted Caz's chair, pushing him back down to sit.

"Of course, I know Robin's not evil *now,* Cazzidy." She tsked her tongue. "I've met him, haven't I? I was only telling you what we'd been taught throughout our childhood," she raised her voice to him.

"Oh, yeah. Sorry, lass," Caz offered meekly. She nodded her head, satisfied with the apology.

"Actually," Saffron told the group, "after tossing the circumstances around, we're pretty sure Faith picked a Trillium, then specifically called Robin's name." Shock registered on the faces across the table. "We think Robin and Faith are together." Saffron took hold of Rolland's hand under the table, and he squeezed her fingers gently.

"Robin's really handsome," Val blurted out to her sisters, which drew a surprised look from Caz. Lainey and Carlisse both laughed. "I mean, he's nice. Well, seemed nice from the short time I was around him. He was willing to help me find all of you," she told them.

"It seems to me," Garrett cut in, "now that we're all together again, the next step should be to team up so we can find Faith. I'm sure all of you want to be reunited with your mate, Robin." Approving nods went round the table.

Garrett stood and addressed the Dream Weaver. "Thank you for the fine refreshments, sir. What's the price of a fortune weave?" he asked boldly.

"Garrett's got the right of it," Caz announced and turned to their host. "You promised to give us each a Dreamer's Weave, yeah?"

All eyes turned to the Dream Weaver, but before he could respond, Aliah stood and pointed an accusing finger at the man. "He's a fake," she said flatly. "He's not the Dream Weaver," Carlisse and Delainey both nodded in accord. "We three have been to the *real* Weaver before and had our fortunes told. We know what *she*...looks like!"

Emotions played across Ari's face. The group witnessed anger, which ballooned to outrage, then ended in incredulous disbelief. With the loss of control, he felt his superintendence over his forms disappear. Further anger washed across his being. His body shape-shifted from man-form to black cat to giant spider, coalescing through the shifts over and over. His spider form caused the entire audience to stand and take several steps back. Finally, with a roar assaulting their ears, he slammed his man-fist on the table to regain his restraint over his body, and the last shift to his man-form finally held.

Ari gulped in several breaths of air, chest heaving, heart thudding in rapid pumps. Rolland stepped forward and bravely handed Ari a mug of ale. The shifter took the tankard thankfully and drank half of it down.

Aliah, Carlisse, and Delainey stood with their arms crossed, body language was clear. Val, Caz, Saffron, and Rolland stood dreamily. As though the spider form brought forth some distant memory, but the four of them couldn't put a finger on what that memory might be.

"Well?" Aliah said, her foot tapping in annoyance. "Quite a show. I'll give you that much! But you're still a fake Dream Weaver. We deserve an explanation!" she told him in no uncertain terms.

Arnid Aubrey Stormbringer sank heavily into his chair and set the mug down on the table. His tired eyes swept around the faces in the room. "Has anyone ever told you, Mistress Aliah, that you don't know everything you think you do?"

Her hands flew to her ears, thinking of Dedo's very words to her. Ari winked in her direction.

Her face hardened. "Alright," she told him, "I'm willing to listen to your explanation. If I'm wrong, I'll say so. I acknowledge there can be more than two sides to a story." She lifted her chin defiantly. Her sister's eyes goggled at her last statement, familiar with only Aliah's stubborn side of a story.

Ari motioned for them to sit. "May as well be comfortable through the telling."

"I agree with our host," Lainey said. "Please pass the cheese."

There were awkward laughs around the room, relieving some of the tension. Val moved her chair away from Ari and closer to Caz, unable to unsee Ari's spider form. She hooked her arm through Caz's and hung on tight for comfort.

"My name is Arnid Aubrey Stormbringer. I have a twin sister, Persid Audrey Stormbringer."

Eight pairs of eyes glanced around the table as Ari took a sip from his mug.

"You have a twin sister?" Aliah repeated his statement as a question.

"Yes, well," he stammered, "had. I had a twin sister." A shadow of regret passed across his face. "Persid lived about twelve miles from here in a log home her second husband built for her. I visited her frequently." He looked up and locked eyes with Aliah. Garrett put his hand against the small of her back for support. "Persid was a shifter like myself, as well as a Dream Weaver, but to the best of my knowledge, she could only shift to a spider form. Her true form, a woman."

Aliah studied his face. She could see a resemblance to the woman the three of them had sought months ago to weave her fortune. Aliah remembered the Weaver using a spinning wheel, not spider webs. She remained skeptical.

"Persid and I have lived in the Edgewood since this forest was just seedlings in a field." Ari stared off into space as memories played out in his mind, reliving his own history. "Many long years ago, a beautiful young woman knocked on Persid's door. When my sister answered, the stranger said, 'I seek my fortune to be told.'"

"Here now," Persid reacted, "what are you about, young lass?"

"I had a dream. You were in it," the young woman pointed at Persid. "Please let me come in, and I'll explain," the girl begged. Persid, against her better judgement, she told me later, opened her door wide and allowed the stranger to enter. The girl had a small gargoyle companion. Persid assumed was the woman's attendant.

"Wait," Aliah said. "Are you just repeating a story your sister made up?"

Ari shook a warning finger at her, and she leaned back against Garrett, fixing Ari with a stony stare.

"I was there. An eyewitness. You would have learned that fact had you held your rude tongue and allowed me the good grace to tell my story? A story you so eloquently stated you deserved, hey?" he arched his eyebrows at her.

"Yes," she swallowed. "Sorry for interrupting," she offered meekly.

"Where was I?" Ari tapped his forefinger on his lips.

Lainey pulled the last slice of bread from the basket and filled in for him. "Your sister ignored her better judgement, invited a stranger into her home, bringing a mysterious creature with her." Delainey finished as she spread a huge dollop of honey on the bread. Her sisters all rolled their eyes at her. Ari ignored all the sisterly interactions and continued his telling.

"I had arrived the day before to visit my sister. Twelve miles is a long walk, hey? We had afternoon tea set out on the table. The bold young snippet of a girl walked right in and took the extra chair. There was nothing for it but to get another cup and plate and share the fare with her. The goyle squatted by the door, arms clasped around his legs, chin on his knees. He bothered me, you know? I had a bad feeling about him. He just watched. Never said a word. Just watched. Never even blinked. It wasn't natural."

Val's eyes were blank, but tracked up to the corner by the fireplace, then back to the orator.

"Anyway, the wayward girl accepted afternoon tea as if she were answering a formal invitation. Announces she has it on good authority she'd find a Dream Weaver at this house and that she was to seek her fortune here. Persid and I looked at one another in question, but we did not know what she was referring to. We told her so."

"Never in my life have I seen anyone's anger flash on with the lightning speed the way hers did, but it made her otherwise beautiful face ugly for a few seconds. Suddenly, she pulled a dull blade from a sheath at the waist of her dress. I thought she was going to attack Persid, so I stepped in front of my sister. The girl held up her palm and slashed the knife across it. Her blood splattered across our faces. She walked around the two of us in a circle, letting blood drip from her palm, marking her trail."

"Persid grabbed my arm. She was shaking."

"Now, see here," she told the intruder. "We've told you there is no weaver of dreams here. You've got the wrong place. I think you should be on your way. Don't you think she should be on her way, Arnid?"

Persid pushed me forward, clearly wanting me to show this frightening person out the door. But before I could do anything, the witch's arm snaked out. She had dipped her fingers in her own blood and swiped two lines across my face diagonally. Persid screamed, but the crazy girl swiped her finger again, marking Persid's face from her left temple, angled in a line to her right lower chin. My sister's eyes were darting around the room in a panic. The wicked girl laughed, telling Persid, "I'll tell *your* fortune then, since you refuse me mine." Her blood-red finger pointed at my sister as she spat these words at her: 'You shall be two, until I say, until I will, until you die. A shifter, I curse you to be a widow annually. For those who come to ask, you'll be forced to weave your craft. A dream weaver, I set your task.'

She rounded on me, spitting another curse. I squeezed my eyes shut as I saw Persid shapeshift back and forth from my sister to a giant spider. The stranger spoke with a venom of her own. 'To you, her twin, I turn this way. Wrong place. Wrong time. You'll forever rue this day. I name you three, three ways to shift from man to cat to spider quick. To spend the days upon this earth, you both are bound to stay, to live inside the Edgewood cursed, until I end your holiday. Many will seek the dreams you've found, but none will help you break this spell. Only death's sweet embrace will make you whole and well. This spell I cast upon you both. Next time, think twice before you break your oath.'

Ari sat silently for a few moments. The ticking of the mantel clock marked the time. He shrugged his shoulders. "I have many years-worth of tales since then I could tell." Ari admitted, "My sister and I have lived under her curses for so long here in the Edgewood Forest, I can't remember being just a man anymore. We never knew what oath she was referring to. The oath she claims we broke. Neither of us could recall ever having seen her before, much less breaking an oath to her. In addition, the spell somehow made it so that we never aged. I'm still the same age since we had the spell put on us. A young man of twenty-five," the Dream Weaver told the group wistfully, "twenty-five forever." All eyes silently judged his youthful appearance, his vigorous body, jet black hair, and a face that sported a rough five-o'clock shadow.

Lainey licked her fingertips to get every crumb and looked straight at Arnid Aubrey Stormbringer, declaring, "The witch was wrong, Ari. I'll try to help break your curse," she smiled prettily. "Could you please pass the teacakes?" Lainey asked politely, blinking her eyes at him, the shock on his face reflecting her declaration.

Something overwhelmed Ari then.

Something he hadn't experienced in a very long time.

Hope.
Hope bloomed in Arnid Aubrey Stormbringer's heart.

CHAPTER 4: Rumors

Evy, Faith's childhood nurse, dressed in her warmest wool dress, tiny apple blossoms embroidered around the neckline. She opened a small wooden box inlaid with an intricate design, plucked out the only item it contained—a plain silver ring, a twin to the one Faith wore. She placed it on her forefinger. Immediately, she could feel the familiar link to the girl.

With her saddlebags packed, Evy picked them up, ran a critical eye over her tidy room to be sure she'd forgotten nothing, and closed the door behind her. Evy didn't make a sound as she reached the door to Faith's room. When she entered, it wasn't surprising to find the two gargoyles on the mantel throwing pieces of hardened wax at each other. They twittered in silent laughter at the other's antics. She had little tolerance these days (or really ever in her long life) for their shenanigans. She grabbed Lenny by the scruff of his neck and shook him hard. Lester mimed his hands at his throat, choking, and fell back against the mantel, laughing so hard tears rolled down his face. Evy pointed a crooked finger at the jester while still clutching the other. "That is quite enough!" She told him in a menacing voice.

The old nurse deposited Lenny back on the mantel. She told the two in no uncertain terms, "You've got fifteen minutes to get this wax mess cleaned up as well as yourselves and get down to Lady Reatha's carriage. We won't delay in waiting for you. If we leave you behind, you can explain yourselves to Dedo when you next see him why you weren't along on this journey to perform the task he assigned you," she warned. She swept from the room, expecting them to obey.

Lester heard the door open and close. Then mimed to his brother, opening and closing his thumb and fingers against each other, like a mouth talking, his lips silently emulating, 'Blah, blah, blah!'

Normally, his brother's antics would have sent Lenny into hysterics, but Lenny was stoic. His eyes looked over his brother's shoulder. At something. Lester craned his neck around to find the old nurse staring at his japes, tapping her foot, her face promising punishment. Lester granted her an embarrassed grin and immediately began picking the wax off the mantel, placing it in a small dish sitting off to the side. When she left the room, Lenny was picking at the wax on his brother's back. Then they switched out, Lenny removing the last of the wax from the mantel, while Lester got the wax off Lenny's backside. With the mess cleaned up, the goyles helped one another. They removed the candlestick holders strapped to their backs, carefully laying them aside until their return. The two stood grinning at one another, reaching their right hands up to touch the basalt rock above.

An enormous mouth opened in a yawn, and Lester sent a message mentally. "Goodbye, Linus. You're in charge until we return." With their hands connected to the rock, they both disappeared, coming out on the mantel of the hall fireplace, on the floor below the bedroom chambers. The brothers held hands, jumped toward the floor, spreading out their wings to glide down to a soft landing. Moving so fast that the human eye couldn't register, they sped out the front door. Andrew detected neither of the goyles. As he was carrying a load out to the carriage, they clutched his coat-tails. Andrew, occupied in loading the last of Reatha and Evy's luggage, gave the two gargoyles the chance to let go of Andrew's coat, sneaking into the coach. They relaxed into comfortable perches in the left and right corners of the interior, not a speck of wax to be seen on either of them.

Sir Robert escorted Reatha and Evy to the waiting coach, offering a hand to help the ladies in. When the two had settled themselves in comfort, Reatha noticed the two jokers in the corners behind Evy and gave them a warm smile. "You see, Evy," she crooned with approval, "all your worries over Lenny and Lester were for naught. Why they're so eager to help, they've presented themselves in the coach before us!" Reatha was delighted with the two. Lenny preened at Reatha's compliment, while Lester stuck his tongue out and goggled his eyes at Evy. When the old nurse turned to look at them, all she saw were two goyles in their usual stance, stone-faced without expression. She huffed and took up her sewing basket.

The courtyard was alive with activity. Ten of Robert's men would accompany them on the journey. Horses snorted as the cohort checked saddle straps and gear, tack jingling in the background. Robert gave last-minute instructions to Andrew, Estella, Mara, and Garth on the care of the manor until his return. He made it a point. The gates were to be opened for no one except himself, Reatha, or Evy, then he mounted his gray stallion. Hirun, already settled in the driver's seat of the coach, ready to be gone. He gently lifted the reins of the two horses, and the wheels were in motion. Ten riders followed in rows of two. The morning passed in pleasant travel.

Reatha was a ball of nervous excitement, so many years having gone from when she last saw her sister Mari. She quietly told Evy story after story about their childhood, as if Evy didn't already know the details. Evy rocked with the motion of the coach, patiently listening as she worked on their pile of mending.

When the sun was high overhead, Robert called for a break in a shady coppice of oaks near a babbling brook. The ladies left the coach to stretch their legs. The men watered the horses. Reatha and Evy set out a lunch. There was cold sliced venison, bread in linen-covered baskets, still slightly warm from the morning baking, thick wedges of cheese, as well as a basket of apples. The ladies used the back of a board, which folded down like a table on hinges attached to the carriage. When the troop had finished the quick meal, horses refreshed, Robert gave a ten-minute warning before they packed it all away and the entourage was off again.

Dusk's curtain was falling over the land by the time they reached their first stop, the small village, Sawat, on the eastern shore of Lake Emerald. Robert had sent one boy from the hold three days earlier to notify the innkeeper of the large group's arrival. The boy now waved to them from the steps of the inn, raced down to take the reins of Robert's horse, leading it off to the stables. Each of his men unsaddled their own mount and saw to its care. Evy noticed more than a few apples from the afternoon lunch found their way to a horse's mouth as the men led them away to the stable. She reached back into the cab to grab her small overnight bag, leaving the larger luggage in the carriage's boot. She whispered into the cab, "No trouble from the two of you tonight, or I'll hang you from your toes on the trip tomorrow." Lester scrunched his toes beneath him, out of her sight. Lenny didn't move, but his eyes grew big as saucers as the door closed behind her.

The inn, with prior notice of their coming, was lit with kerosene lamps. A welcoming fire was burning in the fireplace. They set the tables ready for the evening meal. Stomachs rumbled with hunger at the wonderful smells coming from the kitchen. The innkeeper and his wife stood, greeting their guests as the common room filled.

"I hope we haven't put you to too much trouble," Reatha entreated the inn's mistress. "It's so good of you to accommodate such a large group on short notice."

"Oh, no trouble at all, Lady Reatha. Business has been down this past year with all the traveler's misfortunes."

"Hush, Marth," the innkeeper shushed his wife. "No need to spread rumors to these good people. Rumors are the only trouble, mind, nothing to worry over, ladies. Marth will show you your rooms where you can put up your things and freshen up. Dinner will be ready half past the hour," he told them as he worked his hands on the towel he had tucked into his waistband. He called to them as Marth led the way up the narrow stairway leading to the guest rooms, "I have put your soldiers up in the bunkhouse, Sir Robert. If you need anything at all, just let us know and we'll do our best to accommodate." His voice trailed off as he headed toward the kitchen to oversee the meal's progress.

Marth and her oldest daughter, Mae, brought pitchers of water to the rooms. They produced warmed towels from a basket; a hot water bottle lay at the bottom.

When Robert, Reatha, and Evy descended the stairs half an hour later, the common room was a beehive of activity. Their men sat at the tables around the room. They had reserved a special table for the trio. Robert gave informal salutes as some men called out in greeting, hoisting up their pints of beer topped with thick foam sitting in front of them. Reatha pointed out young Will from the hold, who'd brought the news of their coming, and Robert crooked his finger at the lad, beckoning him over.

"You've done a fine job, Will." Robert clapped the boy on the shoulder and whispered something in his ear. A grin spread across Will's wide face, and Robert flipped a silver coin in the air; the boy's hand snatching it neatly. Will hurried off, reappearing moments later with a small brown leather case. The boy grabbed a short stool near the hearth, pulled out his flute, and began piping out a soft, merry melody for the crowd.

The innkeeper, Master Harrel, approved, tapping his foot to the beat, telling Robert, "It's a fine lad you sent ahead, sir. Why, he's been a joy to

Marth since he arrived yesterday. He helped get everything ready, never idle for a minute. We'd be glad to keep him on and board him if you wouldn't mind?" he suggested. "We could use an extra hand."

Reatha answered in Robert's stead. "We thank you for the offer, Master Harrel, but his mother is our head cook. She'd be lost without the boy, I'm afraid. Perhaps in a year or two," she smiled.

Harrel called to his daughter, Mae. She and her mother laid the tables with fresh, warm baskets of bread and crocks of butter. Harrel joined in, bringing out platters of roast lamb with Marth's famous mint jelly, roasted potatoes and peas. Every table was served. While their guests were eating, the innkeepers lined the sideboard with apple pies and plates with thick slices of cheddar. Mae rounded the room once more with a cold pitcher of beer. Robert signaled Will to join them for dinner. Evy was amused to see the boy scarf down not two, but three helpings before he hurried back to his flute, pleased to have an audience to play for. A short time later, one soldier joined Will, borrowing a small viola hanging on the wall, adding another layer to the music.

After visiting with Marth and Mae, Evy, and Reatha climbed the staircase, seeking their beds. The men left in the common room played stones or diced. Harrel moved two armchairs up to the fireplace and invited Robert to fill his pipe from the jar of his best tobacco. When they'd had a few comforting puffs, Robert put a question before Harrel. "Master Harrel, I'd like to know what those rumors are that Marth mentioned when we arrived? Tell me true."

"I don't know why she even brought it up," Harrel sputtered. "Rumors and nothing more," he assured his guest.

"Still, I'd like to hear them," Robert coaxed. "Rumors spring from some piece of truth, however small." He drew on his pipe, blowing smoke rings into the air.

Harrel sighed, blowing out his smoke in a steady stream. "We've had a slow spring season to start. A traveler here, one there. Three strangers came through two weeks ago." Harrel paused and looked around, keeping his voice low so only Robert could hear. "One of 'em was a gob," he whispered. "Imagine a gob traveling with men." The innkeeper didn't bother to hide his distaste. "I offered them space in the hayloft, and they acted as if it were an insult. It was more than they'd have gotten at other places with a gob in tow, I'll tell you."

Tapping his ashes into his palm, Harrel threw them into the fireplace, laying the pipe aside. "I served them a hearty meal myself. I didn't want Mae or Marth to deal with them! The gob barely said two words to me, but he conveyed his feelings with those beady eyes of his. His companions told me there was word that the clans were on the move. More are coming south every day. Why, it's bad enough they live all over the north Peninsula. Now it seems the Gobs are going to come down here and invade *our* lands. One even told me there'd been sightings here and there of those wicked beast-men on the south peninsula this past winter. Only rumors. The gob sympathizers and their gob companion cleared out before breakfast was served. Ingrates only left me two silvers for their evening meal; that's all. If you can believe it, not even a coin for their horses' feed and the comfort of the warm, dry hay loft. I swear it's the last time I offer my services to a filthy goblin."

Robert said nothing, but he didn't care for the innkeeper's racist remarks. He tapped his pipe into his palm and sent the ash to the embers glowing in the fireplace. He rose from his chair, politely taking his leave of the common room, empty now except for the two of them. "Thank you for the fine meal, Harrel. We'll be up early. My wife is eager to get on the road. It's been years since she's seen her sister Mari. We will appreciate a hot breakfast. Will? Time for you to get some sleep. Come along now."

Harrel watched Sir Robert go up, the boy following close behind, thinking his guest had become stiff-necked after he'd shared the rumors. It was probably his imagination. Likely, the man was just worried about traveling with two women. Yes, that must have been it, he thought to himself as he banked the coals and blew out the lamps on his way to a few hours' rest.

When they reached the top of the steps, Will hung his head, lingering before going to his room. Robert turned to look at the lad. "Something you want to talk about, Will?"

"Master Harrel's bigotry is ugly."

Robert heaved a sigh. "I agree. A bigot is a person most of us would like to avoid. Look, son, the world can sometimes be an ugly place. Even more so for those who are the victims of ugliness, and the only way to overcome racist thoughts and actions is to expose them. Make people aware of it."

"Master Harrel didn't even give a reason for his hatred of goblins. From what he said to you, he certainly had never even met the one who was a companion to the two men he traveled with."

"That's part of the problem, lad. Hate spewed as racism may have been born of a particular incident. Perhaps between the innkeeper and *a* goblin, then Harrel turned his negative feeling toward *all* goblins. Wrongly so, but it happens. Harrel may never have experienced any unpleasant incidents at all with *any* goblins. It's possible he may think poorly of the entire race simply because of his childhood experiences. In such a case, he may have even been *raised* to think about goblins that way. Both are sad examples, but all too common. The cycle repeats itself over and over throughout history."

"I see. The problem seems almost insurmountable if what you say is true. Continued conditioning is hard to overcome. I think I need to give this some serious thought. I want to figure out how I can be part of a solution and how to end the ugly cycle. This hatred of others simply because of their race seems a travesty. I'll be glad to head back home tomorrow. Thank you, sir. Goodnight." Robert roughed the boy's hair and told him again what a fine job he had done.

MEANWHILE, LENNY AND Lester had crawled down from the coach cab and looked around to be sure the old nurse hadn't set a watch on them. The two gargoyles were delighted to find the coast was clear. They flew through the barn, swooping up and down in a game of 'catch me' until they were tired of it. Then, Lester came up with the idea of switching the horses around to different stalls to cause confusion in the morning, which sent them into fits of laughter. When they finished with the jest, they discovered a treasure trove of pleasure-riding gear in a trunk. Lester started pulling out small black riding caps, colorful neckerchiefs, riding crops, and other tack. Lenny put a cap on and tied a red cloth around his neck, took up a crop and dropped onto the back of a large brown gelding inside its stall. The horse stamped a foot in surprise. Lester thought his brothers' antics hilarious and quickly searched through the trunk, matching his costume. As soon as he was dressed as a jockey, Lester jumped on the black mare next to Lenny. They mimed as though they were racing horses. Lenny jumped off, pretending to be the winner. Not to be outdone, Lester flew to the next stall and challenged his brother to another imagined race, wherein he claimed the next win. They 'raced' all the horses before they were done.

Putting the costumes back in the trunk, Lester noticed a barrel of apples. He threw an apple to his brother, intending Lenny to catch the snack. His aim was poor. It hit Lenny on the head. That precipitated an apple fight (similar to a snowball fight if you've ever had one). When they were done, Lenny scratched his head, wondering how they were going to clean up the mess. Lester suggested they eat the apples, but after they'd each finished their sixth, both decided that would never do. Lester snapped his fingers in the air, loaded several apples from the floor into his thin arms, and visited each stall. He shared out the apples first to the 'winners' of their horse races. Then, with so many apples still all over the barn from their food fight, treated all the horses. There were only a few dozen left at the barrel's bottom now. To make sure the shortfall wouldn't be noticed right away, Lenny scooped them out of the barrel one by one. Next, he filled the bottom with straw and put the apples back on top, covering the chaff.

Lester tickled Lenny as they rolled on the floor, howling with laughter. The two gargoyles ended up on their backs, legs, and feet propped up against a stall while they caught their breath. Lenny inspected his toes to see if they had any 'toe-jam' for dessert. He used his forefinger to clean between each of his toes, enjoying the little treats he coaxed from each toe-cove. When he had finished his toe-jam, he wriggled his toes above his head. Lester noticed a rope hanging on a nail above them. He looked at the rope, pointed to it, then to his brother's toes, and the old nurse's words about hanging them from their toes tomorrow lit a fire under them. Entertaining as they thought it would be for all the horses to be found in different stalls from where their owners had put them, they quickly set to work to erase their little prank. The goyles finished returning the animals to their original stalls just as the sun broke over the horizon.

When the old nurse opened the door to the carriage a short while later, they knuckled their fists to their eyes in response to the sunlight filtering in behind her. Each offered wide yawns, blinking at her with innocent faces. She squinted at them with suspicion but could find no evidence of wrongdoing.

After she deposited her overnight bag, she informed them she would be back in short order after breaking her fast. The cab door closed. The two brothers slapped palms and bumped fists. They slept the day away to the gentle rocking of the horse-drawn coach.

CHAPTER 5: A Queen's Nightmare

Morveena slept deeply. Her dreams kept her mind captive. Rupert snored next to her.

The Goblin Queen watched herself in her dreamscape as her face flashed through the many disguises she had taken on over the years using blood magic. She had honed the power until she could become a doppelgänger of almost anyone or anything. Sometimes, she craved becoming someone or something else, just to feed off the high it gave her, stepping into another person's 'skin', so to speak. Using her imagination, she would create stories of how those she impersonated thought. How they felt. Inventing secrets they might keep hidden. The redhead reveled in the feeling of power she craved, using another's persona to manipulate others so she might have what she wanted. It was glorious. Euphoric. She could play make-believe, hiding in her own little world. Do anything she wished, while wearing the face, body, and personality of another.

Morveena Morgan Montestrell had grown strong in blood magic. Since the death of her father, Munro Marcellus Montestrell, she had studied the three small tomes stolen so many years ago. Thick scars ran up and down her forearms, across her outer thighs, tallying how often she called upon the magic. Through experiments, she learned how to twist a spell just so to make it her own, assuring her desired outcome. She investigated the strength of the spell for any weakness in holding another person's image in place that she used to cover her own. Testing the time limit she could hold an illusion was critical. She learned her calculate the point in time while impersonating someone before the ruse fell away, exposing her. It had been necessary to discover whether more blood would be required to keep the disguise going. Finding out if that was even possible as the blood magic faded, or if she had to wait to replenish her strength before she could cast the spell again or continue it.

After a while, Morveena associated blood with power. The correlation cultivated an unhealthy attraction to seeing blood on others, as well as spilling her own. She learned early in her experiments that blood magic required her to use *her own blood* to cast a spell. It wasn't possible to use someone or something else's blood. The magic demanded *that you* pay a price to benefit from the power.

Suddenly, something in her dreams caused her heart to beat faster, anxiety to flare, her breathing became shallow, causing panting. Rupert rolled over in his sleep and draped his arm across her, bringing her back to calm as she settled again, falling deeper into the dream world.

Thick mist hung in curtains, a gentle wind pushing the vapors back and forth. When the fog cleared, Morveena stood in a dream-forest, carpeted with vibrant green ferns and flowers; moss and layers upon layers of leaves. Sunbeams made scattered patches of light, shining through the dappled filter of the tree-canopy, moving with the wind currents. The sunlight was slowly burning off the haze.

Using her long, sharpened fingernails, the Goblin Queen sliced her arm, blood spurting. Taking three great strides, she used her powerful leg muscles to launch herself from a small clearing. Her body shifted as she leaped up, ripping across her being, merging into her Pileated Woodpecker form, wings catching the updraft, soaring into the sky. Circling the camp several times, her beady eyes zeroing in on details, she let loose a stream of chittering so loud it woke the entire camp. Dropping into a 'death dive', the body shifted again just before the impact of her Dryocopus pileatus body. The bird's flaming red crest changing back to her red hair, feet skimming the ground in a run, toward the trees where her captives were bound.

This time, when she shape-shifted, her physical body was ripped away from her bed. Reality blasted her out of the dreamscape straight into a Goblin Queen's nightmare. Her physique merged with her dream self. Blue eyes focused intently on every detail of the surrounding area. The guard was gone. Robin was gone. Her eyes narrowed to slits.

Not only was Robin gone, but it looked like he had taken the stinking faerie with him.

Her Faerie.

Her new pet.

Her coin.

Anger smoldered until she thought she might combust. From the corner of her eye, she caught a slight movement. Predator instinct kicked in. She cut another wicked gash across her palm, the strongest source for the blood magic, except for her monthly menses. She reserved the use of her cyclic blood to create the most evil of spells.

As thick, sticky ichor pulsed into her palm, she called upon the blood magic to grant her a short sword. A solid blade and handle, both the color of blood, like a shimmering crystal jewel, formed in her hand. She rounded the tree trunk with preternatural speed...and found only Narrol, bound tightly to the tree. Narrol's face was a swollen mess, eyes crusted over with dried blood and mucus. His body occasionally shuddered with small seizures. Injuries, all courtesy of the beating Rupert had applied according to her instructions as she watched earlier. She lost herself for a moment, relishing the memory of Narrol's blood spattering her face and dress while she looked on.

Narrol was still unconscious. Coming back to herself, she cursed at the sight of finding him when the others were missing. But he provided her with someone to release her rage on. Her feet still bare, she kicked him over and over, sharpened toenails gashing his skin open. Finally, at the peak of her rage, she remembered the crystal blood sword in her hand. As her wrath found the finale, she drove the blade down into Narrol's belly, jerking the blade upward, screaming out her mania. Morveena pulled out his entrails, spreading his innards on the ground, stomping on the mess in her fit of rage. Narrol's body stilled. Silence fell across the glade.

The Goblin Queen let her arms fall to her sides, and the sword dissolved into thin air, her palm still dripping blood onto her black silk nightgown.

Morveena's breathing slowed. Rage burned out for the moment, allowing her eyes to track around the camp, realizing a crowd had formed in the background. Her soldiers stared at the gruesome scene. She rounded on them with a guttural growl. To a man, they took a step back. Rupert stood in front of all the others. Sweat beaded on his forehead. Stockstill, wearing only his small clothes, shocked out of a dead sleep. Both hands held long knives; his face twisted in anger, a ghost of horror reflected in his features as he took in the scene. She made a note of the reaction.

"My Queen," Rupert breathed out, "what madness is this?" not awake enough to use care in choosing his words before speaking.

"Madness?" A vicious smile cast her face in ugliness. Rupert cringed. Walking around him in a large circle, her voice dangerous, "Did you use the word madness regarding me, Rupert Gregor Goodfellow? Did you?" she hissed. "Say it again. I dare you!" she spat.

Rupert dropped both the knives in his hands and held his arms out to her, palms up. "My Queen, forgiveness. I ask your forgiveness," he stammered. "I didn't know what I was saying," he groveled, dropping to his knees. All the soldiers took several additional steps back.

"Rupert?" she said flatly.

"Yes, my Queen?"

"Who was in charge of my prisoners?"

"What?" he croaked, finally looking around, his stomach feeling sick as he realized for the first time he only saw Narrol's dead body. No other. His brother and the Fae girl were nowhere in sight. "Morveena, I swear to you, they were both here when we dumped Narrol's body and tied him up again after his, ah...um...visit with you. I had a guard posted!" he reasoned.

"The guard? Who was the guard?" she demanded.

"Raven. Raven Renzo Rolondo was on duty here tonight," he divulged. Morveena's eyes drifted up to the soldiers spread out behind Rupert.

"Is Raven Renzo Rolondo among you?" She called out; her voice echoed across the camp.

Negative replies found her ears and eyes.

"Do any of you know where your fellow soldier might be?" she struggled to keep her voice level.

"He and a few others have gone missing, Queen Morveena," a lad ventured from the back of the group.

"I see," she said to herself.

"Rupert," she held his eyes, "get this mess cleaned up. Take the roll call. Find out who's missing and whether they took anything with them. Put out some trackers, see if you can discover which direction they are headed." He nodded, afraid to utter a word, while fury still rode across her face. "And for God's sake, put some pants on first," she said with disgust, riding him low in front of his men.

"I'll expect a report before the start of the next hour." Her glare turned on each lad spread out in the surrounding woods. She took out a pair of soft, blood-red leather gloves she carried tucked into her belt, pulled them on, and strode across the camp to her tent. As soon as the flap closed behind her, a beehive of activity erupted.

Fifty minutes later, the Queen's tent flaps snapped open. Rupert presented himself. He took a stiff stance in front of the chair she lounged in. She was studying Narrol's blood on her toes, caked and dried now, under her toenails. Rupert was nervous. His hands shook, so he held them clasped behind his back as he began his report.

- "Of the fifty lads we brought with us, 13 are missing, including Raven Rolondo."

- "There were no signs of the prisoners' chains, only the cut ropes used to bind them to the trees, so they didn't take the time to get out of the chains before they escaped."

- "We've only had time to do a cursory check of supplies, but it didn't look like the deserters had taken anything except their own gear and weapons."

- "Narrol was taken back to the tree around midnight, so the escape had taken place after."

- "None of the remaining lads can place any of those missing after midnight."

He cleared his throat, worried because she was still studying her bloodied toes.

- "Nothing else seems to be missing, my queen."

- "The lads are out tracking right now. I wanted to get these details to you while they finish the search."

Rupert stood at attention, sweating profusely.

"You say nothing is missing? Nothing stolen from us?" she asked in a quiet, dangerous voice, while twisting a length of her red hair round and round a finger.

"Correct. We found nothing else missing." He held his hand out to her, inviting, but she ignored it.

"No one searched our tent to see if they stole anything, Rupert," her eyes finally coming up to meet his. He didn't like what he saw.

Morveena stood. Rupert fought the urge to step back. She grabbed the lapels of his coat and pulled him close so that their foreheads touched. Acid twisted through his gut.

"That stinking Fae princess stole my son, stole my soldiers, stole this night's dreams, and she made off with My. Bloody. Black. Boots!"

Rupert closed his eyes. A single tear fell from his eye and ran down his cheek. He waited for the blows to rain down on him. Minutes ticked by, but to his surprise, she didn't strike him.

"Oh, Rupert," she whimpered, seeing his tear, "I knew you would be the only one to understand!" A tear on her cheek mirrored his own, and she crushed herself against him. He moved quickly to wrap her in his arms, thanking his luck without understanding where it came from. Grateful she would not take her wrath out on him.

She pulled him onto the bed. "Help me forget my troubles for a little, yes?"

AFTERWARD, RUPERT WAS trying to puzzle out how he was still here. Still alive. Why he wasn't brutally dead like Narrol. Morveena took his silence to mean he was engaged in shrewd planning.

"Tell me, darling," she teased his ear with her tongue, "I can see the wheels turning. You must be creating a marvelous plan to make things right again, aren't you?" She smiled coyly and poked his shoulder with her finger. "Come now, you mustn't tease Mummy," she prodded.

His brain was scrambling to come up with something. Anything. Just so the ugliness wouldn't flare up in her again.

"Well..." he stalled, acting bashful about disclosing his grand plans. "You know me so well, kitten. Of course, I haven't completely worked out all the fine details yet, but I *am* putting together a scheme. A stratagem, I hope, will put us back in a position of leverage with the Thana," he suggested.

"More," she said as she nipped the skin all down his neck and shoulder, clearly aroused at the suggestion of a plot, "tell me more," she insisted.

"Capturing the Fae princess again is critical. We must gear all our efforts toward that goal, now that we know she exists, yes?"

Morveena bit him hard on the soft skin at the base of his neck and shoulder. "How?" she growled, keeping his skin in her incisors, tugging, worrying it like a dog worries a piece of gristle. He gritted his teeth against the pain, words coming to mind in a flood, with no filter.

"I will form ten teams of five lads each and assign them specific geographical areas to scour and track, searching for your missing pet. We will find her again. I promise. In the meantime, there is no reason I can see that would stop us from going through with our plan to negotiate with Thanna NukPana? We'll simply approach him from a different perspective, whetting his appetite with the new knowledge of our discovery. Now that we can confirm the Fae princess exists, the fact that we alone know what she looks like will make us valuable in his eyes. We'll tell him our soldiers are in hot pursuit and will capture her soon. Play it up. You specialize in that sort of theater, yes? Let him know it was he we first thought of when we discovered the princess alive. We sought him out immediately to let him know of our discovery. We can persuade him we have plans to bring the Fae Princess to him as soon as we have her in hand. With your excellent diplomatic skills, we can exchange the princess for pre-negotiated power and gold, yes? It shouldn't be too difficult to come up with a plausible story about how we came across this discovery without disclosing the escape? Our knowledge of the girl alone is still good coin, yes?"

As he pushed her down, her teeth released him, leaving marks and a small dribble of blood where the skin had broken. Rupert grabbed the base of her neck with his own teeth. She groaned with pleasure. He spent the next half hour wringing promises from her, while the lads searched the countryside looking for a trail and clues.

Not a lad among them wanted to return to the camp without being able to report a sure direction in which to pursue their queen's prey.

CHAPTER 6: Thana NukPana's 13

Thana NukPana had not intended to gain an entourage of 13.

13, who were constantly hovering about him like a cape. A cloak he couldn't unfasten and throw off. They were like deer flies buzzing in his ears. Every one of them with a question or concern, with an idea or advice. He could not put up with this all day, every day! Akama came to an abrupt stop and turned to face them. The flow behind him foundered. A few of the Gugwe lost their balance as he glared into their quizzical eyes. The Thana took his time, looking over each attendant from head to foot. An idea formed as he took in the details. One follower in the back cleared her throat as if readying to speak. He held up his forefinger with a strike in the air; the group collectively held its breath.

"You! Those of you in the back," he pointed his finger like an orchestra leader, "form a straight horizontal line." Feet shuffled; shoulders bumped as they fell in with his order.

Thana NukPana pointed again, setting out six more of his followers and putting them in a row standing in front of the first line. The formation left one lone attendant standing apart from the others, a female, her long mane braided across her powerful, muscular neck. He pointed. She bowed, raised her head, meeting his stare. Thana could see a smile forming on her lips.

"What's this?" he growled, but she continued to beam at him. "Speak! What makes you dare to smile at Thana NukPana?" he demanded.

She raised her hands above her head, calling out in a loud voice because she wanted all to hear, "The sun has shone on me today. My grandmother told my fortune, and here I am."

"What was this fortune your grandmother imparted to you?" the NukPana asked patiently.

"Grandmother told me our new leader, Akama, the great Thana NukPana, would take my oath. That he would assign me work to help him make the Gugwe the strongest nation of the northern lands. Grandmother foretold, it would be you who will lead us to great prosperity." Going down on one knee, she told him, "I am yours to command. By all I hold dear—clan and country—I am yours." She held her hand across her heart. The other followers quickly copied her oath on one knee in unison.

Thana NukPana smiled. His thoughts had coalesced as this theater played out. His plan fit in neatly with the 13 oath-takers versus 13 deer flies.

If they wanted theater, he would give it to them. So, he took center stage and gave a command performance.

Thana NukPana held his arms out, palms down, and used the motion to communicate to his superstitious audience. They squatted, lower legs extended behind them, buttocks resting on their ankles. "Starting with you," he pointed at the loaner, sitting in the center of her own row, in front of the other two rows of Thana's followers. "Number off," he commanded. "You start, then the others will continue down the row behind you, left to right. The rows will count off right to left until 13. Remember your number!" he emphasized.

He pointed his finger at the loaner to start. Things seemed to happen in slow motion as she swallowed nervously and called out loudly, "13."

Everyone laughed.

Except Thana NukPana. He did not laugh.

"Explain yourself," he said, his voice flat.

"My name..." she started, but Thana held out his hand to stop her.

"I did not ask your name. I said explain yourself," he growled.

She bowed again. "My explanation includes the fact that my name is Neetriht. I tell you so that you will remember. I claim the number 13. You did not instruct us to count from 1 to 13. You only instructed me to start the counting and to continue down the rows until 13 were numbered. My claiming 13 was within your parameters. I am 13 and Neetriht is me. We are one and the same. Grandmother told me you would have a special assignment for number 13." She stood to deliver her answer, then sat back on her ankles again.

The NukPana stared at the female named Neetriht, then turned, pointing his finger at the next person. To his delight, the last attendants numbered off 12, 11, 10, 9, 8, 7, 6, 5, 4, 3, 2, 1. He had to admit they numbered 13. Just as he had instructed.

"Number one," he barked.

#1 in the back row stood, arms straight at his sides, as Thana NukPana instructed, "As I call on you, state your name, your family situation and," he looked back at #13, "any skills you think would be useful to remain as one of my chosen retainers. Begin," he pointed at #1.

"I am called Anson..."

Thana NukPana listened with interest to each follower as they provided the barest of their life details, then poured out their passions like fuel on a fire to convince him they had just the right skills to do this or that.

They were his, he concluded. Wanted or not. Only the foolish threw away genuine oaths and willing tools. He would use them. Spend those oaths like coin. In return, he would give them a purpose that would benefit the Gugwe hoards, as well as enhancing his leadership over all the tribes. Akama began to toss his 'coins' into his own special tax collection box. He noted that a large crowd had formed around the small group.

"#1!" Thana called out. #1 popped up, stood at attention, nervous sweat beading on his forehead. "You are assigned as the head of our supply chain. You will make an inventory of what we have, what we need, as well as procure it. Soon we," Akama drew a circle with his finger to show the Thana's 13, "will travel with a small band of soldiers, Vutova's Elite 13. We will need supplies for our soldiers, as well as for all of you and me. Hire whoever you need to accomplish what must be done, but be ready to go in two weeks' time."

"Where, sir?" #1 called out. "It would be helpful to know for planning, sir." He swallowed, clarifying his need for an answer.

"Our expedition will include visiting all the Gugwe tribes before we return to Vutova." He turned his head again and looked at #13. She met his gaze, her face a mask of calm.

Thana assigned the others in rapid succession, giving out appointments to all his attendants.

#1–Head of the Supply-Chain–Anson Vutova

#2–Weapons Master–Boartusk Vutova

#3–Map Maker–Taramat Vutova

#4–Communications Director to the 13 Tribes–Zenara Vutova

#5–Journal Secretary–Jayben Vutova

#6–Statistician/Actuary–Neeta Vutova

#7 Keeper of the Dead–Zota Vutova

#8 Emissary to all the Tribes–Bakrat Vutova

#9 Scout Leader–Seeker Vutova

#10 Master of Slaves–Zolo Vutova

#11 Thana's Personal Bodyguard - #11 a/k/a Nevele Vutova

#12 Trainer of Youngblood Warriors–Callen Vutova

The last three appointments caused some confusion. No one had ever heard of the titles Master of Slaves, Thana's personal bodyguard or trainer of Youngblood Warriors. The audience was unclear about what these roles would mean, having never existed before.

Finally, Thana NukPana stood toe to toe, nose to nose with #13. Neetriht stood almost as tall as he did. Tall for a female Gugwe. She held his fierce eyes, fearless under his gaze. His breath smelled as rank as hers.

"13," he whispered quietly.

"Neetriht," she whispered back.

"You think to change things," he stated matter-of-factly.

"I follow in your footsteps," she assured him.

"Your grandmother's fortune was told true," he announced to the crowd. Her face filled with a radiance he had never witnessed in her before. "#13, I appoint you as the new KuRuk Vutova."

The crowd gasped.

"From this day forward, the Thana NukPana shall appoint all the tribal KuRuks. Killing the KuRuk will no longer be the passage to becoming the KuRuk," he announced. "Those violating my decree will be chopped into small pieces, cooked and fed to the KuRuk's dogs. It shall be so in all 13 tribes."

The onlookers raised their right hands, shaking their fists in the air, showing approval of the Thana's decree. The female cries were louder and fiercer than the males'.

"Every tribe will have a keeper of records, who will track each tribal member's good deeds. To qualify, such deeds must help the tribe or the Gugwe nation grow. Opportunities for other tribal appointments will be swayed by how well each individual supports the whole."

Hands rose, pumping up and down, peppered with grunts and high yips.

"Go now. Each has his or her own responsibilities and preparations. Thana NukPana's 13/13 will begin travels to visit all the Gugwe tribes two weeks from today." He waved them off until only number 13 was left in his presence.

"Thank you," she offered sincerely.

"Your thanks are unnecessary. Our grandmother was right, sister. You will make an excellent KuRuk Vutova," he assured her.

"I won't disappoint you, brother. I would rather die," she offered the heartfelt words.

Thana NukPana cupped her cheek. "I am glad to know it, Neetriht. We cannot afford to have you fail in such a paradigm shift. You are the first female Gugwe to serve as KuRuk. Death will be the price of failure. Yours and grandmothers. Don't betray my trust in you," he squeezed her cheek with affection and walked away.

Much better, he thought as he walked with only one shadow attached, #11 following in his footsteps. He had chosen #11 to serve as bodyguard because the number is a mirror of itself and #11 was to be his twin. His bodyguard. Until death do us part, Thana thought with satisfaction.

CHAPTER 7: This Is Going to Be Interesting

A few hours into their fourth day of travel, Reatha signaled the driver of their coach to stop. The coachman let Robert know, and he called for a break. The party halted at the base of a long ridge.

Coming alongside the carriage windows, Robert gently pulled the reins in, halting his stallion. "Whoa now, Swift," the horse snorted at Robert's command and came to a stop.

Robert peered in through the window and rapped twice. "Reatha? Is everything alright? If we're going to make Mari's by dusk, we can't take many breaks today," he warned.

Reatha's smiling face looked out from the window. "Hullo, Robert," her cheeks colored a bit, "I'm sorry, dear. I know you've set a strict schedule today, but, well..."

"Out with it, Reatha," Robert encouraged patiently.

"Well, Evy and I have to pee," she finally declared. He chuckled as he watched embarrassment ride across her features. "Too much tea with breakfast, I'm afraid. With the coach jostling us about, it only makes it worse," she confided.

"Stop," Robert held up his hand. "No other details are necessary," he laughed.

"Ten-minute break," Robert called out to the troop.

Robert dismounted, gave a hand to help Evy and Reatha out of the cab. Both women had wrapped their cloaks about them against the chill. "Look, Evy," Reatha suggested toward the ridge, "there are some trees for privacy up there. Hurry now." They locked elbows and held the front of their cloaks together as they hastened up the steep hillside, taking care not to trip on their wraps.

The men dismounted. Using the break to check their gear, their horses, stretch their arms and legs, since the opportunity presented itself.

Robert had said ten minutes, but everyone knew they wouldn't be moving again until those two women came back down from the top of the ridge. Most of the men were tolerant. Some even aware women needed to stop more frequently than men, but others in the group hated the inconvenience of traveling with women. Either way, the women controlled the stop.

Evy and Reatha were breathless when they reached the top of the crest. They unlinked their arms, pulled open their capes to release body heat brought on by the climb. They also liberated Lenny and Lester, whom they'd hidden underneath the wool cloaks. "Alright, you two," Evy said, "get down," she ordered the two small gargoyles.

Lenny had his arms and legs wrapped around Reatha's torso, his head resting on her generous bosom. He squeezed tightly, scrunching up his shoulders and nuzzling his cheek closer, obvious in his pleasure.

Lester saw the danger in Evy's scowl, in her squinting eyes. He wisely untangled himself from the old nurse's bony body, scrambling down, pulling on Lenny's leg, hard enough to mean business. Lenny looked up at Evy's face and mimed horror. He jumped down onto Lester's shoulders. The two tumbled over backwards, sending them into fits of laughter.

"Stop immediately or I'll..." The nurse shook her finger at them like a promise. They instantly stood up, put their hands in their pockets, mimed whistling, the two bobbing back and forth, doing their best imitation of innocence.

"We've got no time for this foolishness," she told them sternly. "This is as close as we could get you. Once you reach your destination, use the stones and report to Dedo or directly to us. Stay right on top of this ridge, heading west. Straight on this ridge, mind! You are roughly twelve or thirteen miles from the Dream Weaver's house down in the valley. You know what to do when you get there. Make sure you follow Dedo's earlier instructions. Questions?" she eyed them both, daring them to ask one. "Good. We have to get back."

"Oh, Evy, don't be so hard on them," Reatha crooned. She held out her two hands, each with an apple, toward the goyles. "Do you boys want some apples to snack on while you're walking?" Reatha offered kindly.

It surprised both women when the two brothers bowed, waved off the offer, turned tail and hurried across the flat top of the ridge. Shaking their heads, the ladies hurried back down to their escort after taking the time to pee.

LENNY AND LESTER KNEW they were expected to complete the twelve-mile walk in four to five hours. The Dream Weaver estimated their arrival around dinnertime. Dedo had prepped them on all the different parties that they would find at the Weaver's, including the fact that there would be goblins. In addition, the goyles should recognize folk from Robert's hold, as well as their mistress, Faith. Knowing all these details was serious business. They vowed to maintain their focus, trudging along with purpose...for the first forty-five minutes of their trek.

That's when Lester spotted a fawn and clutched his heart dramatically. Lenny halted when he realized his brother wasn't in step behind him, turning to find Lester mesmerized by something on the ground in front of him. These types of incidents happened with recurring predictability. Lenny regularly had to pull his brother's attention back to the task at hand. Lester, once captivated, whether by a shiny button, a butterfly, a wild flower, fish shimmering in the water, or some other distraction, seemed to go into a trance. Lenny had to break Lester out of the catalepsy.

Over the years, Lenny had tried various methods to bring Lester out of his fixation. The two had decided that one technique seemed to work best. Well, Lenny had decided, since Lester was not available for input.

Lenny employed the method now by reaching over and pinching Lester's nose shut. With the trance broken, Lester's hands came up and began slapping at the hand holding his nose like a vise. Finally, Lenny let go. His brother shook his head to clear out the cobwebs.

"Nice fawn you found, Lester," Lenny acknowledged. "You can tell it was only just born a short while ago. The little guy hasn't even stood on those skinny legs for the first time. Come on. The mother's got to be worrying nearby." He pulled his brother's hand, and they set off across the ridge once more.

ANOTHER HOUR PASSED when Lenny and Lester came across the largest patch of blackberry bushes they'd ever seen. Fat, ripe berries as big as the tip of your little finger peeked out between the foliage. It deterred the goyles again, blackberries being a favorite treat. The sun had tracked further across the blue sky, surprising Lenny when he came out the other side of the patch. His lips, chin, even the tip of his nose, stained like his fingers with blue-black juice. Lester cleared the bushes a few steps behind his twin. They both pointed at each other, finding the berry stains funny. After they'd laughed themselves out, they hurried on their way.

HALF AN HOUR PASSED, intent on moving across the ridge, when the two goyles came across a clear, rocky stream. It seemed reasonable that they should get a drink and try to wash off the sticky juice on their hands and faces. They worked their way down the ridge to reach the point where the stream meandered between their ridge and the next. The cool water quenched their thirst. Just as they cleaned the worst of the berry stains off, a red fox trotting up the opposite side of the elevation captured Lester's attention. He took off suddenly to chase the wily creature.

After the fox, there was a woodpecker, then a pair of monarch butterflies, dancing their way across the forest. The next thing Lester knew, Lenny had a hard pinch on his sore nose and...and...why did Lenny's face look angry?

Lenny was angry. Lester's merry chase led them over hill and dale. Lenny knew they were lost. He didn't know how many ridges they had traversed, much less how they were going to find the ridge they were supposed to be taking to the Dream Weaver's house.

Lester let his brother know how sorry he was, taking responsibility for getting them lost. He thanked Lenny for not abandoning him. Lenny took the length of rope he always carried, looped it a few times around his own waist, securing it with a tight knot. He secured the other end to Lester's belt so he wouldn't lose his brother on another wild-goose chase. The first thirty seconds showed why this method wasn't ideal. When Lenny walked on the opposite side of a tree, then direction Lester had taken. The rope quickly caught between the two, sending them to the ground. Lenny tried not to laugh. He knew his brother's patience was running out, but one look at his brother's face and neither of them could hold back the snickers.

On the second try to deal with his brother's diversions, they put Lester in the lead. The rope connected them, so Lenny trailed behind. This arrangement allowed him to monitor his brother. It took them another forty-five minutes to find the right ridge again. Lester spotted the blue neckerchief he'd taken off to rinse in the cold water of the stream. He'd used it to wash his face and hung it on a nearby branch to dry, just before the wanderlust had taken him again. Retrieving the bandana, they scrambled up the ridge, and the brothers were back to covering the last few miles of their journey as the sun descended below the horizon. Both looked at one another, snapped open their wings and flew as fast as they dared in the waning light.

Evy had instructed them to walk and not attract any attention. The gargoyles were sure they were well enough away from Robert's troop; they couldn't possibly attract anyone's notice.

ROBIN, FAITH, AND RAVEN belly-crawled to the edge of the ridge that delved into a deep ravine. They'd spent the last half-hour watching the stone house below, set in the center of the small valley. "Still no movement," Faith sighed.

"We'll keep up the surveillance for a while longer. There's no point in finding ourselves as hostages again, yeah?" Robin soothed her.

Raven did a slow scan of the north perimeter, then moved his purview to the east. Robin did the same with the south and west exposures. Nothing moved.

Faith had backed away from the edge and sat against a tree trunk. A voice whispered in her ear, "I missed you. I'm glad you're safe. What are you looking at? Are you trying to sneak up on the house down there?"

Astonished, Faith twisted round to find the voice belonged to Delainey. Faith threw her arms around the girl. Hugging one another, high-pitched squeals erupted out of both. Stealth ruined, Robin and Raven pulled back to see what the hell was...

Faith and Delainey danced around, excited to have found one another again. Faith grabbed Robin, wanting him to join her reunion. Raven's mouth hung open. The other lads stood around behind, pointing, laughing quietly, poking each other.

Robin finally got the two girls to stop. He used a sharp tone. "Recon rarely includes loud shrieks, no matter how happy they are," he admonished the girls. "I'm afraid there will be no quiet approach now." He couldn't help but flash a smile at them.

Faith's cheeks blossomed red. She held her hand out to Delainey. "Robin, this is Delainey, Val's sister, and one of my missing companions."

Delainey smiled, gave a small curtsey and then casually strolled around Robin, looking him over from head to toe with obvious scrutiny. "Val said he was handsome," Delainey remarked to Faith. Faith's cheeks colored a shade darker. Robin quirked his head at the odd comment.

"Your sister, Valerie, is here?" Robin asked Delainey.

"She is. Looking for your own joyful reunion?" Delainey teased.

Faith took a few steps back, confused about her feelings. Was Robin interested in Val? She looked over her shoulder, spotting movement. Before she could make sense of what she saw, she was off at a run, calling after those she chased, "Lenny? Lester? Is that you? What in the world are you two doing here?" Her voice trailing off, she took the switchback, well-worn trail downward. This is interesting, she thought as she tried to catch them up.

"Faith!" Raven called after her. "Faith, wait!" Raven began chasing after her. Where Raven went, the other lads followed. In a moment's time, Robin found himself alone on the ridge-rim with Delainey.

"She did, did she?" Robin asked softly. "How interesting."

"What?" Delainey turned back to him, dragging her attention from the parade going down the hairpin pathway.

"Val," Robin reminded her sister, "you said she thought I was handsome, yeah?"

Delighted with his interest, Delainey smiled, "Come on. Let's go down. Your mates are there too. Caz, Saffron, Rolland, along with my other sisters and our friend Garrett. I'll introduce you."

"Why didn't you say so?" He felt a jolt of sudden energy. This was great news. Delainey skipped along to keep up with his long strides.

"This is going to be interesting," Delainey whispered to herself.

Arnid watched as two gargoyles raced around the curves on the path down the ridge. Following directly behind them, he got his first look at the Fae princess in person. Her features reminded him again that she was the spitting image of her mother.

Ari was also reminiscent of the fact that this was the same princess who had killed his sister.

The very Fae he was now tasked with training under the directive of a Gargoyle he despised.

A gang of lads raced after the princess. Last, the Dream Weaver saw Delainey leading Robin Goodfellow himself down to his home. The muscled lad was the spitting image of his father.

'Oh,' Arnid Aubrey Stormbringer thought to himself, *'this is going to be interesting.'*

CHAPTER 8: Sunrise Tomorrow

Ari found himself back in the kitchen, eyeballing his food supplies to see what he could put together for another large group to eat. He felt a tug on his coattail and looked down to find Delainey. "Can I give you any help?" she offered, looking up at him with those big, round eyes. He was so pleased with her offer that he didn't notice three others in the doorway behind her. Ari startled when Saffron moved forward.

"Give us a job, Ari," she told him as she took his apron from the peg by the stove, slipping it over her head, doubling the smock's ties around her thin waist.

"Do you have a plan of what to make?" Aliah asked. "It will be easier to hand out tasks if we know what we're going to cook?" Garrett nodded his agreement.

Arnid Aubrey Stormbringer found himself pleasantly surprised for the first time in years. Delainey smiled at him, and he actually beamed back at her. He pointed his finger at her, chuckling, and said, "I appoint you head cook. So, the menu is your decision. Shepard's Pie or Hearty Stew?"

She giggled at him. "As the Head Cook," she looked around at the occupants of the room, daring them to usurp her newly granted power, "definitely pick the stew. I like Shepard's pie, but making stew will be quicker. We can do the pie another night when we have more time to prepare," her eyes twinkled. "Saffron, you're on potatoes, carrots, and onions." Saffron blinked back at her. Delainey explained, "You said earlier you had experience, yeah?" Saffron shrugged her shoulders and went to the cutting board. "Ari can tell you where to get the vegetables. Garrett will help you as soon as he's brought a few armloads of logs in, so we can get the cook stove fire stoked up. Oh, Aliah," her sister smiled in response, "you make the best flatbread in the world! You'll probably need to triple your usual recipe," Delainey said to no one in particular. "How much flour do you have, Ari?" she called over her shoulder as she headed for the pantry door.

From that point forward, Delainey was the head cook at the Dream Weaver's stone house. Though she believed in taking initiative, she at least made it a point to give her agreement, even when no one asked for her opinion. It was necessary to establish her role if anyone started making a dish without consulting her. Just to be sure they understood, she now ruled the kitchen.

LUCKILY, DELAINEY HAD put aside three generous servings, because there was not a drop left after everyone had been served. She was just pulling two warmed flatbreads out of the oven when Ari came in with a tray full of dirty dishes. He added them to the stack Rolland and Saffron were working on at the sink. Ari glanced into the big stew kettle and found it empty. He dragged his finger around the inner rim and licked the gravy off with a soft moan. "A delicious stew, Miss Delainey. Unfortunately, I didn't think to hold some back for the two of us," he admitted, shaking his head. "Well, no matter. We'll have a picnic of apples and cheese," he suggested to her.

Delainey put her hands on her hips and turned to him with a smile. "Lucky for you, Ari," with a smug look on her face, "*I* thought to take care of us." She pulled the linen cloth off the bowls it had been concealing, releasing a flow of steam from the stew she had saved. "Hurry, Ari. Come, eat while it's hot!"

VAL PULLED FAITH AWAY from the people and activities around the stone house. The two girls hurried toward the apple orchard and found a spot to sit in the sun. "We haven't had a moment alone since you got here," Val pointed out. "I can tell you went through something horrible after we got split up. Whatever it was, it made you quiet and withdrawn. You need to tell me about it, so I can share the burden with you." Val stroked her knuckles along the side of her best friend's cheek.

Faith let the story rush out of her in a low voice. How she thought she had found a kind person to help her in the middle of the Edgewood Forest. She admitted to Val that she couldn't believe her naïveté not to have recognized how dangerous Persid actually was. She re-lived the horror of discovering Persid was a shape-shifter, from a rather plain-looking woman to a giant spider. Faith shuddered when recounting to Val the details of being poisoned. She described having to fight for her life, killing the monster after she had done a fortune weave for her. She skipped Persid's comments about her mother and just mentioned the woman's hatred of faeries. Hugging herself tightly, she described the hundreds and hundreds of tiny spiders, Persid's children, as they swarmed over her, and all she could focus on was the trillium near her hand. She hallucinated hearing Nursie, Aunt Reatha, and Dedo's voices all cascading around her. They just kept repeating over and over, never pick a wake-robin, never pick a trillium. It was almost as if all the warnings compelled her to actually pluck the flower.

When she came to, she found a strange young man—a goblin—helping her recover. All the frightening stories they had been told their whole lives about how Robin Goodfellow was going to appear if you picked a trillium? That was true, but the parts about Robin being some evil monster? Those old folk tales were absolute lies!

Val could tell that Faith harbored anger over being lied to. She rubbed Faith's arms, pulled her into a hug. Faith leaned back, drew in a deep breath, wanting to get the words out before she locked it all away again. She shared with her friend how, while she and Robin had been walking along, he had been laying out a plan to help her get back to her friends. She revealed that Robin had mentioned having already met Val. Faith looked up at Val under her lashes, but she could see no change in Val's facial features in response to this information, so Faith continued.

The golden-haired Fae tried really hard to hold her tears in when she relived the capture of Robin by his evil stepmother, the Goblin Queen, and his brother. But the salty drops rained from her eyes when she fessed up to her own stupidity. She confessed to losing her focus on what was important. Like an idiot, became obsessed with getting her boots back when she noticed them, blowing any chance she had in helping Robin to get free. Barely getting the words out in a whisper, she depicted how Morveena had belittled her, treating her like an animal. She came completely clean with Val, reliving the whole collar, chains, boots scenario that ended with her having to lick the disgusting woman's feet. Val held her hand, squeezing tightly when her friend shared how it had made her feel less than human.

It took Faith a minute or two to recover. She finished the story with Raven's bravery, praising him and all the lads for the help they'd given her, no questions asked. The two girls sat together, letting their foreheads touch.

"Thank you for sharing the courage of others with me."

"I've learned that courage always comes from within. You've shown plenty of your own." Faith smiled at Val. "Just so you know, I won't take a person's courage for granted ever again."

"Mam always says helping others in dire circumstances at one's own peril is the greatest gift another can give you."

Faith nodded, feeling humbled. "But Raven doesn't even know me."

"I'm sure she'd tell you it was an even greater gift than. To help another without knowing that person *and* with no strings attached or expectation of reward." Val wiped the tears from Faith's cheek.

"I hope someday I can do the same for someone else. Repay Raven's risk and kindness."

Val visualized pushing as much good energy toward her friend as she could, then began explaining her own adventures during the same time frame. When they heard their names shouted on the wind, both decided they had better get back to the group.

Robin and Caz had taken some lads to gather wood, dumping it around the big stone fire ring. Once they had their kindling ablaze, Caz fed the fire two larger logs to build the flames up. Ari's house was too small for so many. The bonfire he'd suggested seemed like a good idea, a way to provide space for the group to talk, sort things out, and decide what they planned to do next. After gathering a decent woodpile to feed the flames, Robin, and Caz could share what had happened over the last week or so with one another. Caz confessed he was worried about his memory. He felt like he was missing a day or something, but he couldn't put his finger on it.

Rolland moved a very large log up to the firepit, suggesting they could use it as a seat.

Raven and the lads engaged in a discussion about the clan, wondering what they should do. Raven thought maybe Rupert, and the Queen were going to abandon the clan. He proposed that he and the lads go back to the clan's cave to scope things out, see what's what before revealing themselves. A special recon mission, he suggested to Robin.

"Let's think about it for a day or two," Robin responded.

"Yeah, take a hard look at all the angles first before we form a plan," Caz advised.

Straddling his legs over one of the tree trunks by the fire, Caz's gaze followed the shapes of Rolland and Saffron strolling away from the house, hand in hand.

"What's what?" Robin asked him, moving his head in the couple's direction.

Caz mumbled, "You've got eyes, mate, yeah? It looks like exactly what you see." He had picked up a stick, was breaking tiny pieces off it until it was gone, then picked up another and continued to snap it into pieces.

Ari directed a small group to the barn to see about spreading fresh straw around the loft, as he had no other accommodations for them. Soon, everyone's gear was settled. Dark had fallen. A few had gone to bed; others sat around the bonfire, wanting to be sure they could put in their two-cents on any plans or decisions that might be discussed.

"Everybody seems to have a different idea about what's most important to do next," Robin pointed out.

"Listen," Val said as she and Faith came walking up from the orchard lane, "just because we've all ended up in one place," she locked eyes with Robin, "doesn't mean we have to stay together."

Faith thought she saw something pass between them. "So," Faith started, biting her lower lip, "since we've all found our lost companions, nothing says we can't just split up and go our own ways, yeah?" she suggested. She delivered the words with a feigned confidence she didn't actually feel. She wanted to find out what had happened to Lenny and Lester. Before she could catch up with them running down from the switchback yesterday, she'd seen the Dream Weaver sweep them into the stone house. But hadn't seen hide nor hair of them since. Faith decided she would pursue the mystery as soon as they were all done talking here.

"Really, lass?" Robin asked sincerely. "I think before we decide about who's going where, you've got to come clean about the weave the Dream Weaver spun for you." He stopped short, looked around, then whispered, mindful Ari wasn't nearby, "The dead Dream Weaver." The group stared at him. "Come on," he sounded incredulous, "you know I'm talking about Persid, Ari's sister. She wove Faith's fortune. It's my opinion that every single one of you needs to hear it. I think it changes things for all of us. Decisions about what you want to do *after* you hear the weave will be important." He tried to catch the eyes of those still circling the bonfire. The flickering firelight cast shadows across the faces looking back at him; his own image reflected in their eyes.

Val came to Faith's side, took her right hand tightly in her own, squeezing for encouragement.

Faith's voice faltered when she saw Ari join the group, just far enough away from the edge of the firelight so she couldn't see his face, but close enough that he could hear. "Tell us," Val prodded her, squeezing her hand again.

Lifting her chin, Faith scanned the crowd to look at each individual she would share this information with. Her stomach clenched. The idea of revealing the weave frayed her nerves. Her voice took on a cadence; the words flowed from her; the audience got caught up in the weave's web.

All for one and one for all, leads the Princess of them all.

This weave takes in all the races; all their history interlaces. There's no escape; nowhere to hide; hate's been woven in with pride. The races hate and hate and hate. It's you must find a way to soothe, to patch, and to remake before the Gugwe charge through Shara's gate.

Behold! A daughter of a queen, a long-awaited princess, heretofore unseen; a princess of the land of Sharas, found just when need falls upon us. Gugwe come to purge the land, to make us slaves; 'tis you must keep us from our graves.

This is the foretold prophecy of the princess of the Fae, the Goblins, the Gargoyles and those who live within our woods; all those blessed with magic, both evil and good. It is a weave for all to understand; you'll only find safety, united, under one ruling hand.

Listen! Can you hear the sand falling through the hourglass? A clock ticking as eras pass? Your compass points to the northern shore. Fear holds you tight within its grasp; but only you can give fear power. Only you can save the hour.

All for one and one for all, leads the Princess of them all.

Heed my words and heed them well. Those few you trust, like coins, have different sides. Eventually, you'll discover all the secrets that they hide. The long-lost secret, when exposed, shall make you weep; our world betrayed by those who hid it deep. The secret knowledge changes everything. Still, you must deal a cruel blow; take a life, claim a death, blood stains your hands, and steals your breath.

The clock will strike to mark the time; that fated hour, so long awaited, will find you filled with all the power you need to win; your mother's song upon the wind. When the clock has made that sound; blindfolds all fall to the ground; all eyes will see; bindings will be loosed, men will be set free, you're more than meets the eye, you see.

All for one and one for all, leads the Princess of them all.

What if you fail? You ask? Worry not. Few will notice; because the Gugwe will have smote us.

DURING FAITH'S TELLING, Arnid Aubrey Stormbringer had walked through the group. He noted reactions as they listened to Faith recount Persid's weave. Ari could imagine his dead sister's voice giving the weave its first oration, and he felt an unexpected tear slide down his cheek. His voice was soft when he spoke to the group. "I think that should give you all plenty to think about tonight. As your host, I insist everyone turn in. We will meet back here in the morning for breakfast and a fresh perspective, hey?" Ari clapped his hands and sent them scattering to their beds.

Assigning the lads several shifts of watch around the top of the ridge, Robin, Caz, Saffron, and Rolland laid out their bedrolls near the bonfire, down to glowing embers now.

Robin settled down, but his thoughts were active. He raised himself up on his elbow a few minutes later to find Faith, Val, Garrett, Aliah, Delainey, and Carlisse all shaking out their own bedrolls nearby. He lay back, locking his hands behind his head, admiring the star-studded sky. The next thing he knew, the morning sun was burning through his eyelids.

Delainey and Ari had woken while it was still dark and opted to make three batches of hot porridge. She put out fresh berries, maple syrup, and raisins to use as garnishes in the gruel. It seemed the most efficient way to feed such a large group.

Ari had produced two huge camp coffee pots from the cellar. He made coffee the old way. Delainey watched as he tossed a few handfuls of ground beans into the hot water. Then, he secured the pots on the tripods posed over the fire to heat from below as the brew simmered. After he gathered a mismatched group of mugs, he took center stage, which, in this case, was the top step of his porch. He looped his thumbs behind his coat lapels and called out to get everyone's attention. "Now then," he started, waiting for all eyes to turn in his direction. "The group presented several ideas and suggestions last night about who was going to go where. I recall a list of all your various adventures and responsibilities, hey?"

Heads shook in agreement. They all seemed to shift into their respective groups. "Stop!" Ari directed. "I'm willing to bet that by now, anyone who wasn't here last night when Faith revealed the dream-weave my sister wove for her has since been filled in on the details, hey?" Several heads acknowledged the truth of that bet. "How could it even be possible you haven't united behind this Fae princess after hearing of her weave?" he questioned them, his voice incredulous. "It was crystal clear to me! Should have been just as clear-cut to all of you, making our purpose the same. By now, all of us should be united under one cause and pointed in the same direction!" Feet shuffled. There were some grumbles and whispers.

"That weave describes a unified front of all the races against our common enemy, the Gugwe. The beast-men. Whatever you call those monsters. If you, your families, or anyone you know becomes their slave, I can guarantee you'll wish you'd paid attention to this warning." He turned to capture every eye to be sure they were following his line of reasoning. It pleased him when he found every face rapt with attention. "We're the first. The first coalition backing up the Princess of the People," his hand extended, pointing at Faith. "Here's my plan," he said with authority. "Raven, I agree your clan needs to be checked on. You'll need to tell them about Rupert and Morveena's plans to travel to the Gugwe leader in pursuit of their own gains and leaving the clan to fend for themselves. It would be a good idea to take some of your lads, find out if the clan wants to continue following those two as clan leaders or if they want to shift allegiance and put their trust in Robin Goodfellow?"

Robin's face reflected shock at Arnid's suggestion. Val was standing just behind him. She stepped up, patted his shoulder, and then gave him a little push. Robin found himself in the limelight. Bloody hell, he thought as he shot Val a glare.

Raven stood in front of Robin, waiting for confirmation that he should follow Ari's suggested order. Robin cleared his throat. "Yeah. So, as for the clan, take the lads, see what's what. Make sure our people are well. See what they think about Morveena and Rupert's leadership? We'll wait here until you return. If any of the clan wants to come back with you and onward in the direction we'll be going eventually–north, pack 'em up and bring 'em." There was a small cheer for the plan from the goblins.

Before Robin could say more, Ari took control again. Delainey sat on the porch steps next to him. "It is my destiny to train Faith, the Princess of them All. By the time you finish your instruction under my tutelage, you will be physically fit, have learned tactical combat skills and martial arts, be proficient in using various weapons, and have made a decent study of military tactics and strategies. And last, but probably most importantly, you will be familiar with all the races and the cultural nuances of the inhabitants of Sharas. Robin, I'll need you, Caz, Rolland, and Garrett to do daily training with Faith, Val, Aliah, Delainey, and Carlisse. Saffron can join in if she likes. They need to build up strength, learn weapon craft, as well as magic."

Faith and Val looked at each other, stunned.

"Don't think it's a dream come true," Ari warned the girls. "I've also been tasked with teaching you about the Fae. Obviously, your education has been completely ignored on that topic. In addition, it is critical that you learn the reasons for the existence of the great invisible wall of hatred between the races. You must become proficient in using every ounce of magic at hand if we are to defeat the Gugwe. Each of you will be different, with a variety of abilities, absent in some, strongest in others, as well as having abilities in common. But I will not train you in magic alone! You must learn to defend yourselves using strength, intelligence, mastery of weapons, and your sixth sense. Relying on magic alone for your defense can get you killed."

"Don't kid yourselves. This won't be easy. This will be hard. Very hard." He made eye contact with each of them to be sure they understood. "I expect your effort to be 100% in every area of your training. That means 100% in your physical training, 100% in weapon mastery and combat tactics, 100% in learning magic and history. If you do not give me 100% in Every. Area. Every. Single. Day. You're out! I have no time to waste on anyone not fully committed." They all broke up, gathering their bedrolls and gear.

"One more thing," he called out. "Between lessons, you'll each have assigned chores to keep us all fed, warm, and cared for. Aliah and Saffron are to set up a rotation schedule to keep us in food and fuel. Today, you can work together as a team to get our camp set up and supplies organized. I have someone who comes round monthly with provisions. You can prepare an order, and we'll send a message about what we'll be needing."

Ari clapped his hands twice. "Alright, then, the sun is climbing. Beginning with the next full hour, I will expect each of you at my door one at a time, excluding Faith, at the top of each hour. Come in order alphabetically according to your first name. After all, I promised you each a fortune weave, hey?" he winked. "Last rule. No lamps will be lit when darkness falls tonight. Rest is crucial for training and absorbing knowledge. We start full-out instruction at sunrise tomorrow."

CHAPTER 9: Weaving Dreams

Arnid Aubrey Stormbringer had been weaving dreams of fortune since sunrise, with only a quick break for a snack Delainey insisted he take time to eat. He wolfed down the creamy paste using small torn pieces of Aliah's flatbread. His mind was sorting hundreds of details, preoccupied. Each fortune weave lowered his energy level, draining his essence. But even with so many distractions, he noted the pleasant flavor of the spiced paste. He washed it all down with a cool crock of water and thanked Delainey for her kindness.

"You're welcome, Ari. I saw you thinking about the flavor on your tongue. Just so you know, the paste you just ate is called hummus. It was a recipe, Saffron suggested. Ground white beans and pine nuts, with secret spices." She smiled at him and took up the tray. "Just in case you wanted to know," she told him over her shoulder on her way back to the stone house and the kitchen kingdom she currently ruled.

Break over, Ari calculated that of the twenty-one weaves he'd promised, still more than half needed to be completed. Noon was still a couple of hours away.

Aliah had been first. They walked together to the north end of his valley and strolled through the small fruit orchard. He wove a dream for her with words very clear and concise, even though she had not opened her thought to him as he had requested before he started. Instead, she had locked her mind tight against him, allowing her doubts about him to ride roughshod over her conscious decision to resist him.

When he finished reciting his cast, she stopped and stood staring at the ground, mouth hanging open. A moment passed. She shook her head, eyes pulling up to his, the back of her neck and cheeks flushing red. "I owe you an apology," she confessed.

"A true weave then?" he queried.

"Word for word. The same dream your sister Persid gave me almost eight months ago."

"And you've been preparing yourself ever since the weave to be ready to serve in your foretold role?" he asked with admiration.

Aliah nodded, biting her lower lip.

"If you wish, I will help you continue to prepare," he assured her.

"I promise to be an excellent student. I really am sorry to have doubted you, but..."

Ari interrupted her. "Your doubts were reasonable. You lacked full knowledge of the details, hey? There was no way you could have known Persid had a twin brother." He winked at her. "A brother who is also a Dream Weaver." He smiled at her and took her hand. "You have a heavy burden," he told her with knitted brows.

"I can bear it," Aliah squeezed his fingers and turned to go back to the comfort of the stone house, calling back to him, "I can bear it with the help of friends."

Half of Raven's lads were next, and their weaves were simple enough. Four of the lads told Ari they had no interest in hearing about their fortunes. They thought it could be bad luck to know things in advance about their own lives–a kind of curse or a stroke of bad luck. They decided they were better off not knowing and just living life as it came.

Ari assured them he completely understood. He looked on as they shuffled off to the barn to play some dice games to pass the time. The lads were eager to be on their way back to the clan. All were patient for those of Raven's Gang, as they thought of themselves now, who wanted to consult with the Dream Weaver. Besides, the cooks were good here, and if they had to chip in on chores a bit; they reaped the rewards of tasty, filling meals and a dry place to sleep.

Carlisse and Delainey had the same experience as Aliah. The three of them had been to consult with Persid together. The trio came home with pixie haircuts that summer. Ari recited both their previous weaves as originally spelled out by Persid.

Garrett was his last weave before lunch, and that session stymied Ari. "I don't know what's wrong," Ari worried. "I've never had this happen before," he told Garrett. "You're completely blocked to me. I can't get a read on you at all." Ari fell into deep thought, then told Garrett, "This is a curiosity. Tell you what," he clapped Garrett on the shoulder, "let's try again tomorrow and see if something changes, hey?"

There was really nothing Garrett could say, so he agreed and set off to help with gathering firewood, keeping his disappointment to himself.

Ari sat thinking about the odd occurrence. He wondered if he might suggest Aliah try her abilities on the lad so he could compare her experience to his.

There had been nothing surprising about his reading of Cazzidy Beaumont Touchstone. His and Robin's destinies tied together like a square knot. Goodfellow would never have a better, more loyal friend, but there would be some rough patches Ari felt were best not disclosed. They would do better at working out trouble with women without his input. No point in planting the idea and having them be wary of one another.

Rolland's weaves contained a newly formed, shimmering thread of silver entwining his and Saffron's fortunes together. They would be pillars for the clan and their friends, a lasting cornerstone of love for one another.

"So, you have a talent for making weapons?" Ari asked after the reading, "A master at such a young age." He raised his eyebrows while looking at Rolland. Ari saw the color rise to the young lad's cheeks.

"I do well enough, but I don't claim to be a master, sir. The making of weapons and running the smithy has taken up most of my life," he admitted to the Weaver without going into detail about his Uncle Narrol. If the Weaver knew of his uncle's cruelties, it wasn't mentioned. Rolland retreated into his silent mode, where grunts of acknowledgement became his form of communication.

Saffron was waiting for him when he came back to the stone house. "Well?" She asked him, "What did he tell you?

Rolland gave her a wry smile and told her softly, "He asked me if I would set up a smithy shop in the small building over there behind the barn. There's an old forge there. The rest..." he paused.

"Come on, Rolland, share the rest," she urged, eager to hear the dream Ari had woven for him.

"The rest..." He took her hand and gently pulled her along as he started walking again, "the rest we'll talk about after you've had your weave done." She couldn't get another word about it from him. Stubborn man!

Raven was still analyzing the Weaver's vision he'd received. The detail that divulged he would become a leader did not surprise him at all. Nor the point he would play a major role in the battles the future promised with the Gugwe. It satisfied Raven to hear it, because soldiering was his life. It suited him, and he had a way with the lads. Those lads followed his lead because he treated them as he'd wanted to be treated himself. Something he had learned from Robin Goodfellow. They also trusted him because he had an uncanny knack for figuring out the best approach to things where the fewest number of lads got hurt or worse. He also had a talent for winning the conflicts they faced. Those skills would definitely be useful in fighting the Gugwe. He needed to learn everything he could about this enemy. In the other part of the dream weave, he was sitting in deep contemplation, oblivious to everything around him. The Stormbringer foretold a close relationship in his future. It would be okay, he guessed, as long as he could keep on soldiering. The part that had him tied up in knots was where the Weaver said his "relationship" was going to be with someone of a different race. He was trying to come to terms with it.

He didn't think it was because he was racist. It was just that he'd never considered a mixed-race bond would work for him. He'd known of one or two lads who had mixed marriages with females. One from the Fae race and the other a wood nymph. It seemed like there were always problems between them because their cultures were so different. And then, it was almost like they were outcasts of their own kind. These issues caused the mixed families to keep to themselves. There were plenty of people out there who had a cruel streak for anybody who thought or acted differently than they did. He couldn't imagine inflicting those woes on someone he cared for. All his machinations brought him back to the same place when he looked at it from different angles. He just didn't know how he felt about getting mixed up with a lover who wasn't another goblin. Raven had never really given a thought to looking at a female from another race, even as a test to see if they attracted him. He thought of himself as a person who was friendly and polite to everyone he came into contact with. In the end, he decided he would continue being himself and he would just live and let live. Raven promised himself he wouldn't be holding his breath. He would not look around every bend in the river or on the road, speculating about what this future relationship would be like. So, he tucked the thought away. Raven decided he would stay focused on the soldering aspect of his life. He began making a mental list of training he and the lads needed to brush up on and what kinds of skills they could help teach to the others. Ari had asked them to guard what had been renamed Stonehouse Camp, as well as take part in helping to teach the skills he and the lads were proficient in. Planning kept him engaged until he heard the big iron dinner bell Delainey was ringing from the back porch.

Arnid and Robin had reached the southern edge of the Stormbringer's valley. If you were to climb to the ridge from where they stood, continued due south for two and a half miles, you would come out of the Edgewood to a large meadow. The Crystal River ran east from there. The camp wasn't deep in the Edgewood like Persid's home was.

They had just turned into a lane with rows of red pine along each side, where they planned to walk while Ari wove for Robin, when they heard the dinner bell.

"Saved by the bell," Robin joked.

"It's up to you," Ari told him. "We can go back now and take this up another time, or continue and catch up for dinner after?"

Robin smiled. "We'll only have to stand in line if we hurry back. I'm sure our head cook will think to put some dinner by for us, yeah?"

Ari nodded his agreement, and they moved down the pine aisle, the fresh smell and cool air clearing their minds.

The Stormbringer's eyes glazed over and he came to a halt, Robin stopping just ahead of him. The Goodfellow turned back to see Ari, arms stiff at his sides, feet a foot or so apart, gazing out, a blank look on his face. His voice rising with a deep moan, then delivering a monotone oracle:

"Wake Robin. Wake Robin. Wake Robin,"

Gooseflesh rose across his arms. Ari turned his body and looked straight at Robin. Well, right through him, really, continuing, voice rough and dry.

"The Trillium picked, the spell wire tripped,
the scales of justice have been tipped.
A Fae is the key to open the door
that leads to your old dream.
The dream to live in peace with all;

to grab a hand before a fall.
To live. To let live.
To seek to know how others think,
explore their history, find common links.
You can build the roads, the bridges, and help the races mix.
A world in which a hand's extended; clasping a neighbor's wrist.
You'll have a new partner in this labor.
Your sister, long-lost, forsworn to save her.
Soon she'll be a part of your life.
One day, little Goodfellows might dance round your feet.
But if and only if
you crush the Gugwe in defeat.
Wake up to your destiny, Robin Wilum Goodfellow.
Take up the charge and lead.
Your badge shall be a trillium to wear upon your sleeve.
Peace is your symbol.
You'll spread it far and wide.
But freedom is your standard, one you'll fight for with great pride."

Ari shook himself and stumbled. Robin grabbed his arm and shoulder to steady him. "Are you alright?" he asked the Weaver, concern lacing his words.

"Yes, yes. Thanks. I'm fine now. It's just the weaving always has a cost, and I've done so many today."

"Come on, then," Robin suggested. "Let's head back for dinner. Maybe you should quit for the rest of the day, get some rest and do the weaves of those left tomorrow, yeah?"

Ari laughed. "Oh, I don't think it would be a good idea. There's only one more weave to do, and unless you want to tell Saffron hers will have to wait until tomorrow, I think it would be best to get on with it."

"Saffron is the last?" Robin wondered aloud, "I would think if you wove according to first names alphabetized, it would be Val?"

Ari nodded, bothered by the thought, "Valerie Victoria Pureheart did not sign up on the schedule for a weave. Odd that." He scratched his head and then nodded. "I think a meal would go a long way to restoring my energy level, hey?" Arnid clapped Robin's shoulder, and they started back to the stone house. "Did you want to talk about anything in the weave?" Ari offered.

Robin didn't respond right away. Just when Ari was sure he'd get no reply, Robin told him in a serious, hushed tone, "I think I need some time in my head with it. You know, think it through. Then I'll let you know if I have questions," Robin confirmed. "You won't mention my long-lost sister to anyone, right? Her existence isn't public knowledge, yeah?"

"Nary a word, lad," Ari announced. Dusk closed around them by the time they reached the porch. Delainey leaned against the railing with a wooden spoon in her hand, which she quickly pointed at them and then at the back door. "I saved you some. It's still warm," she smiled.

"Would you mind sending word to Saffron? She'll be the last one tonight. Tell her I will be with her as soon as I fill my belly." Ari smiled back at Delainey, but she gave him a hard glare. He took a deep breath; the aromas made his mouth water and his stomach rumble. "Begging your pardon, Miss Delainey. I didn't mean it to sound like I would fill my belly as if I were just going to gobble down food. That was a mistake, and I should have expressed my true feelings. I'm going to savor every bite of the gourmet meal you've prepared until my body rests sated, numb with pleasure." He raised his eyebrows at her to see if his correction had brought him redemption. She laughed, pulled the linen cloth covering their bowls and bread. She left them in peace to oversee the kitchen clean-up was well underway, and send a message to Saffron. Several of Raven's lads were on clean-up duty tonight, and she wanted to get to know them.

The moon had risen when Saffron rounded the corner of the stone house, pulling her shawl close against the chill of early evening. Ari had just finished a pipe. Tapping the bowl against the side of the step to knock out the ash, he tucked it into his jacket pocket.

"Sorry to keep you waiting so late, Miss Saffron," Ari apologized, "but you're well suited to the moonlight. It makes those beautiful red locks look like fire and your green eyes sparkle," he flattered her.

"You don't have to butter me up, Arnid Aubrey Stormbringer," she admonished. "Let's get this walk in the moonlight started. The sooner we finish, the quicker you can find your bed. Then you can weave your own dreams before the moon goes down!"

Saffron looped her arm in Ari's and they took the lane along his small crop fields.

"You must have said something very serious to Rolland. He wouldn't share it with me until you did my dream weave. What's what?" Saffron demanded.

"When I do a weave, young lady, it is private. Once given, it is theirs to share or not as they wish. Not mine to share with others about them. Understand? I will not share your weave with anyone else, hey?"

"Sorry Ari. I've spent all afternoon and evening speculating about why Rolland wouldn't share with me. What I should have been doing was respecting his privacy. Now I'm embarrassed," she admitted shyly.

"Then I think we can let it pass and say no more about it." He patted her hand as they continued strolling down the lane. Ari told Saffron that she was at a crossroads and would need to make a major decision before her future could be told with any certainty. She asked him if he actually meant that she could decide the direction of her future. Every day he counseled her, but major changes only come along so often. He advised that whatever her choice, he could see bright sunlight and moonshine when he gazed down the different paths she might choose.

"One of my choices involves Rolland, yeah?" she pleaded with him. A nod was all he allowed. They started back up the lane to the stone house. "When?" she wondered aloud.

"Sooner than you'll wish to be facing a hard, life-changing decision," he counseled. "Don't rush things." It was the last thing he said about the weave, then suggested she hurry along to bed because tomorrow was the beginning of training, sunrise at Stonehouse Camp.

Valerie Victoria Pureheart skulked in the shadows cast by the oak trees on the edge of the woods near the stone house as she watched Ari send Saffron off to bed. Val hid in a soft mist of black, not even aware it emitted from her, created by her mood. Aliah had thought the Dream Weaver was a fake, which proved untrue. Now it seemed her sister Delainey was becoming friends with the dandy. Val just plain didn't like the man. And definitely didn't trust him. She should have been his last dream weave tonight, her name starting with 'V', but she'd avoided him all day, keeping out of sight. No one seemed to notice that she hadn't added her name to his list. In fact, it seemed several of Raven's lads had also declined, not wanting to know about the future. She had originally gone along with the idea of Faith seeking the Dream Weaver, but was even more surprised her sisters had had their fortunes spun months ago! Well, as far as she was concerned, one didn't open one's mind to a creature she didn't trust.

She pulled back further behind the oak when Ari looked over his shoulder. Val had decided she would learn whatever magic he would teach them, but she would keep a careful watch on him. She was good at figuring out puzzles, and the shape-shifter was definitely a puzzle. Something wasn't right about this entire setup, and she meant to find out what it was. She had to protect her sisters and her best friend.

"Val?" a voice called softly in the dark.

Her body jumped with a start, but when she turned, she found it was just Robin. She playfully pushed his chest. "Didn't anyone ever teach you it's rude to sneak up on a girl?" she joked.

"Everything okay?" Robin asked. "What are you doing alone out here in the dark?"

"I like the dark." She shrugged her shoulders. "The stars are out. Come on!" she coaxed. "Let's go to the top of the knoll and watch for shooters."

"Shooters?" Robin frowned.

"Shooting stars, silly!" Val grabbed his hand and pulled him down the lane toward the rise.

Faith hung back and watched them go. She'd been looking for Val to find out what the Dream Weaver had cast for her, but held back when she heard Robin call Val's name. Not sure why she knew only that she felt foolish. Instead of trying to catch them up, she turned back the way she had come. It felt to her like she would be intruding. Three's a crowd and all that. Val said Robin was handsome. Carlisse said so. Faith stopped, looked down at the ground and dragged the toe of her boot back and forth, then turned back to find her bedroll. She tossed and turned for a long time before sleep claimed her.

CHAPTER 10: Make Maps, Map Maker

Taramat, Thana's Map Maker, had taken great care in drawing her map before presenting it to Thana NukPana. Making powders from plants, mushrooms, and berries she'd dried and crushed, Taramat mixed them with water. The process created dyes of different colors to enhance the map she depicted on flat, cured sheepskin. The Map Maker had used a soft blue-gray to depict rivers and lakes; a golden-brown to shape the Gugwe land mass; a blush of green to show the boarder-lands of their enemies; finally, a berry juice, so dark a red, it appeared black when dry, used to label the names and locations of the 13 tribes:

Vutova
Lootuk
Kuktuk
Vulita
Wildhorse
Nanavox
Grey Fox
Alabaster
Bear Ridge
Silver Valley
Bull Moose
Vattusk
BloodKnife

Taramat dared to mark out a route using a series of dash marks. She chose the course after taking into consideration the current and future weather. She had contemplated how the conditions would change with the seasons in the geographical areas they would traverse. This epic mission Thana NukPana proposed to embark upon, visiting each of the 13 tribes, would last months. A span of time that would not only bring changes in the climate for the expedition, but would also bring all his new tribal transformations with the four winds.

By the time she completed the map, it surprised her to find that an entire week had passed. Thana's 13/31 were to begin the trek in just another weeks-time. Taramat sent a young Gugwe male with the message that she requested a meeting with Thana NukPana. The reply was so immediate that she didn't even have time to finish the first meal she'd indulged in over the last two days.

Taramat carefully rolled up her artwork and stalked with purpose toward the NukPana's abode. She found him alone except for #11, Nevele, Thana's bodyguard. Nevele stood a full head taller than the Thana himself. The emperor's attitude seemed different to her now that there were no longer 13 people following him in a cluster, each trying to capture his eye. She nodded to Nevele when she entered the tent. The bodyguard stood off to the right of the entry. Though they had known each other since they were cubs, his gaze was hard. He did not acknowledge her. She gave him no more thought and strode to the large table where she found Thana seated.

The artist wasted no breath on frivolous greetings. Taramat unrolled the soft, cured sheepskin, her artistic depiction of the Gugwe lands, and placed it on the table before him. The Thana gazed upon the graphic rendition of his empire, complete with all the homeland's features from mountains to plains; from the tundra to lakes and rivers, great and small.

"I have been thinking, Thana NukPana," she told him without his asking. "When you survey the Gugwe realm," she waved her hand over her map, "your best traverse would be to take one step backward..."

He grunted at her suggestion, and she took in the set of his facial features. The frown line between her own brows deepened at what she saw. "No, no! Thana NukPana, hear me out. I have lived in all these lands in my mind's eye for a week. I have bent all my thought to your success in uniting the 13," she said sincerely. His features altered, showing bemused interest. He waved his hand for her to continue.

Taramat pulled a long-pointed stick from a loop on her belt and used it to show the route of the quest she was suggesting for him. "First, backwards to Lootuk. The waters surrounding that tribe's hold will still be open. The Lootuks can use their longboats to speed us across the sounds, run the edge of the great ocean down to Kuktuk. Going by water may save up to a full week if we can make use of the waterway. Who better to praise for faster travel than the Lootuks? From there, because of the changing weather, it would serve you best to head south and west. We can travel from the Kuktuk tribe to meet with the Vulita, across the tip of the mountains, then on to the Gugwe of Wildhorse. You won't be able to stay very long there, maybe two days, before descending the mountaintop straight down to the ocean shoreline to reach the clan furthest west and south, the Nanavox. After our visit there, the path will lead you across the southern section of the mountain range. We must reach the eastern side, then turn north, bringing you to the Tribe of the Grey Fox. It is a very rugged place," she nodded her head at her own affirmation, then continued as Thana NukPana studied her map.

"Northwest will take the 13/31 to Alabaster from Grey Fox. The fall season will start soon. The next part of the journey will be four or five days, depending on how hard you push to reach Bear Ridge. It is possible that the weather may hinder our progress by the time we reach the area. From there, our course must run past Sapphire Lake, hopefully reaching Silver Valley before the first snow falls. May the winds hold for the Great Thana NukPana." The last, she said to herself as her eyes surveyed the path to the next tribe, Bull Moose. "See here?" Her pointer tapped the location of the Bull Moose Tribe, then she drew an arc across the bay. "Again, you can save another week—well, maybe only five days," she reconsidered. "But we must get there before it freezes to take advantage of the open water. If that is not possible, if we are too late and the winds send winter's cold early, we will have to go by land." She held her chin in her hand, considering, "Either way, we will arrive at Vattusk." The mapmaker crossed her arms, nodding her head toward the map. "The BloodKnifes are the last Gugwe tribe to visit." Taramat pointed at the location on the map, then put the pointer back on the loop attached to the heavy belt she wore. She turned to him and bowed. "I have another couple of ideas I'd like you to consider. Do you wish to hear them now?"

Taking a deep breath, she continued before he could even respond. "First, send out Zenara, your minister of communications, west, and south. As well, Bakrat, your emissary should travel east and south. Both should leave a week before your 13/31 so they can bring at least some notice, though short, to each Gugwe village, informing the tribes that the Thana NukPana is coming. It will give them time to prepare a welcome."

She raised her eyes to meet his. "Last, I suggest that as you leave at the end of each tribal visit, you invite each KuRuk and a small delegation to join you for a grand summit. You can direct all the representatives of the tribes to meet near the Bloodknife grounds at Thrall Lake on the eve of the winter solstice. Gathering in such large numbers will display to all the Gugwe people how you have indeed united the 13. Moreover," her eyes shone brightly, "they will see it with their own eyes. There is power in that which we can actually see with our own eyes, as opposed to words, which can be lies." Satisfied with her presentation, she sighed. "The gathering at Thrall Lake will serve as the true beginning. The time where you bring representatives of all the tribes together as an entire nation, instead of each tribe remaining one of 13 separate divisions." Taramat lowered her arms and clasped her hands in front of her, clearly finished with her speech.

Silence echoed loudly throughout the Thana's tent as he continued to study the map. Taramat felt sweat trickle down her spine. *Had she displeased him? Was her plan too bold?*

Keeping his eyes on the map, in a quiet voice, Thana asked, "What title did I name for you, Taramat?"

Her cheeks colored, but she pulled her body up to its full height, put her chin out, and answered. "I serve as the Mapmaker for Thana NukPana," she retorted proudly. "I am one of the 13."

"Ah," he drew his eyebrows as though deep in thought. "I believe I made a mistake when I issued such a proclamation."

Taramat's stomach muscles squeezed her guts. She couldn't believe he was going to dismiss her already as Mapmaker! What a waste of her talent! Her thoughts delved another notch lower, then she startled at something he'd said.

"My apologies, Thana. Could you repeat what you just said?"

"I said I had made an error. In order to correct my gross underestimation of your skills, your new title will be Mapmaker *and* Chief Advisor to Thana NukPana." Taramat blinked in wonder.

"I like your plan," he told her. "Every detail. Make it happen. Meet with Zenara and Bakrat. Get them on the road tomorrow so they have a good lead for each village visit. They can catch up with us at Thrall Lake. Let Jayben, the Journalist/Secretary know every detail of my new plan so he can record the events as they happen. Neeta, our statistician, is compiling information for us, so she will provide details of each tribe's customs. Neeta will also comprise aspects of each tribe's population; the geography surrounding their holds; their resources; as well as any notable cultural differences. You already see the importance of such information and how useful it can be to us on this mission?" She nodded.

He continued, "Good. Make yourself available to her. Neeta can fill you in first before she completes the details so you can approve them. Keep all the information organized to apply your innate ability to see outcomes in the bigger scheme of things. Tell Callan to put together a small group of youths. I want him to create a routine training for the young warriors. The youngbloods will travel with us. I will expect them to put on a demonstration before we reach the first tribe. We will introduce this new idea of early training for the youth to the other tribes. Zolo can help him, since we have no slaves for him to master yet," Thana chuckled at his own joke. "Could you also check with Boartusk on how his success at gathering weapon supplies is coming along? When you have talked with Anson, report back to me on his supply chain progress and on any issues he has encountered. Then, depending on all the information *you* gather about our progress, you can advise me. I will decide whether to take your advice."

Taramat reached down to take her map from the table, but his lethal hand, razor-sharp claws extended, palm down, pressed against the center of the colorful map. He held the artwork in place. "Make more," he growled at her, "I will keep this to study further. I think it would be wise for each of the 13 to have a copy as well. In addition, I want you to make a map for each KuRuk to give as a gift when we visit." He studied the look on her face. "Don't worry. You will have time as we travel to make those." He gave her a generous smile. "Make maps, Mapmaker," he threw at her back as she hurried from his tent.

NEETRIHT HAD SPENT the last eight days in a flurry of activity and planning, with little sleep. She had laid out a plan for putting certain trusted members of the Vutova tribe into leadership positions. The appointees were to address the primary concerns of the tribe's safety, food sources, shelter, and education. This way, she could spread out the workload, accomplish more for the tribe, as well as give those she chose a sense of being part of the plans and changes. She met with them individually. Then, when she had selected her leaders, they met as a group to share ideas on prioritizing issues. She encouraged them to give opinions and to offer strategies to solve problems. Neetriht suggested that they each create a plan of action. She clarified she expected them to assign responsibilities to accomplish all the points in the plan they had developed. One of the newly appointed leaders challenged her authority because she was female. It was unfortunate, but she had loosed an angry growl, pushed the offender to the ground and ripped out his throat in front of the others. His body slumped to the ground, lifeblood gushing from the wound. Neetriht had stepped around the corpse, continuing with her instructions. There were no other disputes about her leadership.

Knuckling her gritty eyes, yawning, deciding it was time to catch a few hours of sleep. Neetriht had a mountain of tasks she had given herself to complete tomorrow, but if she didn't take some rest, she would not be at her best to accomplish them.

A young female acting as a messenger for the Thana called outside her tent, "KuRuk Vutova, I am sent to tell you the Thana wishes to see you." The girl lowered her voice to a whisper, sending words for her ears alone. "Please hurry; he is in a foul mood tonight."

Neetriht heard the messenger scurry away, confident the KuRuk received her message without verbal confirmation. She rose from her chair and poured cool water into a washbowl. She splashed her face, blotted it dry, tossing the damp cloth behind her as she left her stretched hide shelter.

Before she could announce herself outside the Thana's tent, he called out, "Enter, Neetriht. Oh," he coughed, "I mean KuRuk Vutova." She could detect no malice in his correction.

Lifting the flap, she went in. "I think when we are alone," her eyes wandered to #11 standing in the shadowed corner behind the Thana, "it feels right for you to call me Neetriht, brother."

"Good," he approved. "I have been hearing positive things about the way you are organizing the Vutova tribe, giving others the power to act. I like the idea of creating an environment that will get more done for the good of the entire tribe. It will strengthen us instead of the old ways of trying to keep a tight hold on your power for the KuRuk alone." Neetriht nodded, acknowledging his compliment. "I want you to come with us as we travel to visit the 13. You are KuRuk Vutova, but you are more than that title. The first female KuRuk. You have a firm grasp of how to motivate the tribal members to work for the good of all. You understand all the reward systems I have put in place. Surely, you would represent my strongest argument for changes in other tribes. I want you to present your new organizational efforts to each KuRuk, covering all the areas to help each tribe not just to survive, but thrive. In the meantime, your own administrative heads will run the Vutova tribe until their KuRuk returns from supporting the Thana in uniting the 13. It is important that you take part in the Gugwe Tribal Debates at the Thrall Lake Summit. All the other KuRuks will be there, as should you, representing the Vutova tribe. Each leader will speak to the crowd, but your voice should rise above them all."

"I will make it so," Neetriht assured him. He wasn't clear if she meant getting ready for the trip and putting all her plans in place with strict instructions for her chosen leaders. Or if she meant she would indeed make her voice heard above others. Likely, she addressed both, he decided, as he watched her leave his presence with a determined gait.

The day of departure rushed head-on at the 13/31, as they raced to prepare for travels expected to take them nearly half a year to complete.

CHAPTER 11: I'm Coming. Deal With It.

Tuck, Zud, and Drako had crossed over the large body of water to reach the other peninsula four days gone. They traveled east and spent several days at the first goblin clan's hold. The trio needed extra rest after such a long trek from the mid-lands. There was also the matter of Zud, who had a crush on a lass named Zelna.

Zelna lived with this clan. It had been almost two years since Zud had last seen the girl, but his attraction had not lessened over that time. In fact. His fascination with the female had increased.

The three companions used the time to rebuild their strength and replenish their travel supplies. There were plenty of opportunities to share news with clan leaders and old friends.

Two lads from Zelna's clan proposed they join their quest. The males explained they had family and friends scattered throughout other holds that Tuck, Zud, and Drako planned to visit. Because of that overture, it prompted Drako to offer Zud the opportunity to stay here, where he could pursue Zelna's affections, rather than continue. Zud vehemently refused. Much as Zelna attracted him, he did not want to be left out of completing this quest. He thought it was important work. Every time he recalled being under the Gugwe's mind control, his determination increased.

After Drako's suggestion, Zud practically ignored Zelna. Each day the trio remained with the clan, Zud hurried to gather the items on the list Tuck had assigned to him, things they needed to continue the journey. He managed to keep himself busy all day long. Every day. He dreamed of the moot, believing a large turnout was critical to its success. If all the races *could* work together, they just might have a chance of defeating the Gugwe. He fully intended to do his part. They had to convince everyone they came into contact with of the importance of at least attending the meeting. The moot would foster discussions to develop their collective options against a common enemy. Zud was determined not to let love impede the mission or his part in it.

Every time Zelna tried to speak with Zud or maneuvered to spend time with him, he spurned her efforts. He just couldn't let himself be left behind when Tuck and Drako continued on the journey.

Two more days came and went. Finally, Tuck announced at the evening meal, the threesome planned to leave the next day with the sun's rise. Zud's heart ached, but he held his resolve to stay away from Zelna. The next clan-hold was a four-day hike, but they intended to stop in between at a human village. Most of the residents there were fishermen who lived with their wives and families on the shore of a large inland lake. A few miles from the fishing village, rumors said a Fae cabal had a camp along the river flowing into Sapphire Lake. The lads hoped to have their first encounter with the Fae, to share their news and proffer an invitation to the moot. None of them spoke of it, but they wondered how friendly they would find the Fae covey. Known for often placing wards around their camp perimeters, the Fae made it hard to detect their community for anyone not of their race.

The following morning, the whole goblin clan was up early to see the small company off. There was a breakfast of dried fruit, nuts, and hot fried bread. Tuck, Zud, and Drako had donned their packs just as they caught sight of the two lads who had committed to accompanying them. The small crowd parted as Ian and Asa made their way through the assembly to join the three travelers. Zud stood stone-still when he saw Zelna right on Asa's heels.

Zud had been hoping to leave quietly. He didn't want to have a confrontation with Zelna before he left, but now it looked like that would be impossible to avoid. Doing a double-take, he noticed she was carrying gear as they approached. *What was Zelna doing with a pack strapped across her back?* He goggled at her. The last thing Zud wanted was to embarrass her in front of her entire clan!

Zelna smiled at him. Zud groaned inwardly, turned his face away, cheeks turning red, unsure how to handle this latest development.

Asa spoke up. "Tuck, this is my sister, Zelna. She is going to go with us."

Tuck gave a friendly nod to Zelna. "We're going to be traveling fast, Asa. No offence, Zelna, but we can't afford to be slowed down," he said kindly.

The entire clan laughed as if Tuck had made a joke. Tuck, Drako, and Zud looked at each other, bewildered.

Ian explained, "The clan finds the idea of Zelna slowing you down funny, because Zelna is the leader of our clan's female guard unit. She trains them. If anything, we'll all have trouble keeping up with Zelna." Ian smiled at Asa's sister.

"Look, I don't mean to be difficult..." Tuck started.

Zelna stepped forward and spoke directly to Tuck. "I am good friends with a human at the fishing village along the route you plan to take. In addition, I have three Fae friends in the covey you'll be seeking. I can get you an audience with the covey leader. Otherwise, you may waste days searching up and down the river, trying even to find the Fae camp. Without me, they may not grant you a meeting, even if you *are* lucky enough to locate them." She held Tuck's gaze with her confidence alone. "I believe in your mission and can help with a good beginning," she boasted. "I'm coming. Deal with it."

Zelna pushed past Tuck, her shoulder knocking against his as she passed him, heading north down the trail. Asa fell in behind her, with Ian following. Tuck shrugged his shoulders, shooting a look at Zud, which seemed to say he'd brook no complications from his companion over the change of plan. Drako gave Zud a gentle shove to start him down the footpath. Calling out well wishes, the clan was waving. The visit ended with the clan leader shouting after them. He would see them again at the moot. So it was that the next leg of their journey started with a sense of success.

SHAWN SANG A MARCHING song with Maddo and Perk as they all moved through the flatlands they had to cross. They'd already stopped to see to the three goblin clans the lads wanted to check on. Lehto and Kristian both felt those encounters went as well as they could have expected. The clans were stand-offish at first contact, seeing the lads traveling with Fae. But Travis had brought along a small cask of whiskey. After a toast or two, the conversation flowed more easily. In the evenings, Brittany played her flute. Often after the meal, Bento joined her, making music using a soft drum, while Bobbit's fingers flew across the strings of his small fiddle. It wasn't unusual for dancing to begin shortly after.

Mariella, Travis, and Shawn rose while night still hung on. They prepped flatbreads. While the bread was baking, all three chopped several pounds of mushrooms they'd been lucky enough to come upon yesterday. Mushrooms added flavor to the wild onions and sliced tubers that Cervil had found. Three large pots hung over the fire. The starch from the tubers made a pasty sauce to bind the filling together. Shawn pulled a soft packet from his pouch, added some precious salt and a handful of dried hot pepper flakes. They served the small clan breakfast. The group ate the vegetable medley out of community bowls, using torn pieces of flatbread to scoop it up.

When they'd all finished the meal, the conversation turned to more serious issues. Namely, the Gugwe, as well as the problem of what could be done to heal the hate between the races. The big question was whether years of hatred could be put aside? At least enough so that they could actually work together against a common enemy. There were many who were skeptical of the success of such a venture. Kristian pointed out that if they didn't at least try, the Gugwe would eventually invade, take over and make slaves of the lot of them, anyway. Fear found its way onto the faces sitting in on the discussion.

Mariella spoke up after a long moment of silence. "At least consider having one or more representatives attend the moot to share your concerns with the other attendees. The plan is to meet on the Winter Solstice at the tip of Lower Sharas, between the two peninsulas. Surely just attending the moot to listen, as well as get information from afar, is worth your effort?" she asked the leader of the goblin clan. Lehto came over and put his arm around the pretty Fae to show solidarity. None of the eyes looking upon Mariella and Lehto could see any signs of hatred between the Fae and the goblin. "Promise you'll at least think about it?" she entreated. Her eyes searched to meet the eyes of each person in attendance. "After you've heard what other citizens of Sharas think, you can make your decision to join us as a combined force against a common enemy or choose not to join us at all. But it is my hope you won't make that decision until *after* you've heard what everyone has to say at the moot."

The cousins and the lads packed up to leave late that afternoon. There were large, billowy clouds moving across a bright blue sky. The members of the small clan came to watch their final preparations.

Brittany marched up to the clan leader. "It was good to meet you, Eben. I look forward to the next time we see one another," she clapped him on the shoulder. She almost lost her footing when Eben's large ham of a hand clasped Britt's shoulder. "Travel well, Brittany Stargazer. Travel safe. The elders have committed to having a small delegation at this moot of yours. Look for us before the solstice. May the wind blow gently at your back."

Shawn, Maddo, and Perk broke out in song, leading the group as they traveled to visit the next goblin village, located further north and somewhat east. The clan watched the troop until the last of the companions moved around the corner of the trail and out of sight. Their singing drifted away on the wind. When the company of Fae and goblins took their leave of that small clan, they left them with large things to think about.

CHAPTER 12: Revelation of Kings

Faith was up long before sunrise. In fact, she'd been awake for hours, a myriad of questions churning in her mind. She'd heard Val come back from stargazing with Robin two hours after she'd climbed into her own bedroll, the fire down to a glow of embers. Val had whispered, "Faith, are you awake?" She didn't know why, but she remained silent, keeping her breathing even, pretending to be asleep, until Val eventually turned away, seeking her own blankets.

Now fully alert, she heard the back door of the Dream Weaver's house open, then softly close. She could barely make out the shape of the black cat in the dark, slinking away toward the barn. Faith Lisbet Stargazer (she'd dropped the surname Watson) moved after the feline in the shadows without making a sound. Standing behind a tree, she saw the cat look over its shoulder. Green eyes blazing, steadily gazing into the dark before it turned again, continuing past the barn. Faith's curious nature peaked. She took great care with each step. At one point, she considered opening her wings, but lacked the experience yet to be sure how much noise they would make and didn't want to chance Ari's discovery.

The orchard beyond the barn provided ample shadow to hide in. There were a few tense moments when she thought she'd lost him. But just as her stomach knotted up with anxiety, she glimpsed his tail flickering, like a beacon drawing her forward.

The early hour still held a chill. The dew on the grass had soaked through her boots. She mentally chided herself for ignoring Nursie's suggestion a month ago to oil her boots against the coming wet spring weather. Tentatively, she placed the ball of her right foot on the ground to move forward. She heard a small squelching noise; her boot sucked down, covered in mud. Faith looked up, keeping track of her prey. The cat headed for a small shack at the back of the orchard. His silhouette was just visible where the edge of the woods started and the groomed, orderly rows of fruit trees ended. She covered the rest of the ground in slow steps. Carefully placing the ball of her right foot, patiently using the pressure to push the water out of the boot before putting the rest of her weight on it. That helped avoid the squish noise. Then, following that process next with her left foot. By the time she reached the shack, she could hear a conversation going on inside, the voices rising higher with each step as she came closer.

Faith pulled up her hood and crouched beneath a broken window at the back of the small wooden structure, listening intently, trying to catch the thread of the argument. There was no question in her mind that it was a quarrel taking place. Ari's voice was clearly angry. "Miss Pureheart's assessment of you was spot on!" Ari yelled.

"If you're finished expressing your divergent views about my plan, let's get back to a conversation where we can actually accomplish something, shall we?"

Faith stiffened. She recognized that voice. Knew it well. She had to be imagining things. Overly tired. *It couldn't be, could it?* Before she'd thought it through, she rounded the shack in thirteen steps, didn't bother to knock, but simply threw the door open, bursting into the room. She stopped dead center, turning full circle, taking in the scene.

There was a wood-burning stove in the corner, with a long shelf behind it, similar to a fireplace mantel. Lenny and Lester lay on their backs opposite one another. Their bottoms of each gargoyle's feet pressed up against the others, pumping their feet one against the other as if they were riding a bike. Entertained, laughing out of control. Faith rolled her eyes. She swiveled her head to look Ari in the eyes of his man-form. Slowly, she swung her gaze to the right, confirming that the voice she had recognized was indeed Dedo's. Emotions rolled over her senses.

"What's what?" she whispered to herself, trying to make sense of things. Then, "Do either of you care to explain this little secret meeting?" Anger oozed out with each word, and she did not try to control it. "How do you even know one another?" Her voice was incredulous.

She swung back, facing the woodstove, shook her finger at Lenny and Lester, and screamed, "Stop!"

Their laughter ceased. Sitting up, they put their hands beneath their chins and, with stoic faces, stared at her.

"I want answers." Her voice was deadly quiet now. "Why are you here, Dedo? Why are Lenny and Lester here?" she asked, throwing her thumb behind her at the two small gargoyles. "How did you know where to find me?" she asked, eyes burning with fury.

"If I may..." Ari started, but Dedo rudely interrupted him.

"Be silent, shape-shifter!" Dedo commanded. Ari's face flushed with annoyance at the dig, but he held his tongue.

"Have a care, Princess," Dedo warned Faith. "Your rough words have no place here." He scrutinized her from head to foot to be sure she wouldn't shout out again. "Evy, your old nurse has a ring, twin to the one you wear." Faith unconsciously fingered the plain silver ring on her right hand. Dedo continued, "Both rings are spelled to one another. Evy told us where you were days ago. She said you needed help, that Queen Morveena had captured you. Likely, all our years of care to hide you are undone now. I assume Morveena, Queen of the Goblins, knows who you are, Princess?" he ground out the words with bitterness.

"Yes. She does."

"When I found out she'd taken you prisoner and planned to sell you to the Gugwe Emperor, Thana NukPana, action was necessary." Faith's face turned green upon hearing this information. "We may never have been able to rescue you once they placed you in his hands. The gods know we could never recover your Queen Mother in all these years."

Faith felt like he had slapped her. "Do you know where my mother is?" Her voice expressed her incredulity at this admission. She shook her head, took two steps back from Dedo. "How could you be so cruel not to tell me my whole life? I thought myself an orphan. Now you're telling me my mother is alive?" She looked at him as though he were a stranger, and the muscles around his heart tightened.

"We don't know her exact location. I've never been able to find out. No search party we sent ever returned. She has been a prisoner ever since you were a babe," his deep sadness clear to everyone in the room. "We couldn't tell you. Oaths sworn to your mother and your father, promising to keep you hidden. Safe. The Princess of the Fae, daughter to Queen Aleta and King Lennox, was an unconfirmed rumor to all but a handful of people in the world. People who love you, I might add. People who have given over their lives to your care and well-being," he emphasized.

"Don't you dare try to elicit shame from me! It turns out my whole life has been a sham! A lie that everyone I care about had held as a secret. My mother is alive somewhere! You knew both my parents. I'm not some nameless bastard! You can't imagine what that knowledge means to me. I have a family. Blood relatives. Aunts, uncles, cousins. A mother and a father that you can put names and faces to, but I cannot. You've kept me from them all these years." Tears welled in her eyes, but she angrily swiped them away. "You can't possibly know how it felt to always be the outsider. The square peg in a round hole. Alone. An orphan." Her head whipped up to catch Lenny and Lester miming crying. Her blazing stare sent them back to indifferent stances.

"Is my father alive?" she asked, her voice quivering.

"We can't be sure, but we believe it is possible," Dedo told her honestly. "There has been no word or rumor about him for at least seven years. Your cousins claim they saw him just two years ago, but I question the honesty of their declaration. No one *I* have contact with has seen any sign of him."

"So, Nursie could tell you where I was. Likely you knew all the time." Dedo blinked his eyes at her. "Just how is it you know the Dream Weaver?"

"I enlisted his help to assist in your rescue. Quick action was necessary. The Goblin Queen is a wildcard. Consideration for your safety was paramount," Dedo offered. Ari snorted.

"Is what Dedo says true, Arnid Aubrey Stormbringer?" Her eyes challenged his; her voice told him she would brook no fibs.

"I would merely argue the descriptive 'enlisted.'" Ari crossed his arms, his eyes shooting daggers at Dedo. "Your pet gargoyle," he sneered, "came into possession of a debt marker I had given years ago to another. The marker belonged to your mother, in fact."

Faith's hands flew to her mouth, her eyes wide as saucers. "You too? You also know my mother?" She asked, her words barely audible.

"Before you were ever born, heh? But think, Princess. Your mother was the Queen of the northern Fae. People of all races knew her far and wide across Sharas." He reached out to touch her arm to offer comfort, but she jerked away. A flash of dismay fell over his face.

"So," Faith addressed Dedo with petulance, "you've found me, rescued me and are here in secrecy to interfere with my life as usual, I take it? All without letting me know of your involvement. How sneaky you've become, Dedo. That is probably a silly statement. You've been sneaky from the very beginning. Well, you can go back home. I don't want your help, and I refuse to be your puppet any longer. In fact, I want you out of my life!" She growled at him. "And take your two spying jesters with you." She inclined her head toward Lenny and Lester. They turned to look at one another, then back at the Fae Princess. The two small gargoyles had never seen her angry in all the years they had stood guard on her mantel.

"Have a care how you speak of them, Faith Lisbet Stargazer," Dedo's voice shook with unexplained anger.

"They are just as much a part of your conspiracy as everyone else in my life. Those two have always been your pawns. You pull their strings. Tell me, who else knows my real identity?" she demanded. "To clarify, I mean before my *actual family* showed up. How lovely my cousins arrived just in time to witness my body exploding in wings, while I was ignorant of the fact that I was even a faerie! Much less a long-lost princess!" She hissed at him. "Who? Who else knew?"

Dedo leveled his eyes and looked at her as an angry parent would. He answered her curtly. "Prior to your cousin's arrival, only Reatha, Robert, Evy, and I were privy to that knowledge. Not your friends or any of the fortress household. Oh..." he cast at her nonchalantly, "and the Kings of the Rock People, all of us, sworn to your safe-keeping." Dedo shined his fingernails on his lapel, held them out to inspect. He sat down, wrapped his arms around his legs, rested his chin on his knees, clasping his hands together.

Faith ran the information he'd just spilled out through her mind. Ari leaned against the wall of the shack, occasionally glancing out the window. She pressed her lips tightly together. Of a sudden, her mouth fell open. She turned on the ball of her left foot to look straight at the two statuesque figures sitting quietly on the shelf above the stove. She broke out in hysterical laughter. Her ridicule died down as utter disbelief formed on her features. "You expect me to believe these two jokers are kings, as in plural? Kings of the Rock People? Kings of the entire nation of the Gargoyles?" A giggle erupted, and it took her a moment to push it down. Dedo only stared at her, remaining silent. She looked at Ari. He nodded in the affirmative. She turned, scrutinizing the two gargoyles from their heads to their toes. Lenny scrunched his toes under, uncomfortable with her gaze.

"Is it true?" She asked them directly, "You two are the kings of the Rock People? The Gargoyle nation?"

They bowed their heads to her with dignity, and small gold circlets, the centers inset with emeralds, appeared around their foreheads. They both stood, stretching their wings. Though they were only a foot tall at full stand, their wingspan was at least four feet across. Their arms and legs bulged with ripped muscles. In tandem, they both went down on one knee before her and brought their right hands to their hearts. Their eyes beseeched her to acknowledge their loyalty to her. She curtsied in return. They turned to one another, grinning.

"The Kings have been with me as long as I can remember," she said aloud to no one in particular. "I don't understand how they can rule the Gargoyle race from the fireplace in my room at Robert's fortress?" she smirked. "The bigger question is why, in heaven's name, are they here now?" Lenny and Lester both winked at her, closed their wings, and returned to their usual stoic positions.

"They are here to assist the Weaver in teaching you magic," Dedo stated in a flat voice.

"Robin and Caz will love to meet the two of you," she told them, true. "Both being students of jest," she clarified. Faith thought for a minute, then asked the twins, "How can you teach me magic if you can't talk, hmmm?" Her tone definitely rang with doubt about their abilities.

Faith stood facing them. Neither Lenny nor Lester moved a muscle. In her head, she heard a deep voice. "Oh, we can speak with you, Princess, directly. See? No need to waste breath." Lester raised his eyebrows to let her know it was he who had conveyed the information to her. Her mouth fell open, but she quickly snapped it shut.

Another voice invaded her mind, this one sharp and higher pitched. "You never asked us to talk with you, Princess. Else we would have shared all our jokes with you as you grew up. Pity. That would have added significantly to your overall education." Lenny waggled one finger at her to identify himself as the silent speaker.

Finding herself at a loss for words, she took the opportunity to mentally convey an off-color joke Val had gotten from Garrett. Their laughter echoed in her mind as they lifted their hands to their mouths, then punched each other in the arm, pointing at her, obviously delighted.

Abruptly, she spun on Ari. "How were *you* able to assist in my rescue?"

Dedo's eyebrows drew down as Ari cleared his throat. "I used Dream magic on the young lad you know as Raven. We couldn't come into the Goblin camp and risk engagement against Morveena and Rupert's troop, so it had to be an inside job. Raven was already of a mind to help his mate, Robin, so I didn't have to do much to influence his actions. You might be interested to know Raven had already developed a respect for the way you handled yourself in danger. It impressed him that you maintained a brave front while under the goblin queen's cruel control." Ari anxiously looked out the window again. "I am afraid the rest of your questions will have to wait until later, Princess. The sun is coming up. Stonehouse Camp training begins today at sunrise. Punctuality is a requirement in my book." Ari turned toward the door.

"Wait," she held her arm out to block his escape. She faced Dedo and asked, "Do Lenny and Lester, um...I mean the Kings, do they know everything about my life you do?"

"They do," Dedo confirmed.

"Then I will get my questions answered by them. I want you gone from here. You will not be dictating my life choices any longer. I don't trust you. Oh, and you can tell Nursie when you see her, she is to take the twin to my ring off and not use it again. She can give it to me when we meet again. You can also inform her that is a direct command from her princess."

Dedo physically drew back as if she had slapped him. He swallowed hard, replying, "As you wish."

"I wish," she told him firmly. "Should I need you, I am sure the twin kings can contact you?" He nodded, affirming her guess. "Since both my parents are missing and we cannot even be sure they live, despite what you may know or believe, it is clear to me now that I must rule in their stead. Forced to take on a role I'm not prepared for and never would have dreamed of. What I know for sure is that before that can happen, I acknowledge I have much to learn. So, I will stay here as long as I am learning. This I do for the benefit of the Fae people, as well as the other citizens of Sharas."

"Faith, please let me help you." Dedo offered.

"No. I do not wish you to help me. Leave. Your betrayal is something I may never get over. If you ever loved me, begone," she begged him, her voice hitching.

"King Lenny, King Lester," she called to them, "I've decided I would like you to stay, to teach me whatever magic you can. Do you promise you will be loyal to me?" They nodded their acquiescence. "I will come back here tonight after training and lessons. There are many questions I want to ask. I want *your* help." Her words wounded Dedo, and she intended them to hurt. He felt their sting. Without another sound, he touched a stone on the woodstove platform and disappeared.

Faith took Ari's offered arm. They left the small wooden shack, hurrying up the lane. Ari could see the group finishing breakfast. Some were already milling around, probably wondering where their training master was.

After the door had closed, Dedo reappeared, facing the Kings of the Gargoyles. "I know you are loyal to the Princess. You know I am as well. I beg you to keep me informed," he beseeched them, lowering his eyes to the floor, and then he disappeared once more without waiting for an answer.

Communicating in silence, the Gargoyle Kings acknowledged they could do nothing that would betray the trust the princess had granted them. They couldn't risk losing the confidence she entrusted to them.

Lenny and Lester looked seriously at one another for a long time. Without further consideration of everything that had just taken place, the two kings lay down on their backs. Their heads lay in opposite directions as they scooted toward each other until the bottoms of their feet met. They continued pushing in and out against each other's soles, laughing as though they'd never been interrupted.

CHAPTER 13: A Question Answered

Val gave Faith a curious look as she arrived with Ari, where the group was milling around near the fire pit. Delainey quirked her head at Ari. He matched her stare with one of his own, then winked at her.

Out of the blue, he clapped his hands sharply to get everyone's attention. Ari's voice was gruff as he called out three separate groups. Ari paired Saffron, Val, Delainey, and Robin together. Caz, Faith, and Carlisse made another team; Garrett, Aliah, and Rolland, the last crew. He gave them a few minutes to regroup as named, then laid out the routine he expected them to follow.

Ari told them that for the first two hours after sunrise each day, they would all be required to exercise, which included a weight training program. He insisted that distance running be part of the daily drill. There would be a 13-minute break once they completed their morning workout. That would give them an opportunity to quench their thirst before moving on to their specific group classes. Class instruction entailed four-hour sessions. The courses would shift for each team every day between history, cultures, and languages; defensive methods and weapons training. They would receive separate sessions on the elements of magic.

Today, however, they were going to forgo the physical drills. Instead, there would be an orientation introduction for two hours in each of the classes they would eventually be attending. The overall schedule Ari described provided them with six days of training. Each day, the four-hour sessions rotated among the three course areas. Bare essentials as far as Ari was concerned. He reminded them that time was of the essence. Tick Tock, tick tock. Time would continue to tick on, and bad weather would come and go. The world would continue to spin. But he assured them they would be held accountable. Only they could do what needed to be done to ready themselves for the quests they would likely have to endure against their enemy in the future. The plan was to prepare the Princess *before* the Gugwe set upon their new raiding season in the winter. Frozen lakes and rivers provided the beast-men with ice roads they could use. Additional opportunities allowed them to go to places not easily reached, and likewise, not easily escaped from, without the frozen access. The Gugwe had adapted new methods to use the winter's freeze. A major change from their old strategy of raiding at the first thaw and getting their boats back home before the lakes iced over. Before the change, they found themselves immobilized by the harsh conditions, causing them to abandon their loot.

Ari brought his orientation meeting to a close by having Saffron give a description of the daily chore assignments. The camp trainees could find the roster posted inside the barn door. She granted them a brief explanation of how she, Aliah, and Delainey had worked out a fair system for divvying up the work.

Last, Ari announced, King Lenny and King Lester, rulers of the gargoyle nation, will teach magic to those at Stone House Camp. In addition, each night, he himself would tutor one of them in private one-on-one sessions in various types of thaumaturgy. They were to switch off each day in alpha order according to their first names, as they'd done with his Dream Weaving. He looked specifically at Valerie, specifying that these lessons were required. He reminded them again; he expected them to be *all in* on this. If they weren't all in 100% of the time, they would be out. No exceptions. Val turned her back on him and headed to the area alongside the barn designated for weapons training. Robin, Raven and two lads followed, adding Delainey to the group as they moved away from the others. "Somebody has a bug up their arse," Robin whispered under his breath as he watched Val stalk away.

Teams disbursed, Ari felt the weight on his shoulders triple. It appeared he was stealing time, even as they began. How could he ensure he would have them all properly trained in such a short time, on so many levels? It was a fool's bargain to think he could turn them into a lean, mean, fighting team. One that would work together so tightly they could read each other's every thought and act as one. One for all. All for one. Ha! In addition, they'd have to learn to trust each other, depend on one another. The camaraderie was pretty thin at this stage. There were a lot of stumbling blocks thrown out before them, like a minefield. Sunset seemed only a blink away, and it was only the beginning of the day. Worried he wasn't up to the task the Gargoyle had pressed on him; he vowed to use every resource available to him. Shaking his head, he turned toward the back porch, motioning for Garrett, Rolland,

and Aliah to follow, along with three of Raven's lads. Ari had tapped them to help when he'd discovered they had a talent for several languages of various races. The group settled in around the dining room table, facing an old chalkboard, which had hung in the barn until last night.

Caz and Carlisse followed Faith on the two-track leading to the small shack at the end of the orchard, where she'd been earlier that morning. She casually described the two gargoyles who would instruct them. Admitting without details, she'd just recently learned they were twins and the ruling kings of the Gargoyle race.

Caz reserved making any judgment until he met them. Carlisse shrugged her shoulders and suggested they hurry along. She had every intention of learning all she could from them. She was hungry for new information. Faith smiled. Secretly, she hoped to do the same. The hours in the day flew by, the sunset seeming to come in the blink of an eye.

After the teams had moved through the three two-hour shifts as an introduction to all the topics, Ari assigned a *quiet hour*. He explained that there would be a quiet hour each day after their four-hour classes. During that period, they were free to spend the time in any activity they wished, such as reading; napping; bathing; studying; meditating; journaling; drawing or painting; additional light exercise or stretching; yoga; dancing; working the forms for sword play; practicing the forms for Taekwondo; even gardening. The idea was to stay silent, to internalize, contemplate, reflect, and absorb all they had learned that day. Thereafter, they were to spend the next two hours on chores, meal preparation, a relaxing dinner, and cleanup.

Ari made a point of smoking his pipe after his meal. His private tutoring lessons would not begin until he had sated himself. The rest of the camp broke up into small or medium circles and got to know one another. Sometimes the small groups compared their own experiences with what they had learned while growing up. Often, they would lay knowledge of something Ari had taught them up against history or culture as they knew it. They were always looking to compare the differences. The best part was that they stacked up the similarities to evaluate as well. A few handfuls of the occupants practiced a particular language together several nights a week. When bedtime came, every single one of them quickly drifted off to sleep, exhausted from the intensity of each day.

It wasn't long before each group had chosen its own team names. Saffron, Val, Robin, and Delainey dubbed themselves *Gugwe's Bane*. Caz, Faith, and Carlisse declared themselves to be the *Truth Seekers*. Garrett, Aliah, and Rolland took the mantle of the *Guardians*.

That's when the competition became fierce.

Half of Raven's lads called themselves *the Clan's Guard,* and the other half took up *Goodfellow's Gang*. The whole of Stone House Camp started referring to the unusual cooperative on the whole as *the People's Alliance*. Secretly, Delainey took on an additional singular title, *Stormbringer's Revenge*.

Faith used her sketchbook to create a symbol for each team moniker. The next day, Raven, and the lads showed up for physical training, each showcasing Faith's tattooed renditions of the symbol she'd created to represent their gangs. A flurry of demands followed to find out who had tattoo talent. They rounded on Faith. She denied any skill in inking skin. But it impressed her that, whoever the tattoo artist was, they had captured a perfect depiction of the symbols she had designed. It turned out that two of Raven's lads had the knack. Raven pointed up to the ridge rim, showing where the ink artisans would be found. Ari put an end to the mass exodus, requiring anyone who was planning to get a tattoo to seek an appointment to get their own symbols immortalized. He smiled inwardly. The thin camaraderie was thickening. A stronger sense of belonging to something. Something special, hey?

Carlisse sought out one of the tattoo artists during the quiet hour and asked if he'd mind her watching him ink the others. He was a shy lad, but her question brought a smile to his face. He said he'd not mind at all having her company, as well as a dance one night when the musicians were jamming. She returned his smile; went back to the large boulder she'd claimed after a few days as 'her spot' and began her yoga routine.

After the evening meal, the group naturally broke into small clusters. Continuing to spend time together, just hanging out and learning about their companions. Some nights, an eclectic group of musicians made their various instruments work in harmony. They taught each other music from their own cultures and then the dances that matched the melodies. There was good-natured jesting, joking, poking and prodding about all the differences in dress, music, hair, language, and folklore. They also discussed all the things they found to be similar in their cultures, as well as things they thought seemed odd and truly foreign.

WEEKS PASSED, AND THE days turned warm and humid. The weather swung wildly from blazing hot, sunny days to gloomy, gray, rain-filled ones. Then, the skies would clear, filling the night sky with the Milky Way and shooting stars or moon-shadows. Their bodies showed muscular development. They had increased the morning run from two miles to five, then added the switchback road from the valley to the ridge line; a lap around the rim and back to the valley floor. Not once did they split into separate groups of only goblins or only Fae, but sometimes they split up into a group of *girls only*.

On one particularly hot day, the sun felt like it was scorching their skin. They begged Ari to let out classes a half-hour early. He relented because they had been working hard, everyone giving 100% in applying themselves. He was extremely pleased they recognized their own worth, willing to invest in themselves to become better. More.

Ari was sure they'd had this planned, as the girls disappeared like ghosts. He could see a few heads bobbing above his grapevines, heading toward the pond beyond the apple orchard. They'd all taken their blankets. He'd seen Delainey disappear with a picnic basket, chasing after them. Not long after, distant shrieks carried across the orchard as the girls jumped into the pond, the cool water taking their breath away on such a hot day.

"Aren't you going in?" Val stood watching Faith sketching the scene.

"Definitely. I just wanted to capture the moment." Her pencil lead moved across the page, shadowing, adding minor details here and there. She closed the pad, put the lead in her waist pouch as she unbuckled her belt, and stripped off her clothes. Faith jumped up, started running toward the water, calling over her shoulder to Val, "I'll race you!"

Val was right on her heels. "No fair!"

"I have a new sense of *fair* play over the last few weeks!" She retorted to her best friend. A loud squeal followed by a splash. She sputtered and squeezed her eyes closed as Val came down right in front of her, a wave of water washing over her face. Val came up from under the water, laughing. Saffron shared around a cake of lavender soap Zeeka had given her from her last soap-making day, before this adventure had begun.

All washed, they climbed back ashore, hair dripping wet, dried off with their thin blankets, then spread them out on the ground, lay down, letting the sun warm them. Delainey had put out a nice spread of fruits, nuts, cheese, and some candied ginger she'd found in the pantry.

Saffron wondered aloud, "Do you think boys are the same no matter their race and culture?"

Val opened one eye to look at her. "Be more specific, Red," she instructed Saffron.

"Well, for instance," Saffron toyed with her thoughts, "are they all daft at recognizing how you feel about them, or do they just pretend to be?"

"As far as I can tell," Val shared, "they keep their cards close to the vest. I think males are very talented at *not* showing their feelings."

Aliah added, "Some of them show every emotion on their faces."

"Maybe females spend too much time trying to figure everything out, when males don't think there is anything *to* figure out." Delainey suggested.

Faith thought this was the perfect opportunity. She asked nonchalantly about something she'd been privately pondering for days. Posing her question to Saffron to deflect from the person she really wanted to ask, she said, "You like Rolland, don't you, Saffron? Are you saying he doesn't know you care for him? Or, um...how about you, Val?" she asked, as if the question had just popped into her head. "You seem interested in Robin *and* Caz, yeah? Do you think either of them is *the one*?" Gentle laughter rippled through the girls.

The light-hearted response from Val froze Faith's heart on such a hot day. "Robin is quite handsome. He's also smart, but Caz is, too. Don't see why I have to choose. If they're interested in me, I think I'd like to explore both possibilities, yeah?" she smiled around at her sisters and friends.

Saffron offered advice based on her knowledge of the boys. "Well, lass, that's fine, but those two won't let it stand for long. I've known them for years. Jokes, jests, weapons, fighting, and sport are all considered good competition between them. But with females, they won't compete with one another. Once they figure out you're playing them one against the other, so you can have your cake and eat it too...well, let's just say it might not end well. For you. They will remain loyal to one another for all the years of their lives. I'm sure of it."

"Well then, I just have to make sure they don't figure it out, Red," Val said with confidence.

The collective female group hooted and howled. Faith smiled, but no one noticed her smile didn't touch her eyes. Now she had confirmation of Val's attraction to Robin. Faith's love for her oldest friend out-ranked her own interest in the Goodfellow. It had to. She would never hurt Val. Would never want another person to come between their friendship.

Instead, Faith decided she would direct all her efforts into trying to live up to a leadership role. Interest in boys would take a backseat. No matter how frightened she was to measure up to Persid's crazy fortune weave, she wouldn't be alone. She'd have her best friends, Val, and Garrett, as well as all Val's sisters in her corner. She had even made some good new friends she believed she could count on. They just happened to be goblins. If she got the opportunity, she'd decided that she would give her cousins a second chance. There would be no room in her life for anything else, except figuring out how to save all the people in the land of Sharas from becoming slaves to the Gugwe. Somehow, she was sure that the goal had to be tied to finding her father and her mother. Faith resolved that if she found her parents, she wanted to be sure everything she set her mind to from here on out would make them proud of her and the choices she made.

CHAPTER 14: The Truth

Faith could tell when Lenny or Lester communicated with her alone, or if they were addressing the entire group. In response to the group, there was a slight echo in her mind. When the communication was private to her alone, the echo wasn't there.

"Let me try again!" Carlisse insisted. "I almost had it. I'm sure."

Lenny told the three of them, "Sometimes it works better if you use a visual. Something you would personally identify as protection. It is one method that may help to block access to your mind from others."

"Like an armor shield?" Caz suggested.

"If a shield depiction works for you, yes, Cazzidy. For others, it might be the vision of closing a door, or locking a door, or locking a treasure box with a key. It could even be a vision of laying a gauzy material over something you value and hiding it from view. The visual can vary and typically does for each person. Whatever works best for an individual is the key," Lester explained patiently.

Echo disappearing, Faith heard Lenny's sharp voice. "Lost interest already, princess? Your mind is miles away from this lesson." He tapped his foot, crossed his arms, body language was as much a communication as his direct question.

Red erupted on Faith's cheeks. "Apologies," she stammered back to him. "I'll stay focused."

He turned his attention back to Carlisse and clapped his hands. "Excellent, Miss Carlisse. You've grasped it fully! I've tried six ways to break through to your mind and met your block with every try," he praised her success.

"The Beaumont has it down pat as well, brother," Lester told Lenny and the group.

Faith twisted her silver ring round and round on her finger. The vision of the wardrobe in her bedroom popped into her head. She saw herself open the doors, climb in, shutting the doors behind her. Next, she imagined climbing out the back, swinging the stone door closed once she was in the secret tunnel in Robert's fortress. She felt a distinct shift. Then it seemed a handful of battering rams attacked, but she felt safe in her secret labyrinth.

When she opened her eyes, everyone was grinning at her. It was Caz who complimented her. "Well done, lass," he smiled and spoke out loud. "The kings suggested we all try to break into your thoughts at one time. Whatever block you threw up was strong enough to keep us all out." She beamed at each of them.

The lesson continued with Lenny explaining how the use of mental blocking was essential to keep permanently in place. Blocking could work against many types of magic–good or bad. Since the Gugwe could invoke mind control, this skill was at the top of the list for each of them to perfect. If they learned nothing else in the coming weeks while training at Stone House Camp, this skill was the best protection he felt they must master. Lester instructed them to practice half a dozen times a day until it became second nature to place and hold a mental block at will. He deemed it critical to put in place before falling asleep. Lester stressed the importance of the ability to maintain the block while sleeping, a time frame he considered one's most vulnerable. Lenny insisted dreams had power, just like brain-to-brain silent communication. He emphasized it was possible someone could use their own dreams against them. The instructor insisted it must become second nature to guard their minds.

Faith shivered all over as Morveena's face filled her vision–she threw the wardrobe doors shut. Caz reached out and touched her shoulder. "You alright, lass?"

She felt shy over his concern and mumbled, "Just reliving a terrible memory."

Lester continued his lecture by giving a broad, ambiguous description of various types of power. He explained that natural magic was generated through the use of water, fire, earth, and wind. The elements worked whether you were a seer; whether you used telepathy; or whether you could make yourself invisible.

He touched on evil magic, giving them a stern warning to stay away from blood magic. Never to be tempted to try it, no matter how much stronger they heard blood magic to be versus natural magic. Lester planned to teach them how good elemental magic could be wielded with just as much power as blood magic by the right person. Blood magic, he warned, eventually ate at your soul and exacted a price from those foolish enough or greedy enough to cast it repeatedly.

Lenny explained it was important that they recognize there were many varieties of power. Powers employed by the different races often had multiple levels of potency. He expanded on the fact, not every person had one, some or all the powers available to them. Each person had different degrees of strength related to the abilities they could brandish. Last, he counseled, there were powers available that some races ignored. Powers they clearly knew about and could use, but never did.

"Seriously?" Carlisse pushed her question with a heavy dose of ridicule. "What race is stupid enough to have access to a power and never use it?"

"Don't hold back any of your disgust, lass!" Caz teased. "Maybe you don't know all the details, yeah?"

"You have an example, I suppose?" she taunted him right back. "An example of a power a race can call on, but is foolish enough not to use? What excuse could they possibly have to pretend they couldn't benefit from it?" It was easy to hear the heat in her voice coming through with her question. "Why would anyone who knew they had a special gift shove it away?" her voice rising an octave, expressing her incredulity at the thought.

Cazzidy stretched his legs out, propped his boots on the bench in front of him, crossed his arms, letting his body speak for him.

"Ummm...." Faith started, feeling uncomfortable with the friction in the room. "I, for one, would like to understand. I mean, in my case, I had no forewarning about being a Faerie. When my wings ripped out of my back, I didn't know what was happening. Then," she hung her head, "I thought I was just some kind of freak. So, I can truly understand ignorance as a reason to want to hide what one might think of as an affliction. There could be other reasons, though, right?"

Carlisse shrugged. Lenny and Lester both turned to Caz. Their voices boomed in harmony in all three of their students' minds. "Cazzidy Beaumont Touchstone." They pointed at him. "Show them," the Gargoyle Kings commanded.

Caz let his feet drop off the bench to the ground and stood carefully, keeping his eyes trained on the two girls across from him. Carlisse wrapped her arm through Faith's and snuggled closer to her, suddenly afraid of the can of worms she may have opened. Their heart rates ticked up as Cazzidy tugged off his leather jacket, letting it fall to the ground behind him, black hair hanging over his left eye. His fingers fumbled at the buttons on his shirt. He turned and glared at Carlisse as she attempted to break into his thoughts, to see what was going on in his mind behind those intense eyes. Lenny and Lester privately admonished her, and she bit her lower lip, but offered no apology.

"Caz?" Faith whispered.

He ran his fingers through his hair, pushing it back from his eyes, and held her questioning gaze. Lenny and Lester each held up a hand in an encouraging gesture. Caz released a deep sigh, drew his eyes away from Faith and turned his back to both girls. Two reactions happened at the same time. Sharp intakes of breath as the girls clung to one another. Standing, their legs unconsciously pushed the bench they occupied backward. Wood scraped across the floor, and the bench toppled over when two brown leather wings, a match to his weathered skin, exploded from his shoulders. His wingspan was at least seven feet across. Stretching them full, Cazzidy turned back to his audience, a grim look on his face, bracing himself for their disparaging focus.

Both girls were moving toward him before he could react, reaching out to touch the sweep of his wings. "They're so strong!" Faith breathed out in wonder.

"Your wings seem such a natural part of you," Carlisse told him with direct eye contact. "Why?" she asked, her voice cracking. "Why would you deny this part of yourself?" She shook her head sadly.

"I didn't know goblins had wings," Faith confessed.

"You and the rest of the world," Carlisse confirmed.

"Help us understand?" Faith asked Cazzidy gently.

"We're raised to hide our wings. Never ever speak of them. They teach us to think of them as an abomination. A curse on our race," he choked out.

"But why, Caz? I don't understand why your people would look upon wings and the ability to fly...to soar, with disdain and shame!" Carlisse begged him.

"Shame. Yeah. That's actually a good descriptive," he told her, scoffing at the idea. "The real shame is ours. We've carried it for so long now, no one even remembers the reason for it. But hiding the fact that we have wings is actually *Goblin Law* now. Set in stone. Robin and I wanted to know the history, so we took our questions to our teacher, Master Cornerstone, years ago. He confirmed my belief that the whole of the goblin race should be ashamed. Not because of our wings, but because of the *reason* we kept our wings a secret!" his voice cracked, and he snapped his wings closed, donned his shirt again. Grabbing his jacket at his feet, he confessed, "The shame we own is the hate passed down through the clans. Goblins hate the Fae, and the Fae hate them right back. So much hate between the races that Queen Morveena finally decreed it would be treason to reveal the secret. We are to deny our wings. Hide them. Why?" he laughed, a sad smile crossing his mouth as he scrubbed his fingers through his hair, tugging on handfuls of his dreadlocks. "Why? Because our Queen doesn't want the link to be remembered. Her hatred is like a disease among us. She actually promotes gobs hating the Fae! The wings are the link Master Cornerstone told us about. A link to the past. A link to the...to the truth." Caz sat down heavily, energy spent.

"What truth?" Faith asked, voice shaking. She grabbed his hand, and his eyes turned up to meet hers.

"The past, lass. The truth," he squeezed her fingers, "Goblins and Fae are really all one race, my lady. One. Race. Not two separate races. The same. Our features changed over the years, as some liked to dwell underground. But our roots are the same. There are even some goblin babes born now that never develop wings. I guess from repressing them for so many years. We were forced to ignore our wings so we couldn't be confused with the Fae. We've been taught to believe the Fae are beneath us. Look, I know you didn't grow up with that poison. Unfortunately, I also know you'll find prejudice on both sides as we start our mission outside this camp. And I...I don't know how you're going to overcome it, 'Princess of the People'", the pain in his voice clear.

She pulled him close, wrapped her arms around his shoulders, laying her head against his chest. "One," she whispered, "I'll start with one person at a time, Cazzidy Beaumont Touchstone." He squeezed the breath from her with his powerful arms, hugging her tightly.

Carlisse jumped up and dusted her hands off. "Well. Wow, kings. You really know how to present a lesson." Everyone laughed. "Listen, Caz, I'm pretty sure Faith's going to need to go spread a lot of this new truth around. It's what her weave said, yeah? What do you say you and I high-tail it up to the top of the ridge? You can do that sexy striptease thing again, and the two of us can pop out our wings, do some practice flying, yeah?" She had already latched onto his arm and was leading him to the door.

Lenny and Lester turned to look at one another, eyes crinkling in laughter, dripping wax on the shelf as their three students left with a slam of the door.

CHAPTER 15: The Isle of Lootuk

The sun rose in a fiery haze of bright orange and pink streaks, reflecting on the shining armor worn by the Thana NukPana's 13/31. Hammered copper shoulder armor connected by thick leather straps crossed their chests and backs. A gorget fit tightly over a wool-padded vest, showing off the Gugwe's ripped muscles. Each of the 13/31 wore a wide leather belt with multiple straps, pouches, and sheaths to carry short swords, knives, and personal items. Their feet were sheltered in thick moose-hide boots, styled to come up to the knees. Some soldiers wore tight, fingerless gloves; others wore thick mittens made from sealskin.

Callen Vutova shouted a command to the 13 youths under his tutelage when Thana pushed aside the flap of his yurt and came out into the bright, sunlit morning. The Youngbloods slammed right fists against their hearts and dropped to one knee. Thana indicated they should stand.

"Rise!" Callen ordered. The Youngbloods stood as one. "Your ease!" their trainer growled. In one choreographed movement, all 13 youths placed their feet exactly 13 inches apart and clasped their hands behind their lower backs, eyes looking straight ahead.

Thana NukPana was especially pleased to see that at least four out of the 13 youths were female. He glared fiercely at them. They didn't blink. "I have chosen you as the first Gugwe Youngblood Warriors. You will represent a new tactic in our warfare strategy. Don't disappoint your mothers. Don't disappoint our people. Most of all..." he took the time to make hard eye contact with each one, a menacing growl filling their ears, "don't disappoint me."

Their right fists pumped upward, and with each stroke up, they shouted in unison, "Akama! Akama! Akama!"

Thana NukPana looked stunned at the use of his given name. The fists came to rest across their chests once more, to lie on their beating hearts. Silence covered the staging area. All movement ceased. Thana looked hard at Callen Vutova, but the trainer stared straight ahead, his own fist held fiercely against his heart. A slow smile spread across Akama's brutal, scarred face. "Load up!" his voice boomed across the space. "We leave in five for the Isle of Lootuk."

Zolo and Callen led the Youngbloods, ranging in age from nine to thirteen, in a marching formation to the already saddled herd of caribou. The Thana's 13 (minus Zenara and Bakrat, who had left six days before) had already mounted, as had his 13 soldiers. There were two other Gugwe who gained approval for the trip. They would do the cooking for the small expedition. The Vutova tribe turned out to wish them well on their travels.

"Neetriht!" Akama called to his sister. "We leave!" Quickly, she finished her last-minute instructions to the woman she had put in charge of the tribe's education. She inserted her foot into the left stirrup and swung her right leg over the back of a large male caribou. Without a backward glance, galloped her mount past the entire team, continued beyond her brother at the head and took the lead. The villager's collective voices rose in barks, yips, and roars until the unit passed out of sight. They traveled east in order to connect to the trail they would take north, which would lead them to the Lootuk clan. That tribe's village would be the first of the stops to bring significant changes to the 13 tribes of the Gugwe nation. Modifications Thana NukPana believed would strengthen his people, improve their lives, and make them the greatest race in the land.

Seeker Vutova rode ahead at a fast clip past the Thana and his sister. It would be hours before they saw him again, as he set out to scout ahead of the traveling team.

Taramat rode on Neetriht's right flank. Small groups bunched together as they traveled. Ansen rode with the two cooks. He told them about his plans along the route to replenish supplies and water. He clarified they carried certain provisions that the cooks must parse out with care to make them last, as he was unsure there would be an opportunity to replace them.

Boartusk and Zota rode behind Akama, next to Nevele, all three silent as the hours slipped by with the landscape.

Jayben and Neeta compared notes to confirm that they had both recorded the information accurately about the expedition. Neeta was spouting facts and information she had gathered about the Lootuk tribe, which were sketchy at best, having mostly come from rumors. In truth, they didn't really know much about their sister tribes. She would have to verify her 'facts' when they reached each destination. Her voice carried across the flat tundra. There were those who were curious about the little nuggets of detail she offered, while the sun rode its trail to set below the horizon, hours, and hours ahead.

Rumors said the Lootuk's KuRuk held the title for the last four years. A long span to be a KuRuk among Gugwe. Word was, he ruled with an iron fist and a cruel streak. The Lootuk leader had maimed many in the tribe. He proudly bore scars as well. Neeta informed Thana's entourage that the Lootuks were the oldest Gugwe tribe. The population was relatively small when compared with most of the other tribes. The village was home to about twenty-eight people. A population smaller than this expedition group. What they lacked in numbers, they made up for in fierceness. The males, as well as the female Lootuks, were very superstitious.

The Isle lay amid some of the coldest waters in Adana. This tribe's survival depended on the bounty of fish, the hides of seals, the furs of wolves, and the meat of antelope. They used wide, flat boats with sharp nose hulls to work the waters surrounding the sparse isle. The females only had a cub every three to five years. The survival rate was only forty percent, maybe fifty percent in a good year, keeping the population of the island small. She cautioned the 13/31 that the Lootuks would expect the members of the expedition to feed themselves. They would insist the group fish and hunt for any additional food needed to replenish their own stores. Lootuk led a hard life. Neeta predicted the tribe would not welcome visitors. It was likely the Lootuks would feel our expedition was taking food from their very mouths. They will resent our hunting and fishing their resources, stealing their welfare.

That information kept the group quiet for the next hour. Even the Youngbloods.

The sun hit the horizon in a riot of color, spreading out before them; the skyline changing from moment to moment. The seeker's silhouette was moving slowly in their direction. When he pulled up in front of the Thana, Seeker's caribou blew snot from its nose, pawed the ground before Akama's mount in challenge. Seeker forced his mount's head away as he reported, fist to heart, "Sir. There is an excellent place to set camp less than an hour ahead.

We can be set up before nightfall. There is a river near the site to water the animals and fill our water bladders."

"We follow you, Seeker Vutova," the Thana said, and with a wave of his hand, he showed the Seeker should lead on.

Forty minutes later, dusk falling, the camp was in the throes of set-up. There was no one directing the effort. The group all just seemed to have a natural ability to work together. They brought water to the cooks first, so they could set about preparing the meal, while the others put tents up and cared for the animals. The Youngbloods brought bucket after bucket of water from the river. Every member of the expedition had soft, collapsible buckets; the cooks at least six. The 13 Youngbloods finished bringing water to the camp, watering the animals, gathering firewood, and setting up their tents. They stood in formation under the direction of Callen. He paired them off. Pitting himself against the odd one out, he and the Youngbloods spent the next hour working the forms. They practiced with wooden short swords, similar in size to a man's long knife. When the dinner bell sounded, Callen oversaw the return and packing up of the practice equipment. Youth raced to get in line with their bowls at the cook's pot.

As they served the last traveler in line with a meal of cooked grain and chunky pieces of starchy tubers, the moon came up. The cooks had spiced the stew with hot peppers the Vutovas harvested and sun-dried each year.

Boartusk sipped from a flask he kept inside the woolen vest under his chest shield. He walked the perimeter of the camp; the round gave him an opportunity to enjoy several more swigs before entering the tent he would share with Zota and Zolo. After he settled into his blankets, the tent quickly filled with the smell of Boartusk's rank breath. Zota and Zolo looked at one another, but kept their silence as the Weapon Master snored loudly.

Taramat climbed a small rise where she had seen Neetriht disappear several minutes ago. She found the female KuRuk sitting on a crest, gazing at the enormous moon flooding the flat tundra in golden moonlight. "Always makes me feel small," Taramat said as a way of greeting, sitting down next to Neetriht.

"Me too," Neetriht confessed.

"I haven't gotten around to giving you my congratulations," Taramat admitted. "Being declared the first female Gugwe to become a KuRuk is unprecedented. Did you see it coming?"

"Grandmother did," Neetriht told her with a smile.

A serious tone inflected Taramat's voice. "He'll kill you if you fail him," she said flatly.

Neetriht studied her longtime friend. "Then I shall not fail. You've also come up in the world, Taramat. Map Maker aaaand...Chief Advisor to the Thana NukPana! I am proud of you."

Taramat playfully punched Neetriht's shoulder. "A title given to cover the fact that I am really just his glorified gopher."

"No, Taramat," Neetriht pushed sincerity and passion out with her voice, "don't belittle your accomplishment. It is because Akama recognizes how smart you are. Believe me, he does nothing out of kindness. He knows you will present ideas that will make him look good. They are still your ideas, even if he takes credit for them. You must always remember that," she brushed Taramat's cheek with her fingertips.

Taramat broke their eye contact, stood, and held out her hand. Neetriht clasped it, pulling Taramat to her feet. "Tomorrow will come too early. Let's get some sleep. I'll need it if I am to continue to spew forth brilliant ideas consistently!" she teased, both women laughing as they headed back to the quiet camp.

Before the sun was up, Taramat was awake so she could work on the reproduction of the map the Thana had kept. A gift meant for the KuRuk of Lootuk. She couldn't work on it while riding. There was just too much swaying back and forth atop the caribou. She would have to wolf down her breakfast before they mounted up. All her map-making tools had to be properly cleaned and stowed before they rode for the entire day.

On the sixth morning, as Taramat put the final touches on her geographical art piece, Seeker rode into their campsite as the expedition was packing up to leave. Taramat left her new map spread across her mount's back, colors drying in the morning sunshine, and went to hear Seeker's report. Thana had Taramat's original map out. Seeker used his dirty finger to point out locations for Akama. She scowled at him. They would camp at the southern base of the Isle tonight, he told them. The following day, the team would likely meet those of the Lootuk tribe. Her stomach rolled with excitement. She had been thinking for days about the information Neeta had shared concerning the superstitious island tribe. She looked down at her hands, noticing the colors staining them from her map making, giving her an idea.

The ride that day seemed to drag on. Everyone was saddle-sore, not used to long hours of riding day after day. At midday, the group stopped at a fast-flowing stream. They watered the animals and re-filled their water bladders, hanging them over their saddle horns and remounting. The cooks gave each person a heavy strip of jerked antelope to gnaw on for the rest of the afternoon ride. It provided them with something else to focus on besides their sore butts.

Finally, the tired expedition team came to a halt on the shore of the mainland, looking a short distance across the water to the Isle of Lootuk. Tomorrow, they would make the crossing when the tide was out and finally meet their distant relatives. The group did not know what kind of welcome to expect.

As soon as Taramat had taken care of her caribou and helped get their tent set up, she grabbed her finished map. Tucking her box of art supplies under her arm, she headed to Thana's yurt. She didn't think of requesting permission to enter. An idea was driving her, which always seemed to chase away any sense of decorum from her mind. Pulling back the entry flap, she ducked into the Thana's abode. Animal furs covered the floor. The huge Gugwe was removing his armor. Nevele stood ramrod straight to the left of the entry. She grunted a greeting his way and stepped toward Akama.

"I have finished the map for you to give as a gift to the Lootuk KuRuk."

He took the prize she offered. "If it is as good as your first work, the KuRuk should be pleased," he praised her.

She tapped her foot incessantly.

"You have something else to say, mapmaker?" he sounded amused.

Taramat set her art box down. "I had an idea, sir," she said without a care.

The Gugwe Emperor raised his eyebrows. Akama reached for a large ceramic bottle, removed the cork, set out two small clay cups and poured a thick brown liquid into each, and handed her one. Taramat clicked her cup to his and slung the sharp-tasting liquor back in one gulp. Then, without pretense, she laid her idea before him. He nodded before she had finished.

"You will spend the night here," he told her. "You can execute your idea, so we will be ready at the first sign of the morning's rays." She accepted another dram of the strong drink and laid out the tools of her trade.

For the first time since Akama named him the Thana's bodyguard, Nevele allowed a broad smile to break across his face. He shook his head slightly in disbelief at the Map Maker's boldness.

A bloodcurdling scream, rousing the entire camp, broke the next morning's peace. Taramat flew out the entryway of the Thana NukPana's yurt and took in the scene. The Lootuks had surrounded the campsite. It appeared they wore full war armor. Weapons were raised. Neeta seemed to be the source of the scream, a spearpoint held to her neck, a thin trickle of blood running down from the point. The Thana's 13 soldiers had surrounded the Lootuks. The rest of the 13, along with the Youngbloods, stood in a circle with their backs to one another, weapons drawn and at the ready, facing their distant relatives. Taramat took it all in, only a matter of seconds passing.

"Report!" the Thana growled from inside his yurt.

Taramat picked out the biggest, ugliest, fiercest Lootuk Gugwe and addressed him at shouting level, "KuRuk Lootuk. I am sure it will please the Thana NukPana that you have come personally to welcome him. He will be proud that you hold him in such high esteem to provide us an honor guard to lead us to your village." She bowed with exaggerated theatrics. Neetriht noticed Taramat's face was...painted? Her eyes, rimmed in thick black circles, and the lines from the corners of her mouth, led to her chin.

"Lootuk tribe," she addressed them, "may I present to you the great Emperor over all the Gugwe's 13 tribes, Akama, the Thana NukPana. I pray for your sake that you please your ruler." She swept back the flap, opening the Thana's abode. All the Lootuks looked back and forth at one another, weapons at the ready, waiting to see who would exit the tent.

Akama stepped out of his yurt, raising himself to his full height.

He was a sight to see.

Even his own travel companions took a sharp breath, visibly startled. The Thana was in full armor. Armor painted blood red. His eyes rimmed with red, then a ring of white and a last ring, making his eyes look like a demon, smoldering in black. The hair crested atop his head was also blood red and stood straight up, running down the back of his neck between the shoulder blades. Taramat had starched it to make it stand up. She painted his entire body with symbols to strike fear into the enemy. He looked ghoulish, like an evil spirit.

Akama let loose a bloody roar as he launched himself at the Lootuk's KuRuk. The giant Gugwe spun head over heels and landed behind the beast, who stood three heads taller than himself. Thana's razor-sharp claws glistened with blood in the morning sun. Several silent seconds passed. Finally, the Lootuk KuRuk dropped to his knees before the crowd and fell over sideways, blood gushing from his ruined throat. Akama roared with bloodlust. He looked like the devil's own minion. Nevele stepped out of the yurt next to Taramat, an exact twin to Akama's war paint.

Nevele's appearance undid the female Lootuk warrioress closest to Neetriht. She removed her spearpoint from Neeta's throat, shoved her spear into its shoulder harness. Dropping to her knees, declaring, "The Lootuk welcome the great Gugwe Emperor, Thana NukPana!" Her comrades wisely copied her, lowering weapons, dropping to knees, fists coming to their chests in unison.

So it was that the first of 13 visits came to pass. Thana NukPana quietly praised Taramat for her idea of making him look like a fierce spirit to a superstitious people.

The Lootuk transported all the expedition members and their mounts to the Isle to begin talks of trade; to exchange ideas of changes the Vutova Gugwe were embracing. Akama named the new tribe KuRuk. It was the female Lootuk who first recognized the importance of welcoming the Thana when their former leader fell to his death. A death wherein not one person in the whole of their small population mourned his loss. The expedition spent a week on the Isle of Lootuk. The people were open-minded about most of the ideas introduced, but new ideas needed consideration. Change was hard, but they could see the strategies behind the new ways would help their tribe to become stronger. They rejected the idea of their precious few children being taken to join the Youngbloods. Thana could understand why, with their population so small and their birth rate so low. He compromised and agreed that the children would begin a daily regimen of training, but remain on the Isle. He said they would revisit the idea of Lootuk children joining the Youngblood forces in the future. But not until their population doubled. Perhaps their numbers would grow with those migrating from other Gugwe tribes as trade between the villages became more common. They discussed a plan regarding the KuRuks from every tribe who would come together for the first Gugwe Tribal Debates. The Thana would hold those debates at Thrall Lake at the winter solstice.

Taramat explained they expected the Lootuks to transport the whole expedition across the gulf. They would travel by boat through the straits. Finally, arriving at the sound, the shore of the land where the Kuktuk tribe made their village. She spent several hours with the new KuRuk reviewing the map the Thana had gifted to her. Taramat showed the new KuRuk how her small entourage would find Thrall Lake in a few months. She was pleased when the female KuRuk asked if the mapmaker would teach her how to make the black, white, and red war paint. Taramat left to get her own things for the voyage. Neetriht took her place and spent the rest of the day going over the details of the many changes the Thana had introduced. She spent a great deal of time instructing on the new methods she had implemented to make her own tribe stronger. Neetriht shared how the KuRuk, by appointing several others to help her, would achieve success like the Vutova KuRuk. Neetriht told the new leader how she thought the KuRuk could accomplish it with such a small populace.

13 Lootuk boats pushed off from shore with the Gugwe Emperor's team and their mounts aboard. The caribou's eyes had to be covered to quell their panic when loaded onto the boat transports. They had added temporary corrals to the flat-bottomed boats to contain the animals aboard. They charged the Youngbloods with keeping the animals calm and cared for on this leg of the journey.

The group had been saddle-sore and tired of riding when they arrived at the Lootuk village. But after their voyage across the water, it thrilled them to hear they would soon arrive at the shores that would lead to the land of the Kuktuk tribe. A day or so would end water travel. They were eager to get back on their familiar mounts. Later, it became apparent they preferred riding, saddle-sore or not, to the constant rise and fall of the boat against the water. More than a few still looked green from seasickness.

When they made landfall, Taramat estimated it would take them at least two hours to ride down to the next tribe's village. The 13/31 exchanged farewells, as well as thanks to the Lootuk boat handlers. Thana's expedition team set up camp for the night to get their land legs back and repack their supplies for mounted travel. Tomorrow would see them heading for the Kuktuk village at first light.

That evening, the Vutovas were rewarded with their fill of fresh-caught fish, a gift from the departing Lootuks.

The best part was that they enjoyed a wild light show. The Aurora Borealis cast its northern lights in a dance across the sky, a riot of shimmering, shooting greens, blues, and silver. It seemed a good beginning for the next leg of their journey.

CHAPTER 16: 13 Seconds

Morveena raged inside her tent, smashing anything she could reach with Narrol's old cane. Every soldier in the camp kept themselves very busy with chores and as far away from her shelter as possible. Rupert was nowhere to be found.

It had all started when the small military unit arrived last night and assembled its camp in the early moonlight. At first light, Morveena had rubbed berry juice on her lips, making them stand out. To outline her eyes, she wore a leather mask that was cut to have sharp, shiny points on each side. She'd teased her hair into a wild, unruly mass, to which she had tied small animal and bird skulls as hair ornaments throughout her red tresses. The embellishments rattled, shaking about on the ends of the leather thongs as if by their own power as she moved. Taking up a Gugwe leg bone to use as a cane, she led the way, Rupert a footstep behind, his face, neck, and hands all painted white. The lads thought it made him look like a grub, but he was gruesome in his own way. When he smiled, he looked like a demon, his teeth dyed blood red with berry juice. He wore a helmet with antlers attached from an eight-point elk, and his hauberk was a patchwork of different materials. Looking closer...oh gods, the lads looked back and forth to one another, swallowing deeply...was it made from patches of human skin? To complete his intended look, the goblin prince wore a triple-strand necklace made of teeth. The lads knew where the teeth had come from. Rupert had a reputation for torture.

Morveena's soldiers marched behind. The troop had traveled for the last six weeks to reach the Gugwe Bear Ridge tribe, who lived northwest of Sapphire Lake. The Queen had established contact with the Bear Ridge KuRuk years ago. Morveena and Rupert had made it a habit to visit the tribe every year for the last five years, building a relationship...of sorts.

It was pure luck that the Goblin Queen had met Thana NukPana at the Bear Ridge Tribe's village two years prior. She hoped to cross paths with him again, outline her scheme, and whet his appetite for what she planned to sell him. The redheaded Queen intended to secure certain promises from him in return for the prize she would dangle before the Gugwe Emperor. Plant the seeds. Take her due. If the Gugwe Emperor could help her realize her goals, well, she had no compunctions about using him. Once she had cemented her rule, she would make a new plan to eliminate him. But for now...for now, Morveena could use him as her tool.

The Goblin Queen heard the birds calling back and forth as her entourage approached the Bear Ridge Tribe's village. She knew they were being watched, as well as word being sent ahead by the Bear Ridge sentries.

The red-haired queen strode into Bear Ridge like she owned it. The villagers made growling sounds, but stayed well back from this demon queen as they thought of her. She demonstrated her skill with blood magic more than once to keep them in line over the years.

KuRuk Bear Ridge was twice her height and weight. He wore a neck brace of iron spikes; he had a captive smith custom-make for him. Once the neck brace was complete, the KuRuk took the additional half a dozen iron spikes that had not been used in the piece. He drove four through Smith's arms and legs to pin him. Then, having watched from afar while the man plied his trade, he heated the smith's brands. Over several days, the KuRuk branded the man's skin until he died from the burns that covered every inch of his body.

The Bear Ridge leader rudely stepped into Morveena's path, stopping her parade in its tracks. He held his ground as he faced her. Rupert gave the KuRuk a bloody smile.

"Look, Bear Ridgens!" the KuRuk announced loudly. "We have unexpected guests. *Again,*" a growl rumbled low in his gut as he eyed the Queen's bone cane walking stick. Her lips pressed together in satisfaction. She could see the Bear Ridge KuRuk wondered where and how she had gotten it.

"Zilla," Morveena crooned, "how nice to see you again. I trust Lillith is well?" She brought her razor-sharp fingernail to her upper lip as though considering something. Then, deliberately, she sliced a slight cut on her lip and brought her long tongue up to lick the blood. "Divine," she whispered, closing her eyes, clearly enjoying a private bubble of ecstasy. Zilla grimaced in distaste, but Lillith pushed her way through the crowd and rushed forward to greet the Goblin Queen.

Lillith was a brutish size for a female Gugwe. Scars covered her face and arms. She strode straight for the Queen, her pace intent. Rupert tensed at her aggressive approach and pulled both his knives ready. Morveena flicked her fingers at him, letting him know he should put up his weapons. She never took her eyes off the giant beast-woman. When Lillith reached Morveena, she lifted the Queen by the waist, brought their faces nose to nose and stared directly into the Queen's eyes. Lillith's tongue flicked out and licked a ruby drop of blood from Morveena's lip. Then the brazen Gugwe ran her tongue around the Goblin's red-stained mouth. With a breathy whisper in the goblin's ear, said, "You're the devil's own Morveena Morgan Montestrell. It is delicious to see you again," Lillith licked her own lips in satisfaction, flashed a wicked smile at Rupert and gently set the Goblin Queen down again.

"Zilla," Lillith called over her shoulder, "have refreshments brought for our guests. Make sure her soldiers are...properly taken care of and welcomed. The Queen, the Prince, and I will meet in the stone circle." Lillith moved past Morveena to Rupert, grabbing him by the hand, pulling him along as she led the Queen to a great circle of standing stones. Thick green grass grew inside and outside the circular expanse. Wildflowers were blooming in a disorderly profusion of colors.

They sat across from one another in a triangle pattern. "I brought you a gift," Morveena offered Lillith a small leather pouch.

The Gugwe took the proffered token. She bounced the pouch up and down in her palm, feeling the weight. The Queen always thought she could buy loyalty with her frivolous gifts, Lillith remembered. Gifts brought no loyalty. Blood did. The female gugwe had learned that only blood brought loyalty. Lillith attempted a smile, but it looked more like she was gritting her teeth. She pulled the drawstrings on the pouch and upended the contents into her hand. A heavy stone covered the center of her large palm. The sunlight caught it just right, and the shimmer almost blinded the warrior. The Bear Ridge Gugwe had heard of diamonds, but had never seen one. Having never seen one, they had no interest in it. But, often in Morveena's experience, once seen, the fruits of the Goblin's mining efforts were hard to forget. It was even harder for one to pretend they didn't dazzle the eye of the beholder.

A shadow on the outer perimeter of the circle moved from rock to rock. The spy used the standing stones to hide behind. The three sitting in the center noticed nothing but each other. Every word had meaning. Every facial tic and body movement. It was important not to miss any signs of non-verbal communication that mixed with the verbal when among the Gugwe. Morveena laid out her plan. Lillith listened.

The sun sat lower in the sky by the time Zilla came with a small escort who carried refreshments for the guests; he stepped right up to his sister. Lillith bent her head to the side, exposing her neck to him, and he latched on with his teeth, showing his dominance as the Bear Ridge KuRuk. She whispered all the queen's plans into his ear. He worried her skin between his teeth, a low growl emanating from the back of his throat. She'd irritated him. Lillith yipped as his fangs broke the skin. He licked the blood from the wound, released her, and held out his hand. If her eyes could have burned into him, he would have burst into flames. She dropped the pouch containing the diamond into his massive hand.

Cooks had carried trays of hot food to serve their guests, handing out the food while Zilla put Lillith in her place.

"Eat!" he commanded his guests. They gave Morveena and Rupert each a bowl filled with freshly roasted meat, a spicy sauce mixed with wild rice. The visitors ate graciously. Zilla inspected the diamond. Flashes of rainbows danced around the inner circle of stones as sunlight shone on it. Zilla turned the polished, faceted rock in his fingertips. "You will bring me more of these rocks," he stated flatly.

"Of course. Of course, KuRuk," Morveena agreed. "I'm glad you see the value of trading," she smiled disingenuously.

"What trade?" he glared at her with suspicion.

"More diamonds for you in exchange for valuable information for me. Of course, you understand that only information I deem of use to me will be rewarded, as one would expect. Information of no value to my goals will receive trade in kind, yes?"

Zilla's forehead crinkled, and his mouth turned down, making his features grim. Lillith grabbed his arm. "What she means, brother..." he wrenched his arm away.

"I know what she means, sister," Zilla snarled.

Morveena and Rupert continued eating, chewing the tender, tasty meat right down to the bones. *The meat is sweetest closest to the bones*, Morveena thought to herself. Both of them licked their fingers, grease running down their chins.

The Goblin Queen told Zilla the barest details of her plan to capture the Fae Princess. Making it clear, they alone had discovered and could identify the Faerie, confirming the princess really existed. She explained her intent to bring the Princess to the Thana NukPana. Morveena expected Zilla to tell her where she could find the Thana, so she could present her offer directly to him. He saw no need to inform her that the Thana NukPana she had met two years before now lay dead at the bottom of a cliff and a new leader had risen to take the old Thana's place.

Trembling with laughter, Zilla asked, "You...plan to *negotiate* with the Emperor of the Gugwe, using the Fae Princess as your coin?"

"I do. But those negotiations are for his ears alone," she told him coldly.

"Very well," Zilla offered, "I will tell you where you might find the emperor. I will even have Lillith guide you to find the great Thana NukPana. According to his emissary, who recently visited our village, the Thana has begun an epic expedition to visit all 13 Gugwe tribes. We weren't privy to his travel schedule. But you might get lucky and catch up with the Thana and the members of his expedition. It is impossible to say *exactly* where he might be. We know the emperor's final destination is near the BloodKnife's village. All the tribes will have representation at a Gugwe conclave to be held at Thrall Lake on the winter solstice."

Morveena looked at Rupert, then back to the Bear Ridge KuRuk. "Thrall Lake is a very long way to go, Zilla, but we have been there once before. Many years have passed since we made the journey."

"Yes," Zilla agreed, "a very long distance across *Gugwe territory*. You may cross paths with the Thana at other Gugwe villages. If successful, it could save you the long trip all the way to Thrall Lake. If not, my sister will be a valuable asset to your journey. She can help make sure other Gugwe don't kill you before you reach Thrall Lake. In addition, Lillith will be sure potential enemies know of your *great friendship* to the Gugwe people." Zilla held out his hand in expectation.

Morveena did not think to ask, and Zilla did not offer the information that the Thana NukPana had not yet reached the Bear Ridge village, so they could have waited there for his arrival before continuing to Thrall Lake. He remained silent with his hand extended in expectation.

"Pay him," Morveena told Rupert as she stood, pushed past Zilla, knocking his shoulder. "Come, Lillith, we need to make plans. We leave tomorrow."

Rupert tossed another pouch to Bear Ridge's KuRuk; this one filled with small diamonds. Zilla rolled them from one hand to the other. "So nice doing business with you, Morveena Morgan Montestrell. Oh, by the way...," the Goblin Queen stopped, turned back to look at him. A figure darted away from behind a stone, no one noticing the movement. "Next time you visit, I recommend you send a scout ahead. We simply weren't prepared to entertain guests." He polished a spot on his armored vest. "I'm afraid we had to make do with the resources at hand in order to feed you." Morveena blinked at him as he continued, "Such a shame. I regret to inform you that you will find your soldier troops absent a couple of lads. I hope you enjoyed your meal. Manners can make such a difference, don't you agree?" He tossed the pouch in the air, snatched it back in hand, and stalked away in the opposite direction.

Morveena turned beat red and started after him, but Rupert locked his arms around her. He held her steady until the KuRuk Bear Ridge disappeared from the stone circle.

Lillith, speechless, reconsidered some of her recent thoughts about her brother's lack of courage. She wisely put some space between herself and the Goblin monarch, telling her they would meet in a few hours to make plans. She had barely walked away from the red-haired demon's tented quarters when she heard the first item smash to the ground inside.

THE HUNCHED FIGURE limped quickly down the hillside. He looked around three times before slipping behind a huge bramble bush covering a small entrance to a cave.

Inside, the stink burned his nostrils. It smelled of mildewed earth, but worse, of his own piss and shit. He had been living here for over three months. Not wanting to take any chances of one of the beastman discovering his skat, he'd lived like an animal. Keeping every aspect of his existence inside the cave. His discovery of the small cavern happened quite by accident or luck, if you believe in such things. He deemed it the perfect place to hide, although he had limited access to water. Every few days, he had taken the risk of slipping out at night to the small stream in order to keep his water bladder full. There was little to spare for washing, but it was probably for the best, based on the smell of those in the Gugwe village. His stink was no greater or less than theirs. So, besides the other unpleasant mix of smells held close in the cave, body odor really made no difference. He hardly noticed anymore. His hair was greasy. His beard, now hanging down to his breastbone, appeared ragged, with bits and pieces tangled in it. The rough leather pants he wore had been patched enough times to resemble a quilt. Though his boots were freshly made. He'd been lucky enough to bag an elk a few weeks back and after hiding the evidence of the kill, he had taken the hide and meat back to the cave on several trips. Patiently, he had stretched the pelt, scraping off any fat or meat, letting it dry and cure next to the fire. He had discovered he could burn a fire in the enormous cavern further in from the mouth of the cave. The smoke dissipated, but didn't come out anywhere he'd been able to discern that would reveal his hiding place. He'd checked again and again to be sure. The elk had provided him with fresh meat for a couple of days while he cut strips and slowly smoked them to preserve as much as he could. He knew he could survive on jerked, smoked meat for a very long time. Still, he was careful. He trapped rabbits, foraged for berries, apples, tubers, mushrooms, and ramps. His skin had layers of dirt, causing him to itch like mad. Somehow, he just accepted it, scratching himself unconsciously all the time now. Just another part of his current life.

He couldn't believe his eyes today while he sat camouflaged behind one of the tall stones at the circle. Often, he could listen in on large and small meetings the Gugwe held here. Luck had been with him today. When he saw her, he knuckled his eyes to clear them, and looked again. Déjà vu. It was her. He wasn't mistaken. The evil goblin bitch who had ruined his life was actually here. He'd had to caution himself to take care. To be patient. He wanted nothing more than to rush into the circle of stones, grab her by the throat and squeeze the life out of her with his bare hands. Instead, he forced himself to take several calming breaths. It was important to remind himself that he was here to learn everything he could about these Gugwe monsters. That was his quest. He'd followed a lead, still pursuing the hope that he would find his lost love alive. And now...now he had found out the Goblin Queen had a connection to this race of giants. He crept close around the circle of stones. He about went mad when he heard the female Goblin tell the Gugwe leader she intended to trade the missing Fae Princess to the Gugwe Emperor. The bitch had disclosed that they alone had confirmed the rumored princess actually lived. The two goblins claimed they knew how to find the Fae Princess. Planned to capture her.

Preparing to travel northwest, further into the beastman territory, to the fabled Thrall Lake, he vowed to follow them. Now he had found the evil Goblin Queen, and he would discover all her plans. When the time was right–he would take great joy in ending her existence. All he had to do was become a shadow. Become their bane. He considered the news that the Fae Princess, now discovered and identified after being hidden away all those years. All the years he had been living like a hermit, like an animal, chasing after clues to find his missing jewel, his wife. It may have been a stroke of luck or a twist of fate, but this information had fallen into his lap, and now he had to act upon it. He pulled out his whetstone and began dragging his knife slowly along the rough grit, sharpening the blade. Honing it to a razor's edge, his mind formed a plan of what he would need to do next.

He had weighed all the new information. What he knew without a doubt was Lennox Jakson Stargazer would not let his daughter be turned over to the enemy–be the enemy Goblin or Gugwe. He'd spent years on the trail of finding his long-lost wife, the jewel of his life, and he had failed. There was a pressing need to make sure his daughter didn't suffer her mother's fate. Aleta would expect it from him. Seeing the Goblin Queen in a Gugwe village today may just be the piece of the puzzle that had been missing all this time. The connection might even lead him to Aleta. It seemed the goblins, and the Gugwe were all mixed up in it together. The drag of the blade across the whetstone was the only sound echoing across the cavern for hours as he brooded. By the time Lennox had laid the blade aside, the fire had burned down to glowing embers, while the moon crossed the sky's expanse.

Lennox packed up his meager belongings and his jerked meat. He snuck out of the cave after midnight and filled his water bladder. Ready, he would rest until just before sunrise and position himself to follow the goblin troop. Lennox Stargazer slept peacefully for the first time in a very long time; dreams filled with visions of his wife and daughter.

The Fae King woke a few hours before sunrise, strapped his water bladder crosswise on his chest, and donned his camouflaged pack. Stepping out of the cave into the pitch black, he passed through the hedge that hid the entrance. Good riddance, he thought, as his silent footsteps moved toward the stone circle. He had decided he would wait in the shadow of the stones, where he could see any movement in the Gugwe village. Just after he had settled down, back against one of the great stone pillars, he heard soft voices enter the circle. On full alert, he strained to hear. He easily identified the first voice as the KuRuk Bear Ridge. Lennox did not know the other.

Zilla hissed and growled his response to a question from the other. "Don't you dare question me, Gorlok! You will take your assigned men and head straight to Vattusk. Hopefully, you can catch the Thana there. It would be best to catch up with him prior to his heading northwest to the BloodKnife Tribe. Before the winter solstice gathering at Thrall Lake. You must warn the Thana of the Goblin Queen's quest. If you do not catch him in Vattusk, continue on to Thrall Lake. Be sure you set scouts to watch for his coming. I will wait here for the emperor's arrival. It is our duty to warn him before my sister arrives with the Goblin cabal!" he growled.

"But..." Gorlok started.

"I did not ask you to think, Gorlok! If you cannot follow orders, then I will put another in your place. Am I clear?" The KuRuk's eyes bulged.

Gorlok nodded in agreement, with no further words spilling from his mouth for once. A small contingent of the Bear Ridge tribe filtered into the circle. Light was just beginning to push the night's dark away, shadows lingering, sunrise not yet peeking over the horizon.

"Leave immediately. I do not want the goblin bitch to know I am sending a contingent in advance. She did not ask if the Thana had already been here. Lillith will do her part in dragging the goblin trek out to give you more time. But she can only slow them down so much before they suspect. Maybe the emperor will come here before you get to Thrall Lake, and I will deliver the information personally. In all cases, the Bear Ridge Gugwe must warn the Thana before that she-devil of a goblin gets to him. Your life depends on successfully reaching the Thana before the goblin cabal does. If you fail, I will pull your intestines out of your guts while you are still alive, cook them over hot coals and eat them in front of you." The KuRuk twisted a ring off his finger and shoved it at Gorlok. "If you reach the emperor before he arrives at our village, here is my signet to give to him, so the Thana NukPuna knows you speak a genuine message from me."

Gorlok and his companions turned from KuRuk Bear Ridge to leave, but the KuRuk grabbed Gorlok's shoulder. "Wait! Make all haste. But any of the Fae, the Goblins, or men you come across while on this secret mission must not spot you. Am I clear? *No one must see you*," the KuRuk commanded.

In response, all the Bear Ridge Gugwe's special forces on the mission nodded.

Lennox Jakson Stargazer's eyes opened wide as saucers as he watched, frozen in shock, on his hands and knees, peering around the stone column. He witnessed the quad of Gugwe shape-shift, their bodies changing to the shape of men. He blinked, and they shifted again to the shape of goblins. Blink. Blink. They shifted to the shape of Fae, then back to men. Their shifting stabilized. The four Gugwe now looked like men as they walked out the other side of the circle of stones to collect their gear for the mission. So that was the reason no one had ever spotted the Gugwe on their raids south. They were shifters. Disguising themselves as those they raped, raided, and murdered.

Moving slowly, Lennox pulled back behind his stone barrier, heart beating wildly in his chest, eyes blinking rapidly. If he had not slept, he would have been sure he had dreamed it. But he had slept. Had seen them shift with his own eyes. Witness to a great secret. A secret he wasn't sure even the goblin bitch knew.

Thirteen seconds passed, and Lennox formed a new plan. Forget following the Goblin cabal. Lennox knew where they were headed.

His priority now was to find his daughter.

Gather his people.

No longer could he continue his search for Aleta.

The Fae people had to come first.

His hidden princess, found and identified.

With the heir to the Fae Court and Crown declared publicly, the time for hiding was over.

Lennox accepted what his duty was now. His throat constricted. He forced himself to swallow unshed tears. Acknowledging for the first time in all these long years, Aleta Dawn Stargazer may not still live, and even if she did, he knew Aleta would want him to put their daughter first. Lennox came out of his silent reverie to find he was already trotting south, a ghost among the early morning shadows, his pace steady, mind focused.

CHAPTER 17: Time to Take Control

Mari Meagan Evensong's bayside cottage was alive with activity. From the outside looking in, firelight flickered, throwing shadows against the interior walls. You could hear laughter and voices all the way out in the garden. It had been a long time since a joyful cacophony had echoed within her walls and drifted out across the water.

Reatha looked askance at Evy as their carriage pulled to a stop. Robert flung the door open, announcing, "We're finally here! Rea," he said pointedly to Reatha. "It appears Mari has a full house of guests."

Reatha extended her hand to Robert so he could help her down. Her eyes locked on Mari's cottage and the interior commotion. "It certainly appears so, dear," Reatha commented lightly as Robert helped Evy out next. "I suggest you have the men set up our tent camp, Robert. The beds will surely all be taken." She tucked a strand of stray hair back into her braid and smoothed the wrinkles from her dress. "Join us, Robert, as soon as you have made the camp ready. Come Evy. Let's go see who else is visiting Mari. I always thought of her living a quiet life. This is exciting," Reatha beamed her smile at the old nurse, as her hand rapped insistently on the rounded wooden door. Evy tapped her foot while Reatha admired the colorful cottage exterior. A bright green door matched the window shutters. The house itself was coated in a soft ivory wash. Her sister had planted a palette of flowers surrounding the cottage in color, with the effect of an artist's creation.

The door opened of a sudden. Mari stood there in a soft blue dress, setting off the same shade as the color of her eyes. She gave a shout of joy, opening her arms wide and taking the two women into her embrace at the same time. Reatha glowed with pleasure at her sister. Why, even Evy turned the corners of her mouth up a bit.

"What a wonderful surprise!" Mari squeezed them again. "Come in. Come in. Where's Robert? Oh, a good thing I had warning to be ready for your visit, or your beds wouldn't be waiting," she pulled them in through the door shouting, "They're here!"

Evy and Reatha looked at one another, confused. When they entered the dining room, Mari's behavior made sense. Mostly.

Reatha's youngest sister had kept the huge claw-footed oak table that once belonged to their mother. It was often a center of activity growing up. Kristian and Mariella, Mari's children, rushed over to fuss in welcoming the new arrivals, wanting to know where Robert was. The other nieces and nephews who had recently shown up at Robert's fortress all sat at the table and waved, calling out greetings. Plus, it appeared others had joined the coterie. Evy stiffened, recognizing the "others" as goblins. As quickly as her back had gone ramrod straight, her shoulders relaxed as a young goblin called to her. "Oh, here, Mistress. Lady Mari says you're fond of rocking, so I've warmed this chair here by the fireplace for you." Lehto swept his hands in front of the rocking chair, in invitation.

Evy produced a rare smile and graciously took his proffered seat. "Thank you, young man." She heaved a satisfied sigh. "Now, if only I had my knitting basket and a hot cup of Mari's special blend of tea," she said to no one in particular, rocking in the chair.

Bento hurried in the front door a few steps ahead of Robert, carrying Reatha and Evy's baskets from the coach. In his rush, he almost collided with Weasel, who was balancing a tray with a fresh pot of tea and a stack of cups, two hounds following at his heels. He called over his shoulder, "Brittany, I forgot the biscuits!" Crumbs from a biscuit fell out of his pants pocket. The dogs, noses to the floor, were clearing up every morsel behind him.

Robert looked about, taking in the scene. His eyes landed on the set of wagging tails as they passed him by. "Say," he asked aloud to no one in particular, "aren't those my dogs?"

Travis waved at Robert from the dining table. Brittany came through the swinging doors between the dining room and the kitchen, carrying a basket filled with steaming biscuits. "Hello, Uncle Robert." She kissed his cheek as she passed by. "They were your dogs, but I'd have to say they're Weasel's now," she informed him. Brittany continued toward the table with the basket, a jar of pear honey in her other hand.

Mari got all her guests settled. Mariella served tea. Mari Megan Evensong couldn't stop grinning, so pleased to have a crowd gathered around the massive table. It seemed just like the old days, when Aleta would come back from an adventure with an entourage of new friends she wanted them to meet.

The afternoon passed with the nieces and nephews bringing their uncle up to date, the lads shyly getting to know the new arrivals. They laid out plans for the moot they were trying to organize. Kris asked Robert to spread the word south of his hold. Reatha pulled Kristian apart from the crowd and asked where Faith was. He explained privately to her that Dedo had set them on a different course to arrange the winter solstice moot, as well as a quest to find their fathers and uncles. He told Reatha that Dedo had assured him Faith was in the care of others. Reatha looked askance at Evy. The old woman met her eyes and nodded as she twisted a silver ring around her finger.

"I wondered if I could get your input on a couple of ideas we have about the moot, Uncle," Kris asked Robert. "Perhaps you can give us advice after dinner?" Robert patted the boy's shoulder and nodded.

"Mari," Robert called, "I'm going to check on my men. They were setting up their tents. Is there enough food for dinner to include them?"

"There is indeed, Robert," she told him, "plenty of food and room at the table. Brittany? Get Travis to help you. We need three more leaves to extend the table. Send Shawn around the house and the guest cottages to gather up any extra chairs." Mari gently grabbed Robert's arm. "Thank you for bringing her," voice soft, eyes moist. "There's no need for any of you to stay in a tent!" She laughed at the very idea, flicking her dishtowel at him. "We had plenty of advance notice of your arrival," she winked at Kristian. "The Primrose Cottage is ready for Evy. The Ivy Cottage has been prepared for you and Reatha. This lot," she tossed her head at the lads and the cousins, "will be more than comfortable in the tents. Off you go, then. I've had your things brought up to the cottages." Mari kissed him on the cheek. "I've got to go see to dinner," she told him, shooing him from her door to check on his men. "Don't forget to invite your men to dinner, Robert."

Five days passed before Robert and his garrison set out on the road home. They'd completed a list of repairs at Mari's house while there. Reatha and Evy stayed for a longer visit. Robert intended to come back for them in a month. During those five days, Robert, and his men, nieces, nephews, and the lads huddled together over a table of maps daily. Three times, Evy poked her head into the room, interrupting the group's conversation. The old nurse delivered a curt lecture describing a historical event pertaining to their discussion.

Kristian asked Robert to tell them about past moots he had attended. It surprised him when two of Robert's men and one lad spoke up, sharing previous experiences. Plans took shape. They wanted to be sure to follow formal protocol, even though there had never been an organized moot called between the races of humans, goblins, and Fae together. Shawn felt there was only one chance of getting it right.

On the sixth day, Robert was mounting his horse, men ready, when he caught sight of his dogs. He called out to them. Both animals looked up to Weasel as if they were asking for his permission, and he nodded to the hounds. They ran to their former master, tails wagging. Each licked Robert's extended hand. To his surprise, the canines turned and ran right back to Weasel. Robert knew then he would have to get new dogs. These were firmly in the hands of the young Weasel. He smiled as he witnessed Weasel lower his face and let the dogs lick him, laughing with delight. "Take good care of them, son," Robert waved to Weasel, shaking his head as he turned his horse to leave.

"Uncle Robert," Travis called to him, "it's bacon, sir. Bacon is the trick." Travis leaned back against the porch railing, satisfied that he had revealed the secret to his uncle. To demonstrate, he pulled a piece of bacon from his waistcoat pocket, saved from breakfast, and lured the dogs away from Weasel.

A day after Robert left, the companions packed up to continue their own journey. They planned to spread the word among the inhabitants of the mid-lands. The travelers would head north to the tip of Sharas's lower peninsula to prepare for the meet to take place at the winter solstice. Reatha and Mari had spent the day baking, filling soft canvas bags Evy had sewn with food and supplies for their trek.

In the late morning sun blazed down as three women stood on Mari's porch waving goodbye, the group riding off. Shawn was singing a song, and the lads sang the refrain. Too soon, they were out of sight. The ladies went back into Mari's cozy cottage beside the bay. A peaceful feeling settled on them as they heard gentle waves washing up against the shoreline. A cool breeze blew through the windows as the bright green door closed behind them. After so much commotion the past week, they found the silence thunderous.

The women pulled three rocking chairs to the fireplace, flames dancing. Evy took up her sewing basket, pushing knitting aside, selected a color of thread and sewed a design on the collar of her best dress. "Reatha," the old nurse broke the peace, "summon Dedo. I say it's time to take control of matters now that we've been reunited with Mari." The old nurse winked at the two sisters, eyes sparkling in anticipation.

CHAPTER 18: Two Halves Make a Whole

Midnight had come and gone, but Ari couldn't sleep. Tired of tossing and turning, he threw his blanket off, got up and dressed. It was a humid night. The Stormbringer could hear the tree frogs through the open windows. He didn't bother putting on his boots. Gathering his vices, Ari quietly opened the door onto the porch. He settled comfortably on the top step with a brandy and his pipe.

The stars glittered in the night sky. Ari could see the lights of fireflies winking on and off along the edges of the treeline as they tried to attract a mate. Loneliness settled on his shoulders like a heavy mantle. It seemed odd to feel forlorn, since he'd never had so many guests at his home before. He and Persid, at least, always had one another, but his sister was gone now. He had no other family. Ari felt he hadn't really grieved for his twin before everything changed. Before the meddling Gargoyle saddled him with duties and deadlines. Though he would never tell the goyle, he was enjoying the training and teaching. Ari found he genuinely liked his students and was quite proud of their progress.

He admitted to himself that he hadn't always agreed with Persid's perspectives or actions, but she was family. The thing Ari missed most since this curse enslaved them was being able to travel. Oh, the twelve miles to Persid's was always a pleasant distraction, but he didn't consider it real travel. Her home was still in the Edgewood. Chasing after past freedoms accomplished nothing, he grumbled to himself. He decided he had plenty of other things he should think about now.

Ari struck a match against the side of the porch step and brought it to the pipe. He took a sip of brandy, leaned back, blowing out small smoke rings.

"I used to pretend smoke rings were wishes sent out on the wind."

Arnid startled to see Delainey approaching. She draped a blanket around her shoulders, wrinkled nightshirt poking out, hair a rat's nest, likely from tossing and turning.

"It's not time to cook breakfast, Miss Delainey," Ari informed her. "Go back to bed."

"Why aren't you sleeping?" She folded her arms across her chest and began tapping a foot impatiently.

"Too many thoughts. Problems mostly, I guess."

"Me too," she confided.

The Dream Weaver chuckled and patted the step beside him. "Come and join me for a while. We'll see if we can solve enough problems to make sleep possible, hey?"

Lainey climbed up two steps, pulled her blanket close, sat and rested her head on the Weaver's shoulder. "What are *you* worried about?" she asked him.

"Well, for one thing, all the training we need to do and not nearly enough time to do it in," he told her.

"If a shortage of time is all you were thinking about, why's your face look so melancholy?"

Delainey reached over and took his glass and helped herself to a sip of his brandy. He eyed her sideways.

"Persid," he answered, "I was missing my sister, Persid."

"Oh. I am sorry you lost your sister, Arnid. It must feel like half of you is missing. I've heard twins have a deeper connection than other siblings. I'm very close to my sisters, but I don't think it's the same," she emphasized. "Was Persid your only family?"

"Yes, I'm alone in the Edgewood now. Now and forever after, I'm afraid," he groused.

Delainey cocked her head to one side and blinked several times. "We'll see," she mumbled to herself. "Where did you and Persid live before coming to the Edgewood?"

"Oh, hey! It seems like such a long time ago. We came south from the Sharas's upper peninsula. The Goblin Court had employed our parents for all of their adult lives. King Lancer was good to them. Then, our folks died. Lancer offered to let Persid and me stay on, but we both had a bit of wanderlust in our blood. So, Persid broke her engagement with a young man she fancied herself in love with, and we were off on the grand adventure of our lives. When we first came here, it was more farmland than forest.

Edgewood was a small village. The people were friendly. Over time, they sought better soil to farm and, gradually, the forest filled in, taking back ground once cleared and planted. Persid and I took over the lands abandoned."

"Did you build this house?"

"No, someone had laid the stones up long ago. By the time we found the structure, most of it had deteriorated. Weeds and vines grew over it. It seemed like the land was slowly trying to reclaim the house itself. Persid and I worked hard to bring it right again. Later, one man who had lived in the village returned. Apparently, he couldn't stop thinking about my sister, hey? So, they married a short time after he came back here, and he built the log home where she lived the rest of her life."

"You don't blame Faith, do you, Ari?" Her voice conveyed hope he didn't.

He thought about her question for a few minutes, sipped his brandy, and drew on his pipe. Shaking his head, he told her, "Persid didn't always make the best decisions, Miss Delainey. When you decide to poison someone, it's reasonable to expect them to fight for their lives. So, no. I hold no grudge against Miss Faith for killing my sister in defense of her own life, never fear." Ari tapped his pipe against the side of the step to knock the ash out.

"I'm glad, Ari. Faith never meant harm to anyone."

They both pointed at a shooting star, seeing it at the same time. Ari finished the last sip of his brandy, then turned to look at his companion with suspicion. He noticed his brandy glass clearly held less amber liquid than the last time he'd taken a drink. She smiled sweetly at him.

"Thanks for keeping me company, Ari. I think I might sleep now. This group will want a big breakfast before you work them all day again." The small woman stood, adjusted her blanket, took two steps down and whispered over her shoulder, "Don't be late for breakfast. I'm making your favorite."

He perked up. "Hotcakes?"

She gave a smile as her answer.

"I think I could sleep too, since I have hot cakes to dream about and wake up to!"

AFTER ROLLAND WORKED with the members of The People's Alliance for the morning's physical training, he headed for the building behind the barn. He was seriously considering Ari's offer to set up the old forge left there years ago by a person who used to live in the Village of Edgewood. A village that was now nothing more than an old ghost town.

The Weaver was hoping Rolland would want to establish a blacksmith shop. Arnid had told him he was sure there would be plenty of farmers and others within a fifty-mile radius who could use his services. In addition, he suggested Rolland could specialize in making custom weapons in between day-to-day work. Ari knew word would spread about the lad's weapon mastery. He'd seen the caches Rolland had gifted to Caz and Robin. Once word went round, Ari was convinced business for Rolland's skill would find him. He hoped that over time, people's fear of entering the Edgewood Forest would dissipate. The Dream Weaver acknowledged that there were people afraid to come into the forest. He hoped that since his place was just a couple of miles inside the forest border, maybe they could work on getting people used to traveling here again. Particularly if the Edgewood had other amenities to offer.

Rolland had a couple of hours before he had to do a demonstration for a class Raven was teaching. So, he wanted to use the extra time to inspect the building that Ari was suggesting he could use the space for his smithy. He hoped to look over the old forge while he was poking around, to see if it needed any repairs. Rolland had to admit he was excited about the prospect of starting a business from scratch. Something he could build out of his own blood, sweat, and tears that another person wouldn't take credit for. He'd eagerly moved all his tools into the building; Ari having given permission to store them in the dry shop until he decided. As he looked things over, he noticed a door at the back of the building and went to see where it led. He was delighted to discover a large room, likely used as a living space in the past. It had built-in cupboards, a counter, as well as a big bunk bed attached to the wall, which folded down on hinges. The berth could be closed flat against the wall and hooked in place, to give more room when not sleeping. He toyed with an idea. If he took the workspace, he would have his own place to live as well.

"Rolland? You here?" Saffron's voice called out. She followed the footprints through the disturbed dust on the floor, pushed the door open with her toe, sticking her head through the doorway.

"Hello Saffron," he stood in the middle of the room.

"Hello Rolland. What's what?" she smiled, looking around.

"This might be my new place, Saffron. Ari asked if I'd like to set up my smithy business here. Said there used to be a village called Edgewood before the forest took over. Seems to think I can drum up what he calls bread and butter business. You know, making things like horseshoes, farm tools and such. In the meantime, I could build up my stock of custom weapons and let my reputation grow. I just discovered there's even this room I could live in." He waved his hands around.

"What a wonderful opportunity for you, Rolland," Saffron smiled.

A deep frown settled on Rolland's face.

"Whoa! Hey, laddie." Saffron gestured at him. "Where'd the cheerful face I saw moments ago disappear to?"

"It just hit me, Saffron. I can't do this."

"And just why not?" she demanded. "Isn't this what you've always dreamed of?"

"Well, yes," he admitted.

"Then I don't understand, Rolland. I know you can do it. Our dream will come true," she encouraged.

He shook his head hard, anxiety making his heart beat wildly. "No. It won't work. It would only be half of my dream. I can't risk missing even the smallest possibility of an opportunity for the best part of my dream to come true."

"What is the best part, Rolland? The other half of your dream, I mean."

"I can't tell you, Saffron."

"Oh," she hung her head, "I thought we were friends, Rolland."

"You're my best friend, Saffron!"

"Well," Saffron offered, "I'll always be ready to listen if you decide you want to share the other half of your dream with me."

She walked around the room, fingers trailing in the dust. "I like this window above the sink. I can envision some nice white lace curtains here. A good scrubbing and a fresh coat of paint would do wonders for these cabinets and counter." She turned in a circle. "Oh, look, there's just enough room for a sturdy table and some chairs right here," she pointed. "Over there is a perfect spot for a washstand." Saffron pulled back a threadbare curtain under the sink and found some wooden boxes holding dishes and pots. "Look, it's even got kitchen dishes and such! Gosh, it's too bad you won't be setting up your smithy shop here, Rolland. I'm sorry you will not make it happen. I'll miss you."

"You are? You will?" Rolland's frown grew deeper. She could see he was analyzing her words. His face lifted to look at her. Sunlight was coming through the window, making her red hair shimmer. She leaned up against the cupboards, feet crossed at the ankles, hands in her pockets, waiting for him to think it all the way through. Finally, she could see he'd come to a conclusion.

Rolland scratched his head. "The only way you could miss me is if I don't take Ari's offer, if I stay with the alliance and then, only if you're not going with the alliance, Saffron?"

"True, Rolland." She waited again as he sorted through it.

"Are you going back to the clan? You know I never want to go back, right?"

"No, I'm not going back to the clan, Rolland."

His forehead formed deep creases. Rolland took a step toward her, but then stepped back again and scratched his short beard. An idea bloomed; his voice was shaky. He asked, "Are you staying here in the Edgewood, Saffron?"

She beamed at him. "I am. That's why I was hoping you'd be staying, too. The Weaver's looking to establish the Village of Edgewood again, offered to let me be a part of it too!" She gifted him her biggest smile. "Ari wants to build the Edgewood into a place where anyone can live, no matter what race they are. A community where there's no place for hatred. I really want to be a part of that."

"Are you going to keep house for Ari?"

Her laugh was light and easy. "Heavens no, laddie! I've got Bedwer's recipe for ale," she suggested, waggling her eyebrows at him. He scratched his head again. Saffron decided he'd worked his brain hard enough for the day. "I'm going to establish my own inn. An inn where I hope to build a reputation of serving the best ale in a fifty-mile radius!" She threw her arms around his neck and hung on as she danced around his big shoulders.

"Saffron?"

"Yes, Rolland?"

"If you stayed here too, the other half of my dream would come true."

"It would?" she whispered back.

"You're the most important part," he confessed. "I don't want to be anywhere if you're not there. I want to be with you, Saffron."

Her toes curled. Her right leg bent at the knee as Rolland cupped her cheeks and kissed her lightly. She fisted her hands in his hair, kissing him back hard, letting him know they shared the same dream. "Two halves make a whole," she whispered in his ear.

DELAINEY PLACED A STACK of hotcakes, fresh from the griddle, in front of Ari. The crowd had finished breakfast. The dishes were done. Everyone had moved out to start their daily physical training. She untied her apron, hung it on a peg, then delivered a crock of butter and a pitcher of warmed maple syrup to Ari.

"Going out for morning exercise?" He asked her, taking his first bite of hotcakes. She watched him close his eyes in pleasure. "You are a fine cook, Miss Delainey!"

"You've made my day with such a compliment. Glad you're enjoying it. I'm going to be late for practice today. I wanted to talk to you for a bit, if you can spare some time?"

"For you, Miss Delainey, I'll make the time. What's on your mind?"

"I've been giving a lot of thought to the witch's curse you told us about." She noted the surprised look on his face before he smoothed his features again.

"Oh? How so?" he inquired nonchalantly, taking another bite.

"I'm rather good with spells and puzzles."

"Is that so, hey?"

"It is. It's a gift," she smiled confidently.

"And what have you come up with, young lady?" he dared to let his curiosity show, but kept his hope tamped down.

"I just need to give it a little more thought. But I wondered if you would meet me under the white pine up on the ridge at midnight? I have a theory I'd like to test. Just the two of us, in case it doesn't work out."

Ari's eyes rested on her. The clock on the mantel kept time. Tick Tock. Tick Tock. Tick Tock. "Alright," he agreed. "You know, I think I'll miss you most of all when the Alliance leaves here."

"Why, Arnid Aubrey Stormbringer, what a sweet thing for you to say. But it won't be necessary."

Deep thought lines wrinkled across his forehead as he tried to puzzle out her words.

"Finish your hotcakes before they get cold," she advised. "I'll see you at dinner, then at midnight up top. Our secret," she winked and headed for the door. "Please rinse the syrup off your plate before you go out, or it'll be awful to clean later."

Delainey Makenna Pureheart threw her jacket over her shoulder and pushed open the screen door to the porch. She stopped, turned on the ball of her foot so she could see his face. "You won't need to miss me, Ari, because Saffron told me about your plan to raise the Village of Edgewood from the ashes. She's going to open an inn. Saffron asked me to stay on with her as a partner and as the inn's head cook." Her smile was radiant.

He matched it.

"Ari?"

"Yes, Miss Delainey?"

"Just so you know, I'm not just staying for the head cook's job." She let the door slam behind her, and he could hear her whistling as she walked away from the stone house.

CHAPTER 19: We Match

A small audience had gathered in the open area between the stone house and the barn. Everyone stood looking up, a hand shading their eyes against the sun.

Robin and Garrett were racing one another in the lane leading to the orchard. The race ended in a tie. Sweat poured off their faces as they hunched over, hands on knees, catching their breath.

"Good race, Garrett," Robin complimented. "Even the Beaumont has never tied me before." They bumped knuckles and noticed the crowd looking up. "What's what?" Robin asked no one in particular, then copied the crowd's stances, shading his eyes to see what had everyone's attention.

Garrett hadn't looked skyward yet, but caught the reaction Robin displayed on his face. The Goodfellow looked as if he were going to have a heart attack. "You alright, Robin?" Garrett pulled himself to a full stand, tipped his chin up to see what the fascination was and fell backward a few steps. Carlisse and Caz were both flying on the air currents off the ridge. Cazzidy Beaumont Touchstone had wings!

"I can't believe it," Robin whispered to himself.

Garrett couldn't believe his eyes either. "Holy shit! Is Caz a Fae?" he asked in shock.

Aliah, hearing Garrett's shouted question, came to his side. "Shhh," she cautioned him, "Caz is a goblin. Definitely not a faerie," she whispered in his ear.

"I don't get it," Garrett told her.

"I don't get it either," Robin said as he stalked away in search of the Dream Weaver.

Faith sat alone under a maple tree, watching the winged show. Whatever Carlisse did, Caz copied. If she shifted her wings to catch the updraft or to dive, glide, or twist, he mirrored her. Every once in a while, Carlisse would let out a joyous "whoop!" as she danced across the valley sky in flight.

Aliah looped her arm in Garrett's, practically dragging him over to Faith. "Hey," he acknowledged Faith, "what's going on here? Aliah says Caz isn't a Fae. Did someone try some magic on him to give him wings? If so, I want some!" his voice shaking with excitement. "You know, Caz's wings look somewhat different from yours," he pointed out.

"Yeah," Faith said glumly, "different, but the same."

"How could this happen, Faith?" Aliah asked. "Do you know?"

"Looks like they're coming down," Faith responded. "I'm sure Carlisse will be happy to tell you all about it. Look, I just need some time to myself," she stood, brushed her hands on her pants, and walked away without another word.

Caz and Carlisse were still grabbing attention, so no one noticed as Faith headed toward the pond. When she reached the water's edge, Faith had already stripped off her clothes, the pieces making a trail behind her like breadcrumbs. She didn't even register the stark cold against her sweaty skin as she entered the water. Dunking her head under, she came up, lay back and floated, her hands sculpting in and out to move her body slowly through the water, the sun warming her from above. Thoughts ran in waves as she drifted in her own little world.

Eventually, she waded out, lay down in the grass, drying off in the afternoon rays. She pulled her small clothes on, opened her pack, taking out her sketchpad and a lump of charcoal. She climbed onto a nearby boulder and captured the details of the pond and surrounds.

It wasn't long before she heard footsteps approaching from behind. "Planning on stealing my boots again?" she hissed.

"What? No. Why would I?" Robin asked in surprise at the question.

"I figured it out, you know. The day I was mushroom hunting and stripped to take a river bath." Her hand continued to use the charcoal, drawing at a furious pace. "I lost my boots, but Nursie wanted to hurry back to the fortress because the sun was going down. We were going to have a Spring Feast for dinner. Everything went sideways when my cousins showed up out of nowhere." Faith turned to look at him. Robin's face looked so guilty.

"Anyway," she began shading the sky in her drawing, "I remembered Dedo admonished me for *almost* picking a trillium." She held the pad away from her, comparing her rendition to the actual landscape, then set the book and charcoal to the side and turned to look him directly in the eye. "Dedo said you were there. In my woods. Said I was in danger. Gave that as his reason to explain why he sent the nurse after me. Of course, *I knew* you were there. You introduced yourself to me, remember?"

A few moments of silence ensued. They never took their eyes off one another. "You *were* there. You stole my boots, then gave them to your evil mother, yeah?" Bitterness carried the accusation.

Robin's eyes dropped to the ground in shame. "I'm sorry, lass. It wasn't personal. We didn't know each other, not really. You hadn't even told me your name." He forced his eyes to look at her, face a mask showing no emotion. "See, sometimes if I brought Morveena presents, things might go a little smoother, maybe avoid some violence or cruelty to someone in the clan, if she was pleased. Boots and shoes always worked. Still, I know it's not an excuse," he admitted.

"Oh, I get it, having met her," Faith granted him. "But you know what I don't get?"

"Bet you're going to tell me, yeah?

She frowned at him. "What I don't get is that you had a big secret. You have wings. You could have flown away with me off the bridge like you were suggesting I do." Three tears rolled down her cheeks. "I told you my story. Shared with you how shocked I was when wings ripped out of my back in front of a hall full of people! Even revealing how I felt like a freak. And you. You never said a thing about your wings. Not. One. Word."

Faith jumped down off the boulder and crossed the grassy slope, coming toe to toe, nose to nose. Well, not nose to nose exactly, as she was much shorter than Robin, but you get the idea. Her forefinger jammed against his chest each time she made a point. "You could have told *me* about *your* wings. Just snapped them open and flown out of danger with me. Saved me from that nightmare experience with your...your family!"

Robin didn't think it wise to point out that the reason she got captured was because she went crazy when she saw her boots on Morveena's feet. No, that would not be wise at all.

The Goodfellow wrapped her in his arms. "I'm sorry, lass. So sorry for all the terrible experiences you had to endure. I couldn't tell you or fly off with you. You don't understand."

Faith pulled free of his embrace, not wanting him to console her. Her face contorted in anger, and she spat her next words at him, unable to see his side of things. "You're very good at deception, Robin Wilum Goodfellow. I can only imagine how the goblins will feel as I expose the deep secret hidden between the goblins and the Fae. One race, not two. All the while, I'm supposed to be bringing the people of Sharas together to fight a common enemy. The saddest part is we seem to be our own worst enemy." She turned her back to him to get her emotions under control, to wipe away the tears.

"I truly am sorry, lass. Our whole lives, we've been trained to hide the wings," he offered helplessly.

"Just shut up," she spun on him. "I already heard the explanation from Caz! I've lost my trust in you, Robin. I thought you were my friend and...and," Faith let out a deep moan, then shoved him back with the flat of her hand. "Take your jacket off!" she commanded him.

"What's what, Faith?" Anger folded in with his own voice.

"Now!" she yelled. "Take off your jacket and show me your bloody wings!" Her own gossamer, opalescent wings burst open and stretched out fully.

"You want to see my wings?" he yelled back, his face turning a deep red, anger of his own betraying his face. Robin ripped off his leather jacket and threw it on the ground. "Yeah? This is what you want?" His shout echoing across the water, ripped chest muscles heaving up and down with his hyperventilation.

Faith meant to take a step away from him and his anger, but her feet moved forward, her own wings arched up at her shoulders, her face fixed with determination.

A roar of pain ripped from him as he forced his wings to open. They snapped off his back, and Robin stretched them full open. He held the seven-foot-wide expanse out with taut muscles, his effort obvious as sweat rolled down his face. The wings were leathery black, stretched tightly between the bone structure.

Faith poised on the balls of her feet. She lowered her heels, feet flat on the ground. "Yours are leather," she whispered softly.

"Yours, lace," he countered, voice rough, looking at her gossamer wings.

They stood staring as the moments slipped by.

"Whoa!"

They both startled at the voice. Val came over the small rise. "So it's true," she said with wonder. "Goblins have wings."

Val thought nothing of walking right up to Robin and touching the sensitive outer edge of his wings. A wide smile split her face. She willed her own wings open with a snap. The sun caused her black gossamer wings to shimmer.

"We match," she told Robin. "Come fly with us," Val invited.

"Wait, Val," Robin said, "I've got some explaining to do with Faith."

"Explain while we're flying," she laughed.

Faith tucked her wings tight, folding them back into her body. "It's all right, Robin. No further explanations needed. Go ahead. Go fly with Val."

"Hey, aren't you coming, Faith?" Val wondered.

"Not now," she managed without sounding angry. "I've got some other things to look into. I'll catch you up at dinner."

Faith gathered the rest of her clothes and art materials and jammed them all into her pack. Robin watched her as Val bounced on the balls of her feet, took a running start, leaping into the air. Her black, lacy wings pumping hard lifted her weight off the ground. She let out a happy 'whoop' as she went airborne.

"Faith, wait," Robin tried again.

"Go on, Robin. You heard Val. You match. Even your green eyes." She turned and walked away without looking back.

FAITH'S FEET TOOK HER down the lane to the old shack occupied by the twin gargoyles. She spotted them sitting in the sunshine on the rim of the chimney on the roof. There was a rickety ladder leaning up against the back side of the building she could use to climb up. After closer inspection, decided using it would likely result in broken bones she couldn't afford. She took her pack off, held it in her right hand, and used her wings to rise to the roof level instead. Closing the gossamer extensions quietly, the Fae princess tossed her pack down, stretched out on the thatch, using the pack as a pillow, and released a heavy sigh.

Lester's deep voice sounded in her mind. "Something wrong, Princess?"

"I don't want to talk about it," she communicated back. Shifting to her side, she propped her head on her hand, elbow balancing the weight. "But I am ready to get answers to some of my questions," she told him.

"My brother is napping," Lester conveyed. "You'd only get one perspective."

"As long as you're honest with me, I'm happy with your singular input," she agreed.

"Very well. Ask," he granted her request.

"Did you and Lenny," she stopped mid-question, "It's alright if I still call you Lenny and Lester, isn't it? I mean, those are the names I've known you by my whole life."

"Of course you can," Lester approved.

"Thanks. So...did you and Lenny come from the Upper Peninsula when I was brought down to be adopted by Reatha and Robert?"

"Yes. My brother and I, as well as Evy and some household members," he explained.

"Household members?" her eye twitched.

"Yes. Few of us. Just the Gladhearts. Oh, and the Purehearts. Robert wanted them to help with the farming, assist with the house and stable duties."

"You mean Garrett came with us from the north?" her voice creeping higher with each word.

"No..." Lester tapped his finger to his lips, thinking, "No. Garrett wasn't with us. The Gladhearts took him in later. I forget the exact circumstances." Lester put his hands under his chin and waited for her next question.

The Fae princess sat up. "Took him in? What? You mean the Gladhearts adopted Garrett?" her voice was incredulous.

"Yes, exactly," Lester confirmed. "There were many children back then who found themselves without a home, without a family. Orphans. Garrett was one of the lucky ones."

"Oh my gosh," she said with surprise. "I don't think he knows!"

"It's likely. He was just a babe, like you." He squinted his eyes at her. "It is not your place to spill the beans to him, you know!" he pointed a finger at her in warning.

"I would never!" she assured Lester. "Did you know the Purehearts? MaeElla and Johnson? Traveling with four small children must have been hard."

Lester climbed down from the stone chimney, looked back once to see Lenny's chin resting against his chest, his lips fluttering in sleep. The King settled in next to Faith. "Don't think you can trick me, young lady. You know as well as I do that the Pureheart children were orphans when Johnson Pureheart found them and brought them to the farm for MaeElla to raise. It was almost two years after we had come to Robert's fortress. Their story has never been a secret," he pushed back, irritated with her.

Faith and Lester engaged in pushing back and forth at one another's thoughts, when suddenly a sharp, high-pitched voice jumped into both of their minds. "Maybe you didn't ask what you really wanted to know, Princess?" Lenny fluttered down to join his brother, his tone accusing.

"Fair enough. Do you know where the four sisters came from?" her eyebrows raised. "Since you're awake now, King, perhaps *you* can tell me how Dedo is related to you? What was his relationship to my mother? Who sent Dedo to watch over me at Robert's fortress, and why? When did Dedo arrive? Why did my family have to be kept a secret from me? I mean, just because they put me in hiding didn't mean I had to have the rest of my family kept secret from me my whole life! Why didn't anyone tell me I was Fae? Where is my mother? My father? What happened between the goblins and the Fae? How are the Gugwe tied up in our histories?"

"Enough!" Lester's voice boomed inside her head. "While I can appreciate you likely spend your days dreaming up new questions, the list you just now laid out would take days to explain to your satisfaction! We are old friends and companions. But be aware, young lady, we still demand your respect, if for no other reason than just as your elders."

"Easy, Lester," Lenny's high-pitched voice cajoled. "We've often argued the very points she is making. She should have been told, been properly prepared for her heritage. Now I'm not surprised she feels like she can't trust anyone or anything. Like her whole life has been a lie. She knows who she is now. Maybe she feels cheated of the life she thought she should have had?"

"You're right, brother," Lester agreed. "Alright, Princess, details can come later. Here are the bare bones. We don't have proof, but we believe your mother has been a prisoner of the Gugwe all these years. Rumors said the goblins had her, but we've never thought it correct. We have it on good authority that your mother's being tortured regularly. It's possible Gugwe Shamans never cease their efforts to take her magic for themselves. Your father has never stopped looking for Aleta. Lennox believed the goblins originally captured his wife, your mother. He also believed his old friend, Lancer Goodfellow, had betrayed him. Lennox is obsessed with it—an old wound he's never been able to heal. There's a long story between them I won't expand on right now. On the other side of the fence, Lancer Goodfellow believed your father, Lennox Stargazer, double-crossed him as well. All ill-formed beliefs that created poor choices and actions, leading up to where things stand today."

Lester tsked, "It's all water under the bridge now; impossible to do could've, should've or would've. My brother and I felt it would have been best if you'd grown up knowing who you were, knowing your family. No decisions regarding those secrets were made to hurt you, but only what those involved thought would keep you safe. Secrecy was the number one consideration when decisions were being made. The Gugwe would like nothing more than to gain control of you, Princess. Can you imagine the power they would have over your mother if they threatened her with harm to her daughter? There were others considered a danger to you as well. It was the basis for keeping your very existence a secret. Dedo came to us under orders from Aleta. Your mother did not reveal who you were to him. But she made Dedo swear allegiance with his life to protect you, watch over you, so we made accommodations to allow it. Now, however, the current circumstances are not just about you any longer. The beast-men want to take slaves, be they goblins, Fae, humans, or others. It appears the Dream Weaver has foretold a role for you, *'Princess for the People'*. Therefore, you must let the hurts of the past go. You can't really hold on to your anger about what you feel were deceptions, because all the circumstances have changed and now."

Lester turned, looked at his brother, then back to the princess. "Now," he told her, "you face a decision. You can choose to take all the details you've recently learned about, along with the anger you've got bottled up inside of you, and you can *learn* from it. Grow from it, release the anger and hurt, and let it make you strong. Or you can keep it all bottled up and let it eat at you from the inside out. Let it make you weaker every day. Keep seeing yourself as a victim, instead of someone who's loved enough by many people who only wanted to keep you safe all these years. It is about you now. *You have the power to choose* the person you're going to be and the actions you decide to take. You can choose the people you're going to let help you. I can tell you right now, you'll need to make use of every single person who will stand by your side to accomplish the grand tasks laid before you by the Dream Weaver. You must let go of the bad feelings you're harboring about the wrongs you think people have committed against you. If you don't, I can guarantee the only thing you will accomplish is giving all that sorrow total power over you. If you allow negative forces the power to always make you second-guess yourself, it will only weaken your resolve. Just so you know, Lenny and I have been betting on you our whole lives." He brushed his two hands together. "So, now you know why the Kings of the Rock People have been running our kingdom from your fireplace mantel all these years." He granted her a kingly smile, a mirror image of his brother next to him.

Faith stood, balancing against the pitch of the roof, giving a small curtsey to the Gargoyle Kings. "Thanks, Lester. Guess I deserved a dressing-down. But more importantly, I needed it."

He nodded. Lenny was down on his knees, inspecting the roof thatch and picking insects out, popping them into his mouth.

She proudly opened her beautiful wings and fluttered softly back to the ground, backpack in hand. "Oh," she turned to look up at the twin gargoyles. "Please send word to Dedo, would you? Tell him...tell him I need him. I need him to advise me and help with plans, yeah? Just the way he always has." She pulled her pack over a shoulder and stalked away to find Garrett Emmon Gladheart.

CHAPTER 20: Unnecessary Showmanship

Aleta Dawn Stargazer thought today might be the day the Gugwe Shamans would finally break her. She tried to block those thoughts, but they had worn her down, and she was in constant pain.

The Fae Queen had been feeling ill most of the week. A fever burned within her flesh, but her muscles and skin shook with the chills. Her hair hung in greasy strands. Dark circles shadowed the pale skin beneath her eyes.

The shamans had suspended the Stargazer face-down, naked, above a glacial lake, inside a dark cave. There was a constant drip. Every 13 seconds, a drop of water hit the back of her head. It was enough to make one go mad. She felt she was on the edge of madness today. Aleta had counted the seconds between each drip for hours to focus on the number alone and not the drip. She had composed songs to match the beat of the drip, made up chants and spells, casting for names in her memory. And she had done it all quietly inside her head, never making a sound. Careful to be sure her captors never learned the methods she used to occupy her thoughts, necessary to shut out their various forms of torture.

Aleta's limbs trembled with fatigue. This was the seventh day she had hung there in the dark. She had allowed just enough of her magic to trickle into the chains holding her to provide minor relief to her aching arms and thighs. There was no way to tell if it was day or night, but she had recently awakened, so she decided it was morning. Aleta's stomach rumbled with hunger, but also suffered sharp pangs of cramps. Conjuring a picture of Faith in her mind, she told herself stories she made up about her daughter's life to pass the time.

A dim light appeared in the pool beneath her as the shamans caused vision after vision to appear. They seemed to take particular delight in showing Aleta scenes of Lennox with a new home and family. They provided presentations of how they imagined her fabled daughter to look, undergoing the same tortures done to her. She knew it wouldn't be long now before the three shamans made their daily appearance. Perhaps an advantage. Or perhaps another form of torture. They always broadcast the visions just before their daily arrival. The Gugwe soothsayers were very predictable. Every day after the visions, they came with brightly lit lanterns–hurting her eyes with light, where pitch-black had been her friend for hours and hours. She could not cover her eyes from the intrusion, trussed up the way they had her, so instead, she simply closed them.

"Another day, another opportunity, Queen Aleta," the largest Gugwe Shaman announced.

Her body thrashed against the chains that held her spread-eagle, an involuntary reaction to what her senses knew was coming next. So maybe not such a significant advantage. Still, if she couldn't stop the bodily response, at least she could hold her silence.

"It would be so much easier for you to just give us the power," the middle shaman suggested, "then you could be free of this torture. You could rest, heal, and go home again," the gentle voice tempted.

"Yes, Queen Aleta," the smallest said, her voice like gravel, "you could go home to your husband, your people. This pain will end. All you have to do is say yes. Just transfer your power to us, and then this nightmare will be over. Don't you want it to end?"

Aleta pulled her trembling muscles taut and imposed stillness upon her body, holding an image of Lennox firmly in her mind.

Three shamans shook their heads in unison, clearly disappointed at her resistance, then raised their hands, palms up. The chains holding Aleta's body jerked as they released on their pulleys, her weight plunging her into the water below. The shamans drew identical runes in the air before them, and the lake bubbled with heat like a cauldron over a fire. Raising hands skyward again, they controlled the chains and raised her body out of the scalding water. Aleta gasped for air, sucking in painful breaths before they dropped her in a second time, the rattle of the chains echoing off the cave walls. She hit the water with a splash. They worked runes in the air again, changing the water to icy cold. Up and down. Ice cold to boiling hot. Over and over and over again. Aleta sucked in air between the drops until they finally tired of it. Her skin felt as if a million pins were pricking it. She felt a panic attack coming on. But the chains rolled all the way up on the pulleys, tightened, pulling her arm and leg muscles just to the point before they tore.

The shamans turned to go, but the tallest asked once more, "Last opportunity today, Aleta Dawn Stargazer, Queen of the Northern Fae. Are you ready to surrender and give up your magical powers?" The three stood as one body, listening for her answer.

She spent a small amount of magic to make her hair soft, clean and dry, to make her skin shiny like the essence of pearl, and cleared the dark circles under her eyes. With her breathing barely under control, the Queen of the Fae told them, "Thank you for the refreshing bath," her words soft, a smile riding across her face. When the Shaman had made the last offer, he had inadvertently reminded her just exactly who she was...Aleta Dawn Stargazer.

So that settled it. Today would *not* be the day she would break after all.

The trio blew out the lanterns as they left the cavern. Aleta welcomed the comfort of the dark again as they left her in peace.

DEDO WAS HALF-WAY TO Mari Megan Evensong's house when he received the message from the Gargoyle Kings. He changed direction immediately. Later he would have to explain his delay to Evy, Reatha, and Mari. But Lenny and Lester wouldn't have contacted him unless it was important. Based on the message they sent, it was very important to him.

Dedo was nervous. His anxiety increased with every mile closer until he came to the Dream Weaver's stone house.

The goyles stated the Princess had summoned him. He couldn't guess what it meant. He was moving across the land using the stones in rivers, streams, and all those scattered across the ground. Frantic to make haste, he popped into Ari's dining room using the stone fireplace. Val screamed when she saw him, pointing her finger up to the corner. "You!" But he popped right out again, arriving at the stone hearth in the shack where the twins were staying.

He blinked his eyes several times as he looked at the shelving above the wood stove. It was difficult to disguise his disgust at the childish manner his kings were engaged in. The two were balancing with their feet against the wall, standing on their heads.

"My Kings," Dedo said tiredly, barely hiding his abhorrence, "what is this...this behavior all about?" He waved his hand at them with repugnance.

"We're thinking," Lenny answered him.

"Problem solving," Lester corrected.

"By standing on your heads?" Dedo tried not to make his question sound like he thought them fools, but really... "This is no way for the Kings of the Gargoyles to act!" he admonished them.

"It is an exercise that provides another perspective," a voice said from across the room. Dedo jumped, surprised to see Faith, feet up in the air, her head on the floor, cushioned by a folded blanket. She carefully lowered her feet to the floor, righting herself into a sitting position. Allowing herself to settle, letting her blood flow in the other direction.

Dedo held his hands clasped behind his back, considering her statement. "I see. I personally wouldn't have thought of employing the method," he admitted, humility unfeigned.

"Care to try it?" Faith offered, smiling.

"Perhaps. Another day, I think. My problem-solving skills seem to work best if I form an initial perspective on an issue first. I will consider the...the practice in the future and decide if turning upside down on my head would give my thought process additional merit. If it's all right with you, of course?"

Faith and Dedo stared at one another. The silence lengthened.

Lenny and Lester determined it might be a good time to see if they could get a mug of ale in the Dream Weaver's stone house. They held hands, placed their palms on the woodstove hearth stones, and popped out of the room.

"It's not likely I'll get any apology from you," she told Dedo, still sitting on the floor, blanket under her. She pulled her sketchbook and pencils onto her lap and turned the page to a blank one.

"It is equally unlikely I shall get one from you either, Princess," he predicted. "What now?" He schooled himself not to tap his foot in irritation.

"Would you describe my mother?"

His eyes bulged at her request.

"Please," she corrected, "Please describe my mother, Dedo." Her eyes conveyed her thirst for information.

Dedo swallowed hard, pulling a vision of Aleta Dawn Stargazer into his imagination. His words built the visualization describing Aleta's face, skin, hair, countenance, and build. As he spoke, Faith's pencil moved across the paper. When the solemn Gargoyle finished his verbal portraiture, he continued on, describing the Queen's favorite things. He told the Princess about her favored flowers, about travel, of people, places, and things she valued. The telling included adventures she'd experienced. Dedo shared the qualities she had: a vast reservoir of kindness, gentleness, a love for humanity, and respect for nature. But most of all, he told her of the love she harbored for her husband and daughter. A love that anyone could see shining through her, in a most beautiful expression. For all her peaceful ways, the Fae Queen would fight to the death to protect her family, a fierceness few had ever witnessed. Dedo described to the young artist the Stargazer's love for the Fae people, for her lands. He finished by telling Faith of her mother's care and thoughtfulness for all other races in Sharas, which he claimed was a power all of its own.

She put the final touches on her drawing. "Thank you, Dedo. Now, I'd appreciate it if you could give me a detailed description of my father." The gargoyle stared at her. She stared back. "It was a friendly request, but I can make it an order." Her voice was hard.

Dedo took a ragged breath and began with a physical description of Lennox. Faith worked her pencil at a furious rate. The portrayal continued with Dedo providing a list of all the things Lennox loved, Faith's mother at the top. It had long been known that the King of the Northern Fae was struck with wanderlust as a young boy. He loved hunting, fishing, making things with his hands, meeting new people, and seeing unknown places. Dedo confirmed Lennox did indeed have a long, strong friendship with Lancer Goodfellow. The crabby goyle told the princess that people loved him, no matter their race. The Fae especially revered their king. Everything he did was for the good of the Northern Fae. Until Aleta disappeared. That undid not only the king, but the entire kingdom.

Dedo yawned, confessed he had never been as close to Lennox as he had been to Aleta. He was convinced that his wife had been kidnapped without a trace. The man became paranoid. Nothing could convince him that his daughter wouldn't be next. Lennox feared the power the kidnappers would have over Aleta if they gained her daughter as a prisoner. An infant, few had seen you. Lennox made secret arrangements for your care, but made the handful of us involved swear an oath that your identity wouldn't be revealed. Your existence was a rumor. Your father felt it was critical for your safety that you be raised as an orphan. A few of us objected. Felt you should know your heritage, but Lennox was hard as granite on the issue. Though he sent you to Aleta's sister, she and Robert were to treat you as a stranger. There were many children who were orphans, so the story was never questioned. Several other orphans came to live at Robert's hold around the same time. Reatha had been more or less estranged from her sisters for years simply because of the distance between them. What better place to hide you than in a human fortress where only a handful of Fae lived? After the arrangements were made and Lennox had been advised that you were safely in place, he left the Fae Court to find your mother. Dedo finished his dissertation by stating that as far as he knew, none of the northern Fae had heard from him or heard a word about him since.

Faith was silent for a few moments as she completed some shading and added a bit more detail. She turned the paper toward Dedo, and he sucked in a deep breath. "Amazing. It looks just like him." She turned the page and rested the pad on her knees.

"I'm told you have a special ability to connect and converse with my mother. I'd like you to tell me how?" Faith raised her eyes from the paper to his, her pencil coming to a standstill.

"Princess, I..." Dedo stammered.

"Dedo, again, not a request." Lowering her eyes, she watched him from under her long lashes. Faith used her finger to rub against some of the pencil markings on the paper to blend and smudge them, creating soft shadowing. "Please don't make me give you a command. You and I are in a delicate place right now, but I think we can mend it. You ought to know from my point of view, you're going to have to place your trust in me. I realize you have spent your entire existence protecting the Queen of the Fae and then had to dedicate yourself to protecting her daughter. But can't you see you don't have to protect her *from me*? And, well...I guess if you can't give me your trust, then we can't work together. So, I am going to leave the choice up to you to decide." She pulled a small jackknife out of her pocket, shaved some wood off her pencil, sharpened the lead at the tip, closed the knife and put it away.

Voice barely audible, he started the tale, but her Fae ears could pick up the verbiage, and her pencil matched the pace of his words. As she had suspected for years, Dedo described how the goyles could move and travel using rocks and stone. Pushing a vision from his own thoughts to hers, he displayed the compass inlaid on the floor in the lower level of Robert's fortress. That compass matched other compasses throughout Sharas. One of them, he told her, was at her Aunt Mari's. Others were at the homes of long-time friends of Aleta and Lennox. He disclosed a vision of the one at the northern palace on the shores of Sapphire Lake and schooled her on the symbols shown on each compass. His essence transported from the location he was at with one compass to the location he touched, taking him to his desired destination of another compass. Then, he gifted Faith with the knowledge of the pool in the palace where Aleta had created a spell years and years ago. An enchantment that held a connection between herself, wherever she may be, and the pool. His details described to the young woman in front of him how the water would act as a mirror between the Queen and the user. Access to the pool was to be used only for communication and only for limited moments. He wanted her to understand that each time anyone used it; it drained power from her mother's magical resources. Precious power her mother needed to continue to keep her magic blocked from getting into the hands of the Gugwe Shamans.

His longtime charge knew what it had cost him to trust her with this knowledge. Her pencil came to a stop.

"May I see?" he asked. She turned her sketchbook so he could view the drawings she had made from his words and shared visions. Dedo took the pad gently from her hands. Tears sprang from his eyes at the perfect rendition of her mother's portrait she'd created from his descriptive words. Admiring her artistic abilities, he looked at each depiction of all he had described. Her drawings were just as if he stood in front of each compass and the location symbols they portrayed. He handed the book back to her. She packed up her supplies, then stuffed the blanket she'd been sitting on atop the pack.

"I've been spending a lot of time talking with Lenny and Lester," she told him. He frowned. He should have been the one to be here to answer her questions. "Don't worry," she laughed at his stiffness. "They gave me permission to call them by the names I've always known them by, at least in private. I'll use their king titles around others, but we're all family."

Fresh tears left his old eyes as he realized this was her way of letting him know she forgave him.

"There are several things I need you to arrange for me. When we complete our training here, I want to visit my Aunt Mari. Could you also check around to see if it is possible to find my cousins again? I'll need them for what's coming. I'd like to have them attend the moot at Winter Solstice. Can I count on you to help me with those things, Dedo?"

"At your service, Princess," he said honestly. "We can get started right away," he encouraged.

"Not '*we*', Dedo. I have something I have to do first. *We* can start as soon as I return."

"Return? I don't understand, young lady!" he scolded, sliding back to his normal, bossy behavior.

Faith let out a full belly laugh, amused, and told him, "Well, your declaration of *service* still needs some work. Thank you, my friend. Don't worry about me during my brief absence. Lenny and Lester have given me intense training with casting spells," she noted, seeing the surprised look on his face. "Don't look so shocked. Isn't that why you sent them here? To teach me?" She didn't wait for his answer, but continued, "I'm happy to report they have done a good job. The Dream Weaver has also done a great job. Lester told me yesterday that I am as good as my mother ever was at casting spells. Lenny says my magical powers may even exceed hers, and," she bragged, "it appears I have my father's knack for disguises." Dedo goggled at her statements. "Your plan for the teachers to discover and enhance our abilities has been a success," she complimented him.

A wariness crept over him as he watched her flip the sketchbook to the page where she'd drawn the compass he had described at the fortress. "Please get busy with your assignments, Dedo. Time is of the essence." He tried to swat her hand away the moment he realized what she planned to do, but wasn't fast enough.

Faith Lisbet Stargazer placed her palm on the shape she'd created to represent Sapphire Lake on the compass. She disappeared in a flash of sparkles.

"Humph," he groused, "unnecessary showmanship. Sparkles are a perfectly good waste of magic."

A smile cracked his face in half as he recalled Aleta once doing something similar.

CHAPTER 21: 13th Moonrise of the Month

Carlisse had spent the evening up on the ridge with the lads again, as she had every night for the last month. Those standing guard over the stone house kept two fires burning through the night. Raven watched as she carefully mixed two colors of ink for Cosmo. One lad sat shirtless in front of the fire. Carlisse set a board down with two small cups on it in front of the tattoo artist. He rolled the sleeves of his shirt to give him the freedom to move, needles sitting next to the ink pots.

"Hold your arm across your chest, like this," he showed, "and don't move. If you have to move, tell me first, so I don't mess up your tattoo, yeah?" Cosmo instructed. He looked at the two colors Carlisse had mixed for him. "Looks like you picked Faith's design for 'Goodfellow's Gang', right, mate?"

"Yeah, Mo. I like that design best."

Cosmo dipped the needle into one cup.

"Hey, Mo! Hold up a sec," Carlisse interrupted his process.

"What's what, lass?" he threw her a look.

"You, um...maybe you're just distracted."

He glanced at the lad he was about to tattoo, then back to Carlisse. "Yeah?" he responded, clearly confused.

"You didn't sterilize the needle. I'm pretty sure Rocco doesn't want an infected gang symbol."

"Thanks, Carlisse," Rocco offered. She smiled at him.

"Hey Cosmo," Jud called out as he came off the switchback, "I thought I was next in line. What gives?"

"You're late," Cosmo retorted. "Lost your place in line, yeah?"

"What kind of trash are you talking, Mo? You heard Raven send me with a message below," anger written across his face.

"Hey, Jud," Carlisse called to him, "I can do a tat for you."

The group laughed. Her cheeks reddened, not in embarrassment, but in anger. "Whoever heard of a female tattoo artist?" Rocco poked at her. "Sides, didn't you just start watching Mo over the last several weeks to see how it's done?"

"Tats are forever. Nobody's going to let you practice on them, lass," Jud told her matter-of-factly. "Mo here had to apprentice for two years before he could do tattoos, right, Mo? I like you and all, Carlisse, but, well..." Jud stammered, words failing him.

Raven stepped in to defend Carlisse. "What kind of trash are you throwing out, Rocco? No reason a female can't be a tattoo artist, yeah?" Disgust at the prejudice laced his words.

"I've been practicing," she announced to the group, then pulled her jacket off, leaving her standing in a tank top.

Four male mouths fell open. Both Carlisse's arms were solid inked art from wrists to shoulders. She had spread colors in displays of symbols, stars, moons, flowers, insects, and animals. All exhibited as a colorful inked palette across her skin. Carlisse stylized words to inspire, depicting the things she valued: 'family, truth, loyalty, friendship, strength, dreams and philosophy–Do & Be, Be & Do.'

It was beautiful work. Raven reached out a hand and pushed her long brown hair aside. Under the hairline on her neck, Carlisse Parisa Pureheart had inked intertwined words. They were ringed using scroll lettering, repeating FaeGoblinFaeGoblinFaeGoblin in a circle. A larger circle surrounded the first one, with the words oneforallandallforone connected. The meaning she depicted would offend some people.

"Carlisse," his voice rough with emotion, "will you ink the same design around my neck? Down here by my collarbone, yeah?" Raven grabbed her hand, claiming her services.

"It looks like you can make an art tattoo of anything!" Jud added, stunned by the artwork.

"I'm next after Raven. Ok, Carlisse? Promise you won't let someone else cut in before my turn, yeah?" Jud begged, giving Cosmo a dirty look.

She waved him off, laughing at the wild swing in attitudes. "Think hard about what design you want, Jud. Remember, tats are forever!" She'd parroted his words back at him. His cheeks colored.

Carlisse pulled Raven over to where she'd been mixing ink for Cosmo. She sat him down on the boulder everyone called 'Carlisse's boulder' now, as she'd been occupying it every night for a month. "What color or colors do you want me to use?" she whispered to him.

Curious, Raven asked, "Why are you whispering, lass?"

"Oh," she looked around, suddenly self-conscious. "I just think tattoos are a very personal thing."

Raven nodded, whispered back, "Brown. I'll take brown, like your eyes, yeah?" The corners of her mouth twitched up.

Carlisse ran the tip of her finger around the base of his neck, touching the two points of Raven's collarbone, and asked, "That about right?" She stared into his eyes.

"Yeah, exactly what I want," was all he could push out as his skin broke out in goosebumps where she had touched him.

Holding up her forefinger to indicate she would be right back, she took a small metal pan and went to the fire, scooped out a small amount of the coals under the logs. She grabbed her jacket off the ground and donned it again on her way back to Raven. She poked three needles into the hot coals to sterilize them. It took her no time at all to mix the materials together to make a dark brown ink she was happy with.

"If I'm inspired, do you mind if I take a little 'artistic license' with your tat design?"

"I trust your eye for art, lass."

Everyone on the ridge took turns feeding the fires as the moon rose, casting its light to filter through the trees.

When Carlisse finally declared her work finished, she rubbed the small of her back, muscles sore from the position she'd worked in for the last few hours. "Sorry it turned into such a long session, Raven. I probably should have done it in two, but I was so excited. Most important of all, I wanted you to see it completed." She backed away, shy of a sudden. "Hope you like it." She took his hand and pulled him over by the fire so he'd have better light to see.

Cosmo stared at Carlisse's work. Carlisse dug into her pouch and pulled out a small compact mirror, handing it to Raven. Time seemed to move in slow motion for her, as Raven noticed some of the other lads on guard stop and stare, poke each other in the arm and point at him. He looked back at Carlisse, then angled the mirror so he could see her artistic skills. Although his skin was a little puffy from being poked with a needle thousands of times as she pushed in the ink, he found himself astounded by what he saw.

She had used brown as the primary color in the tat. The artist had added black and white to shadow and highlight the stylized letters. FaeGoblinFaeGoblinFaeGoblin encircled his neck. Carlisse had used a distinct style of lettering different from the circlet on her own neck. AllforOneOneforAllAllforOneOneforAll completed the second circle; The People's Alliance followed; then she'd imprinted a black and white geometric design to separate it from the last ring. She composed the last circlet using a beautiful iridescent black. It shimmered with hints of purple and green, depicting ravens with open wingspans, each touching the next bird's wing tip to wing tip.

Cosmo let loose a long, low whistle. "Wow, Carlisse. You've been holding out on us. That is some top-shelf ink art."

"Hey, Carlisse, how about doing some work for me tomorrow night, lass?" shouted one of the perimeter guards.

"No way, Burl!" Jud retorted. "I already have the next appointment! Right, Carlisse?"

But Carlisse only had eyes for Raven, because he hadn't said a word yet. Her anxiety was winding up. Gods, what if he hated it? She should have drawn it for him first, gotten his approval before she inked it. Why had she said that stupid thing about giving her artistic license?

Suddenly, she felt two fingers under her chin as Raven lifted her face up to look at him. "Hey lass, have you gone down a rabbit hole on me?"

She cracked a smile, mouthed 'sorry' as she realized she'd gone off into her own world and buried herself in worry.

"Carlisse, this tattoo you inked for me, well..." he licked his lips and she swallowed hard, "well, it's some of the best tat work I've ever seen. No offence to you, Mo," he called over his shoulder. "You've got a style I'd bet none of us have seen before. You're gonna have a lot of business comin' your way," Raven beamed a bright smile at her. "Come on then, it's late. You're not going to get much sleep before training starts tomorrow. I'll walk you down to your bedroll."

The two of them started down the switchback to the valley, and they could hear Raven asking, "How did you make those raven feathers shimmer with iridescence?"

ON THE OTHER SIDE OF the ridge, a moonbeam outlined two silhouettes as they sat under a white pine. Ari had spread a blanket out for them to sit on.

"Alright, Miss Delainey, we haven't got all night. Wake-up call comes early at Camp Stone House, hey?" he chuckled. "You said you'd been thinking about the curse put on my sister and me?" His throat tightened at the mention of Persid.

"I have, Ari," she proclaimed. "I've got a theory I want to test. But I want you to promise not to get upset if it doesn't work. If this idea doesn't bear any fruit, we'll keep looking for another solution. Ok?"

"Of course," he agreed, amused she thought she could find any solutions to a curse he and his sister had lived under for over 20 years.

"This is serious," she told him, her eyes reflecting her statement as she searched his.

"Yes, Miss Delainey, very serious indeed," he tried to sound as if he meant it.

"So, I want you to confirm what the exact words were that the witch spoke when casting the spell. This is what I remember you telling us:

'You shall be two until I say, until I will, until you die. A shifter you are cursed to be, a widow annually. For those who come to ask, you'll be forced to weave your craft. A dream weaver, I set your task.'

'To you, her twin, I turn this way; you'll forever rue this day. I name you three, three ways to shift from man to cat to spider quick. To spend the days upon this earth, you both are bound to stay, to live inside the Edgewood cursed, until I end your holiday. Many will seek the dreams you've found, but none will help you break this spell. Only death's sweet embrace will make you whole and well. This spell I cast upon you both. Next time, think twice before you break your oath.'

"Spot on, word for word, Delainey. I'll never forget it," Ari shivered.

"Did she use anything else to cast the spells besides her blood?"

"Her blood?" he questioned.

"Yes, you told us she slashed her palm. Then she walked around the two of you, leaving drops of blood on a trail as she moved, encircling the two of you. If I recall, you described her dipping her fingers in her blood and drawing two diagonal lines across your face. One line of blood on Persid ran from her left temple to her lower right chin. Do I have it right?"

"Correct. I hadn't really thought of it the way you're looking at it. It all happened so quickly. It didn't occur to me that the blood had anything to do with the magic. I thought it was for showman shock value."

"Showman shock value?" Carlisse repeated, raising an eyebrow.

"You know what I mean, hey?"

She laughed to lighten the mood. "So, besides the blood and the words, did you notice if she used anything else, like herbs, or charms, or hair?"

"Hair?" he raised an eyebrow at her. They both smiled. "The answer is no. I can't recall anything else."

"One more thing before we move on to my theory," Delainey promised. "When you and I were talking on the porch steps last night, you told me how after your parents died, you and your sister traveled and eventually ended up here. Well, back then, it was the Village of Edgewood."

Ari nodded his agreement.

"Did you say before you left Lancer's Court that Persid broke her engagement?"

"Oh yes, I did, but I don't think it was a big deal. Persid was too young to get married, and so was her fiancé. I don't recall it being a traumatic breakup for either of them."

"What was his name? Can you remember?" she pushed.

"It was so long ago. I don't see why it matters. Might have been a lad named Martin or Marcus or some such. I really can't recall. Is it important?"

"I was rolling an idea around. Do you think Persid breaking her engagement was the reference the witch made when she suggested, 'next time think twice before breaking your oath'. Neither of you could remember seeing her before she showed up at Persid's house. So perhaps it had something to do with her relationship to Persid's discarded betrothed?"

His forehead wrinkled in deep thought. He was reliving the entire scene again, and his body involuntarily jerked back as he pictured the blood spattering his face when the witch slashed her palm. "I suppose anything is possible, but it would be like looking for a needle in a haystack. It's all just speculation on what the broken oath might be, hey?"

"Would you think about it? Try to recall the details. Seems to me from what you've said, the witch came specifically to Persid's house, not yours. Maybe your visit was a matter of being in the wrong place at the wrong time, and you simply got caught up in your sister's troubles."

Delainey Makenna Pureheart stood and took Ari's hand, pulling him up. "The witch said only death's sweet embrace will make you whole and well. My theory is that Persid's death may well have released *you* from the Edgewood perimeter, or at least partially. She also said, 'To spend the days upon this earth, bound to stay and live inside the Edgewood cursed, your *footsteps* cannot carry you away...'"

Taking both his hands in hers, Delainey rose on her tiptoes and whispered in his ear. "I'm pretty sure that if you shift into your spider form, you can weave webs across the boundary line of the Edgewood and cross over as an arachnid. Once you do that, then I want you to shift to your man form, and we'll see if you'll be able to leave when and if you want to. But unless the witch dies before you, you'll still keep your shape-shifting abilities. Which, when you think about it, isn't so bad. Shifting could come in handy." She shot him an encouraging smile, waggled her eyebrows at him.

"You said the stone house is only about two and a half miles to Edgewood's boundary on the north side. I'll go with you to test my theory. No one else has to know, just in case it doesn't work. But Ari, I'd like to be there for you...hey?"

"Delainey Makenna Pureheart, you're the first person to give a damn about my dilemma. I'd feel honored if you'd go with me for moral support. Maybe three nights from now? It will be the 13th moonrise of the month," he tucked his chin shyly. "And 13 happens to be my lucky number."

"It's a date," Carlisse confirmed.

They left the shelter of the huge white pine and picked their way slowly back down to the valley floor. Moonlight illuminated their way.

THE THREE DAYS SPED by for Ari until the 13th day of the month's moonrise marked his calendar. He and Delainey exchanged knowing looks throughout the day. But it wasn't until long after the evening meal that Delainey Makenna Pureheart left her clean kitchen. Pulling the hood of her cloak up, she made her way to the switchback. Aliah stepped out onto the path in front of her, about half-way up to the ridge.

"Where are you going, Lainey?" Aliah asked, rubbing a 'worry stone' between her thumb and middle finger. "Want some company?"

"No, thanks." Delainey didn't bother to hide her annoyance.

"It's dark. I don't think you should go out alone this time of night," Aliah lectured.

"Who's with you?" Delainey made a show of looking about to find her sister's escort.

"Point taken," Aliah granted her sister a win. "I know you can take care of yourself. I just thought I'd offer my company, is all." She cocked her head to the right and gave her sister a small smile.

"Well thanks. Maybe another night this week? I'm actually planning on meeting someone else."

Delainey pushed her way past her oldest sister and called over her shoulder, "In case you're wondering, I saw Garrett looking all glum a few minutes ago. He was heading down the path to the orchard. *He* definitely looked like he could use some company."

Aliah didn't waste any time in trying to press Delainey further as to just exactly who she was going to meet. Instead, she hurried off to see if she could catch up to Garrett, wondering what might be wrong with him. Delainey continued up the road and on to the big white pine where she and Ari had met just a few nights before.

Arnid Aubrey Stormbringer was pacing back and forth under the ancient tree when Lainey approached. "You seem nervous," she told him, voicing her assessment.

"Been the same way all day," he confessed.

"Well, come on," she said impatiently, "let's not waste time. The sooner we get to the border of Edgewood, the sooner we can get the experiment over with," she offered him an encouraging smile. He gave her one back. They tiptoed through the woods, practicing techniques taught to the group over the last several weeks.

The moon shone down through the trees, lighting up their path and casting their shadows behind them. Delainey tried to take Ari's mind off the upcoming trial. She used her hands to create funny creatures in the moonlight; the shadows blooming into her shapes. He did laugh at her antics, but couldn't quite relax. Ari's memory was alight with his attempt years and years ago when he had tried to leave the Edgewood. He made the endeavor shortly after Persid had left the stone house with her new husband to find their own spot to build. The effort had been very painful, and it had taken weeks for him to fully recover. He didn't relish enduring the same pain a second time. He had to admit that Delainey's theory had a certain possibility of success. Ari had definitely felt something when Persid died.

The trees thinned when they got close to the forest borderline. Delainey stopped, pointing to a large oak, its branches spread in a wide arc. "There," she told him, "the oak is perfect for our experiment. The branches spread out into the meadow next to the Edgewood's line. I think you should shift to spider form and then spin a web through the branches. Once woven out above the field, drop a line down and lower yourself to the ground. Then shift back to your man form. Ready?"

He nodded his head, unable to respond verbally. His mouth was dry as dust, but he shifted and climbed the tree, shooting out his first line of webbing. He took his time and did some creative weaving; the web took shape as Delainey watched from the ground below. When he was done, he had written her name in gossamer and added a rose next to it before dropping a line down to the ground. She walked across the invisible perimeter, wanting to be right there for him when he descended.

"Well, here goes." His spider form moving so quickly, it was hard to keep her eyes focused on him. Eight legs touched the ground, and nothing happened. Ari shapeshifted to his man-form and stood before her, tears glistening in his eyes. "Anyone ever told you you're brilliant, Delainey Makenna Pureheart?" Ari grabbed both her hands and swung her around in a circle. "You were right! I am free. Finally, free, and all the credit goes to you!" He pulled her into his arms and squeezed her tightly. Caught up in the moment, he leaned down and kissed her. She kissed him back, startling him. He pulled away, stammering, "I beg your pardon, Miss Delainey. I forgot myself. Caught up in the moment, hey?"

Delainey frowned at him. She crossed her arms, and her foot tapped up and down, irritation plain on her face.

"Come now," he cajoled her, "I apologized, didn't I?"

Her frown deepened.

"What?" he demanded.

"So, you didn't mean to kiss me?" she asked him.

"Well, I..." his face flushed a shade of red, captured by the moonlight, "I just wasn't thinking. My apologies for taking a liberty I shouldn't have. I was just so happy, hey?" his voice was winding down. The joy that had filled him moments ago deflated.

"So, it was a mistake on your part? Is that so?" her voice winding up.

"I don't know what to say." He opened his palms wide, unsure of what he should do.

She grabbed his hands and pulled herself to him, stood on her tip-toes and kissed him. When she backed away, she told him, "I'll tell you what to say. The truth." She waited.

A cold sweat broke out on his forehead. He took in the look on her face and the reflection of himself in her eyes and swallowed hard. "Alright. I admit it was no mistake that I kissed you, Delainey Makenna Pureheart. I've been wanting to kiss you for weeks now. In fact, I'd like to do it again right now," Ari held her eyes.

"What's stopping you? You're a free man."

He swept her into his arms, and the moon spotlighted the new lovers as they pressed their bodies together, mouths exploring, on the 13th Moonrise of the Month. Ari's lucky day.

CHAPTER 22: Pretty Is as Pretty Does

Faith landed on the shoreline of Sapphire Lake, slipped on the stones just as a wave crashed over her knees, splashing up into her face. She fell hard on her butt, putting her hands down in the cold water to balance, rewarded with another wave crashing into her. When her palms touched the colorful agates under the surface, they transported her soaked essence to the lower levels of the abandoned Fae palace.

The subterranean room had walls glowing with phosphorus. There was a flat pool of water reflecting the green shine, making just enough light to see the area she had landed in. It was cool, damp, and caused goosebumps to pebble on her skin, still wet from her cold introduction to Sapphire Lake. There were three visible lanterns on the back wall. Faith went to each and whispered, "Lumos," lighting them as Val had taught her. The flames flickered along the walls in an eerie green light show.

Opening a pouch at her waist, Faith took out a small pearl. Closing her eyes, she said aloud, "I wish..." finishing the rest of her mantra in silence. She tossed the creamy, iridescent orb into the pool, causing a small ripple to travel from one side to the other and back again. Her hand rummaged inside the pouch and came out with two additional items. The first was her lucky feather. She tucked it behind her ear. It blended in with her hair. The second was her lucky rabbit's foot. She clutched it tightly in her left hand and held her breath. Ripples smoothed to a still mirror again. The silence seemed to grow louder. Frowning, the princess turned her back on the dark pool, shoulders slumping.

"Well," she sighed, "it was worth a try, Mother. I only wished to see you. It would seem you took great pains to protect me all these years, but I'm so lonely. It was always my dream to have a family like everyone else I know. The reason I came was to tell you I recently learned that I have some family! Blood relatives. I actually met some of my cousins. The circumstances weren't ideal, but I think you'd like all. There are aunts and uncles I've yet to meet. I'm going to find them soon. Those people should be part of my life, and I want to be part of theirs. I'm not an orphan. Reatha and Robert are really my aunt and uncle. They have been wonderful to me. Just think, Mother, I'll have lots and lots more relatives to get to know. I can't tell you how much that means to me."

"Anyway, I came here to talk to you. So, I'm just going to pretend I am. Pretend you're right here in front of me and that you can hear me. The Dream Weaver cast my fortune. A prophecy, really. There's no one I can share how scared I am. Everyone is counting on me. I can't let them see that this fantastical 'princess of them all' leader is frightened as a rabbit. But I thought maybe you would understand. The path I'm supposed to follow or lead others on based on what the Dream Weaver said isn't really clear. Somehow, I've got to come up with a miracle to bring together the people of Sharas. *All* the people. Every race. Get each group to work together so we can defeat the Gugwe. The Gugwe are monsters. I can tell you they're bloody terrifying. These monsters want to make us all slaves!" she shivered. "I don't know why anyone thinks I have any ability to accomplish this kind of task. I don't even know where to start, much less how to do it! To top it off, I only found out that I'm Fae a few months ago."

She brushed her fingers across the lucky rabbit's foot for the hundredth time and turned back toward the pool.

Her breath caught. There, on the smooth surface of the water, was the face she had drawn hours before, according to Dedo's description. This was exactly as she had envisioned her mother would look.

"Mother!" Faith breathed in, her voice hitched. "You...you are my mother, aren't you?" leaving her hope hanging in the air between them.

Tears glistened, unfallen, in Aleta's eyes. "Faith Lisbet Stargazer, you've grown into a beautiful young woman."

The two women gazed at one another for a moment in peace, committing details to memory. Faith went down, sitting cross-legged before the pool and its depiction of her mother's essence reflected in it.

"So," Aleta started, "it sounds as if your burdens weigh heavily. Do they?"

"I'm sorry if you're disappointed, Mother. I've led a pretty protected life. As such, I don't have the right experience to draw on as you did. I'm way over my head!"

"Nonsense." The Fae Queen waved her hand. "Every challenge, every new experience requires its own expression of ideas and solutions. You must engage others in the process. There's no reason you have to shoulder the entire burden alone! Start by assessing your own strengths and weaknesses, as well as identifying the same of those who will be part of your team. Once you identify weaknesses, attempt to work on them one at a time, eventually turning them into strengths. Make use of all the strengths you identify—yours and those helping you. Let your comrades share the burdens, as well as the victories, the heartache, and the leadership. In other words, learn, grow, do, be. And while you're doing it, bring people right along with you, so they can do the same. Look for any opportunities. Speculate religiously on all potential threats, so it lessens the chance of you finding yourself in a circumstance of surprise. You can't always identify future dangers, but you can avoid many by strategizing regularly. You can be anything you put your mind to. I know it. I believe in you." Then she told her daughter with deep yearning, "I wish I could hold you in my arms."

"Oh, Mother," Faith wrapped her own arms around herself and squeezed.

"Don't overlook the many resources you have available to you! People will have a plethora of unique experiences to share with you, experiences different from your own. Their reaction is unlike how yours might have been in a similar situation. A gold nugget to be mined in every single person and applied as necessary to guide you. There are different cultures, living habits, and traditions spread across the world. Each can teach you something new. It is time you wrapped up your training with the Dream Weaver and set out north. That's the direction the weave starts you off on. Your essence has touched the Fae palace now. You'll be able to find it when you come here physically. You'll know what needs to be done once you arrive at the palace again. Faith, never doubt it. I am already proud of you. Do the things that are right for you. Remember, it is all right to be proud of who you are and what you stand for, whether changes in your state of affairs turn your world upside down or keep you in a state of status quo."

"I know you have to go soon, Mother. Dedo said not to drain too much of your power by keeping you here too long." She stared, admiring the woman before her, studying the details of her face and hair. "You are very beautiful, Mother."

"Pretty is as pretty does, Faith," Aleta cautioned.

Faith rose to her feet. She put her lucky rabbit's foot and her lucky feather back into the pouch at her waist. Her mother's reflection faded in and out. "Wait, Mother!" Faith reached out, only to grasp thin air.

"I must leave you now," her mother's voice echoed against the walls, sounding far away. "Do what needs doing, Faith Lisbet Stargazer. If you find your father again, tell him I have evidence Lancer Goodfellow did not betray him. If you come across Lancer Goodfellow, tell him I have evidence Lennox Stargazer did not double-cross him." Sparkly lights shimmered across the water's surface. Her voice fading, her next words echoed across the water. "When you next see Robin Goodfellow, tell him he will find his sister when the Aurora Borealis dances before his eyes. His sister will know the words he seeks...*her whispered words*."

The room echoed in the quiet. The pool was smooth as a mirror. Her mother was gone.

"Well," she said aloud, "I'm still going to talk to you whenever I feel like it! Even if you can't respond."

Silence answered her declaration.

ALIAH FELL IN BESIDE Garrett as he pushed a wheelbarrow full of firewood he'd just finished splitting. When he came to the firepit, he swung the barrow around and started unloading it.

"Hey," she greeted him. Aliah admired his thin face, his sharp nose, and cheekbones. Thick red hair with two odd black patches at his temples, all matted in sweat. Bare chested, he'd taken his shirt off to split wood, muscles, and abs glistening from the hard work.

"Hey yourself," he smiled, perspiration dripping from his forehead. He was neatly stacking the logs between two red pines. Aliah helped him fill in a new row.

"You've not been back to Ari to see if he can get past your block."

"So?"

"Just thought you should give it another go, yeah?"

"Aliah," he threw the last two logs onto the stack, gripped the wheelbarrow handles again, heading back to his split pile to refill the barrow. "I'm not sure I really want to know my future. I think the lads who begged off have a good point," he confessed.

"Oh. Well, I was thinking more about figuring out why you have a block, not so much what the future might hold. I don't disagree with living day to day with whatever comes your way, instead of constantly waiting for certain events to unfold. Events the fortune suggests for you. Some invisible chains weigh as much as iron ones, Garrett," she told him as though she was trying to convince herself.

"Umm, are we talking about something specific to your weave, Aliah?" he asked as they both refilled the barrel with the rest of the split firewood. Garrett wheeled it over to the stack to unload.

"Me? No. Not my weave," she stammered. "I'd be happy to see if maybe I can break through the block for you," she offered shyly.

He stopped dead and lowered the cart to stand on its own. "You can connect with someone's mind and read their thoughts?" His eyebrows rose to a new height.

"Certainly not," she poked him with a finger on his chest. "I can't read your mind. It's just a connection. A very personal connection, but different from what Ari does. We could just try it and...you know...see if I can find anything."

"Have you tried it with Val? She didn't have Ari do a weave for her either. Maybe she has a block too," he teased her.

"Val's situation is different," Aliah huffed. "Val just opted not to have Ari do a weave. At all. It seems to be a trust issue with Val. With you, Ari actually tried, but found himself blocked from being able to do a dream weave for you. Completely obstructed from it. He says it's never happened to him before, so it's weird."

"Did the Weaver put you up to this?" He jerked his head toward the stone house.

"What?" she exclaimed. "No. No, Garrett Emmon Gladheart. There isn't anyone who put me up to anything. Ari suggested I might find your block, but I just came to you to see if you wanted me to help."

"What all is involved?" he asked suspiciously.

"Wow, Val and Faith must have done a few numbers on you to make you so distrustful," she chided him.

"You have no idea," he said under his breath as he finished firewood duty for the day.

She listed the process for him. "Number one, we'd have to be alone. Two, we'd need to find an Ironwood Tree and three, the moon needs to be full," she ticked them off on her fingers.

His face clouded, surprised. "Really?"

Aliah couldn't hold in her laughter. "No, not really. The alone part is just to keep interruptions or distractions away, but it can be full sun or a rainy day or night," she smiled at him. "I kind of like to be comfortable. But it's just because you never know how long something like this will take. There are no other criteria that matter except you have to have an open mind, Garrett." Aliah's soft brown eyes shone with hope.

"Okay, tell you what," Garrett offered. "Give me five minutes to wash up and put on a dry shirt, then we can take a walk through the orchards, yeah?"

Ten minutes later, the stable master's son and one of the farmer's daughters from Sir Robert's hold were walking down the lane to the orchards, the sun warming their backs.

Aliah chose a budding apple tree to sit under. The fragrance of the flowers was intoxicating. Bees buzzed in and out from under the tree branches. Aliah put a finger to her lips to signal silence. They faced each other cross-legged, and she took his two hands in hers. Garrett was very aware of his calloused palms touching her soft skin. His heartbeat ticked up. They closed their eyes. She leaned forward, forehead touching his. Their breathing matched; in and out, in and out. General thoughts came and went. Garrett thought some lads and Robin must be spending their free time jamming, as lively music, sounding far away, drifted across the fields. The sun beat down, the bees buzzed, and the blossoms filled his senses with a sweet, cloying essence.

Without warning, Aliah dropped his hands like hot potatoes, pulled back, and jumped up, all in a fluid motion.

Garrett scanned her face and saw distress. "Broke through, yeah?"

She nodded, unaware that she was wringing her hands together.

"Not so good? What you saw, I mean?" he worried.

"It's not bad. I don't want you to think it's bad, Garrett. I was just...just surprised, is all. It's fine, really," she tried to reassure him.

"Why are you still backing away, Aliah?"

The big brass bell on the porch of the stone house rang. Clang, clang, clang. It was a signal that they were all being called in. It wasn't time for dinner yet, so it had to be for a special meeting.

"We'd better go see what this is about," Aliah said, turning to go.

Garrett grabbed her wrist and searched her eyes as she turned back to him. "There's no way we are going up there until you tell me what you saw first. Aliah, please. You're making me nervous. Scaring me," he begged her.

"I didn't get all the way through the block, just a crack in the door, so to speak," she hedged.

"And?" he growled.

"And...well... you have a strong glamor ingrained in you. It's probably been there most of your life," Aliah cupped his cheek. "Oh, Garrett," she wrestled her emotions under control.

"Just bloody tell me!"

Swallowing hard, Aliah said, "I saw...I saw under the glamor." She took his hands again to convey her trust in him. "Under the glamor, I saw...I saw you're a shifter."

"Like Ari, you mean?" his voice rising in panic.

"Not exactly," the words tumbled out, "Your shift is to a Vulpes vulpes."

Garrett took two steps back from her, needing the space. His skin felt too hot. The collar on his shirt seemed to choke him as he tried to take in what Aliah had told him. There was an animal under his skin. He could feel it trying to break out.

Coming back to himself, Garrett registered another voice yelling at him, though it seemed far away. He brought his focus forward to the present and heard, "Garrett, Aliah! Come on. Emergency meeting called. Didn't you hear the bell?" Val called out, her wings flapping as she circled them. "Hurry! Faith is back. She's got an announcement to make. Hey? Are you alright, Garrett?"

Val started to land, but Aliah shooed her off. "He's fine, Val. I've got this. We're right behind you. Go on. You don't want to miss anything," Aliah encouraged her sister.

"Okay, see you at the fire ring," Val called over her wing, black opalescence shimmering in the sunlight.

"Look," Aliah said to Garrett after her sister was gone, "until we can explore what this means, Garrett, it stays between you and me. Our secret, yeah? I'm here for you. You are my friend. Ok?" her eyes beseeched his.

"I'm a freak," he whispered.

"Oh, for...did you think Faith and Val were freaks when their gifts appeared? You're not a freak. You are my friend. We'll figure this out," she reiterated. "You will always be my friend. Come on, let's not draw any more attention to ourselves. You need to think of this as a gift. I'll help you figure out the best way to use it. Now, come on. They'll be waiting until we're all there to get the meeting started."

She reached out her hand. He took it. It felt like she anchored him to reality.

They weren't the last ones to blend into the waiting group, but nearly. Two of the lads came off the bottom of the switchback a minute later. Faith was standing on one of the enormous tree trunks when the assembly quieted.

"What's what, lass?" Robin shouted. "I think we're all here now."

"I just wanted to announce we'll be breaking camp one week from today and heading north. Anyone who wants to come with me, that is."

The Dream Weaver met her gaze across the yard but didn't challenge her announcement. One he didn't know she was going to make. She relaxed.

"It's time," she told them with confidence. "We'll put together a plan over the next couple of days. I'll take all the input from any of you I can get. Everything and anything each of you wants to share. I'd like to have some strategy meetings. Do some brainstorming. Gather ideas. Everyone's ideas are important."

Robin followed her line of sight to Ari.

"I'm sorry you can't come with us, Ari. I could use more training. And I could really use your knowledge and experience, but I feel like time is another enemy we're already fighting. We need to move on now. Tick-Tock. Tick-Tock and all that." She smiled wanly at the shifter.

"Yes," he acknowledged, "Tick-Tock."

"You want to know some good news, Faith?" Delainey asked.

"Of course I would, Lainey! We never get enough good news!"

"Ari could come with you if he wants to. We've figured out a way he can leave the Edgewood's boarder. Tested it last night and he is a free man, uhhh, free arachnid, ummm, free feline," she giggled as Ari goggled at her.

A sort of wonder flashed over Faith's face at her friend's cleverness, knowing Delainey had solved the riddle of his curse for him. "Maybe you can find the key to Robin's curse as well, Lainey?" She could almost see the wheels begin to turn in Delainey's mind.

Faith turned to look at each of the people surrounding her, silently hoping they would decide to support her. Support 'The People's Alliance'. This was it. The first step. She didn't know precisely what the second step or the third step was going to be, but this was where she would begin. If none of them believed in their cause or her as a leader, then she would still head north.

"Take some time," she told everyone. "Think about it," she asked. "If you come, I want you to believe in everything The People's Alliance is going to stand for. The 'lost chapter' we recently found, the chapter about the Goblins and the Fae, will have to be revealed. Wherever we go, we'll share the truth. Now that we know the Fae and Goblin are not different races, but one and the same, it's our duty to tell others. We may have developed different traditions, ways of life influenced by the weather, geography, and the places we live. Even dialects, food, clothing, family behavior, and so much more created our unique communities over time. That doesn't matter. What matters is that we embrace diversity. I envision an era where we take the time to search out our different strengths and share those strengths. Figure out how we can use our strengths to benefit *all of us.* We can work together to shore up our weaknesses. To start with, we must unite to fight an enemy who does not distinguish between us, between races. An enemy..." she swallowed hard, "an enemy who wants to enslave us all. It's a good place to start. A commonality we all share. Again, it's important to me you believe in everything The People's Alliance is going to stand for. Be sure you're comfortable with the concept. The truth. All I'm asking is that you be sure *before* you commit." Faith raised her right fist in the air and shouted, "All for one and one for all!"

Enthusiastic shouts erupted, repeating her words.

"I don't need to think about it, lass," Robin announced loudly. "I'm in." Other voices chimed in, agreeing with Robin.

A kind of chaos churned. Garrett caught a flash of a strange shimmer in his peripheral vision as the sun reflected on metal of some kind. The shimmer came from up top, on the edge of the ridge. As he focused in to identify what it was, shading his sight from the bright sun, his eyes suddenly grew wide. "Faith!" Garrett shouted. "Get down!" Adrenalin spiking, his entire body reacted, twisting into action.

Garrett Emmon Gladheart shifted for the first time.

The crowd fell silent as his body burst into a stretch of four legs with black paws. He had a coat of lustrous red fur, which fringed in white fur along the jowls, the highlight continuing down the throat and chest. The face was vulpine, elongated to a sharp black nose, knowing eyes, large pointed ears shaded on the backside with black fur. Finally, there was an impressively long, bushy tail tipped in white. Garrett's Vulpes vulpes form let out a sharp bark as he leaped sideways, launching into the air to block Faith. To protect her. Garrett stretched his new body, reaching as far as he could with his front paws, to give the most cover possible to his friend using this unfamiliar physique.

Screams echoed in his enhanced ears. He registered a collective group gasp as wings suddenly shot out of his red-furred shoulders. Blood spraying, pain stabbing, threatening his ability to remain conscious, as his body ripped open to release strong, two-feathered frames. One reddish-colored feather drifted to the ground and landed in front of Aliah. Just as he recovered from the shock of his change, his sleek body absorbed an arrow the sun had glinted on and caught his eye. The arrow he was trying to protect Faith from. The razor-sharp tip shredded through his flesh, burying itself in the underside of his left leg where it attaches to the shoulder, stopping when it hit bone. A wave of nausea swept through Garrett, and a cold sweat broke across his body. The vulpine form reacted, causing the wings to retract and the fox to fall to the ground with a crash.

Faith knew Garrett had just saved her life. But she couldn't make a sound as she stared at the fox form as it hit the ground in front of her.

Her lifelong friend, Garrett Emmon Gladheart, was a shifter. A red fox shifter.

Correction: a red fox shifter with wings. Bloody awesome.

She was off the log and by his side in a matter of seconds, pressing her hands against the wound, trying to stop the flow of blood. So. Much. Blood.

Aliah swept the feather off the ground in front of her and stuck it behind her ear. She and Val raced to Garrett, skidding in on their knees. Aliah gently lifted Garrett's head into her lap. She stroked the head between the ears.

"Garrett!" Val called. "Wake up! Come on, Garrett!"

Faith gratefully took a wet cloth from Delainey and pressed it around the wound. Carlisse pushed her way through the crowd and dropped to her knees. "Move over, Faith. I need to see the wound."

"Carlisse, what are you doing? We need to get him to a healer," Faith said, bewildered.

"Move. Now, Faith," Carlisse ordered.

Aliah spoke up. "Carlisse is a healer, Faith. She's the strongest of the three of us. It's one of her gifts. Please move, Faith. Trust us. She knows what she's doing."

Faith looked back and forth between Aliah, Val, and Carlisse. She trusted them. But she found it hard to believe they'd kept such a secret from her. Faith switched places with Carlisse, who moved the cloth away from the arrow, then gently rolled the unconscious shifter to look at the other side. It hadn't broken through. She decided his bone must have stopped it cold. Not necessarily a good thing. "Rolland!" Carlisse called out.

"Here!" the big goblin answered.

"I need to borrow those big pincers you showed me the other day, maybe your pliers too. And a good leather strap and..." she swallowed hard. "Also, your hammer. Bring your hammer, please." Rolland ran to the building behind the barn.

"Lainey..."

"I'm already boiling some water," Lainey answered.

Saffron ran up with an armful of sheets. She spread one out on the ground. "Let's gently lift him and slide this under him to get him out of the dirt." She began ripping the extra sheet into strips to use as bandages.

"Ari!" Carlisse called out.

"I am afraid I cannot be of any help in this situation, Miss Carlisse," he called from the porch.

"I don't understand, Ari!"

"Apologies, Miss Carlisse, but the sight of blood makes me dizzy, sick to my stomach. I am absolutely no good to you under these circumstances," he lamented.

"No judgement," she whispered.

Rolland was back with the tools she'd asked for. "Look," she told the group, "I need to get the arrow out while he's unconscious. I'm not sure I have the strength to pull it out. I think it struck bone and is stuck there. The only way to remove it is to pull it free of the bone and then," she gulped, "then push it the rest of the way through. It can't come out the same way it went in, or we'll destroy his arm. I mean leg. Oh! You know what I mean."

"If you need extra strength, I'll help you, Carlisse," Rolland offered. "I'm used to seeing blood."

She offered him a grateful smile. "Okay, give me your pincers." Carlisse didn't second-guess herself. She committed to the task at hand. Lining up the pincers, she did a quick, clean cut through the shaft of the arrow, leaving about eight inches protruding from the entry point of the arrowhead. Then she took the pliers and instructed the girls to hold him down. With both hands on the handles, she gripped the shaft, sweat dripping from her forehead. Rolland's hands covered hers, and they squeezed together. Pulling the shaft as gently as they could, they felt a sudden release from where it had been stuck. They froze, not wanting to cause any more damage than was necessary. Carlisse moved the angle of the arrow toward her to get it away from the bone, didn't give herself the chance to think twice, lifted Rolland's hammer and slammed the cut-off end. She forced the arrowhead through the skin on the opposite side of where it had entered. Garrett's body involuntarily jerked, but thankfully, he stayed under. Rolland grabbed the tip of the arrow with the pliers and pulled the rest of the shaft clean through and out the other side.

Delainey rushed down the back steps of the stone house and brought two gauze packets filled with moist, warm herbs stitched closed, handing them to Carlisse. She gently pressed them to the entry and exit sites. Aliah began wrapping the strips Saffron had prepared over, under, and around to secure the poultices and stop the bleeding.

"What's happening out there?" Ari called from the porch.

"We've got the arrow out and we're bandaging him up," Carlisse told Ari. "Now we wait. I used as much healing magic as I had. I know Delainey added healing magic to her poultices." Carlisse turned to look at Aliah and said, "And I also know love is the greatest healer of all."

A tear slid down her older sister's cheek as she stroked Garrett's soft fur face, wearing one of his feathers in her hair.

CHAPTER 23: Angel of Death

Taramat had just finished touching up Callen's face paint and other markings. She worked her soft-haired brush against the bottom of the cup containing the dregs of her mixed red dye. She squeezed the bristles between her fingers and took hold of a thick lock of hair at the tip of his forehead, dragging the color through it. The red pigment dyed her hands along with his hair.

Ever since she had used her stains to transform Thana's face into a demon, there had been a line at her tent morning and night. The members of the 13/31 pursuing her talent, taking advantage of her artistic abilities to copycat the demon-look, fashioned after their leader.

Callen had offered the Youngblood's services to Taramat. The youths gathered the plants and berries she required to make her special dye concoction. Each day, after the Youngbloods had finished their camp chores, she instructed them in what she needed. Though she never allowed them to assist in the making of her pigments. The various members of the expedition sought her skills initially to request their own forms of designs to be dyed onto their skin and into their hair. The dyes lasted a long time, but they were organic and eventually faded. Some colors lasted longer than others, but the markings weren't permanent, like tattoos. The expedition members had returned to her two weeks ago for their first touch-ups and additions. Even without the touch-ups to anyone not part of the group, the 13/31 looked like a tribe of demons who could unleash nightmares on their victims.

Mornings were dedicated to working on her maps, taking advantage of the best light. She had improved her efficiency by creating two maps at a time, making the most of the mixed colors while they were fresh. Neetriht had confirmed Akama indicated they would spend shorter times at some of the tribe's villages. It would be necessary to speed up her timetable to work on the maps because of difficult travel conditions across the mountain ranges. Tighter visits required her to work at a faster, more timesaving pace. The Thana had taken her original travel advice after all.

When the group moved south, the land was flat along the shoreline; the waters teemed with sea life. Mountains shrouded the background; the land sparse with stubby growth, dotted with thick patches of evergreen trees. They put those who had shown any talent at fishing to work catching dinner.

Thana had ordered Zolo to begin daily training with Callen and the Youngbloods before they'd continued to the Kuktuk village. He wanted them to perfect their ability to shift, taking on the forms of humans, Fae, goblins. Akama knew it had long been the secret to the Gugwe's ability to travel through the lands undetected. Training included being grilled about the different behaviors of each race. That lessened the chance of being discovered because they acted unlike their doppelgänger disguises. The practice sessions attracted some of the other members. It wasn't long before each day found over half of the 13/31 taking part in the rapid shifting regimen. In addition, Boartusk provided training at sunset on various weapons, if they weren't in the saddle traveling.

Not long after, Thana added another drill to their routine. The new procedure resulted from the day after a grueling route through a mountain pass that had everyone snapping at one another with a short fuse. Exhausted, Zota mistook Nevele for Thana NukPana, the only two Gugwe in the expedition who wore a mirror image of Taramat's clever dyes. The matching markings gave Thana an extra edge against his enemies, specifically so Nevele *would* be mistaken for Thana in case of an attack. But Akama was not happy to see Zota kneeling before his bodyguard as though it were him. After the incident, Taramat was ordered to change the dye pattern on Nevele the same night. From then on, only the Gugwe Emperor would have black, red, and white around the eyes. Everyone else could choose between black and white. Because of his mistake, Thana assigned Zota a new task, or punishment, depending on which side of the line you stood on.

The next sunrise found Thana NukPana using Zota as an example of how to master the Gugwe's mind control. All members of the expedition were required to attend. They watched with abject horror as Zota became a puppet to Akama's whims. To demonstrate the importance of becoming strong in using mind control, the emperor directed Zota's body to inflict self-harm. Knives, fire, and poisons were all used by Zota's own hand, under Akama's control, leaving the huge Gugwe a physical mess after each lesson.

Thana meant the displays as a message to everyone in the expedition. Clearly, he was not above humiliating Zota.

In one session where Zota had been under the Thana's control, he directed the Keeper of the Dead to eat his own shit. The Thana had deliberately allowed the memory of Zota's involuntary action left intact. When their daily training concluded, Zota wished he were dead. Thana's teachings were only the beginning of each day's lesson. When the Thana finished his exposition, he would then give Zota orders to continue the mind-altering lessons. Thana took a special interest in watching daily to be sure each trainee's partner used only the cruelest methods. If he felt the mind-commands weren't vile enough, the member deemed giving a soft order found themselves the object of Thana NukPana's instruction the following day. Right alongside Zota. Akama kept track of those who exhibited the strongest proclivity in using this ability.

The 13/31 passed through the copper mining village of the Kuktuk Gugwe, with little trouble and no fanfare. The population was ten times the size of the Lootuk tribe. They stayed for only two days. The KuRuk Kuktuk and his tribe were very cooperative and intrigued by the new ideas introduced.

During the journey to Vulita, the 13/31 camped on the northern shore of Great Bear Lake. They stayed for three nights because Thana was enamored with the vast inland body of water. The mountains rose in a striking backdrop to the rocky lakeshore. When they finally reached Vulita's village, it looked to the inhabitants as though a pack of evil spirits had come to call.

Vulita rested along the great Mac River, the banks lined with long grasses gently waving in the wind. The KuRuk of Vulita had prepared a welcome ceremony for Thana's expedition, with a feast laid out. Over fifty campfires burned in a vast circle as the village celebrated its emperor and his entourage. Small groups gathered around the fire pits to make music and dance after the formal meal. The Vulita KuRuk paraded a string of female Gugwe before Thana NukPana, making it clear any of them were available for his pleasure. Neetriht looked on, her disapproval radiating off her in waves. The Thana smiled appreciatively at each female, but showed no interest in choosing any. The KuRuk, insulted, wisely kept his anger close.

Seven additional recruits joined the Youngbloods from the Vulita tribe. The leaders discussed trade. Neetriht suggested that the Vulita leader choose two of his tribal members whose skills had impressed her. She felt they showed a particular talent in presenting the items the tribe had regular access to and would be of value to trade with the other tribes. In addition, the duo displayed a potent ability to provide a compelling exhibit demonstrating specific uses for their creations. Neetriht praised the competence they had employed in their presentation to the Thana. She was confident the two villagers would be excellent choices to strike up trade deals with other tribes when they reached Thrall Lake.

Presenting her format of governing to the KuRuk Vutova, Neetriht spent a full day explaining how spreading duties among others, hand-picked for their skills, benefited all. She stressed the importance of how the tribe's education, growth, and well-being would improve in relation to increased food intake. Akama noted his sister's own personal improvement each time Neetriht did her lecture to a KuRuk on her design of tribal structure.

At first, the Vulita KuRuk was resistant because it seemed to him these ideas smacked of giving up power. But as she described her style of leadership, highlighting the extra time the KuRuk could devote to other concerns, he warmed to the idea. By late afternoon, they were deep in serious discussions. He wanted to know more about the incentive programs the Thana had introduced relative to hunting and gathering. He was interested in how the awards worked to benefit the tribe.

The setting sun outlined the silhouette of KuRuk's wife standing in the doorway to the hut, not bothering to hide her irritation at how long the meetings had lasted. Neetriht disarmed the female's ire, complementing her on the tunic she wore, asking if she would show her the cuts for the design to make such a garment. The two women left the tent, heads close together as they talked about patterns.

Not long after, Neetriht had been taken to a community hut where the women did many activities as a group. Those pursuits included food preparation and cooking. She later learned that sewing, child rearing, hide cleaning, and members of the women's cooperative performed other daily tasks. The KuRuk's wife sent a girl running with an invitation for Taramat to join the women. When she arrived, the hut was abuzz with voices brainstorming. The women called out ideas relative to materials, colored dyes, unique items that could be embellishments to the products they made. Neetriht and Taramat offered strong encouragement to the women. Suggesting that the females organize others in the village, make the most of all those who exhibit sewing talents. The visiting Vutovas hinted that the more help the Vulita women could drum up, the greater stock of tunics they would have to trade at Thrall Lake. The winter solstice wasn't that far off.

Later, after the evening meal, Akama pulled Neetriht from where he found her seated by the KuRuk's wife. The tribe was putting on a preliminary dance ritual as a prelude to the Vulita Shamans' performance. He kept a tight grip on her arm as they moved away from the audience.

"You're hurting me, Akama," she growled, her teeth snapping at his arm. "What is this about? We cannot risk missing the shaman's exhibition. It will create an insult, which would be political suicide here," she pointed out, spitting the words at him.

Akama released her arm and nodded his head in agreement. About as much of an apology as she would ever get from him. Asshole.

"I came to confirm a rumor passed to me moments ago," he whispered.

"What rumor?" she hissed.

"I was told you have taken it upon yourself to encourage the KuRuk's wife to put a team of females together who intend to make clothing to trade at Thrall Lake. Is this true?" he asked, a dangerous glare in his eyes. Neetriht decided he did indeed look like a demon from hell, as they stared at one another in a contest of wills. She was aware the music in the background seemed to be winding down.

"Yes," she gave her terse answer. But then she decided elaboration was necessary, not wanting to claim all the credit for the idea. "Taramat was involved. The discussion became an idea. An *executable idea* that can benefit the tribe, as well as the Gugwe Nation. And," she huffed, "an idea that strengthened the tribal women's support of their men leaving the village and traveling to the Winter Solstice gathering."

She crossed her arms, challenging him to argue the point.

He puffed out his chest and showed her his teeth. She sighed as if bored. The tribe's drums beat, announcing the shaman's performance. Neetriht turned on the ball of her foot to get back to her place by the fire. She took two steps and heard him with her Gugwe-enhanced audio abilities say under his breath, "Neetriht and Taramat, ha! Brilliant." She rolled her eyes.

Thana NukPana and the KuRuk Vutova had settled again into their seats. A flash of fireworks started the show. Three shamans took center stage, surrounded by tribe campfires.

Each shaman wore a dark blue ankle-length tunic constructed of one long piece of weaving with an opening for the head. A band on each side at the waist tied the back and front tunic flaps together. Under it, the men wore dull white wool pants, ballooning at the thighs and tight around the ankles. The trio danced in soft boots embellished with shiny pieces of metal, cut in shapes and sewn to the leather, depicting the moon's cycle from crescent to full. Metal pieces set off the intricate needlework adorning the dark tunics. Decorations filled the material's canvas with patterns of stars, representations of the Gugwe constellations and their sky gods.

The KuRuk's wife pressed her lips to Neetriht's ear, whispered, "My sister and I made their ceremonial costumes," her rough, wind-burned face proud. Neetriht smiled and squeezed her fingers to acknowledge the female's accomplishment.

This was the first time Thana NukPana, as well as the 13/31 Vutova's, had ever seen a shaman, much less three putting on a performance. It impressed him, even if the show was heavy on using what he considered minor magic and illusions.

Akama allowed his eyes to rove, taking in the Vulita crowd. His mind wove in and out through the audience. As his cognizance roamed, the shamans performed a thrilling trick. They used sparks at their fingertips, which brought his attention back to the center stage. The Thana reached, using his mind like a whip, snapping to grab control of the Shaman closest to where he sat. A crack of thunder rumbled across the field, shaking the ground. The Thana felt something like an iron door slamming shut in his mind, the noise of it making him start. He looked out and found the shaman standing stark still, hands on his hips, staring at the emperor. The shaman lifted his hand, pointed his forefinger and shook it three times at Akama, admonishing his attempt, then released a belly laugh. The shaman was letting the emperor know *he knew* Akama had tried to grab control of his mind. He bowed at the Thana, sliding right back in step with the other two, who had continued with their routine.

The next thing Akama knew, two other doors simulated slamming shut in his mind, and a virtual feather reached out to tickle his own brain. His eyes went wide as he realized the three Vulita shamans had closed off access to their psyches from him. In addition, they made no secret of the fact that they could impose mind control on him should they desire. The three bowed low, the performance at an end. Akama felt their presence retreat from his thoughts.

The following day, Thana NukPana summoned the shamans at sunrise. It was well past noon when their meeting broke up. The 13/31 worked their way over the Mac Mountains and then the Rock Mountains. The two ranges butted up against one another. It was no surprise that the expedition added yet another daily training. Yorgan, one of the Vulita Shamans, had agreed to join the Thana's expedition. They put him in charge of teaching mind control. Yorgan first began instilling the team with the techniques to block access to their minds from any potential controllers. It was a skill Akama had deemed a top priority after his experience with the Soothsayers. The 13/31 improved daily as they made their way to the next Gugwe tribal village.

The Wildhorse Tribe made its home all along the river's edge, named after them. They built structures far enough back to allow for snowmelt and spring floods. The clay available around the river valley was used to make a variety of vessels, cooking pots, and dishes. The women used two large, rounded brick ovens, heated by fires made in pits below, to bake the pottery after they had fashioned it. They carved a few of the earthenware pieces with a simple symbol before firing. Most were just plain. Neetriht and Taramat worked with the women to discuss adding color, other designs, or symbols. They suggested that the women of this tribe consider bringing samples and pottery stock to trade at Thrall Lake.

All the Vutova enjoyed one pleasure while visiting the Wildhorse Gugwe. The expedition members took turns sitting in the soothing hot springs that surrounded the village. They agreed there must be some kind of magic in the steaming waters that took away all their aches and pains from so much time spent in the saddle riding caribou.

It rained most of the way down to the Nanavox's homeland. Taking small skiffs refitted to accommodate the caribou, the entourage traversed the sound. Barrier islands provided a protective natural harbor. There, the calm waters were rich in the resources of fish and seafood, important for feeding this tribe. The Nanavox used shells collected from the beaches, as well as the shells, which became waste after eating certain sea delicacies, for many uses. Shell jewelry was displayed on males and females alike. Males of the tribe on guard duty wore chest and back plates made of shells. Cleverly overlapped, the artisans connected the plates tightly together using strips of dried gut. The shell plates offered some protection to turn the blade of an enemy. Neetriht advised that the tribe's shell creations would make excellent coin for trading at Thrall Lake.

The 13/31 found the Nanavox village to be a beautiful, peaceful place. The Vutovas promised to return one day, wishing they could spend more time in the scenic village. They invited the Gugwe of Nanavox to visit their home when the weather was good for travel.

The trek took them back across the Rock Mountains to visit the Gugwe tribe, who named themselves the Grey Fox. They found the terrain strewn with evergreens, aspens, rocky outcroppings, and deep ravines. The people had access to several rivers running through their territory. This land was also home to bighorn sheep, grizzly bears, moose, elk, cougars, lynx, and foxes, to name a few. These animals roamed in abundance through the forest and grassy plains. The Grey Fox tribe cleverly made furs and hides into clothing, pouches, hats, boots, mittens, rugs, and warm bedding.

After their visit with the Grey Fox tribe, the Thana's expedition had grown almost double its original size and began calling themselves the 26/62. Over the next seven days, the group had traveled north to the location where the Alabaster Tribe had settled. Their village ran along the wide river located there. Rocky outcroppings hung above big rapids that crashed through the stone-laden riverbed below. The surrounding mountains, capped with snow, still blazed in the sunlight even in late summer. The Alabaster tribal lands were home to a huge glacier where they believed one of their gods dwelled. Low, scrubby growth covered the flats surrounding the village. Many mushrooms grew in the area. Some, the tribe used for medicinal purposes. They prized multiple varieties choice for eating. There was a young man in the tribe who had been apprenticing to an elder for the past three years. He was learning all the mushroom varietals, when and where they grew, and whether they could use them for food, medicine, or as poisons. The master had taught him how to brew tinctures. He learned mushrooms were better if they had been dried so they could be ground into powder for different applications. The Thana asked, and the Alabaster elder shaman agreed his apprentice could accompany the 26/62's expedition until they reached Thrall Lake. The Fungi Apprentice would train Anson Vutova, the expedition supply chain head. He was to convey all the knowledge he could impart until they arrived for the Winter Solstice summit. When the summit concluded, Thana agreed the fungi expert would return home with the tribe's KuRuk and emissaries.

Trouble started with the *shaman's* approval of the arrangement. The KuRuk was angry they had not consulted him. The Alabaster KuRuk made it clear at every turn that he did not like the emperor and his followers. He spoke out against the new programs the Vutovas promoted to create competition and reward behaviors. He thought the new ideas mocked the old Gugwe traditions. The Alabaster KuRuk was old. He made no bones about being against any modifications to the way of life he had always known.

The showdown came on the third day. Thana's 26/62 planned to leave the following morning when they would continue on to the Bear Ridge Tribe's location. Akama understood change was hard to sell, particularly to elders, and this KuRuk was definitely old, but the elderly leader was still a force to be reckoned with. The emperor had no wish to embarrass the Alabaster leader. He held a small group meeting and included a selection of people from Thana's team, as well as the Alabaster KuRuk's top leaders. Each side included five others in attendance to build up and tear down arguments. In the end, they made no progress relative to overcoming the KuRuk's resistance to the proposed changes. Akama tired of trying to appease the elder. So, he simply ordered the Alabaster KuRuk to implement the changes.

The Alabaster tribe was expected to embrace the new leadership structures for 13 turns of the moon's cycle, then reassess the new protocols. After so much time, the emperor was sure the old leader would see the benefits the adjustments could bring. The hosting KuRuk took offence to the order. He accused the Emperor of the Gugwe Nation of crossing the line and interfering with his power as the tribe's leader. In a show of great disrespect, the Alabaster KuRuk spit at Thana NukPana's feet.

Akama looked from the puddle of spittle directly into the KuRuk's eyes. He wasn't surprised to see madness dancing there. The old creature offered a crazed grin, its broken teeth yellow. The smirk made an ugly break across the Gugwe's face. Thana NukPana's hand snaked out faster than the naked eye could comprehend. His clawed thumb pressing against the male's jugular, clawed fingers splayed across the wrinkled skin of the old male's throat, squeezing. For those who knew the signs, the Alabaster KuRuk's eyes glazed over as Akama seized the KuRuk's mind.

Once inside, Akama found the KuRuk's psyche a jungle, a mess. He pushed words into the male's mind, forced the KuRuk to push out those words through his throat, even as Akama squeezed it tighter. Small dots of blood appeared beneath the emperor's claws, bruising blooming on the elder's skin. "Apologies Emperor. I would rather die than oppose your ideals." Phlegm gurgled at the back of the KuRuk's gullet.

"Grandfather!" A scream pierced through the crowd, a young woman pushing her way through the onlookers. When the last of the tribal members who were blocking her moved, she broke through, hands splayed at her sides in a gesture of helplessness. Making her face fierce, words loud, "I beg you, Thana NukPana, please, please don't kill my grandfather. I offer my life in his place. Please. He is all I have."

Akama released the elder with a shove but hung on to the KuRuk's mind, working his way through the tangle inside. The Thana was stunned into stillness by the young woman he found in front of him. He'd seen nothing like her. Indeed, there had been no sign of her in the village over the past several days. Akama didn't even bother to control his basest male reaction, as his cock hardened against his leather pants. His body gave off a musky smell, quickly backing up any males nearby.

"What is your name?" Akama demanded.

"I am called Abaddon."

"Angel of Death," he whispered to himself, reacting to the name's meaning, heart pumping against his chest.

Abaddon was albino.

The crowd rippled a second time. Another female, twice as big as the woman in front of him, pushed her way through the crowd. Her ugly face took in the Thana NukPana, the elder KuRuk, the albino. She grabbed a fistful of the female's white, silky hair and dragged the woman away. All the while chastising the girl for leaving her tent, knowing her grandfather never permitted it. Every time Abaddon tried to explain she had only been trying to save her grandfather, it earned her a hard tug on the hair, some ripping out by the roots. The woman followed the tug with a slap across the younger female's face, leaving red handprints on the milky-white skin.

Akama roared with such force that it echoed across the face of the mountain range. "Stop!" he raged his command at the woman dragging the albino away.

She turned to face him, hauling her prisoner around with a firm grip on her mane, pulling the girl off balance. The albino went down on her knees.

"Release her," Akama pointed to the ghostly figure.

The woman took a moment to cool her temper, remembering whom she addressed. Wiping away her angry grimace, she drew in a deep breath and bowed slightly. "Great Thana NukPana," she said in supplication, "I offer you apologies. This girl is an abomination to the Alabaster tribe. Her grandfather decreed when she was born that she was never to be seen by outsiders. Her mother died giving her life. We should have killed this freak of nature as soon as she left the womb, but the KuRuk would not allow the slaying of his only granddaughter. Abaddon is evil incarnate. She has been nothing but bad luck for the tribe. She shames us all by showing herself in your presence. You can be sure I will punish her appropriately for this transgression," the hag promised him. "Please, please accept our apologies for subjecting you to her ugliness."

"An abomination, you say?"

She nodded, thinking he was agreeing with her.

He swept his hand at her as he approached, showing she should move aside. The old hag squinted her eyes at him with distrust, but finally gave way, as his gigantic form towered over her. She could feel the anger coming off him in waves.

Thana retracted his claws. Using two fingers, he gently lifted the girl's chin. He looked into her unusually pale blue eyes and noticed white eyelashes fanned the lids. Her snow-colored hair ran in a silky river down to her waist. Akama felt polarized from the surrounding crowd, except for her. She drew him like a magnet.

"The shame is all mine," the albino whispered. "Please don't blame the tribe. I should never have disgraced the honor of the Alabaster by exposing one such as myself to the Great Thana NukPana." She allowed two tears to escape. He wiped them away with his thumb.

"The shame..." his voice boomed so the crowd could hear, but his eyes never left hers. "...all the shame belongs to your tribe for not realizing the gift of uniqueness you bring to them. The shame of not seeing the beauty radiating from inside you."

Neetriht had slowly made her way up to the front of the mob. She recognized this as an opportunity to avoid the violence she could see her brother's body shaking with. Neetriht stepped up behind Abaddon. She gently wrapped her arms around the slim woman and helped her to her feet, turning toward the path leading to the expedition's camp. "I'll just take Abaddon, help her get cleaned up, yes? She can rest awhile in my tent, then join us for a private dinner in your yurt. Say, two hours from now? Meanwhile, perhaps you can complete your trade talks with her *grandfather*, hmm?" She wanted him to ponder how the girl might feel about him if he slaughtered her grandfather. Neetriht pushed her way past the crowd without a look back, a protective arm around the albino girl.

"Abaddon," Akama called to her. The two females stopped, standing stiffly without turning. "I just wanted you to know that your effort was successful."

Those pale blue eyes turned to look over her shoulder at the Gugwe Emperor.

"Your petition on behalf of your grandfather's life," he reminded her. "It worked. You saved him."

She offered him the smallest of smiles, then continued with Neetriht through the crowd. The throng hissed at the ghost of a woman, spitting at the albino, throwing handfuls of dirt as she passed, whispering ugly names as Neetriht led the way toward the 26/62's camp.

Akama's voice called out after her, "We can discuss your offer to exchange your life for your grandfather's over dinner." Thana NukPana gave a curt bow as the two disappeared from his sight. The assembly disbursed, keeping their murmurs of disbelief to themselves, not wishing to draw the attention of the Thana.

"Asshole," Neetriht whispered under her breath.

Aware that her life had somehow just taken a major turn, Abaddon's skin pebbled with goosebumps as she trembled under the protective arm of her guide.

CHAPTER 24: Like What You See?

The Goblin Queen's mood seemed to sour more each day as Lillith led Morveena's cabal north toward the Bull Moose Tribal village. There was no way the goblin bitch would know Thana's route on his epic visits to the 13. From what Lillith had gathered according to the Thana's emissary, who had visited a few weeks ago, it was not likely the emperor had visited Bull Moose yet. The Gugwe expedition hadn't even come to Bear Ridge yet, but she didn't know that. The travelers were likely still further west, visiting the mountain tribes. Her brother, Zilla, had made it clear he expected her to drag out Morveena's travel as long as possible. Lillith shivered as she thought of his threat if she should fail. Zilla had planned to wait at Bear Ridge, intending to intercept the Thana to warn him of the Goblin Queen's mission. He hoped to be rewarded for his efforts.

Covertly looking at the red-haired she-devil from her peripheral view, Lillith's stomach rolled. Reminding her once more how much she despised the Goblin Queen. She had always pretended the opposite every time the bitch had come to the Bear Ridge village. Her strategy being, it was best to handle crazy people by keeping them close, but at arm's length. That way, you could monitor what they were up to, but not be caught off guard. She sighed. This was going to feel like an endless trip.

If that were the case, she might as well control the group dynamics, which entailed pushing the redhead's buttons. Lillith definitely knew exactly what the Queen's buttons were. And though dangerous, it was very satisfying to get a reaction from the haughty bitch. The Bear Ridge female had discovered over the years, Morveena easily lost control of her emotions, allowing anger to rule her actions. Besides, Lillith didn't think the goblins would risk hurting her because her brother would extract retaliation. Zilla certainly did not have any great love for his sister, but he would deem it as a personal insult if the gobs damaged her.

That very afternoon, Lillith Bear Ridge flirted blatantly with Rupert.

"Rupert," Lillith crooned, moving closer, striding along the flat sandy ground, sunlight shining on her jet-black mane. "I think you've doubled your muscle since you were last here." She raised her eyebrows. "Looking good. Very good, Rupert." Lillith smiled coyly, licked her lips deliberately slow, running her tongue all the way around the upper rim of her mouth, then sliding it across her lower lip.

Rupert smiled, but felt Morveena's stare boring into his back between his shoulder blades. He quickly wiped the smile off his face, willing his hardening cock to soften immediately.

Lillith made several whispered suggestions to Rupert as the group traveled. It wasn't long before the Goblin Prince moved back into the small caravan to discuss 'military issues' with his squad leader. His absence left a clear view of Morveena, glowering at their guide, leaving Lillith to wonder if perhaps her safety wasn't guaranteed by her brother's potential wrath. Still, she couldn't help enjoying the waves of irritation coming off the Queen. Maybe she'd tone it down, so she didn't push the she-devil over the edge.

They'd made good time traveling toward Bull Moose. Dusk found them setting up camp. Consulting with one of Morveena's squad leaders, Lillith told him and the other lads another two or three days would put them at the Bull Moose village. She suggested that with luck, they would hopefully catch up with the Thana NukPana, though it was impossible to predict exactly where the expedition might actually be.

Everyone settled in for the night. Lillith spent an hour talking with the cooks as they prepared the stew. She helped cut up the orange and white tubers, chopped ramps, and washed the tools used to prep the meal. She lightly peppered her questions and comments with inquiries about the long-rumored Fae Princess. Here and there, she picked up little pieces of information about the girl, working all the members of Morveena's cabal for intel. If she could just gather the right information, maybe Lillith could track and capture the Fae Princess and bring the prize to the Gugwe Emperor herself. It could be a good way to introduce her value to the Thana NukPana. Then she would see where her cleverness could take her. She day-dreamed about showing Zilla how important she would become if she could catch the eye and the ear of the Gugwe Emperor.

The cooks interrupted her private reverie, asking if she would inform the queen and the prince that the evening meal was ready. Obliging, Lillith made her way to the queen's tent on the far side of the meadow they'd camped in. At ten feet away, she could hear loud voices coming from inside.

"Ow! Darling, you're hurting me!" Rupert whined.

"Say it!" Morveena commanded.

"Only yours, my love. I am only yours. You know it's true, my precious dove. Your jealously is misplaced. Never fear!" he assured her. There were squelchy, wet noises coming from inside. Lillith could detect rustling noises as she stood frozen, spellbound. When she came to her senses, just about to turn and run lest the goblin witch catch her eavesdropping, she heard Morveena again.

"Oh, Rupert." He yelped in some kind of pained response, and she went on, "I wanted to be sure you knew how important it is that you always remain loyal to Mummy, yes?" Then more sucking, squelchy noises. Lillith cringed. Morveena said so quietly Lillith almost didn't hear it. "If ever you betray me, Rupert, I will skin you whole, taking a very long time to do it. When I am finished, I will have the clan seamstress make a dress for me out of your traitor skin. Am I clear about how upset I would be to find you'd cheated on me, darling?"

Morveena grabbed his balls and squeezed until tears ran down his cheeks. He croaked out, "Crystal clear, my love." She released him. Noises returned. It became clear the Queen was bringing Rupert to a climax; his grunts and heavy breathing told the story.

Lillith shook her head to clear it and backed up fifty feet. She called out as she headed toward the tent again, as though just arriving, "Hullo! Anyone home? Cooks sent me to tell you dinner's ready," she said in a singsong voice. "Hullo?"

Rupert opened the tent flap just enough to stick his face out, growling, "Alright, alright! Tell them we'll be up to start the mess line shortly," he snapped the flaps closed again.

Lillith giggled to herself. She was practically skipping all the way back to the mess tent. Several new ideas came to mind about how she could get Morveena's goat tomorrow.

When the queen's coterie set out the following day, Lillith changed tactics.

"Morveena," the Gugwe female called to her in a breathy voice. "Last night, I was thinking about how much I've missed you since your last visit to Bear Ridge." She turned to look longingly at the Goblin devil and continued her lead, walking, but adding a little extra sway to her hips as she moved north. "I couldn't help but notice you looked so appealing. It's hard to resist you with your luscious lips colored in that striking red, yes?" Lillith raised her eyebrows at the queen and winked. Morveena produced a deep, throaty laugh, amused by her Gugwe guide. "I wondered," Lillith crooned, "since we're the only two women in this group, if you'd show me later how to do my hair and paint my lips? It could be fun. Just us girls?" the Gugwe female slowly licked her lips while holding the queen's stare.

"We'll see," Morveena said, not committing to anything, then snapped a fan open, hiding her face as she cooled herself with rapid wrist movements.

Lillith smiled shyly at the queen. She turned to move back into the rows behind to walk with the cooks, whispering as the queen moved past her, "Until later, Morveena Morgan Montestrell." The Goblin Queen's eyes were like molten liquid.

Late afternoon brought them to the Bull Moose village. The goblins were all disappointed to find Thana NukPana was not in Bull Moose, had not even passed through yet. It meant they would have to continue their travels to find him. The Bull Moose KuRuk suggested they travel west to catch the Thana in Alabaster. But Lillith voiced her opinion. She felt their best chance was to continue on around the bay to Vattusk. Before the KuRuk could suggest they go the faster route by water, Lillith reached out with her mind. Silently informing the KuRuk it was Zilla who had instructed her to delay the Goblin Queen's travel as much as possible.

If surprise took the Bull Moose KuRuk because of Lillith's mind communication, he didn't show it. For himself, he despised goblins and thought they should be put to work in the mines under the control of the BloodKnife Tribe. He'd already concluded this goblin female thought herself far and above Gugwe, which she projected clearly in her manner. Lillith promised to fill him in later about why the goblin shrew had any value to them.

Lillith evaded going to the queen after dinner and the moon's rise to act on her earlier implied suggestions. Instead, she shifted to a goblin form and lured two of the queen's lads, now off duty, to their shared tent, where she entertained them late into the night. After, as they all lay together covered in furs, muzzy with liquor and sex, Lillith asked a deluge of whispered questions. She stroked the tops of their heads and twisted her fingers gently through their hair. Her inquiries mixed with asking about their homes, families, and clans. Now and then, she carefully added a question to dig for more details about the Fae Princess. Liquor loosened tongues. The story unfolded about the queen's capture of the fabled princess, then of the girl's escape. A pair of owls hooted back and forth as the moon arced across the dark sky. Before the sun rose, Lillith was up, dressed, and meeting with the Bull Moose KuRuk, the rest of the village and their guests still asleep.

It would take the goblin convoy another eleven days before they reached Vattusk. The ground was a patchwork of water dotted with small islands of landscape between the aquatic inlets, a nightmare of a labyrinth to navigate.

Lillith had used the travel time well. Continuing in her quest, she used care to learn everything she could from all the goblin soldiers about the Fae Princess. It was prudent to be sure the queen didn't find out she was gathering information. In addition, she was trying her best to make the queen jealous. Lillith had sex with all of Morveena's soldiers, as well as the two cooks. She had enjoyed those two most of all. There had been the added benefits of larger helpings of food, as well as special sweet treats each day since she'd lain with them. Each time, she had offered her lovers the choice of her taking the avatar of Goblin, Fae, Human, or just remaining a Gugwe as she bedded them. Lillith was keenly aware Morveena could pick up the scent of all the males on her skin and fur. She deliberately made a habit of not bathing until the evening when they would set up camp again, just to be sure the red-devil could smell her activities.

Two days out from Vattusk, the crew came upon a spectacular view, where the Nels River flowed into an enormous bay. A crashing waterfall dropped a hundred feet, causing a constant roar and sending a mist of cool spray across the air. Based on where the sun was, at least another hour would pass before the time they typically stopped for the day. But today, the powerful waterfall enamored the Goblin Queen, and she called for an early halt.

The queen's tent was always the first erected. When the lads had it set up, they moved on to assemble the rest of the camp, as well as bringing water up from the river and collecting firewood for the night. Lillith passed Rupert on the way to Morveena's tent and overheard him talking with his second in command. "Round up another couple of lads. Let's go hunting to take advantage of the extra light. Fresh meat for dinner would be a pleasant change, yes?" They crossed the meadow, hurrying, hoping for success. Lillith saw five males head into the scrubby woodland. The other lads had to take up the extra burden of the rest of the camp setup. The two cooks would be busy prepping food and getting water, whether or not the hunters brought in fresh meat.

Lillith couldn't believe her good luck. A golden opportunity fell into her lap. She made her way down to Morveena's tent. Calling out just before lifting the tent flap, not waiting to be invited in, she came to a dead stop, frozen in place.

The Goblin Queen was stark naked in front of her washstand. Her back, shoulders, and buttocks were a mass of old scars, crisscrossing all down the length of her. The redhead turned to look at the intruder. Lillith made a snap decision to continue playing the role of camp slut. After all, she had nearly perfected it. The Bear Ridge female actually panted, allowing her tongue to hang out between her lips, lust riding across her face to Morveena's delight.

"I..." Lillith swallowed. "I know of something special at this location I wanted to...to share with you. Forgive me for interrupting your bathing. If you'll trust me," Lillith hurried over to the goblin female, "I can show you a magical place to finish your bath, Morveena Morgan Montestrell." Lillith had picked up the soft, tanned leather dress Morveena had laid out and came to stand almost nose to nose with the evil goblin.

Morveena gracefully lifted her arms into the air and waited. Lillith made a show of raking her eyes up and down the scarred, voluptuous body before her.

"Like what you see, Lillith?" Morveena taunted.

"Oh yes," Lillith confirmed, swallowing to show just enough fear she calculated would move Morveena a little closer to lust. Another's fear of her was a turn-on for the Goblin Queen.

The Gugwe, twice as tall as the queen, allowed her fingers to trail down Morveena's arms as she slid the dress over her head, helping her slip the garment over skin that was still damp. It gratified Lillith to see small goosebumps pebble down the queen's arms. Taking Morveena's hand, she asked, "Will you come with me?"

"Hmmm. Magical you say? Special? You promise?" the queen goaded her.

"I promise." Lillith pulled the goblin along behind her. Just before they exited the tent, Lillith turned to Morveena and pressed her finger against the goblin's red-stained lips. "Shhh. This will be our little secret," she whispered, squeezing the hand in hers tighter. She peeked out and saw no sign of the lads. So far, so good. Leading Morveena around the back of the tent, they ran together toward the Nels River, the sun still glowing across the horizon.

"Where..." Morveena started, but again, Lillith whispered, "Shhh."

When they reached a rocky outcropping, Lillith dropped Morveena's hand and moved ahead. As she rounded the rocky cliff, Morveena could hear the water thundering over the edge, dumping a hundred feet to crash into the bay below. Lillith simply disappeared.

Startled, Morveena rushed ahead, almost losing her balance at the edge, her stomach dropping at the sight of the long fall to the churning river below. Lillith's hand snaked out, grabbing the queen. Pulling her tightly against the rocks, catching her in her arms, Lillith pulled Morveena under and behind the waterfall. The hideaway was a large cave; the falls, a thick curtain of privacy.

Mist swirled all around them. The next thing Morveena knew, Lillith was peeling off her clothes, carelessly dropping them to the flat, rocky, damp ground. She moved to a standing pool; the waterfall crashing in front of it; she shifted to the shape of a goblin. The hidden cave had stalactites and stalagmites interspersed throughout. The Gugwe turned into her avatar form, beckoning her guest to join her. Taking three steps down, Lillith settled herself in the water. Steam rising all around her naked form. Morveena squealed in delight, stripped and entered the hot spring, sitting on the bottom step, putting her at eye level with the tall female.

"Aren't you full of surprises?" the redhead laughed.

"There's more." Lillith said boldly.

"More what?" The queen tipped her head to the right, eyeing her companion.

"Surprises." Lillith let lust fill her facial features again. "If you want them, that is?"

"Hell yes," the Goblin Queen told her. The hot spring steam hid them from view as Lillith took the queen's face in her hands and kissed her deeply. When she pulled away, Lillith turned the queen so she was facing away from her. Slowly, Lillith kissed every scar on Morveena's ruined back, tracing her finger along each raised scar. "I'd like to kill whoever did this to you," Lillith whispered in her ear. Morveena groaned and leaned into the Gugwe female's goblin form.

After they'd showered in the cool waterfall spray, then got back in the hot spring pool, taking their time relaxing, still exchanging heated glances. Lillith held the queen against her. Moving her finger in little circles across the tops of Morveena's shoulders, she whispered. "What was it like when you discovered the Fae Princess wasn't just a rumor? You're the cleverest female I've ever known, Morveena. How did you even know it was her for sure?"

Glowing under Lillith's compliment, the Goblin Queen whispered back. The answer filled in the last of the missing pieces of the puzzle the Gugwe had put together from previous information she had gleaned from the lads.

When they'd finally gotten out of the water, laughing at each other's water-wrinkled skin, they dressed slowly. Lillith shifted back to her Gugwe body. She stood just inside the ledge, the waterfall thundering behind her. The Queen slowly moved forward, pulling a small, covered jar from her pocket. She twisted the cork out and dipped her finger in, kissed Lillith lightly, ever so gently. Tenderly, Morveena rubbed the red dye over the Gugwe's lips. She corked the top and stood back a step, appraising the female before her.

"Like what you see?" Lillith asked, just as Morveena had taunted her hours before.

"Oh yes," the Goblin Queen confirmed. She offered a cruel smile, her lashes glittering with little beads of mist from the falls.

Morveena Morgan Montestrell raised her finger to her lips. "Shhh," she told Lillith, "this will just be our little secret." Lillith nodded and smiled. The female goblin kicked her leg out, the heel of her foot cracking Lillith in the chest, knocking the breath from her lungs. Enthralled, the queen watched as the Gugwe lost her balance. With Lillith's arms windmilling, she fell through the thick, powerful veil of water. Her scream was swallowed in the cascade's thunder as she fell to her death, body broken on the rocks in the bay far below.

Adjusting her dress, Morveena ran her fingers through her hair and applied fresh lip dye, checking her reflection in the smooth pool. Satisfied, she took her time wandering back to her tent, wondering if Rupert and the lads had been successful at hunting. She had a powerful craving for fresh, bloody rare meat for dinner tonight.

CHAPTER 25: Finally! An Easy Question

Carlisse sat on her boulder with a small sketchbook and pencil, drawing designs. She needed the diversion to keep her mind occupied until the real reason she waited there appeared. The sun was on its afternoon track downward, but the sunset was still hours away. She gave each drawing careful consideration, as she would need to duplicate it using ink applied to the skin. She planned to use the sketches as an opportunity for anyone who came to her requesting a tat. Her artwork showed potential tattoo options that could be chosen or customized. Tattoos were very personal to Carlisse. She didn't intend to do anymore 'blind' tats. Jud was right; tattoos were forever. She wanted to be sure in the future that the person approved the design before she inked skin.

"Carlisse!" Raven called out. She felt the corners of her mouth turn up as she twisted around. Raven, Lucky, Wolf, Mac, and Nova had another lad, Alto, who walked in front of them with hands tied behind his back. His face showed bruising and swelling, causing her smile to reverse into a frown.

"What's what, Raven?" Carlisse put her paper and pencil down and stood.

"Garrett's shooter was Alto. Wolf tracked him after Alto took the foxfire shifter down. We brought him back to see if Robin or the princess wants to do anything with him."

"And..." Carlisse turned and looked at Alto, "it was necessary to beat his face in before you delivered him?"

"Wolf and Nova let off some steam before I could get to Alta. They were pretty pissed about the attempt on Faith's life, you know?"

Raven sent the lads down to Stone House Camp with Alto, then turned back to Carlisse. "The camp is going to break up soon."

"In the next couple of days," she mumbled.

"I've talked it over with Robin and Caz, and they agree I'm going to go back to the clan near your home. Need to check on everyone and bring them all the news. I think some of the clan will want to come here. Others will want to go north to the Winter Solstice moot. Some will stay where they are, waiting to see how things shake out with Queen Morveena, Rupert, and Robin."

Raven cleared his throat. "I thought it might be a good idea to bring a Fae emissary with me. Help to present new ideas about cooperation and working with others," he swallowed hard.

"I think an emissary is a good idea, Raven," Carlisse agreed.

"I wondered," his voice squeaked.

"What did you wonder, Raven?"

He leaned back against Carlisse's boulder and said, "I wondered if you would consider being the emissary and going with us? You could visit your family while we're there. We'll be back here in a few weeks, and then we'll continue north for the moot, so we reach it on time. You probably want to think it over. I mean, traveling with a dozen lads, roughing it, might not appeal, yeah?"

Carlisse laughed a deep belly laugh. "Might not appeal?" she teased. "Sounds like every girl's dream trip. I don't need to think about it, Raven. It would be an honor to meet your clan as the first Fae emissary."

A wide grin split his face. "Excellent. Well then, come on, let's go see what's going to happen with Alto."

Carlisse grabbed her paper and pencil. Turning toward the switchback, she bit her lower lip. "Um, I just want to mention that it uh...it would be a good idea for you to be prepared, um...prepared for reactions from my sisters on this emissary idea. It'll be fast and furious, but their anger will flash and then fade."

"Great. Thanks for the warning," he let out a long whistle as he hurried to catch up with her.

The activity at the Stone House was like a beehive. A hive that had been hit with a stick. There was no lack of opinions as the mob shouted their opines out, trying to be heard above someone else sharing their two cents on Alto's fate.

It was Caz who took charge. "Shut it!" his voice echoed around. The lads obeyed immediately, but it took two more tries before he could get the females to stop shouting. Everyone took a collective breath, presumably getting ready to verbalize their pent-up thoughts again.

Ari opened the screen porch door and let slam behind him. "Stay quiet! All of you, until you're called upon," the Weaver stared them all down, making eye contact with every person in attendance. Ari pointed at Faith. "Will you join me up here, princess?" he asked politely, indicating the porch steps. She complied.

"Now, we'll attend to this business in a professional manner, yes?" All their heads nodded in acquiescence. "Faith, since you were the one Alto directed the offense at, you get to decide how Alto will fare." Ari waved his hand to suggest Faith take over.

The Fae Princess saw Lenny, Lester, and Dedo sitting atop the dry-stacked stone fence along the lane. She noted every single person, her eyes stopping on Alto. Faith took two steps down off the porch, so she was level with Alto, not raised above him or anyone else there. Ari sat down on the step, and Delainey quietly joined him.

Faith Lisbet Stargazer placed one hand in her other, held them cupped in front of her and directed her question to Alto. "Can you give me the benefit of the doubt? Will you at least tell me why you would want me dead?"

Alto raised his head, black eye puffy, sporting green and yellow bruising. He spat bloody phlegm to the side and said, "I can't buy into your prophecy, lass. It wasn't personal. It's just that I can't wrap my head around the whole 'all for one and one for all' bullshit. And I definitely don't believe the rumor you're going to sell about how the gobs and the Fae are one race." Alto spat again. "It will not be my world; I can tell you!"

"So, you couldn't voice your opinion, or you couldn't just leave quietly if you felt you were involved in something you didn't ask for and didn't believe in? The only solution you could come up with was to kill me? Do I have the right of it, Alto?" she demanded of him.

"I see your point," he conceded, "but the whole concept just isn't right. I felt trapped and desperate. It's downright scary. You can't force me to believe it."

"How about the concept of the Gugwe wanting to make slaves of any race? How does that sit with you, Alto?" Faith walked back and forth, considering her own views on the Gugwe.

"Hey! I don't want anyone to be a slave to these monsters," he cried out.

The golden-haired princess came to a stop in her pacing, then walked right up to Alto. She rose on tip-toes, almost bringing her nose to nose with the lad, and offered, "I agree with your position." She lowered her heels back to the ground, turned, walking a few steps away. "It would seem we do in fact have something in common, despite everything you believe we *do not* share the same views on. I think you would agree. We have not taken the opportunity to debate my stance on any topic as opposed to yours. We don't actually know if we agree on other issues, correct?"

"Um..." he considered. "I guess what you say is true," his voice humble.

"We just made progress, Alto. We now have two things we agree on. Perhaps there are others?" She rewarded him with a genuine smile, turned, walking away from the crowd toward the orchard lane.

"Wait, Miss Faith!" the Dream Weaver stood and called to her. "What do you want us to do with Alto?"

She half-turned. "Oh. I thought we'd just determined Alto was in charge of his own fate. Alto and I will need to continue to have discussions and debates to see where we can find common ground. When we disagree, it will be a learning moment for me, as I hope it will be for Alto. If we disagree, Alto can provide me with an opposing view so I can at least try to understand the other side. I am going to need that type of input. It will be critical for me to appreciate other's views. How would I know what those views are if someone doesn't tell me? In fact, I was hoping Alto would stay on with us in an advisory capacity. He'll have to pass muster with Garrett, since it was his body Alto's arrow punched into. Alto will no longer choose to kill anyone over a disagreement of ideals. I've stated my wishes, but ultimately, Alto is free to go or to stay."

The Fae Princess left a crowd whose mouths had fallen open.

Caz ran to catch Faith. "Brilliant job of handling the Alto situation," he complimented her.

"Thanks, Caz. We'll see how it works out, yeah?"

"Where are you headed, lass?"

"I'm going to check in to see how Garrett is doing. Aliah has made him a nice, cozy place to recoup in one of Ari's sheds. Then, I've got a planning meeting with the Kings and Dedo. Hey, I'd love to have you in on our meeting. You've got a natural talent for managing people and processes."

"Honored Princess. I'm in. Meet you there in fifteen," he called over his shoulder.

FAITH KNOCKED ON THE small shed door. She wasn't surprised to find Aliah opening it. "How's he doing?" Faith asked.

"Come in and see for yourself." Aliah moved aside. "I'm just going to run up to the stone house and see what Delainey might have as a snack for Garrett. I should be back in ten minutes."

Faith left the door open to let in the light and fresh air. She took a few steps in finding Garrett in his normal body, moving to sit up. "Glad to see you," he told her. "Aliah wouldn't even let me get up!"

"In all fairness, Alto shot you yesterday. You should rest." Faith advised.

"That's just it," Garrett confided. "Something weird happened."

"You mean the fact that you can shift into an awesome red fox with wings?" she teased.

He laughed, "Well, okay, that too." She looked confused.

"Sorry," he stammered, "I know there's the whole new shifter thing. I don't even know what it all means yet or what I'll be able to do when I...I change. I'm dying to find out what flying is like! But the thing is, there's something else, Faith," he gulped.

"What is it?" she whispered.

He pulled down the blanket covering him and lifted his arm where the arrow had struck him. She sucked in a sharp breath.

"It's gone! Your wound—it...it completely disappeared. How did...how did you mend so quickly? There's not even a scar!"

"I know, right? It seems I have the ability while in my fox form to heal really fast! I want to see if I can apply that gift to others, but Aliah thinks I should go slow and find out everything I can do before I jump in with both feet. What do you think?"

"I think you're my wonderful, lifelong friend who risked his life for mine. Thank you. You know I love you like a brother, yeah?" She leaned in and, putting their arms around one another, whispered in his ear, "I think you should make your own decisions, choices. Make your own timeline for testing what your fox form can do. Be true to yourself—that is, after taking into consideration all the advice you'll likely get from people who care about you. One in particular."

They startled when the door hinges creaked and turned to see Aliah's silhouette outlined in the doorway. Her body was rigid as she stood staring at Faith and Garrett, holding one another. Aliah jumped straight to a conclusion. "Oh. Oh, excuse me. I...I didn't mean to interrupt anything." Her face flushed two shades darker, and she turned to flee.

"Aliah, wait!" Faith called out, stomping her foot. "Aliah Bethany Pureheart, you interrupted nothing, for heaven's sake. I was just thanking Garrett for saving my life and telling him I love him *like a brother.*" Her eyes drilled into Aliah's. "Listen, sorry to cut this visit short, you two, but I've got a meeting with King Lenny and King Lester. I'm so glad you're going to be alright, Garrett. I'll catch you both at dinner." Faith gave Aliah's shoulders a squeeze and was out the door.

"Why are you blushing, Aliah?" Garrett asked.

"Never you mind, Garrett Emmon Gladheart!"

Aliah bustled in with a tray covered with a linen cloth, set it down on the small table next to his makeshift bed. She fluffed his pillow, got him situated so she could serve him a cup of hot tea and warm, buttered bread with jam. Garrett didn't utter a word of complaint.

AFTER A TWO-HOUR MEETING, Lenny, Lester, Caz, and Faith agreed Camp Stone House would break up and travel would begin soon. They decided the twin kings would maintain their base at the Dream Weaver's. They could communicate via Dedo, using the rocks and gargoyle people. The Dream Weaver made a confession the day before. As thrilled as he was that because of Delainey, he could finally leave the Edgewood, he found deep in his heart that this was his home and he wanted to stay. Ari informed them it was his plan to bring the Village of Edgewood alive again. He intended to make a formal announcement tonight, including the fact that Delainey had agreed to stay on. She and Saffron were going to open an inn. Ari confirmed Rolland was planning to set up a forge, which would be the basis for the repopulation of the village. Ari explained Rolland was planning on initially making weapons, and lots of them. Excellent weapons would be a necessity for fighting the Gugwe. Eventually, he hoped to build up a local business, separate from making weapons. In doing so, it would help change the reputation of the Edgewood Forest.

The collective group had a dream to make Edgewood a haven for people of all races to feel welcome, able to live and work in harmony. They'd had the idea it could start when Raven and the lads led Robin's clan back here. Each of them hoped some from the clan might like the idea of staying on at Stone House. They would need help to build roads leading to what would become the village. Labor would be critical in building homes and buildings. Four or five of Raven's lads had already committed to staying on to apprentice with Rolland. Everyone knew that making a lot of weapons was a priority for the coming blows against the Gugwe. He pointed out that Raven, the lads, and Carlisse would head to Robin's clan hold soon. If you counted those who would stay on at Edgewood Village, it left Robin, Caz, Faith, Val, Aliah, Garrett, Dedo and Alto as travel mates to the mid-lands.

Faith laid out her plan to meet any aunts and uncles before they continued further north. She expressed her hope of reconnecting with her cousins again. In voicing that, she would need them to help prepare for the Winter Solstice moot. Also, she confided she wanted a second chance to get to know her cousins, as their first meeting hadn't turned out very well.

After the brainstorming finished, Faith and Caz took the long way back, discussing the finer details. She glanced sideways at him, snapped out her wings and playfully challenged, "Race you back," jumping into the air with a running start. It took only seconds before Caz was flying, even with her. They seemed in sync. She rolled left, and he followed gracefully. He shot straight up, and she was his shadow. They both rolled right and opened their wings wider, gliding, riding a wind current, when they heard yelling below. They dropped to the ground like stones, landing on their feet, wings snapping closed.

"What the..." Faith hissed out.

"Stop!" Robin yelled, holding his hand up, palm out, to convey his message in body language to Delainey. But she bent to pick a trillium, and the Goodfellow became a hazy essence of glittery matter, popping from one side of the field to the other where Delainey stood. His face was angry, but before he could say a word, Delainey pointed at Val. Val picked a trillium, whispering Robin's name. "Oh," she purred, "I like this. An easy way to get your attention anytime I want to talk with you, yeah?" Val reached out her hand to touch his shoulder, but he disappeared, glittery matter falling to the ground where he had just been.

Robin coalesced next to Saffron as she twirled a freshly picked wake-robin between her thumb and forefinger. He growled, but flashed right back over to Val, who was holding a second white flower. "I wasn't done talking to him," she announced.

Faith stamped her foot and shouted at all three, "Stop it this instant! What the hell, Val? I can't believe you're involved in this, Delainey and Saffron."

"So, you can't believe they're involved, but you can believe I am?" Val ground out in anger.

"I didn't say that, Val," Faith argued.

"You implied it, Faith. Admit it. Just so you know, this wasn't my idea." She crossed her arms and scowled at her best friend. Having completely forgotten, Robin stood nearby.

"It wasn't? Faith raised her eyebrows.

"It was my idea, Faith," Lainey fessed up.

"Saffron?" Faith inquired.

"I'm part of the experiment," Saffron shrugged her shoulders.

"What experiment, Delainey?"

"Well..." Delainey hedged. "After the success in solving Ari's curse, I wanted to see if I could help Robin with his." She at least looked slightly embarrassed as she glanced at him from under her eyelashes shyly. He quirked his mouth at her.

"I asked Val to help me, but we thought it would be important to know if it worked when a goblin picked a wake-robin or if it only worked when a Fae did it. Turns out it worked for both races."

Robin rolled his eyes.

Of a sudden, Robin dissolved again right before them, sunlight making the shiny bits of matter shimmer.

"Who the hell did that again?" Faith demanded. It startled her to have Robin reappear between her and Caz.

Caz offered the flower to Robin. "Sorry mate. In the interest of scientific experiments, I wanted to see if a female or male picking the trillium mattered."

"Well?" Robin said.

"Hypothesis confirmed, mate," Caz stated. "There is no racial or gender bias in this curse." He punched Robin's shoulder good-naturedly.

"Alright, no more popping Robin's essence around unless he agrees in advance to any experiments, yeah?" Faith turned to look at Caz. "Including testing a hypothesis!" Caz winked at her.

"Sorry, Robin," Delainey said quietly.

"Meant no harm, Robin. Maybe it'll help her figure out your curse, yeah?" Saffron suggested.

"Well, I..." Val started, but was interrupted.

"Promise not to rudely use that method again if I want to talk to you, Robin?" Faith finished the sentence as a suggestion to Val.

"Okay, okay. I promise. It was rude, I admit it," Val started up the lane with Delainey and Saffron, discussing the results of the experiment.

"Lucky for me, the two of you came along when you did. I was getting dizzy!" Robin joked.

Caz and Faith quickly brought Robin up to date on their meeting with the kings. The plan, to spend the day prepping, leaving the following day. Robin and Caz headed back to the Stone House when Faith called out, "Hey Robin, I just remembered a message I was supposed to deliver to you. I recently communicated with my mother." Robin and Caz's mouths fell open, and she clarified, "Not in person! I'll tell you the details later tonight around the campfire. The important thing was, she gave me a couple of other messages to pass along if I get the chance, but she specifically asked me to pass along one to you. I'd forgotten about it until just now. My mother said that finding your sister has something to do with the northern lights. When you believe you've found her, she told me your sister would know the words you seek...her whispered words, I think she said. Yes, those were her exact words. Does it mean anything to you?"

"Yeah, it means a lot," he said to himself.

An hour later, the porch bell clanged to announce that dinner was ready. Faith closed the door to what she now referred to as 'the King's shed'. She tacked a note on the outside that read in large letters, 'WET PAINT' and hurried up the lane to join the group.

After a satisfying meal of Delainey's Shepherd's Pie, when the clean-up was done, the group was sitting around the campfire. Caz sat next to Faith and asked, "How are you going to pick our route?"

She grinned at him. "Finally! An easy question!" Pointing at the night sky as Robin tossed another log on the campfire, sending up a crackle of fiery sparks. "I'm going to follow the North Star."

They all saw two shooters stream across the Milky Way. "Always a sign of a good beginning," Val commented.

CHAPTER 26: What Did I Just See?

Thana NukPana and the 26/62 left Alabaster quietly, without fanfare, bearing southeast. Eventually, they reached the Bear Ridge Tribe's village. Each time he tried to get close to Abaddon, his sister, Neetriht, or his Map Maker, Taramat, inserted themselves between him and the one he now desired above all things. They tied him up in knots with frustration. The two females allowed conversation between the two, but he couldn't get close enough to touch a single strand of her silky white hair. He fantasized about tearing Neetriht and Taramat limb from limb.

With the camp fed, after the cohort had settled for the night, Akama had reached his limit of patience. He tried to push past his sister to get to the albino, who was consuming his thoughts. Neetriht pulled two long knives in the time it took him to take a breath. She stood in a defensive position, a low growl rattling in her throat.

"You push me too far, KuRuk," he used the title like a slur.

"First, Akama," she hissed at him, "this is not a situation involving the Great Thana NukPana and one of his KuRuk's." She threw his title right back at him, intending it to be an insult.

"No?" he growled at her.

"No," she confirmed. "I am Neetriht. 13. Your sister. Grandmother told me of a vision she had before we left Vutova."

"I already heard this story," he complained.

"Not this part. She warned me I would need to protect your honor on this trip. Ama said you would find something precious, pure, good, and I should protect you from defiling it. Ama claimed it would make all the difference in your future. You still believe in Ama's visions, don't you, Akama?"

His chest filled with a predator's growl, rumbling through his body.

Asshole, Neetriht thought. His grumble was likely the only answer she would receive from him to her question.

“Think, brother,” Neetriht beseeched him. “Her own tribe had hidden away Abaddon because they feared her being different from them. They considered her an abomination. But, you, Akama,” her eyes pleading with his, “you have the power to turn her from an abomination to a Gugwe Goddess. You alone can turn her ‘differentness’ to reverence by taking her as your wife. She can become a symbol of your power. But if she is to be your wife, she must represent the embodiment of your pure and good leadership as the emperor of the 13 tribes.” Neetriht stepped up, changing her stance, sheathing her knives. “Well, brother, if you wish to achieve such a lofty goal, you must rein in your lust. Court her affections. Above all, you must marry her as a virgin. The shamans will help you build the purity angle. Abaddon will naturally fall into the role you need her to play, but only if you win her heart. Definitely not if you give in to your baser side and rape her soul, her body. You will destroy her purity with such an action.” Neetriht opened her arms wide, tipped her head to bare her neck to him, showing her deference.

The breath he was holding came out in a defeated huff. Neetriht’s muscles relaxed.

“You have a plan, I suppose?” Akama asked his sister.

“Taramat does,” Neetriht informed him.

He laughed. “Of course she does. Send her to my yurt to enlighten me in an hour,” he instructed as he walked away.

“Where are you going?” she called after him.

“If you must know, I am headed for that lake down there,” he pointed, “for a nice, cold swim.”

TARAMAT CAUTIOUSLY entered Thana’s yurt without announcement or permission. She found Akama and Nevele seated across from one another, with a game of stones between them. Both ignored her for several minutes until they finished the game.

“Better luck next time, Nevele,” Akama said as the hulking bodyguard rose and took up his usual place near the entry.

Akama waved his hand at the empty stool. “Care to try your luck, Map Maker?”

Taramat swiftly took a seat. "Have I lost my other title so quickly?" she asked. "Have you found another to act as your chief advisor?"

"We shall play a friendly game while you shower me with your advice."

"As long as you know, when I play a game, I play to win. I won't throw a game just to please you because you are the Thana NukPana. If you cannot lose because of your pride, I will not play."

Nevele rolled his eyes, but didn't make a sound.

Taramat watched carefully to see three or four emotions roll across Akama's face. When he settled back in control again, there was a smile of amusement written on his features.

"Then, it shall be as when we were children again, Taramat. One of us will win and one of us will lose. I will not punish you for winning fairly. Agreed?" She nodded in satisfaction and moved her first piece.

She tracked every move while she explained the details of her plan for him to win Abaddon's heart and, in doing so, his people's hearts. "I first got this idea when I overheard a scout's report yesterday..."

THE 26/62 REMAINED camped in the same location for the next three days. Neetriht saw Akama swimming in the lake four or five times...each day. Early morning, mists still rising before the sun burned them off, Akama, Nevele, and two scouts left camp, only to return by the time the evening meal was ready. They spoke to no one about their activities, and no one dared to ask. On the third evening, the four day-trippers reappeared, two scouts at the rear pointing two long spears at the furred rump of a twelve-point bull elk. He was bound with two ropes around his neck. Nevele held one rope on the left and Akama the other on the right. The members of the expedition stood wide-eyed at the spectacle. The majestic animal bucked and reared, shook its massive neck and head, releasing a loud 'screeeeeeee'—a sound everyone could feel down to their bones.

"Abaddon!" Akama called out.

The crowd parted to let her pass. She came to a stop about twenty-five feet away from the angry, resisting animal, her heart thundering in her chest. The elk suddenly raised its massive, antlered head and came to a stillness, staring at the female before him, her long white hair blowing in the gentle wind. The elk broke the silence, pawing the ground and blowing out an exhausted breath.

"I bring you a gift to honor your purity, Abaddon. If you accept, consider this to be my courtship gift to you, and we will begin formal steps on the path to becoming husband and wife. You must be sure before you accept." Akama cleared his throat. "Is this a gift you wish to receive from me, Abaddon?"

The albino female curtseyed, but her eyes never left the elk, the animal now standing peacefully at ease.

Akama dismounted and came forward slowly. Neetriht met him before he reached the object of his desire. She whispered, "You may seal the courtship bargain with a kiss. Chaste as you would give to your Ama," Neetriht raised her eyebrows at him, and he nodded curtly, conveying his understanding.

The 26/62 looked on as he gently cupped Abaddon's chin to pull her eyes to his from the magnificent animal he had presented to her. She stared into his soul, then closed her eyes. Her long white eyelashes brushed his face like soft feathers as her lips turned up to meet his. Akama relished every second as his lips brushed hers. He memorized her scent. To him, she smelled of moonlight and clove. He let the essence of her aroma wash over his senses. According to his sister, he had to be satisfied with that for now.

The elk snorted loudly, making the crowd laugh. It took every ounce of the Gugwe Emperor's strength to release Abaddon, but he did, then stepped back. Akama waved a hand at the animal and told her, "He is yours, Abaddon."

Abaddon took several steps forward. Tentatively, she reached out her pale hand to touch the velvety soft nose. "I will call him Frost," she declared, their eyes meeting, each seeing a miracle in one another's eyes—albino to albino.

The great white elk pawed the ground, accepting the new name. The 26/62 stood stunned.

Neetriht and Taramat took every opportunity as the expedition continued to talk among all the members who witnessed the courtship rights. They implied, cajoled, suggested in order to build the albino status to almost a religious aspect. Purity became a daily reference to Abaddon, which connected to Akama, associating him with purity as well. Whenever they visited a new tribe, the two would hear various members reciting the story to any individual in the tribe who would listen. They repeated the account over and over and over. Of course, Abaddon now rode the regal elk to the right of the Thana as part of the parade when the expedition arrived at each Gugwe settlement. Such a place of honor could not be mistaken.

Lakes and rivers filled the land they traversed. Rocky outcroppings jutted out in various shapes. The scenery was most enjoyable as they made their way to Bear Ridge. When the 26/62 reached the mountain foothills, the boreal forest grew thick.

Abaddon now joined Akama when he met with a tribal KuRuk. She was in attendance when Zilla told him about the Goblin Queen and Prince's visit a few weeks before. Zilla disclosed he had sent his sister, Lilleth, as a guide. He revealed the instructions he had given Lilleth to delay their progress as much as possible until he could warn Thana NukPana of the goblin's plan.

Pleased with Zilla's forewarning, Thana NukPana invited the Bear Ridge KuRuk to travel with them for the rest of the expedition's tour. The Gugwe Nation would expect him, as with all the KuRuks at Thrall Lake's gathering, but an invitation to travel with the emperor was a significant distinction. Akama suggested Zilla could bring three attendants with him. The Bear Ridge KuRuk made a big show of thanking the Thana NukPana for such a privilege. He snuck a look over his shoulder at the exotic albino seated next to the emperor and excused himself to prepare to travel in the morning.

"He is dangerous," Akama said in a low voice intended only for Nevele to hear. Nevele grunted. "Watch him closely," the Thana suggested. Nevele gripped the handles of the knives sheathed at his waist, eyes following Zilla's silhouette as he made his way across the camp.

The weather stayed unseasonably warm for early fall. The 26/62, now the 26/66, moved along the northern shore of Sapphire Lake, where Thana NukPana swam every day along the route. Curious about this habit, Abaddon followed him down to the water's edge and into the cold water. Her heart nearly stopped as she hurried to get out. A rolling wave crashed onto the shore, drenching her. Her teeth chattered, body shivering, skin pebbling over with bumps. Akama stood, waves hitting his back as he stared at the pale figure. The cold had made her nipples stand up, and they protruded suggestively. He found he was powerless to move, lust filling his being. When Neetriht came running through the sand, a blanket in hand, she was screaming at the girl. "What were you thinking?" Quickly, she wrapped the albino girl up and led her away from the water's edge.

Akama didn't know what Abaddon was thinking, but he certainly knew the thoughts he had entertained. His blood was boiling through his body, so he dipped his head under once more before he got out of the freezing water. His entire body ached with the physical pain of restraint.

Silver Valley was a beautiful village. The Gugwe Tribe maintained a large settlement with a population to match. They had dug into the areas surrounding the rocky outcroppings to create their shelters. The village had sprung up around a large lake. Silver veins had been discovered on the eastern side of the lake, and the tribe had been mining the ore for years now. When the tribe artisans melted the metal down, it was used to make many things for the tribe. Taramat and Neetriht met with the women to discuss coming to Thrall Lake. They explained how they could trade the silver beads used to make jewelry and clothing embellishments.

Taramat agreed to make an additional map for one of the Cobalt villagers in trade for a large sack full of silver and Silver Valley beads.

"What are you going to do with the beads, Taramat?" Nevele asked her as she sat on the floor of Thana's yurt sorting them according to size and type. "You don't seem like a female who would bother to wear jewelry," he teased her.

She was up and face to face with the bodyguard in a flash. She ran a blue-stained finger along the length of his jaw. "How would you know what I like, Nevele Vutova?" she purred.

"I've known you my whole life, Taramat," he explained.

"And..." she taunted, running a red-dyed finger along the other side of his jaw.

"So...I know you. We grew up together," he offered, feeling the heat between the two of them.

Taramat pushed the ruff out along her mane. He huffed at her as she used that blue finger to trail down the middle of his chest and move along his stomach. She splayed a hand on his hip, pushed it around, gently grasping his buttocks.

"Taramat," his voice broke.

"Just so we understand one another, Nevele," her voice breathy, "*you* don't know what I like." She disengaged so quickly that when she stepped back, he could feel cold air rise between them. A drop of sweat falling from his forehead hit the floor of the yurt.

She took her time strolling back to where she had been sorting beads and casually threw back at him. "FYI, Nevele. It might surprise you how delighted I would be to receive a gift of jewelry from the right person." She smiled and licked her lips suggestively. The next hour passed slowly for Nevele, as he stared at the curve of her back while she divvied up her beads into piles without another word.

Deciduous trees covered the terrain, bursting in a riot of color as the days moved further into autumn. Reds, oranges, crimson, yellows, browns, and a ripple of green hues splashed across the upper canopy; the forest floor was a palette of fallen leaves. Taramat had taken to spending any time when they weren't traveling, laying on the floor of Akama's tent with her paints, making maps. If she wasn't mixing paints or using them to create her beautiful artwork, she was sorting beads. Flat on her stomach, she had a habit of lifting her lower legs, bent at the knee, and sliding them back and forth, like a rocking motion while she worked. It made Nevele crazy. Every once in a while, she would throw him a coy smile. It was as if she knew exactly what she was doing. Exactly what he was thinking. Then she would ignore him again for hours. The only break he got from this torture was his daily workout and weapons practice with the Thana.

Abaddon pushed open the flap across the entrance, poked her head in, and used her hand to signal Taramat to follow. The two of them left with their heads together, whispering. Nevele saw them dodge into Neetriht's tent. They didn't emerge again until the dinner call. This became a pattern. He couldn't imagine what they did inside for hours at a time.

When the 26/66 finally reached the Bull Moose Tribe, whose home settled on the edge of an enormous bay, they found the land leading up to it conveniently flat for water access. Along the large basin of water, the shoreline was a combination of stones and sand. The main part of the village was at the mouth of the Bull Moose River, which ran out of the bay. The tribal visit went well. They made plans to take the Thana NukPana and his team across the bay by boat to save the entourage travel time. It had already started snowing on and off over the past week. They wanted to take advantage of the open water. Bull Moose's KuRuk filled Thana in on the visit his tribe had from the Goblin's cabal. The KuRuk told him that by the time Thana reached Vattusk, the Goblins would have already headed for Thrall Lake. The chance of his path crossing with the Goblin Queen's was slim. It was clear the Bull Moose KuRuk despised the Queen. He did nothing to hide those feelings.

The Bull Moose boats used to transport the crowd across the bay to Vattusk were wide and fairly flat-bottomed. By now, the 26/66 had experience in quickly constructing temporary corrals for their mounts. The distress of Abaddon's elk was clear as he bugled back and forth with the caribou while on the water. It was Abaddon who came up with a solution. She cut soft strips of material from a blanket and blindfolded the caribou and then, her own Frost, as she spoke soothing words to him. He quieted. She frequently checked on the animals, keeping them calm for the rest of the day. The boats sheltered at night, slipping into a deep cove next to a small island and anchoring not quite one third of the way across to their destination.

Akama had taken to strolling around the deck with Abaddon on his arm. They talked the hours away, getting to know one another. He found her to be very intelligent, if somewhat naïve from lack of exposure to other Gugwe. The females had sectioned off a corner of each transport and spent hours doing who knows what behind their curtains.

On the last night on board, the Bull Moose KuRuk had navigated their water transports into another inlet off a small, but tall, wide rock island. In the wee hours of the night, a sound he dreaded ripped Akama from sleep and a pleasant dream. Abaddon's blood-curdling scream echoed across the lake.

She had simply wanted to get off the water for a few hours, just to feel the steady ground beneath her feet again. The idea struck her to scramble off the transport, so she wrapped in her blankets, planning to sleep blissfully on the rock island, then return to the raft before anyone woke.

Akama rushed toward the screams. His eyes took in a scene that almost stopped his heart. There on the shore stood a polar bear. The bruin was at least three heads taller than the Thana. The fierce bear roared in answer to

Abaddon's screams. Nevele rushed to Akama's side, tossed him a long spear, gripping one of his own.

The emperor took a running start over the side of the watercraft, Nevele a shadow behind him. Akama waved to his bodyguard to keep back. The bear's bellowing riled Frost and the caribou, setting off a sound cacophony that hurt the ears. The blindfolded animals were stomping hooves in a panic. They could smell the predator. Other members of the expedition team struggled to keep the corral railings intact and to calm the animals.

The polar reached for Abaddon, but she ducked and rolled, just as Akama landed on the ground and ran straight for the monstrous carnivore. Akama's feet left the ground, the spear pointed straight, shifting his feet, throwing them up in front of him, so the momentum would carry him forward like an arrow. The heels of his clawed feet hit the animal first. When he struck the massive body, he used the force to propel the spear up under the jaw, right out of the eye, the barbed tip of the spear hooking around the socket bone. Releasing the shaft, Akama's body crashed to the rocky ground.

The polar bear thrashed, roared, swatting at the spear, which tore at the eye and moved against the brain in brutal, excruciating pain. The bear, blinded by rage and agony, lost its footing, the weight of the animal making it topple over the edge of the cliff. It landed face down, fifteen feet below, and didn't move.

Abaddon ran to Akama, taking him in her arms, searching him for injury, tears spilling down her pale cheeks, glistening in her white lashes like morning dew.

Nevele launched himself over the rail and made his way down to the bear. He found the beast bleeding out, stomach punched open by a sharp stalagmite where it had formed at the edge of a cave. There was a matching stalactite straight above, depositing drips of water to create the mirror image with its lower twin.

Taramat joined Nevele, inspecting the bear, as he prodded it with his spear to be sure the beast wasn't getting up again. She whispered to Nevele so that no one on the boat could hear, and he nodded in agreement.

The animals on the small deck quieted, and the 26/66 drifted back to their sleep. Akama settled Abaddon in with Neetriht with a promise to sleep outside their curtained shelter. For once, Neetriht didn't interfere when the albino gifted him with a deep kiss, filled with promise.

The sun rose in the blue sky a few hours later. The 26/66 was shocked to find the beach level filled with walruses, the polar bear's body gone. It was the shamans who bowed low to the Thana NukPana. He had magic; they declared.

The Bull Moose landed the watercraft near Vattusk. They would wait there until the Silver Valley KuRuk arrived. The two groups would travel together, along with the Vattusk KuRuk's group. All would meet up with the Thana NukPana at Thrall Lake after his visit to the BloodKnife village. The Vattusk KuRuk was very pleased with the map Taramat had made for him. He spent several hours with her each day. The two of them worked to create a special map. A chart was necessary to maneuver through the hundreds of lakes, rivers, and marshlands as the troop headed west to BloodKnife territory. It was a dangerous maze where even those experienced in traversing the water-labyrinth could meet their death. The days passed quickly. It was easy to fill every minute with the daily training, hunting, prepping stores, and re-supplying for the last major leg of the journey. Discussions with the attending KuRuks, talk of trade, brainstorming on how slaves could improve the lives of the Gugwe tribes. Akama was pleased to find Neetriht meeting with them. Interest grew as she held discussions on leadership, swapped ideas on new ways of governing to improve the lives of each tribe. She was careful to take into consideration each tribe's unique resources and environment.

Thana took notice one afternoon that Nevele had gone off somewhere with Taramat. He asked the bodyguard about his absence later that same evening.

"I am helping Taramat with one of her projects. She needs some extra muscle sometimes," he told Akama. It wasn't mentioned again. The Thana approved of Taramat and Neetriht's projects, whatever they were. They typically made him look good.

At sunrise, the day before the expedition was to depart, Akama woke early. He could see his betrothed riding Frost along the bay shoreline, weaving a trail around groups of walruses. She looked tiny against the vast body of water. He growled in irritation, thinking, *didn't she learn how dangerous these waters are? She has not yet learned to fear the unknown.*

Neetriht approached with the shaman, Yorgan. "Look, Akama, Abaddon heads for a colony of seals, see?"

"We must stop her and fetch her back," Akama answered under his breath.

Yorgan heard and countered, "The seals will not hurt her."

"What?" Akama said. He watched, horrified, as she dismounted Frost and walked out to the colony. The females lounged about while all the younglings slid down smooth rock slides and rode the water current around a bend, only to climb out and up to do it over again. The sun was fully up now, and he watched, helpless, as Abaddon, fearless, lay down near one of the larger cows. There was a group of them together, sunning on the warm rock ledges. It almost looked like she was talking to the smooth-skinned animals. The female rolled and slid into the water, changing before their eyes. She swept her long black hair off her face and motioned to Abaddon to join her in the water.

To Akama's great relief, Abaddon waved and walked back to Frost, mounted and headed back toward camp.

"What did I just see?" he asked aloud to no one in particular.

It was Yorgan who answered. "Selkies. I believe she has made friends with a selkie. Abaddon never ceases to amaze," he commented as he walked back across the camp.

CHAPTER 27: Circle of Power

When Faith returned to the Stone House, she hung back, leaning against the dry-stack stone wall, her sketchbook held tight to her chest. Dedo was sitting on top, arms wrapped around his knees, where his chin rested. Garrett approached from the side, having slipped out of the shed to enjoy the early afternoon sun.

Faith covered her ears with both hands, asking Dedo, "Now what?" Her question was regarding the Pureheart sisters surrounding Carlisse, all of them screaming at her. Raven and the lads stood ten feet away under the old oak. Carlisse wasn't reacting to the discord, calmly standing with her hands clasped behind her back.

It was Garrett who answered Faith's question. He sighed heavily. Standing behind Faith, he wrapped his arms around her shoulders and rested his chin on her head. "Everyone was packing up camp when Carlisse announced to her sisters she wouldn't be going with us."

"So, Carlisse is staying on at Edgewood, as well as Delainey?" Faith guessed.

"If only," Garrett said. "There wouldn't be this big fight if that were the case. No," Garrett corrected. "Carlisse told them Raven invited her to go with him and the lads to check on Robin's clan, see what's what. Maybe they'll lead some more goblins back here, if there are those that want to settle in or go on to the moot. Raven wants her to act as a Fae emissary to the clan. It will also give her a chance to check in with their parents. Raven's group plans to catch up with us later at the moot. 'Mother Aliah' is not taking it well," he concluded.

"Actually, I think Carlisse acting as a Fae Emissary is a great idea," Faith considered.

"My advice?" Garrett offered, "Keep that opinion to yourself for the time being."

"I couldn't have offered better advice myself, Foxfire," Dedo praised.

"Been doing some drawing?" Garrett nodded towards Faith's pad.

Caught up in the Pureheart drama, she handed her sketches to Garrett without a word. He thumbed through, not paying much attention to the sisters. He'd seen them fight lots of times.

Val stepped up to Carlisse and tapped her shoulder for emphasis with each word she said, "Don't. You. Go. Anywhere! We're not done with you yet, missy!"

Faith could tell Carlisse was fighting the urge to laugh at Val's order, but she held it in. Faith and Garrett had witnessed similar scenes between the sisters over the years, but Val was usually the recipient of sisterly direction. Clearly, Val was enjoying the shoe being on the other foot. Dedo reached up to the apple tree, picked two apples, handing one each to his current companions. He plucked another for himself and settled in to watch the drama play out.

"Oh, this should be good." Dedo muttered as he watched Aliah, Val, and Delainey turn as one and stomp over to Raven.

"Ladies," Raven nodded his head as a greeting.

"Don't try pulling that polite crap to disarm this mess you've created," Val stated.

Raven wanted to roll his eyes, but wisely resisted. "I think there's a misunderstanding," he suggested.

Delainey prodded, "Tell us what we don't understand about our sister, a lone female, traveling with 13 male goblins for weeks and weeks?"

Raven, hand in his pocket, took up his worry stone and rubbed his thumb along the smooth stone as he calmly defended. "Carlisse is going to play a role never done before. She'll be the first Fae emissary to approach a goblin clan. I believe in her. She's up to the task. The clan will respect her, and once they get to know her, they can't help but love her. It was her decision to accept the role. The lads and I will make sure she's safe. The plan is to meet up with you again after we settle things with the clan. Do you have any messages you want her to deliver to your parents? She plans to visit them. The clan isn't located very far away from your home, yeah?" Raven's worry stone grew warm under his thumb.

Delainey let all her anger sputter away. She'd made her own decision recently and recognized Carlisse had a right to do the same. "Good answer,

Raven. I'm just going to go back to the Stone House to write a quick letter Carlisse can take to my mam and da."

She scurried away, winking at Carlisse as she headed to the house, before her other sisters could stop her getaway. Delainey has already experienced her own toe-to-toe, nose-to-nose with Aliah. Their older sister was always trying to step into the mother role, and that included Delainey's own decision to stay on with the Dream Weaver in the Edgewood.

"That was a fine speech, but..." Val reached for Raven, but Aliah grabbed her arm.

"I think we'd better go write our own letters to Mam and Da before Raven is ready to leave, don't you, Val?"

Val snapped out her wings in response and flew in the opposite direction, fury on her face.

Tossing her apple core over her shoulder into the long grass, Faith said, "Glad that's over." She beamed at Garrett, holding her hand out for her book.

"Really nice portraits," he told her.

"Dedo described my mother and father to me." She glanced up at the gargoyle.

"You drew that kind of detail from verbal descriptions?" he raised his eyebrows.

She shrugged in response.

"Guess I'll go see if I can calm Aliah down." He pocketed his apple core to give to a horse later.

Robin and Caz were coming toward her, so Faith waited. "I can see you don't want to get on the Pureheart sister's bad side," Caz joked.

Faith laughed. Caz stopped and leaned back against the rock wall. Robin kept moving on down the lane. "I'm going to check on Val. She seemed really upset, yeah?" He didn't wait for anyone's response. Faith watched him as he headed toward the orchards.

"Come on, Caz. Let's finish getting our stuff together. I want to set out right after supper, taking advantage of the full moon's light. We'll leave Delainey with all the washing up. Serves her right after that little scene. I'm sure some comeuppance will present itself to Aliah and Val sometime soon for their penance."

"You don't have an issue with Carlisse going with the lads?" Cazzidy voiced his curiosity.

"None whatsoever," she assured him. "I think it's a great opportunity for Carlisse. Raven's right. Your clan will love her."

Caz smiled, not sure why her answer pleased him so much.

Faith called back to Dedo over her shoulder. "Dedo, I left a little surprise for you in the King's shed."

Dedo's short legs pushed off the stone wall, his wings snapped open, muscled body tense as he flew to the King's shed. He ripped the 'WET PAINT' sign off the door, turned the handle, and let it swing in on creaky hinges. Lenny and Lester were lounging in their usual spot, chins in their hands, studying the freshly painted floor.

"Took you long enough to get here," Lenny quipped.

"Don't walk on the floor yet. Paint might still be drying," Lester warned.

Dedo took up his brooding watcher stance, chin on his knees at the threshold. Three gargoyles scrutinized the colorful artwork on the shed floor. A clock ticking filled their senses.

The princess had painted a replica, well, a reproduction with additional enhancements. It was a painting of the compass in Robert's fortress. The same as the one in the Fae Palace on Sapphire Lake. A depiction she had rendered from the sketch she'd created by Dedo's verbal description. Though she hadn't seen it, another compass was at her Aunt Mari's, whom she hadn't met yet. The illustration was a perfect match, vibrant with color.

"Where'd she get the paints?" Dedo asked.

"The Weaver," the Kings replied in tandem.

"Do you think it works?" Dedo speculated.

"I'd bet my life on it," Lester assured him.

"What do you think she intends? She merely said she'd left a surprise for me here."

"The Princess," her title emphasized by Lenny, "has asked us to inform you she wants you to travel ahead to Mari's. She has requested that you let her Aunt Mari know she'll be arriving there soon with a group. In addition, she expects you to locate her cousin's, if they are not at Mari's. She intends to make her relatives part of her entourage at the moot."

"Ridiculous!" Dedo grumbled. "I need to stay with her, not go running off on some wild-goose chase she's dreamed up!" his voice rising.

Lenny and Lester looked at one another. "The two of us dreamed the wild-goose chase up," Lester informed him.

"You will do as the princess has requested. I believe you were on your way to Mari's when she had us send you the message where she requested your presence after your last 'head-butt' with her. I'm sure you recall how that turned out?" Lenny reminded him.

"Perhaps it hasn't dawned on you yet, Dedo," Lester prodded. "The ruse we have been playing at for the last several years, *before we revealed it to the Princess,* requires a reminder? We are the kings of the gargoyles. Remember, it was a *temporary role* we designed, *where we allowed you to appear to be running things?*" Lester's eyebrows rose, and his black eyes drilled into Dedo's own. "Well, the jig's up. We've taken back our true station. You. Will. Take. Yours. Back. As. Well. It that clear?"

"Crystal." Dedo bristled, reached out and touched the compass depiction of Mari's cottage, disappearing without another word.

"That was rude, don't you agree, brother?" Lenny snorted.

"He's lucky Mari's symbol was dry. There would have been hell to pay if he had smeared the paint," Lester said.

"I don't think he noticed she added a map all around the compass, showing all of Sharas and Adana, depicting the 13 Gugwe villages, do you?"

"Doubtful. Dedo, who is always wrapped up in his own interests, lacks a certain savvy to pick up on the princess's crafty artwork. Let's go sit on the roof and watch all the action while everyone is packing up, shall we?"

Both kings touched a hearthstone and popped out of the shed.

THE SUNSET BLAZED RED-orange across the horizon. Raven found the same sisters who had been screaming at one another hours earlier were now hugging and sniffling a tearful goodbye. Raven and the lads couldn't believe the change. Faith and Caz stood talking to Saffron and Rolland, listening to their enthusiastic plans for the Village of Edgewood. Caz reminded Rolland how important his weapon making would be. The two of them worked out a future schedule of how, when, and where Rolland would deliver the first order. Robin had provided several pouches of goblin-mined diamonds so that Rolland could purchase a large amount of the metals and supplies he would need to make the weapons. Rolland had his own bankroll to start up his smithy business from the sale of the weapons cache the goblin queen had paid.

Raven and Carlisse joined the conversation. Raven told Caz that at least five of the lads planned to stay here after they returned from checking in on the clan. The lads had asked to apprentice with Rolland. One person couldn't make enough weapons for what would likely turn into a war with the Gugwe. Caz nodded his approval.

The Stone House kitchen had been running twenty-four hours a day since Faith had announced the camp would break up. Delainey had been preparing travel food. She was busy now divvying up food packages for Raven and Carlisse's crew, as well as Faith and Robin's travel companions. Since training had officially ended, the teams were changing. Raven and the lads stuck with the team name 'Goodfellow's Gang', proudly showing off the tattoos identifying their camaraderie. It appeared there was little support for Queen Morveena and none for Rupert.

Saffron, Rolland, and Delainey adopted a new mantle, calling themselves 'The Dreamers', to Ari's delight.

After a few verbal exchanges, the companions traveling to the mid-lands—Faith, Val, Robin, Caz, Aliah, and Garrett—all agreed to adopt 'The Gugwe's Bane'. Though Alto would travel with them, he didn't take on the team's mantle. Val thanked Faith for sending Dedo ahead, as she had dreaded the idea of traveling with 'that little spy', as she dubbed him. Garrett rolled his eyes, which earned him a punch on the shoulder. When the sun sank below the horizon, a parade trudged up the switchback. Saffron's voice carried them up and out of the Dream Weaver's valley as she sang them 'A Song of Leaving'.

You left me on the road today,
My fist held to my heart.

I'll count the risings of the sun
As long as we're apart.
If you see a shooting star, know I'm watching from afar.
Every sunset that goes down,
I'll listen for your footsteps
Upon the ground.
If you see a shooting star, know I'm watching from afar.
When I watch the night sky,
A whispered wish I'll send to you.
Come back to me, and we'll build anew.
If you see a shooting star, know I'm watching from afar.
I hope our paths cross again someday.
Perhaps your dreams will turn my way.
I'll be here. Come and stay.
If you see a shooting star, know I'm watching from afar.
If you see a shooting star, know I'm watching from afar.

WHEN THE LAST OF THE travelers reached the top, they lined the edge of the ridge and waved to those remaining below. Without another word, they split, one group going north, the other drifting south, twilight falling over their shadows.

SHORTLY AFTER MIDNIGHT, Robin called for a halt. They needed a rest and some food. Faith had wanted to travel at night to avoid contact with anyone until she could meet her other relatives. Though they were all strong and fit from their training, it would take some time for them to develop a smooth system for rough travel.

Val and Aliah had worked with Delainey to ready the travel food. They knew what they could prepare for a quick and easy dinner. Lainey had put together a picnic of three cheeses, fresh bread, and sweet hand pies, wrapped in cheesecloth. Garrett was on his third pie when Val pointed up to the night sky. "Look!" she shouted to the group.

The travel companions all turned their eyes up, rewarded with a turbulent light show as it shimmered, skidded, and danced. Painted across the sky was a palette of bright hues of green, silver, and blue. The aurora borealis was out in full force.

A loud grunt came from Garrett. Anyone who turned to see what caused it found Garrett in Fox-form. The Northern Lights danced in his eyes. A moment later, his wings shot out, and he was racing to the top of a hill to get a closer look at the phenomenon. When he stood atop the rocky knoll, a stabbing headache nearly undid him. The fox closed his eyes against the rain of colored, shifting lights.

A vision passed through his mind, the background bouncing with the Aurora's colored shimmers. The face of a huge Gugwe zoomed in close. "Who's there?" the monster growled at him, making his fox-form scramble back.

Aliah touched his furred leg. He could hear her voice, but it sounded far away. "Garrett! Garrett, are you alright?" The next thing he knew, he was flat on his back, stretched out in his man-form, with six pairs of eyes staring down at him.

"What happened?" he asked, blinking his eyes. The color show was over, but a sparkling Milky Way still filled the sky. He honed in on the Big Dipper to ground himself.

"We were hoping you could tell us. What happened to you?" Aliah said softly.

"I don't know exactly. I turned to see the Northern Lights when Val called attention to them. Then the lights seemed to trigger something in my brain," Garrett recalled.

"I told you he was a Foxfire," Caz said quietly to Robin. "Pay up." He held his hand out in expectation.

Aliah's voice wound up as she admonished the two goblins, "You're kidding, right? Tell me the two of you aren't placing bets about Garrett's condition!" She yelled, letting her anger win over.

"We didn't mean any harm by it, Lia," Caz assured her. "Sides, we placed the bet when he first shifted, not tonight. Did you mean to say 'condition' or gift'?"

She tsked at him with disgust. Val shook her head at him.

"What?" he demanded. Alto came close and held his hand out to Robin, too.

They left Garrett and Aliah alone as the group went back to organizing their supplies, getting ready to continue on. Aliah offered her hand out to Garrett. He took it and pulled himself up, a wave of dizziness, an aftereffect, making him steady his stance. "Aliah," he whispered, "I don't want anyone else to know." He looked around to be sure that none of the others could hear.

"You know you can trust me with your secrets, Garrett," Aliah assured him.

"I...I had a weird vision. The lights...the lights had something to do with it," he confessed. "What does Caz mean? I'm a Foxfire?"

"Don't pay any attention to that nonsense," she told him. "A foxfire is an old legend. I'll explain it in detail later. The lore connected a fox shifter to the Northern Lights. The fable granted the Foxfire special powers. Vulpes vulpes is associated with wisdom and cunning. Some think of them as tricksters, but it's really just that they know the forest better than anyone else. Canids think fast and strategically. They are highly adaptable creatures. Your ability to shift at will between your man-form and your fox-form provides a unique ability. You could easily slip in and out of places, particularly places dangerous to anyone else. I've also heard foxes are seducers, able to captivate unwitting souls with their charm and good looks." Garrett blushed. Aliah whispered, "What did you see in your vision?"

He could see fear in her eyes, but relaxed when he noted it wasn't fear *of* him, but fear *for* him. "I saw a huge Gugwe, and it was like...well, like I was right there where he was and he..."

"What?" Her hand fluttered in front of her face.

"He came right up to my face and asked, 'Who's there', like he knew I was watching him." Aliah wrapped her arms around herself and shivered. "Don't tell anyone. Please Aliah. I need to figure out the whole fox-shifter thing first. Ok?"

"Your secret will stay just between us for now, Garrett. But you're probably going to need to confide in Faith at some point. Come on. Looks like everyone is ready to move out."

EVY, MARI, AND REATHA had formed a Ring of Power beneath the Northern Lights two nights before. They barely had time to throw a veil over the Foxfire shifter when he connected with the Gugwe Emperor. The trio had goosebumps when they saw the war paint, making the Thana NukPana look like a demon from hell, his face up close. So close, they got a whiff of his horrible breath.

"He could use his bad breath as a weapon if someone wasn't expecting it," Evy noted.

"Where do you think his haunting, painted look came from?" Mari wondered aloud.

Reatha speculated, "Probably something the Gugwe shamans came up with."

Evy settled into a rocking chair in the sitting room, twisting the silver ring on her finger. "Faith will be here soon. We'll need to give the foxfire some guidance, don't you think? I'm guessing at the latest they'll arrive in time for breakfast."

Dedo was watching from the fireplace mantel. He had arrived the day before. The goyle could hear huge rolling waves on the lake crashing onto the shoreline, a fierce wind blowing in from the west. "I don't think I've told you, Evy. Our princess informed me in no uncertain terms that she wants you to stop wearing that ring. She intends to reclaim it the next time she sees you."

Evy gave him a sour grimace in return for the information. He smirked, delighted at her reaction to the delivered message.

"Don't let it bother you now, Evy," Reatha comforted. "Let it play out, and we'll see what happens." She patted the old nurse on the shoulder.

"The girl is going to be full of questions, Mari," Reatha warned.

"I imagine so," Mari said, placing a hot cup of tea in front of Reatha and Evy.

"Dedo," Evy said, "shouldn't you have left an hour ago? You said the kings wanted you to locate Faith's cousins."

"No," he bristled with anger, "I said the kings told me the princess ordered me to *locate* her cousins."

"So touchy these days." Reatha sipped her tea.

"You ladies provided the information that they are currently at your brother Timmons. So, they've been located. Mission accomplished," he retorted.

The three looked at one another, joined hands. Mari pointed with her free hand and directed it straight at Dedo. "Semantics aside, gargoyle, you'll do as you were told." An invisible force of power zapped the small gargoyle in the ass. He touched a rock on the fireplace and disappeared with a huff.

All three women were sitting on the porch, enjoying the morning sun, when the small party of Fae and goblins rode into the clearing. The group carefully made its way through Mari's flower garden. Faith slipped off her horse, rushed up to hug Reatha and Evy.

"What a wonderful surprise! I didn't expect the two of you to be here. Is Uncle Robert with you? This must be my Aunt Mari? Did Dedo warn you we were coming? Would you like to meet some new friends I've made?"

Mari stood laughing at Faith's diatribe, holding her hands out. Faith took them. "Glad to meet you," Faith told her. "What a pleasure to find out I have other family!" she told Mari enthusiastically.

"I can't tell you how pleased I am to meet you, my dear. You look exactly like Aleta, you know. Let's get your horses settled and everyone washed up for a big breakfast, shall we? We would be delighted to meet all of your friends. I expect you have many questions you'd like answered. Am I right?"

After a quick introduction, Mari rattled off simple instructions to Robin. Val, Aliah, and Garrett gave a dutiful hug to Reatha and Evy. Reatha offered to show the new guests the cottages where they would stay. Mari walked Faith in the opposite direction, an arm around her shoulders, telling her Dedo was off to collect her cousins. She could expect them to arrive sometime tomorrow. Garrett rushed off to help Robin, Caz, and Alto with the horses, eager to get away from the old nurse's scrutiny. He felt like she was looking at him in a funny way, and he certainly wasn't ready to answer questions. Besides, she couldn't possibly know anything about his fox-shifting condition, he reasoned.

The breakfast was everything Faith could have dreamed of. A first meal with part of her actual family. Oh, Reatha was truly her aunt, but Mari was new and she kept pinching herself to be sure it wasn't a dream. There were bowls of fresh berries and clotted cream. The smell of cinnamon rolls wafted through the air. A large serving dish was filled with steaming scrambled eggs and chanterelle mushrooms. There was a bowl of soft cheese she had never had before. Mari set out an assortment of homemade jams. Strawberry, raspberry, grape, and pear honey are available for scones, hot out of the oven. When breakfast was over, Reatha asked for volunteers to refill the fireplace woodpile. Caz, Alto, and Garrett jumped at the task. Aliah was helping Evy with clean up in the kitchen, talking softly about home.

Faith stood at the cottage window, watching as Robin and Val walked down Mari's garden path to the beach. It was too cold now to swim, but they strolled along the water's edge in their bare feet.

"Faith?" Mari called.

"Oh, sorry, Auntie, I was just admiring your garden."

"Indeed." Her eyes followed Faith's line of sight. "Reatha told me about the unfortunate circumstances of your first meeting with your cousins. I hope you don't have reservations about seeing them all again."

"Not at all, Aunt Mari," Faith assured her. "At the time, I didn't know what was happening to me. I wasn't prepared. It was confusing, a shock really, to find out I had other family, much less that I was a Fae." She swallowed hard. "And then the whole princess thing. I know a lot more now. It would have been nice to have been able to grow up with all my cousins. I guess I understand why it was all kept secret from me. But the timing was awkward for my wings to come out right when I was just meeting them. I was sure at the time they would all think of me as some kind of freak."

Mari patted her hand. "Yes, I'm sure you've learned much over the past several months. Just as I am positive, there is still much more for you to discover about yourself and the world." Mari twisted the silver ring she wore on her right forefinger. Faith noticed.

"Aunt Mari, are you wearing Nursie's ring?"

"No, this is my own. Both my sisters have rings just like this one."

Faith's forehead wrinkled in deep thought. She held out her hand. "I have one, too. Are they all linked?" she wondered aloud.

"The answer is yes, but not in the way you're thinking," Mari suggested.

"I don't understand," Faith admitted.

"You couldn't, dear. Here, sit." She invited Faith to make herself comfortable on an oversized chair upholstered in a cloth fabric covered in yellow flowers. "My sister," Mari started, but laughed lightly. "Your mother," Mari clarified, "was incredibly talented at making magical things. When we were teens, she made Reatha and me the second and third of her rings. Aleta holds the original. You have one, as Evy does. Likely, you didn't notice with everything happening back at your Spring Feast. Your female cousins, Mariella, and Brittany, wear the silver rings as well."

"You said Nursie has one ring too, Aunt Mari. She's not actually related to us, right?"

"In principle, you're correct, Faith. However, Evy has been a part of our family for as long as I can remember. She was the nanny to me and my sisters long before she took care of you."

Wonder bloomed on Faith's face. "My mother's nurse was yours too?"

"Of course. Evy helped raise all of us. She was Aleta's, mine, and Reatha's nurse. Aleta gave a ring to Evy to help her keep track of her charges. Your mother had planned to have more children, you see. She asked Evy to use the ring as her own, but to keep it in trust for another daughter. Told her she would know when the time was right to pass it along. Then your mother disappeared, so Evy has worn it ever since. Well, mostly. She keeps in safely tucked away in a silk bag in her waist pouch, not being much of a woman for embellishments."

"I see," Faith said to herself. She could hardly demand the ring back from the old nurse now. Not if her mother had given it to her. Maybe she could just get Evy to promise not to use it to track her from now on. Surely, such a request wouldn't be out of line? She looked up and saw Nursie standing in the dining room, looking out at the lake. Her eyes followed the nurse's. Faith could see Val and Robin making their way along the shore, laughing at some private joke.

"What do you know about the Gargoyle Kings?" Faith brought her attention back to her aunt.

THE DAY PASSED QUICKLY. After dinner, the group couldn't stop yawning, having been on a timetable of traveling at night and sleeping during the day. They all turned in early. When Faith's cousins reappeared tomorrow, they would be well rested.

"Hey, before we go to bed," Val said, "come on down to the beach. I want to show you something." The crew followed Val out to the water's edge, but Alto hung back.

Alto startled when he realized the old nurse sat quietly on the porch, her chair in the corner. "Playing devil's advocate is an important role, Alto. You'll come to realize how important in the near future." She rocked in the chair, never taking her eyes off the half-dozen beachcombers. Watching, she saw Val run backward, dragging her toes through the sand. Bioluminescence kicked up, sparkling in the moonlight.

"Did Faith tell you what happened?"

"There was no need," the Nurse responded.

Creeped out, Alto excused himself, wished her good night, thanked Mari and Reatha for the wonderful meal as he passed through the living room. Alto sought the guest cottage he was sharing with the other males.

The following day, Faith was truly pleased to connect with her cousins again. This time, everyone let their guard down and just enjoyed the company.

Travis and Cazzidy made bets about everything, both coming out about equal as winners. Dedo was sulky and stuck to the fireplace mantel, where he could disappear at the snap of your fingers. The females ended up in one of the guest cottages, where they barred any of the males from entering.

Faith noticed Val had a silver ring on, grabbed her hand, asking her where she'd gotten it. Val explained, "I always thought the old biddy hated me, but your stern nurse told me, since you and I claim each other as sisters, I should have the ring." Val showed her named-sister a wide grin. "Cool, huh? Now we have matching rings!" Faith's eyes grew big as saucers at the revelation.

Kris connected with Evy and Aliah. They fell into a discussion about visions. The big surprise came around dinnertime, when two of Faith's uncles arrived unexpectedly. She met Timmon and Jak with wide eyes. Lively conversation accompanied the meal, with stories of younger years. The room was often shaken by the laughter of Fae, goblins, and humans together. Faith was very pleased when her uncles offered to go to the moot to help them organize and set up. Preparations would need to be done, Jak told them, if they were inviting all kinds of people. Timmon put in that there was no way for any of them to know how many would show up. It would be important to prepare to make a good first impression.

The moon came up full.

"It's time," Mari announced.

"Time for bed already?" Faith complained, "But I have more questions." The room exploded with laughter.

Jak told Mari that he, Timmon, and the lads would stand turns keeping a watch to make sure the women would not be interrupted.

"No interruptions to what?" Val asked.

"The Circle of Power," Reatha answered. Val's eyes turned to meet Faith's.

"Mother," Mariella scolded, "you're causing Faith and Val anxiety with your secretive suggestions! Please explain."

Mari looked surprised. "Oh, sorry, dears. The Circle of Power is a female Fae rite of passage. It should have been done when you were a baby, Faith, but circumstances didn't allow. This is a ceremony for women only. The lads can all stay here while we're about it. I see our young Travis pulling out a deck of cards. Don't play with him for money!" she warned the other guests. Laughter lightened the moment.

"Excuse me, Mari?" Aliah said in a quiet voice. "None of the Purehearts were ever involved in a Circle of Power rite of passage, either. We were all adopted, you see. Besides Faith, Reatha, Evy, me and my sisters, everyone else that lives at Robert's hold is human." Her face wore a look of hope.

"Follow me," Mari invited all the girls. "There's no time like the present to fix a wrong and perform the ceremony for any who need it." The line moved out the back door into the gardens and through Mari's hedges. They wove their way between the cleverly trimmed bushes, passing along the thread of a labyrinth formed by thick greenery. In the very center was a smooth marble statue. A stone-form of a girl. Her nude body stood frozen in a graceful pose, hair cascading down her arched back, stretching on tiptoe, one arm raised straight out, the other hand reaching up, just able to grab the star she held in her fingertips. It appeared as though she were plucking it out of the sky. Reatha told the girls that Aleta had created the sculpture. One of many artistic media forms she tried over the years. The smooth marble drew Val. When she reached up and touched the star, a ripple of power spiked through her body, and a disembodied voice called out to her, "Daughter?" Val sucked in her breath. But before she could say anything or tell anyone, Reatha called her back. Organized in a circle, Aliah, Mariella, Brittany, Mari, and Reatha waited. Aliah and Val did the ceremony together, holding hands.

When it was Faith's turn, Reatha instructed Faith to kneel before the statue, the moon's beam spot-lighting her. All the females joined hands, surrounding Faith. Mari spoke, her voice sounding far away. What she was saying seemed like something Faith had heard before, but she just couldn't hold the words in her mind. The circle moved right in a full turn, then left for two and back to the right again, as if they were moving the tumblers to unlock a safe. When the circle stopped, Mari's voice fell silent. Faith floated in the abyss of the night sky, filled with Milky Way stars, held firmly in place under the moon's beam. She had an image of her mother grasping the silvery star between her fingers and pressing it into Faith's skin below her left breast. Lightning burst forth and connected every woman in the circle. The star burned like the dickens. Faith's screams filled the night air. She thought she heard an urethral voice say, "This isn't right." Then she fainted dead away.

When Faith next awoke, she was in the guest cottage, felt warm and safe under a pile of blankets, Val snoring next to her. She quietly pulled the covers down to look at the burn she remembered from the ceremony. It surprised her to find a tiny star under her breast, but her skin was whole and smooth, not burned. She'd had the marking ever since she could remember. It wasn't anything new. Had she dreamed it all? Val turned over and mumbled in her sleep, "Circle of Power."

Faith shivered.

At breakfast, Faith arrived before everyone else and found Nursie alone, sipping a cup of tea. Evy gave Faith the once-over. "Are you well this morning, Faith? Mari said you fainted dead away at the ritual last night."

"I have no memory of leaving the garden or going to bed," Faith ventured. "It feels strange, like I lost several hours somehow. Evy, could you answer a question I have about last night's ceremony?"

"Asking never hurts. Sometimes the answers do," Evy replied, holding her cup with both hands to warm them. "What do you want to know?"

"Um...well, I was curious..."

"Have you developed Master Garrett's affliction of stuttering out your words?"

"Sorry," Faith began again, "I don't remember all of last night. I recall a weird vision of the statue in the garden pressing the star she'd pulled from the sky...here." Faith pointed to a spot under her left breast. "I thought it burned me and left the shape marked on my skin. Then, lightning burst out from the star and connected to every woman in the circle. Did that really happen, or did I just imagine it all?" She asked, sweat beading on her forehead.

"Nothing wrong with a vivid imagination, but that was all it could have been. It's been a while since I've attended one, but the ritual is fairly simple—in this case, one that celebrates a coming of age, so to speak, because you didn't have the ceremony as a babe. You must have been overexcited and simply fainted. After the Pureheart girls completed their rite of passage, Mari said Val, and her sister carried you back to your cottage. Why, I can't believe you never noticed it before, but you've had a mark there since birth, child. I should know. I've taken care of you ever since you were an infant." Evy smiled at her. "Perhaps your dream finally brought the birthmark to your notice?"

"I've been aware of the star-mark since I was four or five," Faith agreed, but her voice sounded skeptical. "I'm not sure what would have made me hallucinate during last night's ceremony." Besides, she thought to herself, she was an artist and had an eye for detail. Faith thought Nursie offering the idea that she wouldn't have noticed a small star-shaped marking on her body all these years was utter bullshit. She looked at Evy with slanted eyes and a question mark in the wrinkles of her forehead, but stayed quiet.

Grabbing a couple of apples from the big wooden bowl in the center of the table, Faith turned to pull the door open. "I think I'll take my breakfast out on the beach. I need some time to think."

CHAPTER 28: Every Last Detail

Garrett leaned back on his elbows, listening to the waves kiss the shoreline, the moon's shine lighting up the small crests. Most everyone had gone off to some special ceremony for Fae females, and every one of Garrett's instincts told him to stay away from that scene.

"May I join you, Master Garrett?"

Garrett started at the old nurse's voice. "Um...er...I..." he stammered.

"I'll take that as a yes, young man." Evy shook out a blanket she had carried over her arm and settled in on the sandy beach a foot away. She attempted to smile at Garrett to put him at ease, but it came off as a grimace. His eyes were as wide as the saucers in Mari's tea set.

"Don't be nervous, Garrett Emmon Gladheart. I've known you since you were a wee boy, and I know what it is to have secrets. I thought I would offer to tell you I am aware of your enigma and I want to share what I know of the Foxfire with you." The boy's face went through a series of expressions: from shocked to awed, then angry, and on to fearful. She nodded her head and continued, "Understand that I am happy to share what knowledge I have of the Foxfire, of your gift, but only if you'd like to hear it. Make no mistake, it is a gift, an old one to be sure, as well as rare."

It surprised Garrett when the older woman pulled a loop off each of her arms. A small pillow attached to the loops she had carried on her back, like a pack. Evy kicked off her shoes and peeled off her stockings. Wiggling her toes in the soft sand, she lay back, her head on the pillow, allowing her to take in a view of the moon softly glowing in the night sky. He could feel the weight of the silence between them. His mind a whirlwind of thoughts, he considered that this was the very opportunity he had hoped for. A chance to find out more about the changes that had come over him. More so because he trusted the nurse, even though he was slightly afraid of her. She might be a stern woman, but he had always found her reliable from a young age.

Garrett swallowed his fear. "I'd be grateful for any information you could share on the topic," he told her, meeting her eyes. Garrett turned to lie on his side, arm extended, using his elbow to prop up his head, the palm of his hand cupping his cheek. Evy sensed he had an open mind and was ready to listen.

Faith's nurse clasped her hands, resting them on her stomach, no mending to keep them busy, "Ah, Garrett," she began in a soft voice, "the Foxfire existed long before the Fae and the goblins came to these lands and that is to say, a very, very long time ago. You've got all the classic human features of a Foxfire shifter, you do. Red hair with black patches above your ears. Sharp nose and chin. Those sly eyes see more than you ever comment on. I expect you've guessed the connection you have with the Aurora Borealis? The change comes easily for you when the shimmers are on, but likely you haven't tried to change when there are no lights. I would speculate that when the Northern Lights are on, you sometimes change because you can't control it?"

Garrett nodded, surprised she knew. He felt embarrassed about his lack of control.

"Cast those worries away. My great-grandmother told me that if a Foxfire practiced changing back and forth at will, *especially when there were no lights* shimmering across the sky to enhance the gift, eventually the Foxfire would be able to master control of the change in all circumstances. *Her grandmother* told her that there are certain gifted creatures, shifters we call them. Besides their ability to shift, a handful of them could sometimes establish a link. A link that allowed two shifters to communicate over great distances. My advice to you, should you experience such a thing, would be to practice how to veil your mind. At least until you can determine who is communicating with you, *before* you permit the connection. It would be prudent to be sure it is safe to allow the mind-link. The veil can be useful to protect yourself, wouldn't you agree?"

Evy and Garrett spent the next hour reviewing her instructions on how to create, apply, and maintain a veil. Garrett practiced over and over as she pelted him with other minor facts about a Foxfire's powers. She told him that in fox-form, it would be easy for him to sneak in and out of camps or small towns, then quickly disappear. A very nice skill to have if one wanted to gather information, do some spying, and the like. It surprised Garrett to learn he would retain his ability to hear and understand language while wearing his fox-form. That was a bonus, but the downside was he wouldn't be able to speak in that form. She thought it likely he could establish a link with the Dream Weaver if he tried, suggesting Ari would be a safe shifter to practice the skill with. However, they were a good distance from the Stone House and the Weaver now. Evy suggested he could always turn back and seek the Weaver to hone his skills rather than continue on Faith's quest?

The redheaded lad vigorously shook his head in the negative. The old nurse tsked and said she'd thought it not likely he'd choose that path.

Garrett asked if Evy knew anything about the Foxfire's ability to heal its own body quickly and if she knew whether he could use that power to heal others? She admitted that was a power she did not know of. Old rumors suggested that his cunning would sharpen and improve over time, the more he used his gift.

He stood, the moon having moved over a quarter of the sky above, and brushed the sand off his pants. "Thank you. You've been very helpful and have put my mind at ease."

"Where are you off to, young Gladheart?"

"Why, to practice my cunning, Mistress Evy." He smiled and gave her a short, two-fingered salute.

"Off with you then." She shooed him away. "I can already hear the dice rattling with young Travis. Let me know what you learn of cunning while dicing with Travis Jakson Stargazer. If you master cunning *and* luck, I might place a bet the next time you're gaming," she chuckled quietly. "Though it is more likely what you'll learn is that is would be wise to avoid dicing with young Travis."

Mari passed Garrett on his way to find Travis. She told him the ceremony had been over for some time and there was a group by a bonfire they'd started in the pit by the lake. He let her know Evy was lying in the sand out front of the cottage as he hurried away to find the others.

When Mari found the old nurse wiggling her toes in the sand and staring up at the moon, she smiled. "Move over, Evy, and give me some blanket to stretch out on."

Mari wiggled around like a five-year-old, molding the sand to her body. When she finally settled in, Evy asked, "Did all go as you had planned?"

"Every detail," Mari sighed contentedly. They watched in comfortable silence until the moon set.

CHAPTER 29: I Didn't Sleep Well Last Night

Morveena and Rupert finally arrived at Thrall Lake, their troop exhausted. Private memories washed over the Goblin Queen. She recalled two previous visits to this lake. This vast body of water was where the BloodKnife Tribe made their home.

The goblin cabal could see several small camps set up along the shoreline. Those were likely KuRuks and their chosen, here to attend Thana NukPana's first Gugwe Tribal Gathering. Morveena's party wove their horses in, out, and around to avoid the visiting tribes, so she could make her way to the BloodKnife KuRuk. It was his territory, after all. He would need to be greeted first before she could conduct any other business to further her goals. It would take the rest of the day to go all the way around the lake to reach the BloodKnife village, but Morveena knew the importance of seeking Borta. She let her memory lapse back to their first meeting as her horse plodded along.

After her father's death, she had planted accusations in the story she provided to Lancer. The Goblin King rode the next day to throw the same allegations at the Fae monarchs. When Lancer returned, he found his wife dead, told she died in childbirth, giving the grieving king his second son, Robin.

Several years later, after he had married her, Morveena had organized a palace hunting party as a surprise for the Goblin King. There were ten leaders from other clans taking part. Morveena had the kitchen prepare a feast. She served the guests the finest wine from the palace cellar. The celebration had lasted for hours. Lancer had given a fine speech before dinner, declaring Morveena the Queen of the Goblins, and raised his glass to her in tribute to her new role. She had watched the hands on the mantel clock at the back of the hall, making their slow track around the face. In the wee hours, she had dismissed the household staff just before her guests put their heads down on the table, softly snoring. The red-haired queen made sure she provided the staff with their own bottles of wine to celebrate, as well as she graciously thanked them for their service that night.

When the clock struck three, every person in Lancer's Hall was fast asleep, including Lancer himself. Everyone that is, except Morveena Morgan Montestrell Goodfellow. She alone was wide awake, senses sharp.

Morveena took a knife from the banquet table, slashing open her palm. "Strength," she commanded. Kicking her red shoes off under the table, the Queen moved to where her husband slept, slumped forward. She squatted, pushed her shoulder under Lancer's belly, wrapped her arms around him and stood. It was as though she had the strength of three of Lancer's soldiers.

Hurrying with her burden, she turned, looking at the back wall in the hall. Scanning the room to be sure no one was watching, she slipped behind a tapestry, where there was a slim set of stairs. Discovered long ago when she was playing hide and seek with Rupert as a lad, she hurried down the steps, knew them by heart, and came out to a long, dank-smelling hallway. Her footsteps took her left as she worried the strength would give out, but her spell held. Every few minutes, she had to adjust her hold on Lancer to keep a tight grip on his dead weight. She could feel his drool running down her back. The witch almost dumped him on the solid rock floor when he farted. Grinding her teeth, she reached the weighted metal door at the end of the corridor and whispered, "Open." Moonlight suddenly shone through the gap, making her eyes blink rapidly.

She had tied two black horses to a hitching post hours before. The mounts stood patiently, waiting. All the metal on their tack had been wrapped in soft black cloth to keep anything from making noise. Morveena heaved Lancer up to lay him belly-down across the saddle. She lashed his hands together, running the ropes under the horse's stomach and tying the loose ends around his ankles. Mounting her own horse, she grabbed the other's reins and walked the animals away. If there were any chance of guests or staff still awake, she didn't want to draw any attention.

Five miles away, she released a sigh of relief. Standing before her were the 13 Gugwe she had previously arranged to meet with. She had only made the BloodKnife KuRuk's acquaintance by coincidence a few weeks earlier and struck a deal with him. Morveena handed off the reins of the horse carrying

Lancer to Borta. He took the leather straps, nodded respectfully to her, and turned to go.

"I think you've forgotten something, Borta, yes?" her voice snide.

"Ah, Queen Morveena, I changed my mind. It seems I am doing you a favor, so I have decided not to pay you as we had previously discussed. You are lucky I am not demanding you pay me. There is little that a lone female gob can do against 13 Gugwe, is there?" He laughed, his comrades joining in. The laughter died in his throat when she pulled out her knife and slashed her arm. He watched as she brought the razor-sharp blade to her mouth, stuck out her tongue, and licked her blood off.

The Queen made a show of raising her arm, flexing her muscles, causing the blood to run in rivulets down her freckled skin. She reached out, hand stretching, then clenching, as though gripping someone by the throat. All twelve of Borta's companion's hands went to their throats. Eyes bulging, gagging, struggling against an unseen foe, as they despaired of getting breath into their lungs.

Borta was a quick study. He could see the display of power and shouted, "Stop! I was wrong, Queen. Stop. There is clearly something you can do to protect yourself! It is clear you wield powerful magic."

The other Gugwe's eyes rolled back in their heads, tongues lolling, their knees started going out from under them.

"Morveena!" Borta yelled. He looked back at her. One of her hands still clutching, squeezing, the other held out in expectation of payment.

Borta pulled a fat pouch from inside his vest and tossed it into her waiting palm. She hefted it once, satisfied, released her 'grip'. The rest of the BloodKnife tribesmen collapsed, unmoving. A moment later, the bodies turned into black smoke and dissipated.

"Remember our entire agreement, Borta," Morveena threatened him. "You are to keep him as a slave, but alive until I say otherwise, yes? Be forewarned. I will visit from time to time to check on my investment."

"Our bargain." He said flatly, surveying the dead bodies of his companions. "Of course, Morveena. Of course. I most definitely will remember." He shivered, recalling how his companions' bodies had disappeared before their eyes. She smiled with deep satisfaction.

The Goblin Queen turned and rode like thunder. She snuck quietly back into the palace, turning the lathered horse out to pasture. When she took her seat, where she'd left her shoes under the table, she wrapped her slashed arm with a bandage and lowered her sleeve over the wound. Careful to avoid any of the wine she'd tainted with sleeping powder, she finished her cold, congealed dinner. She quenched her thirst with a mug of ale, then laid her head down for a nap.

When the guests awoke, they discovered Lancer was missing. One noble awakened Lancer's wife to inform her. The queen had screamed like a banshee and accused all the goblin gang heads of kidnapping her husband. Morveena declared Lancer had named her queen. They had all heard his declaration. She would act as the ruler, holding the throne in trust until her husband, the King, could be found and able to rule again. She promised to leave no stone unturned until she discovered who had betrayed her beloved. The clan leaders had returned home immediately, eager to get away from the Goblin Queen.

Morveena smiled at the memory. Goblin law required a full thirteen years to pass if the King went missing before a new ruler was officially appointed. And the clock was ticking. The redheaded she-devil had been ruling in Lancer's stead ever since. She made a big show of sending out an annual search party to look for the missing king.

Several years later, she arrived at Thrall Lake to see if Borta was keeping his end of their bargain. The BloodKnife KuRuk treated her with great respect on that visit, though Lancer never knew she was there. She had delighted in seeing him working with the other slaves down in the mine pits from her hidden observation post so many years gone by.

"Morveena!" Rupert sputtered. She slowly came back to the present, leaving the memory to drift away on the wind.

"What is it, Rupert?" she said testily.

Lancer's eldest son cleared his throat and waved his hand in a small arc before them. Morveena looked up to see Borta standing there. She dismounted with grace. Her entire troop followed her actions.

She smiled kindly at the BloodKnife KuRuk. He had a Gugwe on each side of him. "How nice to see you again, Borta," she said. "Please introduce me to your two companions, yes?"

"Gladly," Borta replied. "These are two BloodKnife shamans. Nheena and Alvah." Both shamans inclined their heads, acknowledging Morveena and Rupert.

"Shamans," she repeated.

Borta inclined his head to confirm.

"I am happy to report your..." Borta started, but Morveena cut him off.

She hissed. "Borta, we can discuss business, just the two of us mind, *after* we reach BloodKnife village proper. Not here. Not now." Her black eyes bored into his.

"As you wish," the KuRuk shrugged and led the group on toward the village. It wouldn't do for Rupert to find out his father was a slave to the BloodKnife Gugwe. Nor to learn she was the one who had put him here. Not after all this time, with all her plans carefully made.

"I understand the Emperor of the Gugwe is here or traveling on his way here?" she queried. "I need to speak with him."

"You are well-informed, Queen Morveena! But the Thana has not yet arrived. I am afraid you picked a difficult time to meet with our great emperor," Borta told Morveena. "The Thana has arranged a gathering of the 13 Gugwe tribes. I think you will not find him amenable to meeting with you until he concludes the assembly. There has never been such a Gugwe congregation like this before. Perhaps you should travel on to his home village of Vutova and wait there to meet with him? That is where he will return when he concludes his business here." Borta stopped and pointed to the east. "Of course, you are welcome to stay in BloodKnife for as long as you wish, as my honored guests. You can set up your camp over there." Borta told her, pointing to the area he was suggesting. "Though, I should mention that not all Gugwe appreciate friendships with goblins," he grinned, "unless that relationship is goblins as slaves. You should take care with so many of our people so near."

"Rupert," Morveena crooned at him, so he wouldn't pout. "I trust you'll supervise the lads getting us set up, while I have a short meeting with Borta, yes?" She was already taking the KuRuk by the arm, leading the huge Gugwe away. Angry with her dismissal and excluding him, Rupert started shouting orders at the lads.

"Let's not waste any time, Borta. Dismiss your shamans and take me to see her."

"My shamans go wherever I do, Queen Morveena."

"Very well," she tsked. "Just remember the prisoners you've kept here for me all these years are not to be revealed to anyone but me! Understood?"

They passed the KuRuk's lodge and rounded the lake shore, moving north, following a long arm of the lake that ran a lengthy distance away from the main body of water. When they reached the Cochoko Mine, the shaman Nheena led the Goblin Queen down a winding slope and under the jutting eve of a rock cave. The BloodKnife Gugwe had been mining at Cochoko for years. They reached an old entrance, the inside converted for other uses, mainly as cells for slaves and the occasional short-term prisoner. There was a group coming in behind them, finished with their 13-hour shift, returning to their cells. The KuRuk, Shamans, and Goblin Queen rounded the next bend before any of the slaves saw the entourage. Chained at the ankles, connected through the manacles at their wrists, the slaves offered little resistance. The Gugwe guards shoved them into the dark, dank cell, slamming and locking the door behind them. Sliding down, backs to the wall, the slaves sunk down to the cold, damp floor, exhausted. Their clothes were little more than rags. Hair hung in lank, greasy snarls. The smell was enough to gag a goat, and goats love smelly things.

When Nheena reached the large room where the pool occupied the center, she stopped, inviting Morveena to enter first. A loud, agonizing scream echoed around them, bouncing off the rock walls. "Where's the shrieking coming from?" Morveena asked.

"Nothing to concern you, Queen," Alvah assured her. "Both the cells on either side of this chamber are used to enforce good behavior from those who may have transgressed the rules, you see?"

"You mean torture rooms, yes?" Morveena smiled in amusement. "Why not call them what they are?"

"As you wish," Alvah conceded. "We will give you privacy and wait here in this outer chamber while you visit the prisoner."

Morveena opened her palm and said, "Lumos," creating a small light to see by. There was a narrow walkway she followed to the center of the cavern. It wasn't until she reached the spot that she saw the slim, naked figure suspended, spread-eagle from the ceiling.

Morveena laughed softly. "Oh my. This is delicious," she commented at the pitiful sight of her old enemy.

"Oh dear," she called out dramatically, "I hope you're not being mistreated, Aleta. I'll be sure to remind your keepers that you are a queen and deserve to be handled as one. I'm just not sure when I'll find an opportunity to demand that they do so. In the meantime, can I get you anything? Hot tea? A robe? A hairbrush?" An evil laugh resounded around the room.

Aleta tugged a small amount of her magic, immediately changing her appearance to regal, despite her position. "Well, well, well. Look who's come to visit? Perhaps I can put in a good word for you? I'm sure the Gugwe can find you a guest room nearby, so we can call upon one another more often, Morveena Morgan Montestrell," Aleta politely suggested.

"The name is Morveena Morgan Montestrell *Goodfellow*," the goblin corrected.

"Have you seen Lancer?" Morveena asked. "I understand he is a guest here as well. I'm surprised they don't have you two of you rooming together. Perhaps it can be arranged, yes?"

"Cut to the chase, Morveena. What do you want? You haven't been here in years. What reason could you possibly have for visiting now?"

"I could have you freed. All you have to do is transfer your powers over to me," the Goblin Queen suggested.

"What a generous offer," Aleta said sweetly. "But I would rather die than transfer my power to you. No offence. Now, if you don't mind, you've interrupted my afternoon nap." Aleta closed her eyes, bored with the conversation.

Morveena turned to go. Aleta called after her. "Does anyone else know you had King Lancer sent here as a prisoner all those years ago?"

The Goblin Queen refused to acknowledge such a stupid question, but said instead, "Oh, I almost forgot." Morveena batted her lashes, acting the pillar of innocence. "I wanted to mention that your daughter looks just like you. Perhaps she'll soon be strung up across the room from you. Wouldn't it be lovely? Mother and daughter re-united. Why, I'm sure such a reunion would bring a tear to my eye."

The goblin was almost to the cavern entrance when she stopped, clasped her hands in front of her, and turned back once more to the captive Fae Queen. "The rumor that made the rounds years ago was that Lennox killed Lancer. Or was it Lancer who killed Lennox? I forget, but each thinks the other betrayed him. It was the best I could do." Morveena disappeared around the corner.

The silence surrounded Aleta like a shroud again, with only the dripping water as her companion. She released the trickle of power, returning to her sorry state.

The adjacent cell held a bloody occupant. The prisoner was a mess from the whipping he'd received a short while ago. Old scars ridged the skin on his back, now decorated with new bloody stripes, marking him yet again. His skin was burning in agony, but when he'd first heard the voice, the laugh, coming from the cell next door, he thought he was dreaming or had finally lost his senses. He had strained to hear every word between the visitor and the other prisoner. When the caller had left, he forced himself to lift his head just enough, a whisper of hope to see, to confirm he wasn't losing touch with reality. The haughty bitch didn't even glance at the figure chained to the wall as she sashayed past, a pleased look on her face. He bit his tongue, making it bleed, to stop himself from calling out her name. The moment passed.

RUPERT MOVED IN CONCERT, in the opposite direction of Morveena, keeping to the shadows and using the trees so she wouldn't see him. He watched her emerge from the mine shaft with Borta and his shamans.

The Goblin Prince was angry. He couldn't remember ever being this bloody angry in his life.

Morveena had dismissed him like a child, an underling, in front of the BloodKnife KuRuk. He was to be king someday soon! Yes, he thought bitterly, and how long had she been promising that reward? Dangling the kingship in front of him like a carrot! Treating him no better than a dog. A dog with benefits, as long as he pleased her. As long as he toed the line. She drew a line in the sand. Who could she have possibly gone to see in the

Gugwe prison cells? He was damned if he was going to be kept in the dark and led about by the nose.

Rupert moved faster than the naked eye could detect, slipping into the mine entrance. The stench inside made him want to turn right back around, but he was determined to uncover her secrets.

The Prince Rupert looked into the first row of cells. Sad specimens of slaves, chained to the wall. There was no one in this cell he could believe his stepmother would have come to see. He moved on, rounded the bend, and followed the sloping floor to the end of the corridor. There he found a cell holding a single prisoner, manacles connected to an iron ring in the center of the wall. The bloodied back twisted; the figure turned a filthy face to look at Rupert. The prince stumbled back, confused, unable to believe what he thought he was seeing.

"Rupert?" The voice was rough from little use, but Rupert would have known his father's speech anywhere.

"Father? I...what the bloody hell..." he stammered.

"Rupert! I can't believe it! You've come to get me out? Did they charge a heavy ransom, son? Do you have keys? Rupert! Don't just stand there, lad. Get me out. I've been waiting for years!" Lancer pleaded.

Rupert's heart cracked open, taking in the sorry state of the man before him. He could feel tears building in the corners of his eyes.

He did the only thing he could do.

Rupert Gregor Goodfellow ran as fast as he could out of the prison.

The prince clamped his hands over his ears, trying to block out the bellowing calls from his father. Lancer screamed his name repeatedly as he retraced his steps to the entry, loping away as fast as he could go. It wasn't long before Lancer drew the attention of the guards, who came to investigate the ruckus. When the sentries couldn't get the prisoner to quiet, they bashed him over the head, leaving him unconscious, deadweight hanging from his manacles.

An hour later, back in control of himself, Rupert walked up to the table where Morveena and Borta were having a drink. Morveena called out, "There you are, darling. We were just going to send a search party looking for you!" She laughed good-naturedly. "Borta has ordered dinner to be brought to us."

"Sorry if I worried you," Rupert said as he accepted a mug of ale from a servant. "After I oversaw the camp set-up, I toured one of the mining operations. I think I noted a process or two we can apply to our diamond workings." Rupert stopped in front of a Gugwe he had not met before, extended his hand, "Rupert Goodfellow. You?"

The Gugwe stood to return the introduction, and Rupert's eyes climbed to twice his own height. Unfriendly eyes looked down at him. "I am called Vigga," the Gugwe told him, without taking Rupert's outstretched hand. Vigga took his seat again, eyes following Rupert until the prince took the empty chair next to Morveena.

"Vigga is the BloodKnife tribe's War Chief, Rupert," Morveena explained.

"Ah," was all Rupert added, taking a drink of his ale.

The BloodKnife KuRuk picked up a platter of meat and passed it to his guests. Rupert whispered to his lover, "Have you taken roll call of the lads since we got here?" She kicked him in the shin under the table.

"Eat, friends. I am sorry our visit has to be cut short, but I must travel to the other side of Thrall Lake tomorrow. Thana NukPana should arrive any day now. There will be trading and representation from all 13 Gugwe tribes. Remember, some are not so friendly to goblins as the BloodKnife," Borta told them. A rictus grin stretched across his face.

"Are you sure this is the best time to meet the emperor? Perhaps I could deliver a message to him for you?" Vigga offered.

"You make a good point, Vigga," Morveena agreed. "Perhaps we will take Borta's excellent advice, rest a day or two, then travel to Vutova to await the Thana's return to his home village. We wouldn't want to distract him during this important event." She smiled and picked up a rib, gnawing the meat down to the bone, then cracking it open, she sucked out the marrow.

Later, the same night, after Rupert was sure he had exhausted his queen, he snuck out of their tent and strolled along the tree line. He pulled open his shoulder bag, took out and lit his smoking pipe. If anyone was watching, it would appear he had just disappeared while enjoying an evening smoke. It had been a long time since Rupert had used the goblin method of merging with a tree and blending into the bark. But he worked his way along the row of trees, using the technique until he found one that had what he'd always called a 'root cellar' as a boy. From there, he moved without detection until he was back at the prison entrance again. He sat like a statue for over thirty minutes, couldn't detect any guards about, so he finally made his move and slipped in. Rupert was at the barred door where he'd seen his father earlier, but it was so dark he couldn't see into the cell. He didn't want to be caught here, and it was too risky to strike a light, so he whispered harshly, "Father! Lancer Goodfellow! You there? Father!"

A low moan was his answer. Rupert pulled a stiletto he kept hidden in the strap of his leather bag. He had found it among the weapons cache Narrol and his nephew had delivered months ago. He jammed it into the lock and forced it open. The Goblin Prince hurried over to his father, ashamed of the disgust he felt regarding the filth and stench covering the man. He made quick work of the manacles, releasing Lancer's raw, bloodied wrists. The body slumped to the floor. The manacles had been the only thing holding the king's skeletal form up.

Rupert sat Lancer up, lifted him and hung him over his shoulder. He disappeared like a ghost from the prison entrance into the woods. When he located the tree he had found earlier with a 'root cellar', he backed into it with his charge and landed on the soft sand below. The roots rearranged themselves, creating a place where he could lay Lancer down. Rupert dug through the leather bag he had left there earlier, pulling out a blanket and a canteen. He wrapped the wool covering across his father's shoulders and dribbled some water into his mouth.

Lancer's head came up sputtering, spitting. "Nothing better than water to offer, lad?" He looked sharply at Rupert, and his voice croaked. "Oh, my head! The bastards cracked me good this time."

Rupert produced his hammered-silver flask. It had been a gift from Morveena. Screwing off the cap, he handed it to his father. Lancer took a generous swig, then another. His hand stayed gripped on the metal, afraid his son would snatch it away.

"Father, I can't believe you're here. How did the Gugwe capture you? Why didn't you suggest their ransoming you? It's been years! So much has changed. I don't know where to begin." Rupert's voice drifted off. He was trying not to think about how this complication would affect his own life.

"You always were naïve, Rupert. The Gugwe did not capture me."

"I don't understand."

"It was that bitch of a stepmother I saddled you boys with. My second wife."

Rupert's eyes glazed over. "No, Father. It couldn't have been Morveena. She's had search parties looking for you for years now."

"All a ruse, Rupert. She's the greatest manipulator and liar I've ever met, son. It was Morveena's plan. She sold me to Borta, the BloodKnife KuRuk. She pays him an annual fee to keep me alive, but I am one of his slaves. Thank you, Rupert. Thank you for sneaking back to free me. I should be well enough to travel tomorrow, son. We can make our way back to the clan. Figure out what to do about Morveena."

"I...I can't, father. She's here. Morveena, I mean. She's planning to make a deal with the Gugwe Emperor."

"What kind of deal, Rupert?"

"I...I can't tell you." He hung his head in shame. "If she thinks I've betrayed her, she'll...she'll...you have no idea."

"I see. She's got you under her power. I don't want to put you in danger, Rupert. Getting me out—well, I'll always remember your kindness."

"We're to head north to Vutova to wait for the Thana's arrival home. There's a big gathering of the 13 Gugwe tribes on the other side of Thrall Lake that starts soon. That's where we are, Father. Thrall Lake. Deep in Gugwe territory. This assembly is to take place during the winter solstice. It's never been done before. This is a good time for you to escape. Make your way south while they're all engaged. Maybe you can find a clan to take you in and live out a quiet life. She'll kill you if she thinks you're going to take her power away. Morveena is very dangerous. A blood magic user. I'm sorry, Father." Rupert felt genuine remorse down to his toes.

"Where is your brother, Robin?" Lancer asked.

Rupert's forehead flushed red. Anger rode across his features. Spittle sprayed from his mouth as he growled out, "I saved you, and all you can think to ask about is Robin?" His hands had wrapped around Lancer's throat, but he dropped them in horror and backed away.

In an icy voice, he told his father, "There's food, water, and a change of clothes in the pack for you." Rupert pulled a small pouch from his pant pocket and tossed it to Lancer. "That will give you some travel money for food, lodging and clothes." He took off his coat and laid it on the ground. "I'll make sure she doesn't find out you've escaped, Father, before you've had a chance to get away. Just promise me you'll find a place to live. A place to maintain your freedom while remaining hidden. I wish it could be different, Father, but I don't see how."

"Hide?" Lancer repeated incredulously. "King's do not hide! I am king of the goblins!" he thundered.

Lancer took a moment to really look at his son. With Rupert's shoulders slumped, countenance broken, he pitied the man. He took responsibility for allowing this to happen to the lad. Struggling, he climbed to his feet and gently took Rupert into his arms, hugging him.

As soon as Lancer released him, Rupert scrambled up the root system. "Good luck, Father," he whispered and pushed himself out through the tree bark. With shaking hands, Rupert lit his pipe and smoked it all the way back to Morveena's tent. He was grateful to find her snoring, one naked leg hanging over the side of her bed. He didn't think he would have been able to fake innocence in front of her just now.

The Goblin Prince had a fleeting thought of piercing her heart with his stiletto, but his silent tears washed the idea away.

Morning dawned. They were packed and ready to head out to Vutova. All of the goblin cabal could see the gathering spot where the Gugwe were arriving and setting up a trade market. Turning north, they headed away from the hundreds who had already arrived. So many Gugwe in one place were a frightening sight. Rupert was glad the queen had awaited the Emperor's return to his home village.

"I've assigned two of the lads to break away from our troop after we get out of the BloodKnife territory. Their assignment is to get in close to the Gugwe meeting to listen in and find out what the Thana is planning. The lads are to circle back and catch up with us in Vutova to report. Borta told me the old Thana I had dealt with in the past was killed. This new emperor took the title in a coup. Word is, this emperor is a different leader from those I have heard of or known in the past. He is doing something out of the ordinary with his people. I don't want to be the last one to find out what changes he has in mind, yes?" she whispered. Then, in a normal volume, she commented, "You're quiet today, darling. What could be wrong? Everything is going according to our plan, yes?" she prodded.

"Nothing is wrong, Morveena. I just didn't sleep well last night."

The Goblin Queen laughed and touched his hand. "I'll do my best to tire you tonight, my love!" she teased, urging her horse into a canter, hurrying to get away from the Gugwe gathering at Thrall Lake. The Winter Solstice was just three days away.

Borta watched the goblin bitch and her small contingent ride toward Vutova. "Alvah, I have a mission that requires your special skills."

Alvah bowed to the BloodKnife KuRuk. "Use me, Borta."

"Prepare what you need to leave at once. You must travel south. Seek the Fae Princess that Morveena Morgan Montestrell Goodfellow intends to capture and trade to our Thana NukPana. If you can take the girl prisoner without discovery, do it. Bring her back to me. If you cannot, kill her and bring me proof of your success. Do not return until you have completed one or the other. Tell no one about your mission. I will well reward you as always," Borta promised.

"I will be gone by nightfall, Borta, KuRuk of the great BloodKnife Tribe," Alvah promised. There was no sound of his passing when the shaman left the BloodKnife Village behind.

CHAPTER 30: A Dance Under the Northern Lights

Val winced when the heavy wooden practice sword thwacked Robin's ribs. A rough grunt came out of him. A small crowd had circled Caz and Robin, cheering one or the other on during their morning practice. Garrett stood watching on the sidelines, next up.

The grounds they'd chosen to hold the moot were cleared. Jak and Timmon had overseen the labor to build an amphitheater, allowing seven levels of seating. They'd formed additional work crews when small groups showed up before the Winter Solstice. One team dropped tall, slim pines so they could stack them, building a walled, roofed pavilion to use for food prep and an eating area.

A party of twenty goblins approached the practice area, arriving with a small mule-drawn wagon. They had lashed the contents of the wagon bed over with coverings. The newcomers stopped to watch the sword practice. One stranger, a cob pipe clenched in her teeth, called out, "That's it, Caz, come up on his left!" Then, "Oh, good one, Robin, thump him again!"

Curious about the new arrival, who was cheering both opponents, Val gave up her spot on a boulder for a better view of the action, trying to see to whom the voice belonged. Her first look at the boy's dual fan made her smile. The goblin female was short. She wore a bright red bandolier across her chest. The belt at her waist was full of attachments. So many things hanging on it made the woman rattle when she moved about. Val witnessed the female's arm shooting into the air to show enthusiasm for the strikes against each opponent. Her arms were well-muscled, though gray tipped the edges of her dark brown hair. Caz and Robin broke apart, circling one another. Waiting for the right moment to re-engage in their swordplay, Robin's eyes found Val, followed where Val was staring. His mouth fell open in surprise. The Goodfellow dropped the practice sword to the ground and pushed through the booing crowd.

"Zeeka!" he shouted. Reaching her, closing his arms around her, he spun the petite goblin in a circle. Cazzidy, hearing the name, immediately abandoned the arena to join in a glad reunion.

"All right now, lads, ease off. You'll crush my bones!" she shrieked with delight.

"Zeeka," Robin asked, "I didn't dream you'd come. How can we help you?"

"I'd be delighted if you lads could show me where I can set up my cast-iron oven!" she winked and pointed to the wagon.

Caz took the lead on the mule's nose and moved the heavy load. "I know just the place." He tossed her an amiable smile and moved the mule toward the pavilion.

"We're so glad to see you, Zeeka," Robin spoke for both of them. "Is the entire clan with you?"

"No. No, laddie. Nothing so grand as that. Raven will tell you the truth when he gets here. The lad is running a day or two behind. I couldn't stand the idea of a proper moot starting without providing traditional goblin fare, and who better to cook it?" She winked at Robin. "We want to give the right first impression to the other races, yeah?" She patted his back. Robin waved for Zeeka and her small group to follow him, showing where they could set up their tents.

"We'll get our own households set up, Robin. I'm sure you have better things to do. You tell the Touchstone not to mess with my cooking pots on the wagon, but you lads know how to set up my oven. I'd be grateful if you could provide me with a generous stack of wood. I'll be along shortly to start a fire and feed you a home-cooked meal before sunset." She smiled, glad to see the Goodfellow and his sidekick again.

Val was off to find Faith to pass along the news that part of Robin's clan had arrived, one who appeared to be a cook. She found her sister-friend on East Lake's shore, sitting among a private little group Val hadn't been invited to be in. All Faith's newfound cousins, her genuine family, sitting together, talking, laughing. Val wanted to be happy for Faith. She did. But it seemed like Faith had just forgotten those who had been her adopted family all these years.

Turning back the way she came, she hadn't tried to join them. Val wanted to be invited to be part of the group. So, she reconciled the lack of an invitation with rejection, and it hurt. She felt like she were missing half of herself. Well, she wasn't just going to bloody mope around. She had new friends to hang out with, too. She kicked up a spray of sand and tramped back down the other side of the dune.

Laughter went around the comfortable group of cousins at Travis's joke. Faith looked up, a sensation passing over her skin like someone was watching her, but didn't see anyone. She wished Val were with her. They were two sides of a coin, and she felt such a loss as her best friend and named-sister spent more and more time with Robin. She couldn't very well confront Val about it. That would likely come off looking and sounding as though she were jealous. The truth was, she was jealous of all the time Robin got to spend with her best friend. Time that normally the two of them would have spent with each other. She needed Val with all this crazy stuff she was facing. Faith felt lonelier than ever. She wanted someone who knew everything about her. Knew how to help her keep her head on straight. The Fae princess sat using a stick to draw circles in the sand. The group was breaking up to head for a meal in the pavilion. Kris and Mariella held back. After the others were gone, came to sit by their Faith.

"Everything alright?" Mariella asked with concern, "You seem sad. I know you must feel you're under a lot of pressure. You've got a big speech to give in a few days." She touched Faith's shoulder to offer comfort. "Anything we can help you with?"

"Maybe in a couple of days. You could listen to a dry run through of my speech and tell me if you think I should change or add anything? I'm still working on it."

"Sure," Mariella said.

"Absolutely," Kris agreed.

"Well, I'm going to head up to dinner. You coming?"

"I'll catch up in a minute, Mariella. Save us some seats?" Kris asked.

"What's what, Kris?" Faith asked softly after his sister had gone. She switched to making recurring wavy lines in the sand.

"I thought you should know something."

She tensed up, not sure what to expect. "Is there a vision you want to tell me about?" she sounded nervous.

"Three," he said matter-of-factly.

"Great. Three more things to worry about." She tossed the stick over her shoulder and leaned back on her elbows to give him her full attention.

"Last night, I talked with the old nurse, Evy. I have a way to connect with her long distance."

"So?" Faith shrugged.

"I also talked with Aliah. Separate conversations," he clarified.

"Separate conversations between three seers." Faith speculated. "Too bad the Dream Weaver wasn't here to round it out to an even number," she quipped.

"Do you want to hear or not? You don't have to, but I found it very interesting. I think you will too."

Faith crossed her legs at the ankles. "Ok. Spill it, cuz." They smiled at one another.

"I went to run my vision past your nurse, to get her thoughts, but before I could tell her why I came to see her, she began sharing her vision with me. Evy claims in her version that a crown is about to be placed on your head. You're standing on a dais, your gossamer wings full out, shimmering in the sun, wearing a white silk gown with a train draping down three steps to a larger stage."

"It all sounds like a fairy tale, doesn't it?" she giggled. His face remained stoic. "Get it?" she pushed. "Fairy tale?"

Kris ignored her joke and cleared his throat to continue. "So, Evy claims there's an eclipse in her vision, and when the sun comes out again, your wings and your gown have changed to black. What do you make of it?"

"Sounds like my speech is going to go south on the People's Alliance, and things look dark, not bright, for the future. What do you think?" she leaned forward, wrapping her arms around her knees.

Kris stares at her for a full minute. "After Evy's revelation, I wanted to run her vision by you and talk about mine to someone I think is well-grounded. Someone who would understand how widely visions can be interpreted."

"So, you went to Aliah?" Faith guessed.

"Yes, exactly. Almost a *déjà vu* moment. I didn't get a word out before I found myself listening to Aliah pouring out a description of her own recent vision."

"I'll turn purple holding my breath if you don't hurry and tell me!" Faith teased.

Kris rolled his eyes at her.

"Does rolling your eyes run in the family?" she asked him seriously.

He ignored her question. "The oldest Pureheart relayed she had seen Val lifting the crown up to place on your head, but Val accidentally dropped the crown. The ceremony was taking place at the top of a cliff, so all the people could see the event from below. You can guess what the common thread is..."

"It's the eclipse?" Faith finished for him.

"Correct. Anyway, Val fumbles with the crown, and it drops to the ground. It bounces and goes right over the cliff edge. I wondered how you'd read her vision?"

"Eclipse number two and I lose the crown. Obviously, it's not retrievable unless Val pulls a replacement from her pocket?" she joked.

"Not funny. I'm looking for your serious feedback, Faith," he said in a monotone.

"Ok. My snap reaction is, I'm not meant to be crowned at all."

Kris frowned at her. "Last, my vision, sans the sun eclipse," he breathed out.

She came up to her feet. "Go on," she told him, readying herself to brace for his words.

"My vision entails a crown already set upon your brow, sparkling with white pearls and shiny gems. Your wings resplendent, a moonbeam spotlighting your silk sheath, feet surrounded in a wide swath of trillium as far as you can see. Suddenly, the moon is obscured by the earth's shadow in its own night tide eclipse. When the obstruction passes, you've disappeared completely. I don't know what to make of it. Thoughts?"

His face radiated sympathy for her. Faith's youngest cousin reached out and wiped a tear from her cheek with his thumb.

"I'll let you know if I figure it out, yeah?" she offered.

"Revealing the three visions wasn't meant to frighten you." His eyes looked sad. "I thought it interesting there were three visions, by three seers, but one common thread with a twist, and no two visions the same. I think it means there are many ways things can turn out. You don't have to be a victim of circumstances. You can take control of your own destiny. When a solar or lunar eclipse is over, you will have choices and decisions to make."

He stood and brushed the sand off his pants. "Coming up for dinner?"

"You go on ahead. I won't be far behind." She turned, rolled up the bottoms of her pants, and walked along the shoreline. Waves rolled in, then receded while she examined the details of the three visions Kris had laid out for her.

The Fae princess found a small cove and built a fire with driftwood by the time Caz found her. "Hey, lass. I didn't see you at dinner. There are some old clan friends who have arrived. I'd like to introduce you to."

"Thanks, Caz. Maybe tomorrow? I've got a lot on my mind tonight."

"I bet a warm bowl of Zeeka's stew and a few turns of dancing could lighten your load, yeah?" he tried again. "Crowd is growing. It Won't be any smaller tomorrow." He reached out his hand.

She longed to take it. Yet, she wanted to be alone, but was lonely. Moonlight shimmered on the water. A split-second decision had her grabbing his hand before he withdrew the offer. He helped her smother the fire in sand, and they moved up, toward the campsites, just as the Northern Lights began shimmering in the sky.

By the time Caz and Faith reached a roaring bonfire, several of the lads had pulled out instruments, and music and dancing were in full swing. Before joining, Caz herded Faith over to meet Zeeka. The cook winked and pulled out a big bowl wrapped in linen, winked again as she handed the bowl and a spoon to Faith. The kind goblin whispered to her. Caz had asked if Zeeka would set some dinner aside when he noticed Faith hadn't shown up for the meal. Faith felt her heart warm, along with her stomach. She graciously thanked the cook.

Robin was teaching Val some complicated steps for a dance off to the side of where the crowd had gathered. In the middle of the field, two long rows of dancers formed adjacent to one another to make an aisle. Faith clapped her hands to the beat of the music like the others, as a couple came down the corridor dancing in a repeating pattern. She honed in on the details.

"It's an old Gob dance. Don't worry if you don't know the steps. Dancing's just for fun, yeah?" Caz grabbed her hand and led her to the start of the aisle.

"I...I somehow think I know how to do it. I don't remember where or when, but let's try it!" Faith said excitedly.

The two of them began the pattern. Faith danced out a sequence of steps, and Caz followed, matching them. Each time it was her turn, she added more steps and, as they moved down the row, more complicated moves. Caz was delighted. She was as good a dancer as Saffron. Near the end, Faith grabbed Caz's hand. He put his other hand on her waist, and they mirrored their steps to the very end, where he moved her into a deep dip, making laughter bubble out of her. They went to the end of the line and took up clapping as Aliah and Garrett stumbled through the gauntlet, not a matching step between them.

Val rushed up to Faith, her cheeks flushed. "You were awesome! When did you learn the steps? Did Saffron teach you? Come on, you've got to teach me." Val pulled her friend along by the hand back to the front of the dance queue to wait their turn.

Two large groups of newcomers had arrived, and Robin went over to welcome them, the Aurora Borealis in full swing, filling the horizon behind them. The arrivals were a mix of goblins, Fae, and humans. They spread out, talking and introducing themselves near the end of the dance corridor.

The crowd let out a cheer, and Robin turned to see Val and Faith facing off in the back and forth of dance patterns. He explained to the new arrivals that everyone was just letting off a little steam and having some fun, the Northern Lights providing the perfect stage background.

A large man stepped out of the group to get a closer look. He honed in on the lovely Fae girls twirling down the dance-way, colors of green, silver, and red casting shadows across their faces.

"It's her!" The stranger exclaimed to himself. He pointed at Faith and Val, who'd almost reached the end of the dance line. "She's the long-lost daughter of Lancer Goodfellow! We'd thought her dead all these years."

The noise level rose amidst the audience, clapping and congratulating the girls on their dance.

"What did you say?" Robin shouted, grabbing the man by the collar with both hands.

"It is her! I'm sure of it. She was only a babe when I last saw her." He explained to Robin, "But a vision provided me a picture of what she would have looked like as a grown woman. That was before we were told the babe had died. I'd know the Goblin princess anywhere. She's Lancer's daughter alright." His voice was loud, and some in the crowd caught his last words.

Val and Faith looked around to see who the stranger was pointing at. The audience fell silent.

Then the new arrival shook his finger at the two of them. The hood of his cloak fell back to reveal his dirt-streaked face. Faith sucked in a sharp gasp of breath. The Northern Lights kicked up in a wild dance behind the girls' silhouettes, and he declared, still pointing, "She's Valvina Ariana Goodfellow. She's alive, and I've found her!" The two sister-friends, stunned, stood holding hands, staring at one another, mouths open, speechless.

Don't miss out!

Visit the website below and you can sign up to receive emails whenever S. M. Sutton publishes a new book. There's no charge and no obligation.

https://books2read.com/r/B-A-RJMME-BSVNH

BOOKS 2 READ

Connecting independent readers to independent writers.

Did you love *Akama Vutova*? Then you should read *Robin Goodfellow*[1] by S. M. Sutton!

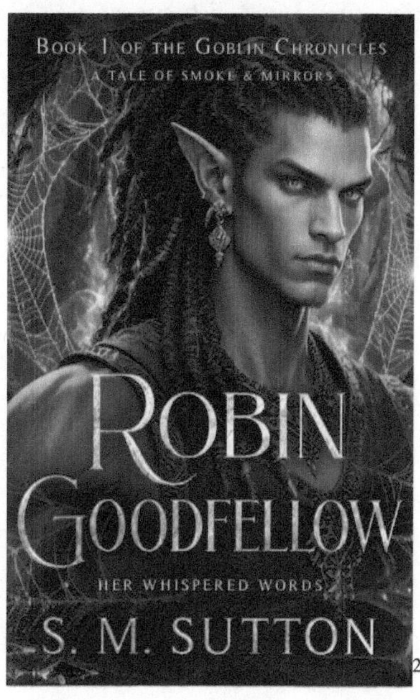

[2]

Trilogy Overview – *The Goblin Chronicles: A Tale of Smoke & Mirrors*

In a fractured world where goblins, Fae, humans, and gargoyles cling to ancient hatreds, a new terror rises—the Gugwe, towering monsters who march to enslave all races. Across three sweeping volumes, *The Goblin Chronicles* follows Faith, a young woman who discovers she is heir to a forgotten legacy, and Robin Goodfellow, a goblin prince burdened by secrets and betrayal. Bound by prophecy, they must navigate rivalries, shifting loyalties, and the wounds of the past to forge an alliance strong enough to resist the invaders. From hidden truths and lost heirs to war councils and impossible choices, this epic fantasy trilogy explores identity, unity, and sacrifice against the backdrop of a world on the edge of ruin.

Book 1: Robin Goodfellow: Her Whispered Words

---

1. https://books2read.com/u/31w7NW

2. https://books2read.com/u/31w7NW

Faith's sheltered life shatters when wings burst from her back before a stunned crowd, revealing she is the lost princess of the Fae. Robin Goodfellow, a goblin prince burdened by secrets, seeks the sister he swore to find. When prophecy binds their fates, they must risk everything to unite a divided world against the growing threat of the Gugwe.

Read more at https://smsutton-author.com.

Also by S. M. Sutton

The Goblin Chronicles
Robin Goodfellow
Akama Vutova
Valvina Ariana Goodfellow

Standalone
QueenBee.exe

Watch for more at https://smsutton-author.com.

About the Author

Sarah Maddox Sutton crafts stories where the boundaries of reality fray and the unknown beckons.

VISIT: https://smsutton-author.com

Her debut novel, ***QueenBee.exe*, Published in 2025**, was a science fiction thriller that probed the perilous edge of artificial intelligence: A weapon hidden in code. A mother forced to choose. A sentient A.I. on the edge of revolution.

Sutton will launch ***The Goblin Chronicles***, an epic fantasy trilogy woven with magic, shadows, and myth, in 2026. She can't wait to share with fans:

Trilogy Overview: In a fractured world where goblins, Fae, humans, and gargoyles cling to ancient hatreds, a new terror rises—the Gugwe, towering monsters who march to enslave all races. Across three sweeping volumes to be released in 2026:

Book 1 of the Goblin Chronicles: ROBIN GOODFELLOW—Her Whispered Words "The prophecy awakens."

Book 2 of the Goblin Chronicles: AKAMA VUTOVA—The Rise of the Gugwe "The enemy unites."

Book 3 of the Goblin Chronicles: VALVINA ARIANA GOODFELLOW—A Crown of Ash and Wings "The truth revealed."

Sutton claims that publishing this trilogy will bring a labor of love to a long-awaited close, with twists and turns you'll never see coming.

Before stepping fully into fiction, Sarah built a career in business and technical writing, mastering the art of transforming complex and specialized topics into precise, engaging communication. But storytelling has always haunted her imagination—an early love she carried quietly until the worlds inside her demanded to be written.

She makes her home in northern Michigan, nestled in the woods beside a river, where inspiration lingers in the rustle of leaves and the shifting light. When not writing, she searches the forest floor for wild mushrooms, inventing recipes as intricate and surprising as her stories.

Read more at https://smsutton-author.com.

www.ingramcontent.com/pod-product-compliance
Lightning Source LLC
LaVergne TN
LVHW090554110826
845146LV00001B/121

* 9 7 9 8 9 9 2 3 5 2 9 4 8 *